BLITZ LOVE

INTERTWINED

By RiKa

Copyright © 2025 by Rika

All rights reserved.

No part of this publication may be reproduced, distributed, or transmitted in any form or by any means, including photocopying, recording, or other electronic or mechanical methods, without prior written permission of the publisher, except as permitted by U.S. copyright law. For permission requests, contact at authorrika@gmail.com

The story, all names, characters, and incidents portrayed in this production are fictitious. No identification with actual persons (living or deceased), places, buildings, and products is intended or should be inferred.

First edition. March 25, 2025.

Trigger Warnings-

Provocative language
Racial discrimination
Sexual abuse
Rape
Strong language
Trauma
Car crash
Violence

Dedication-

If you picked up this book for the sake of learning more about a sport,
sorry to disappoint you!
Just kidding, it is just football!
wink *wink*

Chapter 1- Riya

Spoiled. Bratty. Snooty. Blabber. Smart. Beautiful. Sassy. And obnoxiously rich. These are some of the words people use to describe me. I have been raised like an entitled princess and one thing I hate is uncertainty.

And the man sitting in front of me, makes me feel the one thing that I despise- nervous. Because if I get nervous, I open my mouth. If I open my mouth, I find it difficult to close it back. And no, it does not help me or the other person. I need to take charge. "Let me be very clear from the beginning. I am not a journalism major. I am only taking this class to fulfill my credits and nothing else. I have other things to focus on and DO NOT HAVE ANY EXPECTATIONS FROM ME." I force my mouth shut.

He presses his lips in a thin line and furrows his brows. His brown hair is glistening with sweat and his ocean blue eyes bring back hazy memories that make the back of my head hurt.

"I can't guarantee that the article I write will be selected in the paper, so if you want someone else, I will be more than happy to step aside." I say when he stays quiet for too long.

"All I wanted to say was- 'Pass me the menu'" he does the air quotes. I feel my face get hot in the early cold January. I turn to look away, and suddenly the footpath tiles seemed more interesting. I wonder how they laid the cement!

I awkwardly pass him the menu without looking at him. He grabs it out of my hand and I hear him exhale loudly in frustration. "So are you not even going to tell me your name?" he leans his elbow on the table and battles his long lashes at me. *Why do men have long lashes? It's not fair!*

"Riya." I say as I arrange my books.

"Hi Riya" he offers me his hand. "I am–"

I shake his hand sternly. Just how dad had taught me. "Marcus James Williams. I know." he shakes his head in agreement and stares at me creepily. As if he knows my dirty little secret.

More like OUR dirty little secret.

After he holds on for a second longer, I pull my hand out of his grip. Even his small handshake sends electric currents in my body. *No. It is the static current!*

He scratches his stubble and leans back in his chair. "You do look very familiar..." he says. Oh God No! I'd hoped he was drunk enough to not remember me.

I mean I did leave before he woke up! But I took his shirt with me. Maybe he noticed that it was missing? I'm sure that I was just another hook up for him. Just another one of the 100 girls that he has slept up with! I really pray that he forgets that night!

Because I can't remember it for heaven's sake!

A week ago-

Justine keeps walking back and forth in her new heels that she has been trying to "break in" for two months now. "Why are you even taking that class then? If you hate it so much!" Justine, my roommate and my best friend asks me. Justine and I live off campus in an apartment, which is at a walkable distance from the campus.

She is a Psychology major and so am I. But I also added Biology in my sophomore year. I thought that it should be a piece of cake but I am struggling hard to finish the majors with my study abroad semester in Australia. Don't get me wrong, it was fun! Until I came back and realised how much I had to do to graduate on time next year.

Justine and I were roommates in freshman year and moved off campus in our Sophomore year. She is pretty cool. But she is a social butterfly, maybe because she is that girl who can juggle parties, social life, boyfriend and grades altogether.

The most important thing about me is that I go to parties only once a month, because there is only so much embarrassment that I can handle once I have opened my mouth.

"You're doing it again." Juju shakes me.

"Sorry. I swear to god that I was listening to you. I am taking the class because all the other stupid classes are full and I need to complete this useless class to graduate on time." I sigh.

"But Journalism, Ri? Out of all classes? You know you hate it!" She pats my shoulder.

I plop on our living room couch. Frustrated with my own stupidity."I know, I do! But I enrolled for my classes late in the semester. You know I was busy with the wedding." I had gone back to India for my cousin sister's wedding and we had such a blast, so much so that I forgot to enroll in all my classes. I literally had to beg the Professor to let me take this class so that I graduate next year.

She sits next to me and takes her heels off to reveal bruised red feet and tosses them to the side. I have no idea why she still wears them. Those heels are so uncomfortable that it feels like you are walking on thorns. Plus they are half a size small for her feet, but I know that she is going to wear them until they split her feet in two.

"Well, you do have to go through it now! There's not much you can do. Besides, you can pick that PhD guy for your interview! Is there anyone else you recognize on the list?" Juju asks me. We have this stupid final project which is the only grade that will determine our entire grade in the course.

Basically we have to interview and write an article about the person we interview. The best article will be printed in the college paper and the local Daily Times. Great! I am not interested in it. I just need a good grade so that it doesn't bump down my GPA.

I pout my lips and make a puppy dog face.

She massages her sore red feet to relieve some pressure and hisses in pain. "Of course you don't. Well in that case. You can just pick random people as your second and third options to interview. I'm sure you'll get the PhD dude that you so badly want to bone." She chuckles and hits my back.

I groan and sink lower into the couch in embarrassment. "Juju... One- I do not want to...bone him! And two- he is not the PhD guy. He has a name. And a very cute name at that- Raj." I blush slightly.

Raj is the PhD student that I work with in my lab who is smart beyond my thinking and has such a unique perspective of looking at the world. Not to mention he is irresistibly handsome!

"That's the most stereotypical Indian name and you know that!" I laugh at that. She is not wrong. But he's still cute.

She suddenly props up with energy that I have no idea where she gets from. It's like she is high on coke half of the time. *She's not!* "Okay, I know one thing that will take your mind off it. Jake's friend is throwing a party at his house tonight, why don't you come with me? It'll be fun!" She picks me up by my shoulders and walks me to my room and towards my closet.

I groan and protest with every step that she pushes me ahead. Jake is Justine's boyfriend of three years and they are so cute together that it makes me want to throw up. But she's happy, so that makes me happy! The heels that she was wearing were actually a gift from him. And despite me telling her several times to return them, she was too pleased with the sweet gesture and wore them to their every single date.

I throw my hands in the air and get out of her grip. "I just went to a party last weekend. And you know that I couldn't stop blabbing about how the divorce rate is increasing and is at an all time high worldwide. I am not embarrassing myself more by talking about how aliens exist at this party. My embarrassment metre is at an all time high!" I sulk and pout. I blab when I'm nervous and social gatherings of any sort make me nervous. And I hate that feeling.

I think I blab so much that Juju has learned to tune me out after the fifth word. "I will be there with you. I will zip your mouth shut everytime you open it." she promises. And I am not sure how much to believe, because knowing me, my social meter is almost out of battery. But I also know for a fact that there is no winning against Justine. If she wants me to go to a party, I have to go to a party. Especially, since we missed out on partying together for a semester of Junior year when I was away in Australia.

"Fine. I'll go." I entangle my pinky with hers.

A few hours later, Juju and I are ready and tipsy enough for the party. Her pregame regime is brutal. I don't like to drink a lot at these parties, mostly because the cheap alcohol gives me a migraine the next day. So we drink the expensive whisky that I brought from Australia. I have a higher tolerance than Juju, when she drinks one shot, I have to drink two!

"Okay, I am at level four right now on the drunken meter. Where are you?" I ask her. She stands up and loses balance. "I would say 6." I say quickly as I catch her.

"I won't drink much there anyway. So that's great." She chuckles as she grabs onto my red top that clings onto my body like skin.

It's dips in the front which displays a nice cleavage, but makes me more conscious, but at least having loose jeans makes me feel good enough about my legs being covered. Justine on the other hand, is wearing a see through net top and a neon yellow bra inside and a black mini skirt with leather thigh high boots. Only she can dare to wear it in the early January cold.

Not that my clothes are in any way weather approved, but at least I won't freeze my ass off. Juju at least has a boyfriend who can make her feel warm. If you know what I mean. *wink* *wink*.

"Jake's here." she says, looking at her phone.

We head down and Jake drives us to the party. He promised that he has a friend who is going to stay sober and drive us back, but I might skimp early.

We reach the party and you can hear it from a block away. Disco lights and drunk people out on the lawn. Great! I take a deep breath and brace myself for the crazy night ahead.

"Shots! We need shots!" Jake says as soon as he pulls us in the crowded room. I can't hear him over the loud and meaningless music beats. Justine looks at my face and immediately pulls her mouth to my ear and screams. "I know that look! You are going to enjoy!" Ugh! She knows me too well.

"I will try." I say as I look around. I see the room is full of people dancing, some making out in the corner, there's a usual beer pong table, a sucky DJ who has no taste in music and a kitchen full of people making the most disgusting concoctions known to mankind.

Jake returns with five shots in his hands, barely juggling them. I take three out of his hands. I take a look at Justine and she is in no condition to drink. So I drink all the three shots myself and they hit me like a truck, bumping me up from a level 4 to level 6.

"That tastes disgusting! What was that?" I say after I feel the burning sensation in my stomach adding up to my nausea.

"Tequila and whiskey mixed with vodka." He says and my expression is blank and he chuckles taking the shot glasses away from me. He's trying to get me killed.

"Let's dance, baby." Jake says as he takes Juju's hand into his and they head to the dance floor. So much so for enjoying the party.

Juju grabs onto my hand and drags me with her and I hate it. I hate being the third wheel with them, it makes me feel embarrassed. But not like I have any other option, because I don't know anyone here. After a couple more awkward moments on the dance floor, I head to the kitchen to make a proper drink for myself. Whiskey and coke, my favourite!

I reach there to see that there is no coke left! Ugh! Well, at least there is a decent whiskey instead of the cheap shit. I pour myself a glass and dilute it with a little sprite.

It'll do! I say to myself and gulp the glass. I don't know how people sip on their drinks, I am hasty and just chug it. Unless it's wine. When I am drinking wine, suddenly I feel like a heiress of a multi-billion dollar business.

I am left alone when Justine is dancing with her boyfriend. And everyone else seems to be busy doing whatever they were doing. A couple more chugs later I am at level 9.

It is time for me to go home! There comes a point when I start drinking, when I know that I have had enough and can't keep going and I just go home.

I look around for Juju and just then, in the living room, I see a gorgeous man sitting on the leather sofa. A blonde woman is sitting in his lap, who is basically stroking his crotch with her tiny thighs. His chiselled jaw has stubble and his deep blue eyes which I can spot from a mile away.

Damn, his biceps are probably bigger than that blonde's thighs. She's tiny in front of him.

He leans his head back and then looks ahead and his brown hair falls beautifully off his face. They look so smooth and silky that he could easily advertise for a shampoo brand. Perfect length too! Neither buzzed nor too long, just long enough for me to run my hand through and grab onto.

If this was a movie, violins would be playing in the background right now. He pushes the blonde off his lap and I see him walking towards the kitchen. I think he catches me staring at him, but I head away from there as I feel the urgency to pee.

I head towards the bathroom and he passes me and our hands graze. It sends chills down my spine. *Get a grip!* I realise that he is actually taller than me too. I am wearing four inch heels and even then, he probably has a good five or six inches on me.

I come from the bathroom and on my way to the dance floor, vodka is poured down my throat by some drunk shit. Some just glide down my mouth and down my throat to my chest and disappear in my cleavage. It feels gross and sticky. That just bumped me from level 9 to level 10. Abort. I need to get home. Now!

That's the last thing I remember, before I wake up in bed next to Mr Handsome in nothing but what looks like an oversized shirt on me and my panties. My head is pounding like hell. I have zero recollection of how I got here and I have no fucking idea, where I am!

All I know is that I need to get out of here, before he wakes up. Although I take one more look at him, just for good measures. You know in case any tests come out positive after this. I'm sure that even level 10 drunk me would be smart enough to not let a man come inside her. Or do it without a condom in the first place.

Hopefully.

I don't even know his name, remembering his face is the best thing I can do.

He looks at peace. Perfect nose and high cheekbones. His chest rises and falls in a rhythm which is music to my ears. And damn was I not imagining his biceps. They're huge but his chest is probably bigger than mine. With defined abs like they were chiselled on a stone. Long lashes which make me envious.

And pink full lips.

I am almost tempted to know what they feel like. But I won't. I look around and I spot my jeans and tip toe to grab them. I can't find my bra and my shirt for god's sake.

Ugh! Screw it. I'll keep his shirt on. Not like he will miss one shirt, right? I put on my heels and tiptoe outside his room to enter the hallway which leads to stairs down to a huge living room, which is thankfully empty.

I head for the main door silently and decide to sprint outside. Just then the main door flings open before me and a swarm of men walk inside. I quickly turned around! Fuck. Thankfully no one has seen my face yet.

"Um...You okay?" someone asks me. I nod and scooch past them, facing my back against them and sprint outside! I covered my face with my hair, so there's no way they knew that it was me, right?

Why did I do that? Now they're going to think their friend slept with some ugly bitch.

That was the worst experience of my entire life!

Present time-

"Are you sure that we haven't met before?" Marcus asks me.

"Positive! I am a Biology major and you are... well...a jock! So no way in hell is there a chance that our paths will ever cross." I say almost too quickly. Maybe I am coming off as too defensive. I am still not sure how much he remembers, because I have hurt my brain trying to think about it.

His expression is that of annoyance. Maybe I should change my strategy here and keep anything related to that incident entirely out of discussion."Okay... so why did you select this jock?" he points to himself. The way he says jock makes me feel guilty for saying that in the first place.

I clear my throat, not daring to meet his eyes this time. I stare at my shoes as I speak. "Well... as you know that in the journalism class, we were forced with none of our choice of people to interview and well, write a stupid article about it." *Please stop talking, Riya!* "I am not a professional but I'll need some info about you in regards to that. And let me emphasise on how you were not my first, second or third choice!"

Now would be a good time to zip up but I keep on going. "I hate that Angella got Raj!" I sigh loudly and Marcus chuckles in a husky voice.

I immediately lift my gaze towards him. His laugh is so genuine and innocent, completely opposite of how he looks. *Snap out of it Ri! He's a playboy who has slept with more than half of the women on campus and god knows how many more! He's the definition of manslut. Or at least those are the rumours.*

But he does have the looks for it. I will admit it. Because even the drunk me wouldn't sleep with him if he wasn't this good looking.

He clears his throat and looks at me with those deep blue eyes that make me go weak in the knees. "Okay Riya. So, you want to insult me and interview me at the same time, for free? What do I get out of it?" His gaze changes and there's lust in his eyes. He swipes his thumb over his bottom lip and that jolts my body. I gulp hard and my lips part as a soft sigh escapes my mouth.

I force myself to snap out of it. I will not let his charms work on me anymore! "I don't know. I thought that you were just supposed to do it! Why else would they assign us this stupid assignment then?" He grins now. All I want to know is what is going on in that sexy brain of his? Sexy? No, I meant jock brain.

He leans closer to me."Yes, I mean I should get something in return." He wets his lips and bites his lower lip now.

"You know what? I'd rather fail this class than ever sleep with you! Screw you. I'm done." I stand up abruptly. I know I said that I would never sleep with him, but I already did! Too bad we both don't remember.

He holds my hand and his rough calluses brush against my soft skin. Why does that turn me on?

I'm weird!

"I'm not asking you any of that. Those books you're carrying... Are they yours?" He points towards my textbooks.

I roll my eyes at the obvious question. "No, they are my grandmother's. She's a freshman here." I know my name is Riya, but my middle name is sarcasm. Just kidding. It's actually Chandran. I know! That's why I only go by my first name.

"Is your grandmother as smart and hot as you then?" I know I shouldn't but I couldn't help but blush a little. Not that I care that he finds me hot!

"Smarter and definitely way too hotter." I say.

He clicks his tongue. "Too sad that I'm not into older women." He pouts.

I take a step out of the booth but he stops me. He holds my hand again and this time I don't brush it off. I let it linger just a while longer. I feel my pulse getting stronger with every second. My body has never reacted this way before. Then why him?

Why Marcus?

Chapter 2- Marcus

I've been having a great year so far, especially since my transition to being a captain this season. I know my team has great potential, we reached the semis last season, but when my captain got his heart broken just before the game, he'd been out of his game and led us to a loss.

The moment I was asked to be the captain, I decided to get my head in the game and focus on just football. I cannot afford any distractions. I want to lead the team to the victory that they deserve.

I have become more disciplined but that doesn't mean that I don't have fun! I have slept with more women than I can count, although ever since becoming the captain, I have been going to less parties, limiting my drinking to only weekends and some weekdays. Okay maybe I still drink but not as much as I used to.

People often relate jocks to being dumb, but I do like to think that I am at least smarter than most jocks. Majoring in Computer Science has been the best thing I decided to do.

Coding leaves me at peace.

Maybe because I have been coding since I was a kid. My mom had her own software company and taught me coding immediately after I learned how to read. But all the screen time ruined my eyes and I have to use glasses when reading and using the computer. The boys make so much fun of me for that.

"It's Beck's birthday baby!" George jumps on the sofa with a thud.

Not a good sign. Beck knows how to throw a party! Fucker even brings in strippers if he's feeling good, and if it's his birthday, I doubt that he will go lowball.

"We have early morning practice assholes, unless you want to do it hungover. Coach Belkis is gonna work our asses off. He was already pissed that Nate didn't show up for the last one. Is he still banging that chick? Even after she accused him of knocking her up?" I plop down in the armchair next to the sofa.

Daniel sighs, leaning on the couch. "I guess so. He said he's in love or some shit with her. Man, I hope he doesn't screw it up like Harold did." Harold was the captain before me, the one who screwed up.

"Coach Belkis is not at all forgiving when it comes to personal matters. Don't know who broke the poor man's heart, he's more bitter than Marcus when it comes to relationships." Siddharth laughs as he sits with a beer in his hand. I just roll my eyes at him.

They will never understand it! All relationships are just doomed to end. So, why bother going through one when you're just going to end up hurt? "It's a distraction. And anyway, with college and all the games, I don't have time for a girlfriend and blah blah." I say.

Siddharth, George and Daniel are my teammates and also my roommates. George Daniel and I are Juniors and graduating next year. Siddharth is a Sophomore. Siddharth and George want to go pro just like me, but Daniel, despite being an amazing mid linebacker, will take over his dad's business. Even if he has no interest in it.

I sometimes wish I could knock some sense into him, but Daniel's father is not one to mess with. He is a very powerful businessman, who hides behind his fists when he is angry and raises his hands on his child. I have seen Daniel's bruises when he came back from Christmas, it was the first time I'd ever wanted to gut someone. Daniel is like my brother. All my roommates are, but Dan and I have the most understanding relationship of all.

George walks in the middle of the room. "Back to the party! Beck invited us all. Said there are going to be some strippers coming in too. Now that's a way to turn 21!" He laughs and cheers and hoots. All of the boys in here are manwhores, including me. We have slept with more women than we can count. But the only bro code we never break is you never sleep with the same woman.

"Fine. It's a Saturday anyway." Dan joins in.

"I'll go but I'm not drinking" I say with a sigh.

"Don't be a spoilsport man!" Siddharth or as we like to call him Sid, chimes in.

"Well, somebody has to make sure that your asses get back home so that they can be whipped by Belkis tomorrow." I chuckle and they all groan in union.

"You're no fun, cap." George says.

I hate going to practise with a hangover, especially since I'd taken over being the captain. Coach Belkis is someone who seems like he hasn't gotten laid in a decade and has been banned from jerking off, so he is always so pissed. Because I have wondered so many times how one can be this angry at all times?

Also, I am the worst person to be around when I'm hungover.

I shrug and the boys groan in frustration.

"Ugh! Fine. You can be the sober cop." George sighs.

As soon as I make my way to the party, I am swarmed with people. The usual– women throwing themselves at me and all. And I am not bragging by any means. I make my way through to wish Beck on his Birthday and he sends me back a stripper with me.

As if it wasn't that obvious, she's tiny and petite, blonde hair and too small in front of me. Definitely not my type. I like girls with thick thighs. I think it's the hottest thing for a woman.

Don't judge me!

Some people like to eat meat which has fat. Not in a literal way guys...I am not a cannibal! But a man is allowed to have a type of woman he goes for.

"So, you want to go upstairs or to your place?" The blonde asks me as she sits on my lap. I roll my eyes at her and I spot her...

Chugging her drink like there's no tomorrow. She proceeds to make another drink. She fills half her glass with whisky and adds sprite to it and gives it another chug. Her black hair falls on her shoulders after she places her glass down and shakes her head. That was a strong drink! Her red top is practically highlighting how beautiful her tits are and I see everyone who passes by takes a look at them but she doesn't even notice.

It makes me want to strangle each and every one of them. Her long earrings make me want to play with them. I wonder if they would dangle as I thrust into her. She pushes her hair back with a flip and my dick twitches. Her eyes land on me and it sends blood straight to my pelvis.

Just then the blonde moves in my lap and literally strokes my cock with her thighs. She is probably thinking that she got me this hard.

What is wrong with me? Her one look got me hard! I roll my head back and adjust myself. I take a look at her through the corner of my eyes and she's still looking at me.

I push the blonde stripper off me and make my way to the kitchen. I can see that she can't take her eyes off me either. But as soon as she sees me get up and walk towards her, she starts to look away and walks past me.

Our hands graze and it sends electricity up my body. What is wrong with me? I have slept with more women than I could remember, but I would beg this woman to let me touch her.

I stay in the kitchen for a while until I spot her again as she makes her way back to the living room. Some drunken asshole holds her face and starts pouring the cheap vodka down her throat. She is clearly drunk at this point. But he doesn't stop. The vodka glistens down her shirt until it disappears in her cleavage and I see him checking out her tits.

I can't stop myself from going over to him and smashing the bottle on his head. She finally pushes him away and holds her head in her hands. Losing balance. I run through the crowd towards her. She lands on my chest and wraps her hands around my waist immediately.

Fuck. I am so hard right now. She looks up at me and her eyes sparkle with the most beautiful shade of brown. It reminds me of the great oak tree for some reason. And then I see the smallest mole just under her left eye. My heart melts as I get flashbacks of blue eyes with a small mole just under the eye.

I immediately let go of her, but she doesn't.

"Do–do you. *Hiccup* Do you want to fuck me?" she whispers in my ear.

I gulp hard. I take a look at her plush lips painted with red lipstick. It would look so beautiful around my cock. But I won't.

"You're drunk." I say because she is holding onto me like a pillar and she will fall the moment she lets go of me.

"I'm not *Hiccup* drunk." she pouts at me.

I take a look around to see if anyone is coming for her. "Who did you come here with?" I ask her. I need to make sure that she goes back home as soon as possible, so that I can go back and jerk off this erection.

She pouts as if she is in deep thought. She points towards the dance floor. I look around to see who she is pointing to. "Let's go dance." She yells and holds my hand and drags me to the dance floor.

I hate dancing.

I don't dance!

The song changes to a sexy one and she starts swaying her hips. Damn! Her ass is huge. I'm sure it would jiggle when I smack it. Her back facing me, I keep my one hand wrapped around her waist so that she doesn't fall down while she keeps grinding on me. This is my personal hell!

But I can't. She's drunk. And never in my life have I ever fucked a drunk girl, not even a tipsy one. Unless they're sober and I am sober, I am not fucking them. Period. I don't want to take advantage of any woman when she's under the influence nor do I want to force myself on someone when I am under the influence.

"It's hot in here." she says as she moves her hair to the front and exposes her neck to me. I just want to bury my face in her neck and make her come on my fingers so badly.

Before I can say anything. I see that she's trying to take off her top. I immediately hold her hands down and turn her around to face me. She falls on my chest with a thud.

"You need to go home, sweetheart! Now!" I say holding my inner animal inside me.

She hums with her eyes closed. She's wasted. I can't leave her here. She tried to take her clothes off in the middle of the dance floor. I don't know where she lives or who she came with. Hell, I don't even know her name.

"Do you have all your stuff with you?" I ask her, knowing very well that I am going to regret this. But I can't leave her here.

She just nods her head.

"I'm going to have to ask you to hold my hand and not let go under any circumstance. Can you do that for me?" I ask her as I lean my head down to hers. She smiles at me and her eyes close when she smiles. It twists a knife in my stomach. It again takes me back down the memory lane with my mom when she used to smile at me like that, her eyes would close whenever she smiled when she was actually happy. Maybe that's more the reason that I can't leave her here.

And I know how fucked up it sounds that I am having such vulgar thoughts about her!

I hold out my hand for her and she holds onto it firmly. I make my way through to the room in the back, where my other teammates are getting a private strip show. I roll my eyes at them and signal them that I am leaving. Dan nods his head at me and assures me that he will take care of them.

I make my way outside and the chilly breeze hits my face and suddenly I feel so much better.

She is still holding onto my hand. Good.

I help her get in the passenger seat of my car and strap her in. She immediately bends down to remove her heels. Or at least she's trying. Red bottoms. They would look better laid on my shoulders as I thrust into her and she moaned my name.

Snap out of it, Marcus!

This girl is turning me on, on a next level. I bend down and help her remove her heels and she shivers as my hand touches her ankles. She is wearing anklets and they have dancing bells on them which make a sound when they move. I wonder if they would curate the music to our dance when I am inside her or when I make her legs shake with pleasure.

"I got it." I say and she sits back up. After removing her shoes, I get in on the other side and drive us off to my place. It is about a 10 minute drive, but I drive slowly. She was already half asleep when I started the car.

"I'm sleepy." she says as her head falls on my lap and I almost swerve the car into a tree. But I regain control.

Okay...I'm fine. We're fine. It's not the first time a girl's head was so close to my crotch while driving. I won't lie, I have gotten a blowjob before when driving, but seeing at her red lips, I am hard as fuck right now thinking how good that colour might look around my cock.

I pull the car over and gently tap on her head. "Wakey. Wakey, princess." I lift her head from my lap and she's passed out. I slowly move her head back on her seat and run to open her door.

Let's get you out. "Can you wake up for me, Raven?" I hold her hand and undo the belt.

Mhmm... she nods and immediately wraps her hands around my neck. I can feel her breath on my neck and that sends jolts down my spine. What is this girl doing to me?

"Shoes..." she mummers. I pick her up with one hand as she wraps her legs around my waist like a baby and I pick up her shoes in my other hand.

"Are we home?" she asks in a husky voice.

"We're home." I say as I walk through the door. I think of letting her sleep in the living room on the couch, it is comfy, but I know that the minute my asshole friends walk in, they're going to try to disturb her and I don't like that. So, I carry her to my room.

"Are you going to fuck me now?" she says in a sleepy voice and I can't help but laugh.

"I'm going to get you to bed." I say.

"But, I can please you. If you give me the chance." she exhales on my neck and my dick twitches again. "I want to feel you inside me. Is that so wrong? I can make you come hard." She says in a breathy voice. I stop midway as she says that. No! I am not taking advantage of a drunk hot and sexy woman whose name I don't know.

"Maybe later." I say trying to shake off all the dirty thoughts off my mind, which is impossible to do at this point.

I put her down slowly on her feet and throws her shoes to the side.

She dry heaves a couple of times. "I feel like I'm gonna throw up!" She says.

"Bathroom! To your right." She sprints to the bathroom and I run behind her to hold her hair back but I'm a little late. Her top is ruined and a little bit of her hair too. Once she empties her stomach. I sit her up on the edge of the bathtub and get a wet washcloth. I knew I was going to have to care for one of the assholes, but all I was going to do was carry their dumbasses home and throw them on the floor and let them sleep it off. This was not on my list, but honestly, I don't mind one bit.

"You're sweet. I would even let you come inside me." And I choke on my spit. No woman. And I repeat no woman has ever talked dirty with me as much as her. Usually it's just me who's dirty talking, but it's a good change for once. Except for the fact that I want to jerk off really badly, but I can't.

"Maybe you can tell me that tomorrow." I start wiping down her hair. My eyes fall on her eyes and the small mole under her left eye. I want to plant a soft kiss on it so bad. It makes me tear up.

My mother passed away five years ago and I still haven't been able to get over it. I can't. Never.

She smiles, ear to ear and her eyes disappear. "It's hot in here." she says and proceeds to pull her shirt over her head. I know I should stop her or at least turn around, but I don't. I have been dying to know what she's wearing underneath.

A red lacy bra.

Fuck me!

Her tits are beautiful.

I want them in my mouth.

She proceeds to remove her bra too, but I stop her. As much as the innate animal inside me wants to open her bra with my teeth, I can't. Not when she's drunk.

"Sleep. I want sleep." She says as her head falls on my chest. I carry her in my arms and carry her to my desk. I placed her on the chair and put a shirt of mine on her. She immediately takes off her bra after that and tosses it behind my cupboard. I can see her stiff nipples through my shirt.

She gets up and then proceeds to take off her jeans as well. I let her because my shirt is like a dress on her and she looks adorable in it. I just want to throw her on the bed and cuddle her to sleep. It's weird, I know.

"Sleep." she says again. She walks to the bed and falls on it with a thud. The shirt rides up ever so slightly and I am intrigued to take a look at what's underneath. One thing I can say is that she has thick thighs and a big behind, which jiggles as she falls on the bed and I am turned on again. I pull the blanket over to her waist and pat her head. She looks peaceful while sleeping.

I brush my teeth, jerk off to the thought of fucking her and take off my shirt and jeans and crawl in bed next to her. She shifts in the bed as I sink next to her.

"You know...I have never done it sober." She mumbles. "Because the drunk me is confident in her body, the sober me craves that, but will never show it. Maybe that's why I never had sex sober." She pulls a pillow between her legs and snoozes back.

It crushes my heart to hear that. Doesn't she realise how beautiful she is? I have seen the way everyone was checking her out at the party, how could she not notice? Some were practically drooling over her.

Something in my heart breaks off after hearing this nameless stranger's deepest darkest secret.

I get up before my alarm, because I couldn't sleep at all. I'm sure I have dark circles right now. But I cannot bring myself to close my eyes and not look at her face. I assessed her every feature.

She's beautiful.

And that mole under her eyes twists a knife in my heart, but I love that pain.

I get ready for practice slowly and leave her a note saying my name and my number, in case she wakes up while I am gone.

I am the first one off after hitting the shower. My personal best again. I want to race home to see her and ask her name. I want to talk to her. I want to fuck her.

I race upstairs to my bedroom to find her still asleep in my bed. She kicked off the blanket and my shirt rode up high to expose her matching red lacy panties. And I am hard. Great! I slide back in bed with her and her back is facing me now. I see a small matching mole on the back of her neck and I feel the urge to kiss it. But I shouldn't. I just lay there and I close my eyes and don't even know when I fall asleep.

When I wake up, she's gone.

A week later she is sitting in front of me, assigned to interview me. I had signed up for that stupid thing as I had lost a bet with Sid. I knew George would never stop having sex in the common area, I don't know why I bet against it!

But I have never been more lucky to have lost that bet.

She says her name-

Riya.

Chapter 3- Riya

As if this assignment wasn't time consuming enough, now he wants me to take some more time out of my day and for what? Tutor him? I'd bet him five hundred bucks that he would run away within the first five minutes of my tutoring. I am not patient when teaching dumb students. It is one of the reasons why I never signed up to be a tutor or anyone's mentor.

I have barely a teaspoon full of patience.

"I am not tutoring you. I don't have the time or the energy." *And I can't be with you in a room, without the constant urge to jump your bones.*

"Then, I am not letting you interview me." He says as he folds his hands. God, he's cute. Adorable even. Yet so handsome and sexy at the same time. Snap out of it Ri! Don't fall for his charm again.

"Fine. Works for me. I will ask for someone else. Maybe I can get Raj..." a wide grin is pasted on my face as I think about spending time with Raj.

"Who is this Raj?" He leans his elbows on the table. "Actually nevermind. I don't want to know about your boyfriend." Is he jealous? No! Why would he? He doesn't remember me and for him this is the first time we are meeting.

"Give me one reason why you can't tutor me?" He flashes those beautiful blue eyes at me.

I have a hundred reasons. I roll my eyes.

"I want just one." He says as if he read my mind.

"You play football! And it is not even football..." Okay, I may have a thing against American football. I think it's disrespectful that they call football as soccer and some other game which has nothing to do with feet as *Football!* "What position do you play anyway? Goalkeeper?" I ask him and he bursts out laughing. God his laugh is warm. His eyes close when he laughs and I think that is the most adorable thing ever.

"You are too funny, Raven." *Raven.* It feels like a deja vu.

"My name is Riya."

He nods and apologises. Although I wouldn't have minded being named Raven. It sounds so mystical and beautiful compared to Riya. "Although...you are my Raven." He smolders. And I hate it. I can easily tell that he is trying to do something that is not his cup of tea, because he looks hideous, smoldering like that.

I stiffen a chuckle and gather my books, "I am not yours. Period. Now, if you will excuse me, I have actual stuff to do." *I don't.*

"I'll see you next week then." He huffs in a husky voice as I leave. That did not go as I wanted it to. Now I just have to pray that Professor Bart, my Journalism professor, will let me switch people. Maybe I will switch with Angella.

The old hag stares into my soul like Voldemort. As if I am the one destroying all her Horcruxes. But for that she will have to have a soul, which she does not.

"No." She says blatantly with her glasses sitting too low on her nose bridge.

I take in a deep breath and tell myself to calm down a bit and not say what I want to. "But, he said that he doesn't want to do it with me." I argue with Professor Bart.

She is being completely irrational! "I haven't received any official email from him. I cannot assign you to someone else if he doesn't have a problem with it." I want to roll my eyes so bad!

"But I have a problem with it." I protest.

"And that is not my problem." One tiny push and she will break her bones or at the most sprain something that will make her stay inside her home for weeks. But I am not going to do it.

"I said it on the first day and I will say it one last time. The interviewee can change the interviewer not vice versa. Now, Miss Riya. I have other things to do and I suggest you work out your issues and get started on the project." She turns around in her chair. Classic 80's villain move!

Bitch.

I sigh and open my email to draft an email to Marcus asking to set a new time to meet. He instead replies to me with his phone number. Great!

I just leave it on read. I have too much on my plate right now. And Marcus James Willliams is the one I would like to take my time with.

With graduation nearing, I am thinking about grad schools. I was leaning towards studying the effects of treatments and how it differs with the psychology of the patient. Until now, I have studied very bad accidents, where people on the brink of death survive, because of their will power, whereas I have seen cases where people have passed away at funerals of their loved ones or because of grief, accident patients who pass away even after minor injuries.

Although, there are a lot of factors to be considered here, I think that patients who are recovering are the ones who need the utmost care. Their life will never be the same, they will carry the scars- both physical and emotional, for the rest of their life. But that recovery period is very crucial. I don't take mental health casually, because even though I am a babbler and I love to talk, I love to listen to people even more.

I put myself in their shoes subconsciously and try to reason myself if I would do the same. Justine, despite being a Psychology major herself, often tells me that I am her therapist. And it sounds fun. Natural. I know that everyone has their fair share of struggles, some more than others, but one thing I've known from my personal life experiences is that *change* is the only constant in your life. Nothing is ever going to stay the same way it was, it will change for better or for worse.

"Nothing. I was free, so I called you. What are you doing?" my sister-Maura says on video call.

She has been very busy lately. Not just with work, but perhaps also her personal life. Her boyfriend to be specific. I have always had a ick about that guy. Then again, nobody could ever be good enough for her in my eyes.

I roll around in my bed and wrap the blanket around like a burrito and plop my feet out to balance the heat. "Nothing much. Just had some homework to catch up on. What about you?" I flip through my Biology textbook on my bed. I am bored out of my mind and this is me trying to do my best to do something about it.

"I just…I was thinking of quitting my job." I jerk up my head towards her in shock.

That is the first that I've ever heard of. "What? Why?"

She sighs out loud, clicking her pen on her head. "I was thinking about opening my own fashion boutique or something like that. Nothing too fancy, but I don't know if I will be able to… I mean Keith said that I should stick with this job. It's stable."

Clearly she's disappointed.

My only wish is for my sister to see herself through my eyes and maybe then she will realise how precious she is and how she deserves much more.

Growing up, we were inseparable. When she went to high school, we both pushed each other away as we both went through the awkward teenage phase. We finally reconnected when she graduated her bachelors, I thought we were all good until... I don't want to think about it.

My sister is a pure hearted person, she sees good in everyone. And I know that she doesn't know how badly her words hurt me when she indirectly chose her boyfriend over me. But as long as she is happy, I am happy.

I want to slap her and hug her at the same time. Slap her because she needs to put her dreams before anything and a hug because she doesn't put her dreams first. "I think you should do what you feel is right. And opening your own boutique will give you more freedom. I mean the ultimate goal of this job anyway was to open your own fashion line, right?" I ask her.

She doubts herself further. "But I don't know what mom and dad will think about it. Plus Keith..." another loud sigh. But I am not going to interfere.

She is the glue which holds our family together. She is mom's favourite and I am dad's favourite. Okay, maybe she is both of their favourites, but I am happy that she is. She deserves it. So she has nothing to worry about.

Mom and Dad moved back to India when I was in 4th grade, my grandmother- dad's mother, fell sick and was diagnosed with lung cancer and could not travel to the US for treatment, so my parents moved back to India with me and my sister. I completed the rest of my education there and came back for undergrad.

"Why don't you directly talk to them about this?" I ask her.

She pouts. "I don't know. They were pretty pissed when I told them that I was going to New York instead of New Jersey. I mean our house is still there, closed, collecting dirt." My sister chose to stay in New York and she works for a fashion company.

She always wanted to be a fashion designer, she has always had that potential in her. That's why I would always steal clothes from her closet. We used to live in New Jersey back then, but I chose to go to Massachusetts for Undergrad.

Winston University offered a better Psychology program and it's closer to Boston. I've wanted to experience both the city life and the small town vibe.

Despite having enough money in my bank account, I still worked on campus, because I used to feel lonely in my free time. And the library is not a bad place to work.

India had just started to feel like home and then I had to leave to come back here.

Hiraeth. It feels like I have no home anymore.

I thought that it would again start to feel like home here, but it doesn't. Maybe because mom and dad are still in India and they don't want to leave there. Understandable.

"That was more than 5 years ago. I am sure that they are over it. Just let it go and do what your heart says and screw whatever Keith is saying." *He is not the boss of your life.* I wanted to say that, but I didn't.

My words make her just as uncomfortable. "Ri...please don't...he just wants what's best for me." she defends him again.

"Okay. Fine. I will call you later, I am doing my homework and don't stress too much. If you have enough resources and think you will be able to handle your own thing, which I think you can. Go for it. Okay?"

"Okay. Take care." she flashes me that weak smile.

I hang up and sulk again.

All my life, I have only ever seen relationships crumble around me. Maybe that is the reason why I am a commitment phobe. I know it's not going to last, so why bother yourself with the heartbreak?

But you know what? Being alone sucks just as much. There are times when I love spending time with myself and thank god that I am single, but there are other times when I crave to be loved.

Whatever.

It's no big deal.

"I was going to order take out for both of us." I look at Justine as she comes out of her room all dolled up. "You said we were going to watch a rerun of Harry Potter, Juju!" I flash my puppy dog eyes.

She shuffles and dances in her same uncomfortable heels. "Jake wanted to go out on a spontaneous date. Isn't it so sweet of him? I couldn't say no to him! Sorry Ri." She pouts. Ugh! I hate seeing people in love. It's cringe.

"Fine. Have fun I guess." I swell my cheeks like a pufferfish and Juju comes and kisses my cheek. I roll my eyes at her.

"Sorry babe. Maybe next time. I have shaved everywhere for this date." she squeaks with the pre-sex glow, or maybe that's just the highlighter she's wearing. "I won't be coming home tonight. So you will have the whole house to yourself." She winks at me.

"TMI Juju. TMI."

She scratches the back of heel and I can see that she is already in pain. I grab her by the shoulders and sit her down on the kitchen aisle bar stool. I walk to the other side and pull out the box of band-aids.

I take her shoe off and find her skin peeling on the back. Why does she bear so much pain? Only because he bought the heels for her?! I will never understand it! I carefully apply the band-aid on her heel and she hisses in pain. "Oh come on. You definitely know more than that. But have fun and I'm sorry." she laughs it off.

I laugh along to alleviate the awkward tension.

I put her feet back into the heels and give her a slight push towards the door and plop on the couch. I am happy that at least one of us gets to "Go have fun and use protection, kids." I wave to her from the couch as she exits.

What should I do? I have all this free time.

I go to my room and pull out my portable vibrator from my desk. I put a towel down on the bed and prop myself on the bed.

I turn on the vibrator and as soon as I touch it on my clit, I am immediately teleported to that party last week when I first spotted those blue eyes.

Fuck.

His gorgeous face would look beautiful between my legs. He looks like a man who has hell of skills. I feel an ache in my lower belly as my back arches. I imagine his gorgeous deep blue eyes staring down at me as he thrust in me.

Judging by his size, I am sure *his size* is also bigger. I wonder if he will fit in me.

I remember seeing his hands. They were huge too. Even his two fingers would stretch me. But most of all, I want to know how his mouth would feel on me. I mean he could have already done that, but I don't remember any of it and I didn't wake up with that tingling post-sex sensation between my legs either.

Mmm...

I move the vibrator around until I find the perfect spot and it takes seconds for me to orgasm. My personal best. This is the first time I have ever thought of someone while coming. Damn, it feels different.

I turn off the vibrator and fall back on the bed catching my breath. Out of all the people I could think about, I thought about Marcus.

Why?

Ugh!

It's better to stay away from him as much as possible. His presence itself is intimidating yet makes me feel light whenever he laughs in his deep voice.

My phone lights up as a call notification pops on it, I shove the vibrator in my purse next to me and pick up the call. It's an unknown number.

"Hello?" I say in my post orgasm panting voice.

"Are you at the gym?" A male voice asks me.

"Sorry, who is this?" I ask.

"You didn't save my number, Raven?"

Marcus.

Chapter 4- Marcus

I had to jump through so many hoops to get this girl's phone number. When I sent her my phone number in the email, I expected an immediate reply.

I checked my phone every five minutes and every time it beeped with a notification, to see if it was her. What is wrong with me? I am not someone who mopes over a girl. But she is not just any girl. Her eyes...that tiny mole under her eyes and her red lips...I could go on and on.

I was pissed at myself when I fell asleep and she left my place last week without telling me her name. And then she pretended that we didn't even know each other when she met to interview me. That hurt.

I had called up Beck to ask about her, and he said that she was his frat brother- Jake's girlfriend's best friend. He gave me his number. So I called up Jake and asked him for Riya's phone number.

He was hesitant at first, but he agreed to give me the number after I made a reservation for him and his girlfriend at one of the finest restaurants in Boston and he couldn't refuse. He sent me Riya's number and said that he was going to take his girlfriend out on a date tonight and thanked me.

Works for me. That means that Riya is then probably free tonight. I hung up and saved her number as Raven immediately in my contacts.

I hit the call button and wait as the call rings.

"Hello?" I hear a panting voice.

"Are you at the gym?" I ask her.

"Sorry, who is this?" she asks and it ignites something competitive in me. She didn't save my number.

"You didn't save my number, Raven?" I say in my signature cocky voice.

"James..." she says and I freeze. It's like all the air in my lungs escapes and I suddenly forget to breathe.

"Hello?" she says after I don't respond for a couple of seconds. I shake off that feeling.

"It's Marcus." I correct her, taking in deep breaths.

"Yes, Marcus." she pants softly and then clears her throat.

"Are you at the gym?" I ask again. *Curiosity killed the cat and blah blah.*

"No. I ...am at home." she says hesitantly.

"What are you doing?" I ask and there's a long pause. Is she with someone who is making her pant like this? My blood boils. I can't bear the thought of other men touching her.

"Nothing...um...I was just...reading." She lies.

"You are panting. If you are with your boyfriend, you can just tell me that." Then I remember her mentioning someone named Raj twice during the interview. The way she smiled to herself after saying his name made me feel...what? I barely know this girl!

"I don't do boyfriends and no, I am alone. Like I said...I was cycling." she says.

"You said you were reading before, Raven." I laugh with...relief? She doesn't do boyfriends...*Interesting.*

"Yes. I was reading and cycling. What's with all the questions? Are you my dad or something?" She sounds annoyed.

"No, but you can call me daddy." I smirk. Okay... I admit it! Even for me, it was cringe. But the words had left my mouth and I couldn't take them back.

"If your smirk had a noise, I'd be able to hear it through the phone right now. And ew. That was cringe. Does that line work for you?" She says, sounding intrigued. Man this girl knows me and it makes my heart race. A wide smile spreads across my face.

I rub my hand through my hair, smiling to myself. "Is it working?" I ask.

There's a long pause. "You wish." and I just know that she is smiling ear to ear right now.

"If your smile had a voice, I'd be able to hear it through the phone right now." and she chuckles. I wish I was there to see her smile like that.

"What do you want, James?" she says, clearing her throat.

My brows furrow and my heart paces again as she calls me *James!* Don't get me wrong, I don't hate it, it just...drives me crazy in a way that I'm still figuring out if I love or hate. "Why do you call me James?" I ask her out of curiosity.

"Why do you call me Raven? At least your middle name is James. Raven has nothing to do with my name. Anyway, what do you want?"

"I was–"

She cuts me off and her tone is now that of realisation. "James, how did you get my phone number?" *Shit.* How do I tell her?

Jake had specifically asked me not to tell her that he gave me her number. "I have my sources." I say, not wanting to explain how many hoops I had to jump through and I definitely did not want to out Jake.

"Sure. What do you want? And no, I am not tutoring you."

"We'll talk about that." A challenge. I like that.

"I'm hanging up now." she says.

I had received a "prompt out" email from Professor Bart, regarding this situation and I told her that I had no issues whatsoever and was in fact looking forward to all the interviews. "If you don't tutor me, I am not doing the interview. And I know that you cannot change your partner unless I complain about it. So, Raven, be a good girl and help a man in need here." She sighs.

Maybe I am evil. But I love being evil, as long as I get what I want.

"You can dream on, Marcus. I'll gather information about you from the internet for the interview. Now stop wasting my time and lose this number. Bye." she hangs up on me.

I am speechless. This is the first time someone hung up on me. No one hangs up on me. I call her back and she picks up on the last ring.

"I thought I told you to lose this number." she grunts.

"Send me your address. We'll talk about this in person." I say as I pick my car keys and head outside.

"I am not telling you shit, Williams." I stop in the middle of the flight of stairs.

"I am not playing here, Raven. Send me your address. Now." I say in a more serious voice. Usually women are the first ones to send me their address even when I don't ask them to, but her... *Mmm*. She wakes something primal inside me.

"You can fuck yourself. I am not telling you shit, Marcus." she barks at me. And I am teleported to the night we met, when she was telling me all the things she wanted to do to me. Damnit! I'm hard as fuck now.

I was going to hold onto this card for longer, seeing how she didn't remember anything about that night. But it's a shame that I have to use it this early into the game. But I guess, I'd take this win for now. "That's not what you said that night. I remember clearly what all you wanted to do to me, Raven. And fucking myself was not in the plan." I tease her and there's silence.

INTERTWINED

Ah! I got her.

"I...What– I..." she is nervous.

"Your address." I say clearly.

"I–I'll text it to you." a wide grin spreads across my face.

"Good girl." I say and hang up the call. I have never been so proud of myself for staying sober at a party and not sleeping with the most beautiful woman I have laid my eyes on.

Her place is about a 15 minute drive from my place. I knock on her apartment door and I hear the sound of dancing bells. The same ones that she wore to the party. I take a deep breath in and out.

When she opens the door, her hair is in a messy bun, she's wearing loose pyjamas and glasses. I wonder how it would be like to come over her glasses. No, Marcus! We are not going there!

She just points inside the house in an annoying way and groans as I walk inside and close the door behind me.

"That's one way to treat your guests, Raven." I chuckle.

"It's the only way to treat intruders, Williams." She is feisty. I love that she always has a comeback for whatever I say.

I walk into the living room and see food laid out on the table. There's enough for four people, but I don't see anyone and her roommate is on a date with her boyfriend.

I walk towards the table and take a seat. If she is calling me an intruder, I might as well act as one. "Did you order food for me? That was so sweet of you, Raven."

"Can't you call me Riya for once?" she pouts.

Adorable.

She is freaking cute.

She sits on the couch and presses play on the TV. Ignoring me completely. I guess she wants me to feel at home! So I sit right next to her and grab a spoon for the food. She doesn't mind it when I do that, so I play along.

"What are we watching?" I ask her.

"I–" she emphasises. "Am watching Lust stories." she says as she takes a bite of her food.

"Okay. And whose lusting on whom?" she turns to look at me with that look on her face as if she's turned on right now. I'm not sure though. It's difficult to read her.

She grunts in an annoyed way looking at me and turns her attention back on the screen. A woman on the screen starts to pant on screen. Is she–? Yep. She is having an orgasm in front of what looks like her boyfriend or husband, his mother and some other woman. My gaze adverts towards my Raven.

She's biting her lower lip watching that. I wonder what she would look like, coming on my tongue. And I am more hard now.

She shifts in her seat and crosses her leg over. I know what she's doing and that's just turning me on. Fuck. This is torture.

I move closer to her and lean in her ear. "I can make you come better than that." I whisper in her ear and her body stiffens. I can see goosebumps on her ear and I can't help but chuckle.

She finally turns off the TV and turns to face me.

"You said that you remembered that night?" she gets straight to the point. "So you're saying that you weren't drunk?" I see she's going to ignore my comment earlier and jump straight to the point.

"That's exactly what I am saying." I look straight into her eyes and she's nervous. And then I remember. *I have never done it sober.* She'd told me. She probably doesn't know how sex feels like then. Something primitive inside me awakens. I could make her feel that. No, I want to be the only one who makes her feel that.

"I thought that..." she takes a deep breath in and out. And god, I want to kiss her. "I thought that you were too drunk to remember me, because you didn't bring it up when we met that day." she nervously plays with a strand of her hair which falls out of her bun.

I turn to face her. "I didn't bring it up because it seemed like you didn't want me to."

"I thought it was because I was bad at it, that you didn't have fun." I'm confused now. Does she think that we had sex that night?

"Raven–"

"I'm sorry if it was bad, or if you didn't have fun." she looks down at her feet. How do I tell this woman that she could make me come with just her gaze, with her words. How do I tell her how hard I am, fighting the urge to bend her over right now and make her moan my name until the sun rises again. I gulp hard and bring my hand towards her face and tilt her face to face me.

"We didn't have sex, Riya." I say in a monotone.

She looks up at me with that same gaze which could make me come so hard. It's her big beautiful brown coloured doe eyes! I am definitely going to jerk off to this look when I go back.

I spot a subtle note of disappointment in her tone and her expression. And even though it sounds like relief, I am going to tell myself that it was disappointment. "We didn't?" she asks me. I just nod to her. Then her expression changes.

She looks away from me, towards the TV and says, "Yeah, I mean it makes sense. Duh! I know I am not the type of girl you would go for."

If only you could read my mind right now, Raven.

Chapter 5- Riya

I have never felt so embarrassed in my entire life as I am feeling right now. What was I thinking? Of course I am not the type of girl he goes for. I have a belly and I have thick thighs and I don't have those long legs. His type is probably those girls who look like supermodels. With a perfect figure. Long legs, flat stomach, thigh gap. You know the list.

He holds my hands and pulls me closer to him, slides his arm around my waist and looks at me as if he wants to devour me right now, right here. And my heart is literally thumping out of my chest right now.

"I didn't sleep with you because you were drunk. I don't sleep with drunk women, Raven. I am at least that much of a gentleman." I can't take my eyes off his lips. I wonder what they would feel like on my body. I take in a sharp breath and he notices that.

He growls softly and his eyes fixate on my lips. "Don't do that, Raven." he says and suddenly I feel very mischievous.

"Don't do what?" I slowly lick my lips and bite my bottom lip and I visibly see his eyes darken. From the blue you see in shallow waters to the one where the water dips deep. The beautiful dark ocean blue. I realise that ironically I am playing with fire right now.

He lets go of me and adjusts himself. And for some very weird reason, I feel disappointed.

He takes a deep breath in as if he's trying to calculate what to say next. "You need my help and I need yours." he turns to look at me.

"Why me?" *I know why, because I am smart.*

"Because..." He tucks a lock of my hair behind my ear and it sends chills down my body and a current to my pussy. "This way, we can help each other out. And I saw the books you carry. I know you are smart. Don't act coy." he tilts his head to the side and stares into my soul with those deep blue eyes of his.

"I will admit that I am smart. But I don't have the time to tutor you, James." He freezes for a second and I can see his expression go blank.

"Marcus. It's Marcus." He says looking at his feet.

"I like James better. I think it suits you more than Marcus." I really do. I like the name James better than Marcus. Marcus feels...distant. Feels like he's just *some guy*. But he's not! No matter how much I hate American football, I cannot deny the fact that he is a part of the team, just because he's an average player! Winston is known for their American football.

"Why?" he asks me with real curiosity in his eyes.

"Well, Marcus is a good name, but James sounds like a sweet and caring guy's name. Not saying that you are any of those. But I don't know why, James just suits you better than Marcus. If you don't like it I won't ca–"

"No. I like James." he looks at me. His eyes twinkling.

"Are you crying?" He looks away and wipes away the tears in his eyes. Damn it! I can't see people cry. And for some very weird and protective reason, I can't see tears in his eyes. It makes my heart squish. "I'm sorry, if I offended you. I won't ever call you James."

He huffs and smiles. "I like James better. It just–"

I place my hand on his shoulder to console him and he flinches, flicking his gaze at me. "Please don't cry. I can't see you cry." I say the second part subconsciously and he flashes me a small smile now.

"It reminds me of my mother." he finishes. I don't know anything about him or his family, all I know so far is that he plays football, the type of football which does not have a goalkeeper. But I want to know more. I want to know the reason for his tears. I want to pull him for a hug and tell him that everything is going to be okay and then I want to make everything okay.

"Your mother?" I say as I tap on his shoulder. He brings his hand to my face and runs his hand over my face under my left eye.

"You remind me of her." he smiles for real this time and his smile is so warm that it fills my heart with joy. The way he is looking at me right now, is making me really happy when it shouldn't.

I stay quiet, not knowing how to react. I can feel my heart thumping in my throat.

"I'll tell you about her later. For now, let's settle on a day when you can tutor me and then another day for the interview." he pulls his hand off my face.

There is no way I am winning this, so I give in. "We can do both on the same day. It's fine. I know you must have practice and all too. So, we can adjust."

"No." he protests immediately. "I mean…I am slow at learning. So, it will take me time to understand and learn and you won't have enough time for the interview stuff. I have a lot of stuff that I want included in the article. You know, in case it makes the paper. It will be good for my image as a captain."

I raise my eyebrow in suspicion. "What makes you think that I will write all good stuff about you? And wait, you are the captain?" he chuckles at that. And I immediately feel at ease now. He looks better this way.

"Yes, I am the captain, Raven. So please make me look good in the public eye." he battles his eyelashes at me.

"I wouldn't hold my breath." I wave my hand at him and he laughs.

We eat dinner which I'd initially ordered for Justine and I. It was more than enough to feed four people. But we manage to finish everything. Athletes do eat a lot!

I walk James back to his car. We talked so much. He really loves to talk. And I didn't mind listening to him. Okay fine, I liked listening to his story.

"So, I'll see you next week then?" he says as he opens his door.

"Yep. I'll be at your place. Don't worry, I'll text you before I come over, so you can finish up whatever you are doing." I laugh to myself but he doesn't. Okay. I guess that was not funny.

"You don't have to worry about that." he says as he closes his door. He starts his car and rolls his window down. "Good night, Raven."

"Good night James." I wave him as he drives off. A night well spent. Yes. I had fun tonight.

I texted James before I left class that I was leaving to go to his place, but he still hasn't responded. Now, I'm debating whether or not I should go into his house or just leave from here.

I get out of my car, lock it and head inside. I am immediately greeted by three huge and very handsome men. All of them are so gorgeous. So beautiful! And so buffed!!!

"You must be Riya." The blonde and the biggest one comes and hugs me tight.

"Don't be an asshole, George." the one with the black hair shouts and George lets go of me. "Don't mind him Riya. George can't keep his hands to himself when he sees a beautiful woman." I suppress a smile. "I'm Daniel. But you can call me Dan." he offers his hand to shake. He's the classic beauty. A total Prince charming beauty.

I shake his hand. "Hi Dan." I smile at him.

"And that's Siddharth." he points at the other man standing in the kitchen stirring the pot. He smiles and waves at me. "Marcus is upstairs in his room. But I would not suggest going up there right now." He presses his lips together as if he's trying not to smile.

"Okay..." I take a seat on the couch. "Wouldn't want to walk on something which is not PG-13." I mumble.

"You want some pasta?" Siddharth asks me. I turn to look at him and he is flashing me the cutest smile ever. Hi wheatish complexion and matching brown eyes and frizzy hair make him look hot yet adorable.

I open my mouth to say no, but my stomach growls in protest. "Does it have seasoning other than salt and pepper?" I raise my eyebrow and everyone starts laughing.

"Good question." George sits beside me and the leather couch sinks on his side.

"Yes. It does. Does it look like I would make *white people food* here, Riya?" he rolls his eyes and I can't stop laughing looking at how offended George and Daniel are. Man he's funny.

"I can grab a bite." I flash a short smile. I am starving. And it doesn't look like James is going to be done anytime soon.

"You fucker." some woman shouts from upstairs. I can hear her heels clanking on every stair. "You don't respond to my texts, and when I show up at your place, you don't even want to fuck me and then I find this." I hear her shout. I see George get up from next to me and make his way to the kitchen. Daniel is right behind him.

Dan is washing an onion and George is fighting with Siddharth to stir the pot.

I hear James. "I promised you nothing. It was all in your head. I never once mentioned that I liked you or anything. Fuck, I don't even remember your name. Is it Betty? Bethany? Bianca?"

Ouch!

He didn't have to be so mean to that girl. I can see her heels and all I see is legs. Until I can finally see her wearing the miniest mini leather skirt I have ever seen with a matching leather bralette.

"No, you didn't. You just fucked me once. And then this whore." She holds a red bra up. "And FYI my name is Melanie." She throws a red lace bra at his face. I just stare down at my feet not trying to look at anyone or make it obvious that I am in here. "I was falling for you." She caresses his face.

"I don't do all that bullshit. And you knew that from the beginning." *Bullshit!* He was pretty heartless there.

"Fuck you." she slaps him hard and my eyes widen. Scared that Marcus might hit her back and I won't stand that. Although, that girl didn't have to hit him like that.

He doesn't do anything. Instead he walks to the door and just stands there, indirectly telling her to leave.

"I'm sorry if I led you on." His gaze lowers to the ground and his words catch me by surprise. What the fuck just happened?

"Goodbye Marcus." She leaves crying. It is early January winter in Mass. It's fucking freezing outside. And I did not see any other cars around their house. I hope that the girl doesn't freeze herself to hypothermia.

James closes the door behind her and walks to the stairs to pick up the red lacy bra and then looks at me.

"Let's go to my room." he says with a tired look. I look at his friends who are in the kitchen who are not very surprised by whatever just happened. Their lips are pressed together and they are trying their best not to burst out into laughter.

"Um…Yeah. Sure." I follow him up the stairs.

He stops midway and turns back. "Daniel, at least peel the onion before washing it." he chuckles as if he wasn't slapped a few minutes ago.

We reach his room and it's all messy. The bedsheet is undone and the clothes are on the floor, the drawers are flooded open. And I give him the benefit of the doubt that the not-so-sweet lady trampled over his room.

"Sorry about the mess..." he exhales. I can see that his cheek is all red. The slap from earlier must be stinging bad!

"Sit here." I tell him to sit on the bed and he listens to me. I gently graze my hand on his cheek and his eyes are fixed on mine. "Does it hurt?" I ask him.

He just smiles at me and nods.

"Stay here." I run down to the kitchen and ask Dan for the ice pack. He and the boys make some fun about it and after making me listen to their entire slap count, he hands me the ice pack. I can't believe that among these four men, they have been slapped 52 times. Daniel raking the highest amount of slaps, clocking in at 23 slaps. Maybe he is not the Prince charming afterall. I shake off the thought and run back up.

James is just where I'd left him, tidying the bed sheet. I walk towards him and place the ice pack on his face.

He stops when he sees me and stares at his feet. "I'm sorry you had to see that." I think he's feeling embarrassed.

I stay quiet.

"This is yours." he says as he hands me the red lacy bra.

Shit!

It is mine. From that night. I grab it out of his hand quickly as flustered.

"I'm so sorry. I forgot it here and..." I take a deep breath in as realisation sets in. That girl probably slapped him because she thought that he was sleeping with me- the owner of the red bra.

His expression suddenly shifts and he gives me that cocky smile. "You can make it up to me if you want."

"I'm not going to sleep with you." I say immediately and he chuckles. A raspy laugh as he presses the ice pack against his cheek.

"No...have dinner with me."

Dinner? As in a date? I'm very confused!

"As friends." he says as if he can read my mind.

"Let's get to work and then we can talk about it." I smile at him. "And keep the ice pack on so it doesn't get worse." I press the ice pack on his cheek and he holds my hand. And he looks at me with those deep blue eyes. He looks at ME! He LOOKS at me! HE LOOKS AT ME LIKE NO ONE EVER HAS!

I quickly pull my hand out of his grip before I do something I'll regret.

"Let's start then." I get up and make my way to the desk. "We'll start with the biology of cells."

We study for about two hours and whatever he said about being a slow learner? Lies. He is really smart. But he did pretend to not understand it sometimes. One thing Marcus James Williams is not, is an actor. He can't act.

I close the textbook and sigh with relief! "Okay. I think you should be set for the first test now. The Professor does focus on elaborate answers so don't write anything she's not asking and you should be good." My stomach growls immediately.

"Hungry?"

"I'm just going to drive back and pick something up on the way." I say as I pack my books.

"Or you could stay and eat and then leave." He shrugs.

I know that Justine is working tonight, so she will be home late, so I will be eating alone and besides we will just be eating anyway. "Siddharth was offering me pasta, but you dragged me upstairs." I pout.

"Oh...I'm sorry. I didn't even ask you for water." He shakes his head.

"It's fine. I should get going, I have to get up early for work anyway." I give him a fake smile and it's like he can see through me.

"I insist. We can order in if you want. Come on, Riya." He says my name in a way that makes me fall in love with my name.

"Fine. But I am leaving immediately after. What do you want to eat?" I ask as I pull out my phone.

"You tell me" he pulls out his phone. No uh! I am not letting him pay. I never let men pay for anything, because then they think that I owe them something. When I don't! "I'm ordering it." He takes my phone out of my hand.

"No way am I letting you pay for it." He holds my phone with his hand above his head. I jump and try to get it but he jumps with me as well.

"Give it back, Williams." I say laughing.

"Get it then." He gets up and runs around the room with my phone.

I run behind him until I jump on him and he falls on the bed behind him. He holds my waist and I fall on him. "Got it." I say after I snatch my phone from his hand but I realise that I am on top of him with his hand around my waist. My breasts pressed against his chest. Eyes locked. Deep breaths. Fuck. I want to kiss him.

I immediately get off him and accidentally poke my elbow in his stomach and he groans with pain and rolls over.

"I'm so sorry." I say as I rub his back.

"No you're not." he chuckles. "And I already got us pizza." he flashes me that cocky smile. I was literally in the mood for some pizza in fact that is exactly what I was going to pick up later. "Do you want to watch something in the meantime?" he asked me.

"Sure."

We head down to the living room which is silent now. There's no one.

"What do you want to watch?" Marcus asks me as he passes me a small blanket to pull over my legs. My feet are ice cold and the blanket feels so nice and warm.

It's two am and we're still binging the second season of Modern family. James snuggled in the blanket and I didn't even realise it. Suddenly the door jolts open and we hear a trail of moaning and kissing.

George stumbles in the living room making out with a girl. His hands are wandering all over her body. "Come one man. You know the couch is my favourite place to do it." He complains like a baby and walks away to his room. I immediately stand up and throw off the blanket.

"How dirty is this couch?" I ask and Daniel chuckles as he walks in the door.

"Don't worry. We get it deep cleaned every other weekend." he sits beside me and closes his eyes as he exhales. I can smell the alcohol from a mile away.

"They're drunk." James says. It seems like they were just coming back from a party.

"Why didn't you go to the party? I'm sorry if I held you back." I tell James. Dan chuckles with his eyes still closed.

"Because he likes you." he says in a drunk voice.

The light from the TV is very dim, but I see James turn visibly red. "Fuck off, Dan." James is flustered and I can't help but blush. He turns towards me. "Come on. I'll drop you off. It's late." James gets up and turns off the TV.

"I drove here." I swing the keys in his face.

"But–" he stops and recalculates what he was going to say. "Text me when you reach home or if you need anything and keep your windows closed and doors locked and go straight home. And text me or call me. Whatever you prefer." I try to hold in a smile.

"Yes dad. Will do." he chuckles when I say that.

"Or daddy. Whatever you like, Raven." he flashes me that cocky smile again.

He walks me to my car and opens the door for me after I unlock the car. Such a gentleman.

"Thanks for tonight. I'll see you..."

"Wednesday." I start the car.

"Tomorrow." He says. I raise my eyebrow. "Dinner. Remember? Let's do it tomorrow. If you have time." He smiles at me and it makes my heart flutter. I would agree to go to hell with him when he flashes me that smile.

"Tomorrow then. Bye James."

"Bye Raven."

I pull out of his driveway and have only one thing on my mind.

James.

Chapter 6- Marcus

I almost get tackled on the field by Zackery. "Where is your focus, Williams?" Coach Belkis shouts from the side. "Stop snoozing and get your head in the game." he yells at me.

I have only one thing on my mind right now. Dinner with my sweet Raven.

I hit the showers ready to race home to get ready for dinner. I know it is not a date, it is just a dinner with a friend. But I wouldn't want her to think that I am shabby, that's why I am putting in an effort.

"Marcus." Coach Belkis shouts. "My office. After you're done." Great! Just what I needed. I change and head to his office.

I knock on the door.

"Come on in, Marcus." he says. He is the most difficult man to read. His face stays numb regardless of the news he's going to give- good or bad.

"We made it to the finals, that's great. But it's against Fritz. I know we still have some time but I wanted to discuss some strategies with you." Fritz University is our biggest rival. And the captain of their team- their middle linebacker Cole James Harriett is my biggest rival. It is funny that we once played for the same team in high school.

The rest is history, but we are rivals and I want to win this game at any cost, not just because of Harriett, but this is my first year being a captain and I really want us to win. The boys deserve this win.

"I have been working on it, coach. I know our offence is great as of now, but I am working on our defence with Daniel. I think we might have a good chance of bringing the title home this year." I say with confidence.

In the six games I have played against Cole, I could see that his style has changed a lot. He got more aggressive towards me with every game. This time, I want to crush Fritz University.

"Good. We will go over it tomorrow with the team." I stand up to go just then he calls for me again. "Williams..." he says in a stern voice. "I have high hopes from you. Don't let me down like Harold did." The finals are in a few weeks and if our defence improves a bit we might be able to draw the entire match on our side. But it's Fritz...

Let's say it's a 51-49 chance of winning and losing. And since it's a home game for us, there's more pressure to win.

"Got it coach." I say before leaving the office with a weird feeling. I am not falling for anyone and screwing up my chance to be drafted in the NFL.

My father- Micheal Williams is a football legend. I want to walk in his footsteps and make my name in the NFL. I don't mind when people know me as the great Micheal Williams' son. But I want my game to be known by my name. Not his.

I head home and text Riya.

I'll pick you up in an hour.
Sure. I'll be ready by then. Where are we going though? So, I'll dress accordingly.

It's a relatively fancy place. That's all you're getting from me.
Fine. *eyeroll*

I chuckle as I put the phone down. I love teasing her. Just friends. I remind myself.

She walks towards my car and I forget how to breathe. Her black dress is hugging her curves in the perfect places and showing just enough cleavage that it keeps me wanting more. I get out and open the door for her.

"You look..." *You have to speak Marcus. Words. Any words.* She raises her brow at me. "Spectacular." I finally manage to say and she laughs. Her dark red glossy lipstick would look so good on my neck. Fuck. "You look really beautiful." I hold her hand and press a soft kiss on her cheek. God she smells so good!

Delicious.

Devourable.

Delicate.

"You look good yourself." She eyes me from head to toe and then meets my eyes with a similar expression on her face.

I help her get in the car and swoop her dress in and close the door. I spot her anklet around her ankles. The same one with the dancing bells. Fuck. This woman gets me hard just being around her. I take a few deep breaths and head in through the other side.

I drive us off and I can feel her gaze on me the entire time.

"You can just ask me whatever it is." I finally break the silence and she clears her throat.

"I just..." I can feel that she's flustered. "You look really good. That's all." she presses her purse in between her legs and I wish I was that purse. Pressed between her legs. But why do her compliments make my heart flutter? It boosts my ego to a next level.

"Thank you, Raven." She smiles in that cute way which makes me think about all the dirty things I want to do to her.

We reach the restaurant in a few more minutes and I park the car. I tell her to wait and go around to open the door for her and offer her a hand to get down.

"So..." she drags on but doesn't finish.

"So?" I ask her curiously as I lead her to the restaurant.

"I wanted to ask you something, if it's okay." she hesitates.

"You can ask me anything. Anything!" I wink at her and she chuckles.

"Why football? I mean, from what I could tell, you looked like you weren't that bad at coding." This is probably the first time I have been asked that question.

In all the answers I've prepared for all the interviews I've had so far, I never told anyone about this one. "My father played football and I want to walk in his footsteps."

"But then, why computer science? I mean doesn't it make life more difficult for you? You could've chosen any dumb major." I can't help but laugh.

We reach inside and the server leads us to our table. I pull a chair for her and take a seat across from her. "My mother taught me coding when I was a kid." I tell her. And she bursts out laughing.

"When you were a kid? What were you? Bill Gates?" I chuckle myself at the weird comparison.

"I wasn't Bill Gates, but I wasn't *dumb* either." I smile and she stops laughing. God! I am talking about my mother. I haven't done that in a long long time.

"My mother was very competitive. So when my dad used to teach me how to throw on weekends, my mother would teach me coding on weekdays. She wanted me to be a better coder than a football player" I smile remembering those days. They would bicker like kids. They were so much in love. Until... my smile immediately fades away.

The silence drags on for just a second longer before she cuts in. "That's sweet. So, what do you like better? Coding or football?" She raises her eyebrow. "Is it like asking to pick between your mom and dad?" She has absolutely no filter.

I suppress a smile. I don't think I have ever smiled when talking about my mother, at least not since she passed away. "Coding makes me feel at peace and football pumps up my nerves. So, it depends what mood I'm in."

"I see...So, your dad taught you how to play?" She keeps her elbow on the table and leans her head on her hand.

"He did." I smile. "You have no idea who my father is, do you?" I chuckle.

"Messi?" She raises an eyebrow. "Ronaldo? I know it's not Mbappe. That dude is our age. Almost."

Until now, every person I have ever met in my life has asked me for my father's autograph at some point. This woman sitting in front of me is telling me that she has no idea who my father is and still wants to spend time with me makes me feel the proudest.

"Who is it?" she shouts. Frustrated.

"Just some football player. American football." I correct quickly. By now, I have picked up on her hate for the sport!

"I hate that game." she rolls her eyes at me.

"Even the players?" I raise my brow and I can see that she is trying not to blush.

"Especially the players." the corner of her mouth curves up.

"Maybe I can change that." I adjust my jacket and she chuckles.

"You can try." she challenges me, giving me that seductive glare.

We talk about random stuff the entire time. She tells me about her family. Her smile fades away when she mentions her sister, and I understand that it is a touchy topic for her. I tell her about my dreams and my father's dreams for me. I tell her a little about my mother and she smiles in a way that makes my stomach churn with happiness. I have never talked this much ever. Mostly because no one really wanted to get to know me, Not like she does.

"So you're telling me that you have never heated up ice cream because it was too cold to eat?" she asks me with a serious tone and I am laughing my ass off right now.

"It's called 'ice' cream babe. Not hot cream." I emphasize on the ice.

She points her finger at me, which again, not something anyone has dared to do before. "Not your babe and you are missing out on life then." she shrugs as she takes a bite of her dessert.

"Wouldn't melted ice cream just be a milkshake at that point?"

She nods her head saying no.

"Milkshakes are cold. You're supposed to heat up the ice cream. You should really try it. It's a super lazy snack. You don't have to chew anything."

"No way." I exclaim. "You bite into your ice cream? You're a psychopath!" she bursts out laughing.

"Says the person who sleeps with both feet inside the blanket. It's a universal rule to always have one leg outside the blanket. You're the psychopath." I laugh so much that my stomach aches. And for some reason I don't feel conscious or embarrassed about the things I share with her. She has a way of making you feel not judged.

I love that this woman has no filter and I love how I don't have to have a filter when I'm talking to her either.

She yawns big.

"Geez. Sorry for boring you." I pout and she immediately shakes her head saying no. And another yawn.

"I haven't been sleeping much these days. And last night I barely got any sleep before work. I'm really tired. Can we leave? Sorry." she says softly.

"Why are you apologising? We can leave whenever you want. Let me get the cheque and I'll drop you off."

"I'll get it." She pulls out her card.

"Like I'm letting you pay. No way."

"But you paid last time."

"Riya." I say and she immediately jolts her eyes at me. I like that. "Respectfully. No."

"But–"

"I asked you out for dinner. End of discussion." I interrupt her.

"But..." she pouts. "I don't like it when men pay for me."

I laugh out loud. "You are probably the first girl I know who has ever said that."

"It's true." she shrugs. "It makes some people. Emphasis on some..." she says. "That I owe them something and I hate that feeling."

My heart mellows. "You don't owe me anything, Riya." her eyes jolt up to meet mine as soon as I call her name. Why does that make my heart flutter? "I asked you for dinner and you said yes. Now please let me be the gentleman I am and get the cheque for you as well." I genuinely smile at her and she blushes. That's a first! I love that I can make her smile like that. It boosts my ego even more.

"Fine. Gentleman." she snorts.

"Ouch, Raven. I have been nothing but a gentleman tonight." I say adjusting my suit.

"That you have." she bites her lower lip and that immediately sends blood to my groyne and dirty ideas to my head.

I get the bill and we head out. I help her get in the car and five minutes in, she's fast asleep.

I pull up in the parking lot of her apartment and just sit there. Studying her breathing pattern. She's so calm and at peace. She nudges a little and her eyes slowly start to open. And because I don't want her to think that I am a creep, I increase the volume of the radio and Lover by Taylor Swift starts to play.

"I didn't know you were a Taylor Swift fan. Don't most guys hate her or something?" she says in her sleepy voice and it's so hot.

"I'm not most guys, am I, Raven?" I flash her my signature cocky smile and she chuckles and rubs her eyes.

"Where are we?" she looks around. "Why didn't you wake me up?" she stretches her arms over her head.

"You were snoring, so I thought that you might need all the sleep you need." she punches my arm. "Ouch. You sure know how to throw a punch!" It does hurt a little.

"I know I don't snore. Liar." that glare turns me on! Shit! I can't let her see how hard I am right now. "Well... Thanks for tonight. I really had fun. I'll see you tomorrow then!" She gives me a small smile as her eyelids are droopy and she yawns again.

"Let's do this again sometime." I push my luck too far knowing that she's going to say no.

"Umm..." she hesitates.

I regret these words before they even leave my mouth. "As friends I mean. I had a lot of fun too."

If I'm not wrong, she almost looks disappointed when I say 'as friends'. "Sure. Friend." she says in a sarcastic way. I can't believe that I friendzoned myself.

"Good night James." She closes the door and walks away.

"Night..." she's already walking away. "*Raven.*"

Chapter 7- Riya

Friends. Sure. That's exactly what we are. I mean what else was I expecting? He thinks that girlfriends and relationships are bullshit and I don't do boyfriend stuff. Not that I think that it is bullshit though.

Nevermind. I keep overthinking in my lab.

"Riya." a known voice calls my name and I forget everything.

"Raj... How have you been?" He pulls me in for a side hug.

"Where have you been stranger? How was Australia?" he asks me.

"You know. I just missed you guys so much that I had to run back here." I chuckle.

"I missed you too." he says with a straight face. And it makes my heart melt. *Aww...* I missed him too. Okay, so maybe I have had a little crush on him before I left for Australia as well. But he doesn't need to know that.

"Want to grab lunch later?" he asks me. I was supposed to meet *my friend* for the interview. But I'm sure he won't mind if I am a little late.

"Sure. Let's catch up." I smile at him and get back to deconstructing the paper I was studying.

We walk to the diner near our lab and my phone starts to buzz. I don't even need to check it to see who it is. I silence the call and put the phone away. We take a seat at the booth and my phone buzzes again.

"You can take it. It's fine." Raj says.

"Sorry. Excuse me." I walk outside and pick up his call. "What?" I say angrily.

"Where are you?" he asks me.

"I'll be a little late." I don't know why I am being so rude to him.

"Okay... That's not the answer to my question, sweetheart." He says in his sweet voice and my stomach does the flip-flops. It's probably out of hunger.

"Sorry, do you still like curly fries? And chocolate milkshake?" Raj pops from the back and asks me.

"Yes. I do. You remember!" I am smiling ear to ear right now. I quickly note the change in my voice and tone when I talk to Raj...It's such a cute and sweet voice that I fake around him!

"Of course I do." Is he flirting with me? *Holy shit!* He totally is. He touches my shoulder and walks back inside.

"What were you saying again?" I ask James on the phone. My voice tunes back to the bitch mode subconsciously.

"Am I disturbing your date?" he asks.

"Um...I'll be a little late. Sorry about that. But I'll see you soon." I cut the call and push back my smile and walk inside.

If I thought that Raj was flirting with me before, I was wrong. He is flirting with me right now. And I am not holding back either. We're making good conversations, but there are times where I have to fake a laugh. He does not have very good humour but that's fine, I have enough for both of us.

"There you are." a panting voice next to me has his head down.

"What are you doing here?" I get up and glare at him.

He lifts his head and takes a sharp breath and his eyes lock with mine. I can see something wild in his eyes this time and it makes me rub my legs together.

He doesn't say anything, just slides next to me in the booth.

"James." I bark at him but he doesn't say anything, just glares at Raj.

"Marcus." James shakes his hand with Raj and Raj introduces himself. And James' eyes immediately wander to find mine. I might have mentioned Raj once or twice by accident before. I bite my bottom lip.

"Have I seen you before Marcus?" Raj asks James.

"I play football."

"Wait, you're Marcus James Williams?" Raj's mouth falls wide open as if he's star struck. And James just smirks. Ugh! Annoying.

"You're a celebrity or something, Williams?" I whisper in his ear.

"Not for you." he whispers back and I gulp hard.

"It's nice to meet you man. I didn't know Riya had famous friends." I want to roll my eyes out of my eye socket, if it is possible. Raj and James give each other that 'bro hug'. "Can you get me your father's autograph?" Raj asks sheepishly. I probably imagine it but there is a tiny bit of disappointment on his face.

"I'll see what I can do. Anything for my favourite girl." he wraps his hand around my shoulder. I wasn't even listening to what they were saying.

"Huh? What? Yeah." I say something.

"I didn't know you were together." Raj raises his brow at me and then I see his hand around my shoulder and quickly nudge it off.

"No. We're not." Raj narrows his eyes at me. So different from the way he was looking at me before. "We really are not, Raj." I reach for his hand across the table and give it a squeeze. I see something *red* from the corner of my eye. Yep. It's James.

"Okay..." Raj forces a chuckle. This is obviously very awkward for him too. I quickly retract my hand.

"So Raj, since when are you and Riya dating?" I choke on my spit and start coughing uncontrollably. Raj offers me the milkshake and James offers me water. I chug some water and exhale.

"We're not dating." Raj is very blunt with his tone. And that stings somewhere. "We're just good friends." he adds. This is the second time I am being friendzoned in less than 24 hours! I think this is a way of the universe telling me that I am going to end up alone. Because it has to be me!

I turn to James "Just like you and me. *Friends.*" I flash him a sarcastic smile and I almost think that he is trying to suppress a smile.

We finish lunch and James offers to drive me to his house for the interview. I drove to campus, but it would be weird going in two different cars.

"I'll see you later, Raj." Raj pulls me in for a full frontal hug and gives me a squeeze which makes me chuckle.

As Raj walks away, James exhales and says. "You've never hugged me like that."

I glare at James. "I'm just saying." He throws his arm around my shoulder and pulls me to his side. I know his arm is on my shoulder but it sends blood to my stomach and arousal in my pants.

"What are you doing?" I stop walking and ask him. He doesn't budge his hand.

"What? We're friends, right? You shouldn't mind this. Unless you feel differently and we're not just friends for you." he's teasing me. Two can play the game, Williams.

I hold his hand which is around my shoulder and start walking.

"Not at all, *friend.*" I emphasise.

The drive to his place is intense. It is obvious that there is some sexual attraction between us, but we're both enjoying playing this game of who gives in first and it is not going to be me.

"What are you doing this weekend?" He asks me to break the silence.

"Anything that doesn't involve being around you." I throw this one at him from my box of sarcastic comments.

"I thought I was your favourite person to hang out with!" He takes a quick glance at me.

"Sure. Let's say that. What about you?" I tap on the windowsill, slowly.

"I'm going to Jersey with my friends. Thought you might want to join for fun." he shrugs. Why would I go on a trip with all men to a different state when I don't even know them properly?

"I'm going to New York to see my sister."

"You're kidding." he widens his eyes.

"Nope."

"Maybe we can meet up to do something or..." he goes astray. I am not meeting him because it is getting very difficult to keep my hands to myself around him or to not think dirty about him.

"You have fun with your friends. Why are you going there anyway?"

"There's this event thing. It's kind of like a gala." So when he was casually asking me to go with his friends, was he asking me to go with them as one of his *buddies* or as his *date*? I'm almost 100% it wasn't the latter.

"Gala?" I raise my brow.

"Yeah, Daniel's father is hosting it and he invited us all. It's for charity."

"So, you donate money?"

"Why yes, I do! I am not as bad a person as you think I am, Raven." there it is, his signature cocky smile.

We reach his place and I interview him about his game and his future plans about getting drafted in the NFL. I take notes about when he explains to me how the game works.

"So, it is just a bunch of people tackling each other like bulls and running on the field across a couple lines?" He laughs out loud on that one. I don't know what part of that was funny.

"No one has ever described it like that. But I guess, yes."

"Doesn't it hurt? Getting tackled?" I can only imagine the intensity of the game.

Growing up I used to watch rugby with my uncles in India and would play Kabaddi with my friends. Kabaddi is a sport where you get tackled and thrown outside the court by either one person or seven. And the goal is to not get tackled. Being the daddy's princess that I was, I had only been tackled once by my brothers and after that I never lost a single game.

But that one time that I was tackled by my three brothers, I broke my wrist and fractured my forearm. So I can only imagine the pain that these boys go through on the field, constantly being tackled!

He holds his left hand out and holds his pinky. "Broke this one at least seven to eight times and I still continued playing." He brags about being a macho man. So I hold his arm and twist it behind his back just the way I was taught in the taekwondo class I took last year in Australia. Only difference, James is huge compared to me. My chest presses against his as I hold his hand behind him. And there is not an inch of pain on his face, so I twist his hand more.

"Are you trying to get fucked, Raven?" he asks me in a very low voice with so much lust in his eyes and his whisper gives me goosebumps. I let go of his arm immediately and move back but he brings his other free hand around my waist and pulls me towards him.

"I asked you something, baby." he whispers again. Why is he whispering in his sexy low voice? It makes my panties wet. I gulp hard. Words have escaped my mind. I can't formulate sentences. I don't know how to speak.

He brings his mouth to my ear and I inhale his scent. God he smells so good. Leather-y and woody and fresh. "Just say the word and I will make you come like no one ever has." a soft gasp escapes my mouth.

He moves back and winks at me.

I hold his gaze and act as if I am not affected by his sexy demeanor at all. "A- I'm not your baby. Don't ever call me that and B-" I gulp hard not believing what I am about to tell him. "No one ever has...you know." I know that my complexion is wheat-ish, but

I am 100% sure that my cheeks are red. "No one has ever made me come anyway." his gaze changes. I think he took it as a challenge. I don't have any idea why I told him that in the first place, but my body is not in my control right now.

He sighs and closes his eyes and I wonder what he's thinking. I'm sure the other women he's been with were very experienced. I've only slept with men when I was drunk, so I didn't feel much and I didn't remember much either. Not like I've slept with tons of men, but I guess three and a half is still more than one.

"Fuck. I can't fathom all the ways I could make you come, Raven." That's what he was thinking about?

"Yeah? Tell me your favourite one." *Who am I? Am I possessed? Where is this confidence coming from?*

He nudges me slightly towards him and drags his hand through my hair. His calluses rub against my cheek. "I would make you sit on my face and eat your sweet little pussy." I know his arm is draped just around my waist, but suddenly I can feel it all over my body. I want to.

But what comes out of my mouth is- "I wouldn't want to suffocate you. I weigh a hundred and fifty pounds."

"Are you trying to insult me, Raven?" the pad of his thumb brushes the naked skin on my waist. "I bench more than twice your weight. And being squashed by your pretty ass seems like the only way I'll ever make it to heaven." I want to kiss him. My legs rub together and he sees that. "Seems like she wants it too." he smirks looking at my pelvis.

She does.

I am fully clothed but I feel more exposed than I have ever.

I lean in to kiss him and just when our lips are about to meet the door swings open and I immediately pull back. But he doesn't budge his hand. " Hey cap, there is a package for you." George walks in with a package in his hand.

What the hell was I doing here? He is a fuckboy, and like every other girl he's slept with, I was falling for his charm! *Get a grip, Ri!* Don't fall for his sexy grin and dirty talk that you really loved. James is still looking at me. Not daring to move and not letting me move either.

George comes and sits on the bed and starts opening the package.

"I really ought to teach you guys some manners." he finally breaks off his gaze and looks at George. He undoes his hand around my waist and it feels so lonely. I fall back into my chair as I feel my legs shake with excitement and my knees buck.

"What the fuck is this?" George pulls out a glass artwork which says FRIENDS. "It lights up too? Aww, that's really sweet of you, M. But we all already know that we are friends. Is this a decoration for the house? I'm plugging it in the living room." I am really trying to hold back a laugh, pushing it back physically with my palm but I can't. I burst out laughing. George looks at me as if I am possessed.

"It wasn't for us, asshole." James snatches the package from his hand.

"Geez...alright. By the way, dinner is ready. We also made some for you, Riya." I look at James and then back at George. I wasn't going to stay for dinner.

James senses my awkwardness and tells me that the dinner was actually just made by Siddharth and not all of them. Not what I wanted to know or hear.

"Okay kids. Let's go. Enough study." George pulls my chair away from James and turns me around. He lifts me up effortlessly and makes me stand on my feet and wraps his hand around my waist and pulls me closer to him. My eyes widen when he does that.

"That's better. A hot girl closer to me. And all is right in the world." Okay so maybe, James isn't the biggest playboy here. But up close George looks devastatingly handsome. I get why it must be easy for him to pull girls. They must be falling at his feet. If I was into blonds, I would definitely sleep with him!

James glares at George as if he's going to tackle him right here, right now. And without saying anything, George lets go of my waist and takes a couple steps away from me.

"Thank you, but I should get going. I have early classes tomorrow. James, could you drop me back on campus? My car is parked there." I gather my notes and my bag.

"Dinner will hardly take half an hour, Riya. Stay?" *Riya?* My heart wavers every time he calls me by my name. Which is stupid! I know. James' eyes mellow as if he's saying please with his eyes. Those puppy dog eyes... how can I ever say no to them.

"What's for dinner?" I ask George.

"We made thai curry and rice and there's 'take out spring rolls'"

"Sure. I'll stay for dinner then."

George walks like a happy duckling to the door and bows. "After you." His behaviour is very contradictory to his looks sometimes.

"Such a gentleman." I laugh and walk out the door. James is right behind me.

Dinner with the boys is loud. They talk a lot, mainly about football and they eat. They eat four times what I eat. I feel sad for Siddharth who I'm sure cooks all the meals.

"The curry is really good, Siddharth."

"I thought I told you *we* made it." George points towards Daniel and himself.

"Stirring the pot doesn't count as helping cook, George." I squint my eyes at him.

"Sure it does. At least I know more than M." I look at James.

"I can cook, asshole. Stop spreading false rumours about me."

This feels so natural. The last time I had dinner like this was when I was in India. The boys told me each other's embarrassing stories. It took me back to my life in India, when I used to have fun with my neighbourhood friends. I better text them before sleeping.

I'm missing them like crazy.

After dinner, James drives me to the campus parking lot where my car is parked. I am texting my friends back home and a smile appears on my face after a certain person texts back on the group chat. I might have liked him from the moment I met him back in fourth grade. But it's just an innocent crush, nothing else. I like to admire him from a distance. James pulls the car over and probably sees that I am blushing and smiling ear to ear.

He snatches the phone from my hand.

"I was asking you something, Raven." he looks at my phone and sees that I was totally stalking that friend of mine.

I try to snatch my phone from his hands "Give it back, *James.*"

Chapter 8- Riya

On the train to New York, I can't stop thinking about James. I almost kissed him. *Almost*. Since then we've been acting as if nothing happened. Texting normally. Well, I have been acting as if nothing happened. But he has his usual flirt on, nothing more, nothing less. I have to remind myself every time that I am just one of his conquests. And I am done with one night stands. Although I am scared of intimacy more than anyone, I would like to experience it at least once. I know...I still don't do boyfriends. Maybe I have bipolar disorder. Or maybe I am just shaken to the core about everything when it comes to relationships.

I know I have a difficult time trusting someone emotionally. Perhaps that is one of the reasons that I am the way I am.

My phone buzzes and I am pulled back from my thoughts. It's my sister- Maura. I pick her call and she sounds like a cheerful puppy. "Did you leave yet? I am so eager to see you!" she squeaks. This is what I can focus on– My sister.

"Yeah, I did about an hour ago. Will be there in about three hours or so. What do you have planned for the day?" A sister's weekend is all I need right now. To relax and just have heart to heart girl conversations and reminiscence in our childhood. After being with my cousins all the time in India, I found it very difficult to adjust to living with just one roommate. No offence- I love Juju a lot, but I don't think she would ever tickle me until I cried or add salt to my tea just as a prank. I miss having fun with my cousins.

"Wait, where are you? Are you not driving here?" Eek.

"No. I didn't want to drive in New York. It's awful there. I did it once and never again." she starts laughing.

"Ri...you drive in India. Nothing is worse than that." She's not lying. My mom always says that if one can master driving in India, they can drive anywhere in the world.

"Yeah, I know. But I wanted to rest up during the train ride. It's my break. What are we doing when I get there?" I ask her again. She's avoiding the question.

"Keith wanted to take us out for lunch." I roll my eyes out my eye socket.

"Sure. okay. Well. I'll call you la–"

"Also..." there's a huge pause. "Nothing. Nevermind. I'll tell you after you get here." Something tells me that I am not going to get to experience the sister's weekend that I had in mind.

"Is everything okay? Do I need to buy something to break someone's bones?" I ask her cautiously, not mentioning anyone's names. But obviously, she is smart enough to know who I was referring to.

"Yeah. All good. I'll see you. You need me to come pick you up at the station then?"

Do I? "Yeah, that'd be great." I would do anything to spend some time alone with her without always being on the edge around her boyfriend.

"Got it. Text me twenty minutes before you get here. Bye."

I'm here. I text my sister again after I get off the platform. I texted her fifteen minutes before reaching the station, but she didn't reply. I wait for five minutes, then ten and then she finally responds.

So sorry, could you take a cab here instead? Got caught up with work. I don't even bother replying anymore, instead I head out with my luggage in my homeless clothes and bed hair and hail a taxi to her place.

The traffic is crazy. I finally reached her place in Manhattan after half an hour. She rents a one bedroom apartment with Keith, because she's saving up to start her own fashion house and my main goal of this trip is to boost her confidence and push her towards her dream. *Be her biggest cheerleader.*

She greets me with a huge hug when Keith takes all my stuff inside their apartment. "I missed you so much." I squeeze her and sweep her off her feet. She's light as a feather. And looks beautiful. So beautiful. Her brown dyed hair falls on her shoulder beautifully and her face lights up.

"I missed you too." I finally put her down and walk into her apartment.

It looks clean, with a view of the concrete jungle. It looks particularly beautiful at night time. But all you can hear from here is the constant sound of sirens.

"How have you been?" Keith asks me and I tell myself to let bygones be bygones.

"Good." I look back at my sister and hold her by her shoulders and stare into her eyes. "You better start your own fashion line. You have the potential and don't let any motherfuckers tell you otherwise. You know this is your dream and you shouldn't give up on your dream for anyone. Not a single fucker. You get that?" I finally feel so much better now.

"Ay ay Captain." She salutes me. And we both start laughing and sit on the couch.

"No, but I am serious. Don't let anyone tell you otherwise. I know you the best, right? So, trust your little sister and take the leap."

"There are a lot of things that go into starting a fashion line. You need to have a vision accordingly. It's not like University, fantasies and fairy tales. This is real life, Riya. Not University." Keith throws that invisible and undodgeable punch at me.

"I'm not a kid, Keith. I know that it is not going to be easy. But then again if it is easy, then your dream is just not big enough. And I know my sister better than anyone to know that she can do it." I throw one back at him.

It hasn't even been five minutes since I stepped inside the house. "It is not some nonsense romance novel that you read and fantasise about. Your sister has a stable job right now. If we get married tomorrow and decide to have kids, she will be able to take time off to take care of the kids. She won't be able to do that as whatever it is she will be." I look at my sister and her jolly expression has been long shipped to Antarctica. Something tells me that this has been going on for a while now.

I fly off the handle of the couch and stand on my feet. "A CEO. She will be a fucking CEO. And if she can't take care of the kids, maybe you can. I'm sure she will make more than enough to take care of the house and everything if everything goes according to plan." I give him a venomous smile telling him *two can play the game*. My sister is not alone anymore.

"Let's grab lunch." Maura interrupts our obvious rant. And I give Keith my special, *it's not over yet* look. Signal him that I'm watching him.

We get to the fancy Italian restaurant down the lane and place our order for food. Keith and I keep bickering about what my sister should do in the future.

I look at my sister who has been playing with her plate of food for the past twenty minutes. I give her a nudge with my elbow and she jolts her eyes up at us. "I don't think it matters what we think, Keith. What matters is what she thinks and wants."

"What?" she was definitely not paying attention to us.

I repeat what I said to her and she just nods like a puppet. She's shaking her head, but I know that she's still not paying attention to what I'm saying.

"It's our future." Keith reaches for her hand and I just want to stab his forearm with my fork and then give him a sweet serial killer smile.

Maura nods her head giving a half-hearted smile. Something is cooking in her head and I need to talk to her about it.

"I need to use the ladies room." I get up and nudge her again. "Are you coming with me?" she nods and almost runs ahead of me as if she's been wanting to do that the entire time.

We enter the ladies room and she takes a deep breath as if she can finally breathe. I turn to her and glare at her, I know how uncomfortable it makes her and she blurts out everything. This entire time, she hasn't opposed Keith once or even supported what I'm saying.

"Nothing. You don't want to use the–" I hold her shoulders and shake her.

"What's going on here? You are acting really weird." I ask her, *Why are you with him?* Is what I wanted to ask her. But I don't.

"He mentioned marriage and kids and I don't know...it sounds too scary right now, Riya. I mean I do love him and do want to marry him, but it's too early right now. And kids...I never even thought about it. I don't even know if I ever want to have kids." she's almost shaking, her voice cracking.

I hold my sweet not so little sister in my embrace and pat her back as she lets go of her mask that she has been wearing for a long time. "You don't have to figure out everything right now, Maura. Just focus on what matters the most to you. And I know that it is this fashion line. It's been your dream ever since I can remember. Whatever you choose, make sure that you won't regret your decisions later." She sniffles and hugs me tighter. *This.* This is what I wanted. Not in a public bathroom. But in the comfort of her home.

"Thank you for coming here. I really mean it." She takes a deep breath and splashes some cold water on her face. Of course, she's not wearing any make-up. She's naturally beautiful. Not like me, who needs to hide under ten layers of makeup and shapewear to look at least presentable.

"Hey, you can also do some cost-cutting by modelling in your own clothes, Maura." I say seriously and she chuckles as if I made the funniest joke. Maura is gifted. She is 5'8" which is decent for a model and her lean and curvy and effortless figure makes her the perfect model. And her beautiful and sharp features are just an added bonus!

We head outside and go shopping and empty all my earnings before heading back to her place.

"I'm so tired." I fall on the couch with a thud. I hear Maura and Keith silently whisper something and pass looks at each other. But neither says anything.

"You don't have to whisper. Unless you two are talking about something explicit, then I don't want to hear it." I love sleeping on couches, so I don't really mind crashing on her couch if that's what they are uncomfortable about.

"Um... Do you remember I said that I wanted to tell you–no, ask you something?" Maura sits besides me.

I sit up and she and Keith exchange careful glances between each other. "What is it?" Now I'm anxious.

"Could you sleep over in our house in Jersey? I got it cleaned and ready for you." I don't think I heard it right. She is kicking me out of her house and shipping me to Jersey? Why? Because I took her side? Did I overstep my boundaries here?

"What?" I can't say anything else. I am just that shocked.

"Keith and I will be working on–"

"I was going to sleep on the couch anyway." I feel so embarrassed. I was boasting the entire time how much I know my sister and now she does this?

"It's just..." she doesn't finish the sentence, because I am already up and packing my stuff. I hear a small silent snort from behind where Keith is standing and he has an evil smirk on his face. Telling me that *he won.*

"Riya...I hope you don't misunderstand this or anything." No I won't because I am literally putting off doing my work and assignments to actually be with her just to be humiliated in the worst way possible.

"Did you see my phone?" I look around for it and finally find it. Great, it's at 5%. I can't stay here anymore and ask her to lend me her charger and embarrass myself more.

"Keith and I can drop you off there, if you want." I don't even respond to that. I am calculating how the fuck am I going to make it to Jersey. I can't take the subway, because I don't know the way there and I need charging in my phone to know the route.

"I'll manage. I'll take a cab or something." I'm sure my phone won't survive until I book a cab either. But no way am I telling her that. I am just too hurt right now. And I can't cry. I can't cry. Not in front of them.

I pack my stuff and don't even look back or hear what she says. I think she said goodnight or something. I don't give a fuck right now. As soon as I am out of their sight I break down. I don't know what to do. I can't think straight anymore. And only one name comes to mind, so I open call logs and dial the number. He said he was going to be in Jersey today and it's not that far, is it?

"Miss me?" he says in a smug voice.

I can't hold back anymore and right now I am bawling. "*James...*"

Chapter 9- Marcus

"Get your asses up assholes." I turn over on my back on the floor. I don't know why I thought that drinking something made by George would be a great idea. We're all fucked up from last night. George makes the worst concoctions. It's twelve pm and we were supposed to leave for Jersey at around ten.

"Fucking George." Daniel presses a pillow on his head.

"Wakey wakey ladies." George waltzes in and just behind him is a similar face. But I am too hungover to open my eyes completely to see who it is. "Bye babe." He kisses the blonde bye as she walks out the door.

I am on the floor with a pillow under my neck, Daniel is on the couch and Siddharth is arched over the bean bag.

"You guys are lightweight." George sits on the floor beside me and opens another beer. This asshole is built differently.

"You couldn't even give me a blanket?" I finally sit upright.

"Be thankful I gave you a pillow." I am too hungover to tackle him right now. "The blonde was all over me."

"You fucked her anyway asshole. My ass cheeks are numb from the cold floor." George laughs. But it's true. I can't feel my ass and my back hurts like a bitch. "Poor Siddharth. His back is gonna be done for the–" There it is. The urge to throw up. I race to the sink and empty my stomach contents. I am never touching anything that George makes, ever again! Daniel is right behind me in line to the sink to empty his stomach and poor Siddharth is still passed out.

"Pussies." George laughs from the living room.

"Chauvinist." Dan grunts behind me.

"Hey, not saying I hate pussies. They're my favourite. I worship them and I thank god everyday for making them." I don't know if I should laugh or slam dunk George.

"I'm gonna take a nap before leaving. Let's leave later in the evening. Unless Dan..." I turn to face Dan who looks more awful than me. "Nevermind. Evening. Don't wake me before that or I'll kill you." I make my way upstairs.

"I could drive." I hear George.

"Like hell. I am not trusting you with my drinks, let alone our lives." Dan is right behind me and I laugh.

"So, nobody gonna help Sid?" George yells from the living room.

"You are!" Dan and I yell in unison.

"Turn up the music, M" George yells from the back. "Your playlists are the best. Could you share this one with me?" The first thing George did as soon as we sat in my car was connect my phone to the bluetooth and play songs. The sun has already set when we leave. We're probably going to get there pretty late. You must be wondering why leave today then?

The gala is tomorrow and we could get there tomorrow morning, but we made reservations at the hotel for today and George insisted that we go shopping for the gala in New York. Which we were supposed to do today, but we'll be done with it tomorrow.

Siddharth is still fast asleep in the back. We were scared that he was dead when he didn't move even after we poured a glass of water over his face before. But he's alive.

We are all fed and now ready to get to Jersey in one go. No stops.

We are fifteen minutes away from the hotel when my phone rings and the infotainment screen lights up. It's the last person I was expecting to call. My Raven. Before I could disconnect the bluetooth and accept the call, George accepts the call. Dan, George and Siddharth all go silent.

"Miss me?" I say in my cocky voice, eyes still on the road.

I hear sobs and I hit the brakes hard without looking anywhere. Dan almost breaks open his skull like a watermelon.

"James..." She cries my name.

"Where are you?" I swallow whatever liquid was in my mouth until it's dry. Panic sets in. I stiffen my grip on the wheel after hitting on the gas again.

"Could you.." she sniffles.

"Where are you?" I ask her again.

"I'll send you my location." she sobs again. My world comes crashing down around me when I hear her cry. She said she was going to New York to meet her sister. What happened? Why is she crying?

I look behind at George, who has already opened the maps and started the route without me saying anything. It's about a thirty minute drive.

"Stay on call with me, alright?" I try to take a few deep breaths as I try not to think about the worst.

"I can't. My battery is–" and the call ends.

"Fuck!" I hit the wheel. I should've just forced her to come with me instead. "George–." He had already called her number, before I finished my sentence. The call goes straight to voicemail.

"Fuck, M. Do you want me to drive?" Dan asks. He can probably see how rash I'm driving right now. I don't have time to care about all the tickets I'll receive. All I know is I need to be with my Raven right now. I need to know that she's safe and okay.

"She was saying something about her battery. Maybe her phone died. I'm sure it's nothing that bad, M." Siddharth pats my shoulder.

"She was fucking bawling. Of course it's fucking serious." A series of scenarios going through my mind. And each and everyone pushing me more and more over the edge. What if she was harassed? What if she was hurt? She called me. As far as I know her, I'm sure I'm the last person on her list to call in a crisis situation. Which means the situation is that bad!

Where is her sister? Why did she have to call me? Did something happen to her sister? I look at her location and I don't see any hospitals nearby. *Fuck.* What happened?!

I get us near her location in about twenty minutes. The road ahead is packed with cars and there's no way I will get there in time. "Dan, take the wheel." I grab my phone from George's hands and open the car door.

"What the fuck do you mean by–" I don't hear what Dan was saying as I close the door and run to her location. Pushing through the New York crowd on a Saturday night. My heart is thumping out my chest. *Please, just be safe. Just be safe.* That's all I'm praying for right now. I take a look at my phone and I am at her location, but I don't see her. I call her, but it goes straight to voicemail. *Shit. Riya, where are you baby?*

"James?" I hear a faint voice and turn around to see her. Her eyes are swollen and red. Her cheeks are puffy. I check her from top to bottom. I don't see any injuries. I run towards her and hug her. She breaks down on my chest and suddenly the air feels so much thicker.

"Are you okay? Are you hurt?" I hold her face in my hands and she nods her face. Wiping her tears with her loose grey sweatshirt. All her bags are in her hands. "What are you doing outside?" I pull her closer to my chest. She can probably hear my heartbeat since I can almost feel it in my throat.

"I–I–" she doesn't say. "Thank you for coming, James. I didn't know what I'd do if–"

"Not a chance." I don't even want to think what would happen if I wasn't around. I just don't want to.

"Can you take me somewhere?" she asks me in a soft frail voice. She sounds tired. Not just physically, but emotionally. I want to ask her what happened, but I don't want to push her, right now. I am looking for her confident, sarcastic self, but I don't see that. I just see a person who is tired.

"Anything you want. Did you eat?" She nods her head but doesn't say anything.

"Good." I pull out my phone and call Dan, to pull the car around to pick us up. Dan is there within two minutes. George is sitting in the passenger seat with two ice cream cones. Siddharth sitting behind with two in his hand too.

She gives my jacket a squeeze "Can you not mention the crying or anything to the guys?" Battling her watery lashes at me, she says "Please?" The way she's looking right now and they heard her crying before already, but I won't tell her that. I just want her to smile at me the way she used to in her cocky way. I want her to tell me to shut up.

I hold her hand in mine and bring the back of her hand to my lips before kissing it.

"I won't." I flash her a painful smile that I manage to pull. I just hope that the boys don't act differently around her or act as if they know that she was crying.

"For the queen or sarcasm." George hands her an ice cream cone from the passenger seat and she snorts. It would almost be classified for a smile if her eyes weren't so droopy right now.

"Thank you, George." She whispers to George. Her voice is gone.

"Cap..." Siddharth hands me another cone.

"Why are all of you here? Weren't you going to leave in the morning?" We all simultaneously hit George.

"Because these fuckers can't handle a drink. Lightweight." he scowls. She raises her brow. And the boys start explaining to her the details of last night.

"George fucked us in the ass, or at least he did M." Siddharth chuckles and winks at me.

Her head turns to see me at a megaspeed. Eyes wide. "No." George and I yell in unison.

Sid chimes in, "What were you saying this morning about not being able to feel your ass, Cap?" Riya chuckles and man I would really get fucked in the ass just to hear her chuckle right now. Not fucked, but fingered. *Whatever.*

"M is not my type, Sid. He's too big for me to fuck him." She starts laughing now. Is it wrong to tell the boys that I love them for pretending that nothing happened? For making my Raven not just smile or chuckle, but laugh?! Nope. I'm never telling these fuckers that.

"Did he really?" she whispers in my ear and it makes me laugh how innocent she is.

"You think I can let him, baby? My ass is all yours." I wink at her and she tries to suppress a blushing smile which makes my heart waver.

"Not your 'baby'" she whispers and does the air quotes. There she is! She's back! My feisty Raven.

"I'm letting you sleep on the fucking grass next time, Sid. So much for keeping the secrets secret." George rolls his eyes.

The rest of the ride to the hotel is just the boys making Riya laugh until she is genuinely laughing. Dan pulls the car in front of the lobby and all fall quiet.

"I'm not staying at the hotel with you all, don't worry. You can roam around naked in the room all you want." she huffs.

"That's a shame, your highness. Because what's the point of getting naked if a hot woman like yourself isn't there to ogle us?" George is quick to pass his comment which makes her laugh. She turns to look at me and then whispers slowly telling me that she has somewhere to go.

"Right..." I run my hand through my hair. I turn to the guys and tell them to check in the hotel and tell them that I'm dropping Riya somewhere.

"Don't wait on my account. I'll get a key from the counter." I tell them as I close the door of the driver's seat. Riya sits next to me, all strapped in. She waves the boys goodnight.

"We weren't going to, anyway, asshole." Siddharth comments from the back as he walks away. I just roll my eyes and drive us a little further and then look at her. She falls silent and her smile from a few seconds has faded away.

"I can put the address in your phone." she doesn't even look at my face.

I hand her my phone before saying something which I should've given a second thought. "You can stay with us, if you want. We have two rooms in the suite. Me and someone can crash on the couch or adjust—"

"Please, James... I can't. I'm already very embarrassed. I don't..." she takes a deep breath. "I don't cry like that in front of other people. I don't know what happened. But I can't take any more favours from you." Her words tug my heart around in a tightrope.

"I'm not doing you any favours, Raven." My voice is soft, but I am trying not to let the obvious pain be visible in my words. I'm really not doing her any favours. I am just helping myself, by helping her. One thing I can't tolerate is tears in a woman's eyes. It's my biggest weakness. And Riya is not just any woman. She is one of my closest female friends. Hell, she is my only female friend. She is more than a friend, at least for me.

"James, please."

I hold her hand and give it a squeeze. "I'll drive you anywhere you want, *Raven*."

Chapter 10- Marcus

The house I pull in front of looks like it hasn't been lived in for a long long time. There's weed almost the height of my Raven in the lawn around the house and the lights are off.

"Are you sure we're at the right address?" I ask her, looking around. It's all very quiet.

"Yep." she throws her bags on her shoulders but since I am a gentleman, I take them from her. Did she stuff rocks in them? "Thanks." she says with a forced faint smile.

"They weigh nothing for me." I flex lifting the bags up and down which brings out a real chuckle out of her.

"Not just for that. For coming to my rescue, James. Thank you for picking me up on such a short notice. I'm sure you had other plans with your night. I won't hold you back late." She quickly makes her way to the door past me. How do I tell her that no plan is better than spending time with her?

She opens the door and holds it for me. "You can come in if you want." I am hit by a whiff of dust and old wood. All furniture is covered under white cloth. It is clearly evident that nobody lives here. How am I supposed to leave her alone here?

"You can put the bags there." she points to the cloth covered couch. I put the bags down and she pulls a water bottle out of her bags and gives it to me.

"Thanks." I drink some water while taking a good look around. The house isn't the cleanest, but the floor looks like they were wiped recently. "Can I ask you something?" I choose my words carefully.

"Why is my sister not here with me?" She reads my mind. I wasn't going to frame it like that but I was going to ask her just that.

"You don't have to answer it if you don't want to." I don't want her to cry again. I can't see her cry again.

"Just know before I tell you anything that my sister is not a bad person. She's just a little naive and she would rather suffer herself than let the other person know that he's hurting her." *He?* Okay...

"I won't think like that. I promise." Or at least I'll try not to.

"My sister wanted me to stay here so that she and her boyfriend could do their work or something like that. I didn't wait to listen to the entire explanation." Her eyes well with tears but she looks away and wipes them too quickly. It hurts me that she doesn't trust me enough to let them flow. Does she think that I will judge her for crying in front of me?

"So, why are you here then? You could've booked a hotel or something."

"This is my family's home." She gets up from her seat and looks around. Assessing every nook and corner. I can see a bittersweet expression on her face. "Or at least it used to be." She sighs and faces me.

I get up and walk to the fireplace which is very dusty but I see some dusty frames on top and really want to see her childhood photos. It's not a shabby place. It's pretty big and has a rustic taste. Not something old and rusty, but rather antique. I pick up the frame and clear the dust off the photo. It's probably her mother holding her two daughters on the lawn outside. I can immediately spot the small mole under her eye and it is enough to tell me that it is my Raven. She was adorable! Still is.

"I thought you were an international student." I put the photo down and walked towards her. She's eyeing the kitchen carefully. Reliving her memories.

"We moved back to India when I was in fourth grade. My grandmother fell sick. She passed away a couple years after that. I was glad that at least I got to know her before that. But then, dad said it felt like home and decided to stay there." She turns around to look at me.

"He bought this house when I was born." She looks at the ceilings. "He always said that I was his lucky charm. We weren't always rich. My mom and dad struggled in the beginning. A lot. And now, here we are. I have a really big family back at home. We live in the biggest house with at least fifteen people. It's awesome having my cousins by my side." She genuinely smiles. It is evident that she misses her home.

"Can I tell you something?" she asks shyly.

I just want to turn her around and hug her from behind. Wrap my arms around her stomach and pull her into me, inhaling her scent as she tells me all her childhood stories. *Snap out of it Marcus!*

"Anything."

"I never once called any place that I lived in, home. Except for my actual home in India. That is the only home I have. Even this..." she points around the house. "Just feels like a house. Not home. Maybe because my home is my family." her eyes tear up. I just want to pull her in for a hug and take all her pain away.

She looks at the watch on her hand and then looks at me. "It's late. I don't want to hold you back late."

"Are you sure?" I ask her one last time.

"What?"

"That you don't want to come with me to the hotel?"

She gives me a sad smile. "I'm sure. I know it looks very shabby. But it's just for a night." Just then we hear a noise from upstairs.

I immediately push her behind my back and take a few steps back. She's obviously scared right now. And I wouldn't blame her.

"That can't be your sister by any chance right?" I whisper to her and she nods. Clutching onto my shirt from the back. I pick up the lamp from the table and slowly head upstairs. The wood floor creaks as I take every step. The only sound there is the sound of her panicking breath, the dancing bell anklets, my shallow breath and the creaking wood.

"Stay behind me, alright?" I whisper under my breath enough for her to hear it. We finally make it upstairs and we hear a lamp fall to the ground from one of the rooms. I make my way towards it and slowly push open the creaking door, all ready to attack whoever is there.

We hear a squeaking sound and a mouse jumps out of the corner and towards her. Riya is jumping around until she is in my arms. Eyes closed shut, arms wrapped around my neck. It takes me down the road of ideas of what I would do to her right now. The mouse runs off, but she's still frozen in my arms.

She flutters her eyes open and pierces my soul with her pretty brown eyes. Yep, I'm hard. She wiggles a little and I put her down gently.

"Sorry, I must be heavy." she tucks the few locks of her hair behind her ear.

"You really know how to bruise a man's ego, don't you?" I chuckle and she doesn't understand why I'm laughing.

"I can lift you in one hand sweetheart. You weigh nothing." *Actually…I did lift her with one arm that night. All the way up to my bedroom.* I don't say that. I remember that feeling when she had wrapped her arms around my neck similarly, but so childishly. Something changes in her eyes. Lust? Nah! I must be imagining it.

"I'm sure you can, musclehead." she smirks at me.

"Musclehead? Really?"

"Sweetheart? Really?" Spitfire. She's back to being sassy. Thank god!

A yawn releases from my mouth and I see that she is tired too. "So…"

"So..." she folds her arms behind her back and looks at me with those big doe eyes. I know I am tired and sleepy but man do I want to fuck her right now.

"Where are we sleeping?" Her brow immediately arches up as I say that.

"We are not sleeping here. I am! It's late, you should get back. Thank you, James. For this... But I won't hold you–"

I corner her in the room from which the mouse just ran outside. "Either you let me crash here or else I am halling your ass over my shoulder and putting you in one of the rooms in the hotel."

"You wouldn't dare." She challenges me.

"You think I can't throw you over my shoulder? Are you challenging me, Raven? Want me to prove it to you?" I take one more step towards her until she is trapped between the wall next to the door in the dark room. There's no light in here, but I can tell that her eyes are piercing mine with lust right now.

"You won't dare." That's all it takes for me to find her thighs and lift her with one hand and hall her over my shoulders. I am so tempted to smack her juicy ass right now. But I am using all my strength to keep my free hand in my pocket.

"Put me down. James...Put me down!" She's moving around. I make my way down the stairs. She weighs nothing. Literally. "James. I'm telling you...Put me down now!" She chuckles and hits my back with weak punches. "Fine." she stops hitting as I approach the couch. "You win. You are strong. I get it. Now please, put me down. Please..." Fuck. I can't say no to her. So I put her down gently. She adjusts her hair and sweatshirt which slightly exposed her stomach when I put her down.

She scrunches her nose and narrows her eyes at me. So adorable! "You're an asshole." She hits my biceps.

"You like it." I say and she rolls her eyes at me and finally chuckles after meeting my eyes. I would carry her for the rest of eternity if that meant she would chuckle like this. "Say Raven...What are you doing tomorrow?" I ask her with the cute expression that George taught me. He said that women will drop their panties and fall on their knees to suck you off if you ever use that look. Not that that's my motto here. Not that I would mind it either. But right now, that is not the goal. *Not right now.*

"I'm not sure. But I know for a fact that I am not going to see my sister if that's what you wanted to know." Not why I asked the question. But it breaks my heart to know that her sister hurt her that badly.

I press my lips together in a thin line. "I was wondering if you wanted to go shopping with me and the boys. We were going to this gala. I told you about it right? Do you want to tag along?"

Her eyes widened as if I just asked her to accompany me on a one way trip to Mars. "I... I mean when you put it like that, it feels like you are just asking me out of pity." she forces a laugh.

I cough out loud. "What? No! I would love for you to be there. Both shopping and the gala. You know I'd ask you before, too. But you declined my offer. Nonetheless, I would really be happy if you came with us. God knows the boys need some help with their fashion."

"Just the boys?" her eyes narrow. Challenging me. "You sure you don't need my help either?" she licks her lips and that makes my dick twitch.

"You think my fashion sense is bad, Raven?" I tickle her and she falls on the couch pulling the white cloth. It wraps around her. I wrap it further, immobilising her and tickle her for a good five minutes.

She gasps for breath between her laughs. "Okay. Stop. You have an amazing fashion sense. Stop tickling. Please."

I hold her down. "Say you'll go with me tomorrow."

She repeats while laughing.

"Shopping and the gala. Both."

"Alright, I will."

We are in the fifth store and I have never been so exhausted. I hate shopping and I hate shopping with George and Sid even more. These motherfuckers always have something to comment about every single thing that everyone tries on. And to add to that, my sweet Raven is brutal with her comments.

She made George shut up, for which she was heavily applauded by all of us. "I don't understand why I couldn't go with my idea of painting a shirt as an option." Only George can think of something like that or even pull something like that off.

"Why can't I wear my hoodie?" I complain.

"Because you can't." My Raven looks so upset with all the boys, including me. We gave her hell. But she struck back stronger. At least that distracted her from everything else. I have never been thankful for having such annoying friends.

"Isn't it a black tie event, Dan?" Daniel is looking out the window. All zoned out. I know he didn't want to go to his abusive shit of a father's event. But his father threatened him to come to the event. I couldn't let my brother walk into the lion's den alone, so I agreed to go with him to distract him from the lion in the den.

"Daniel?" Riya shouts from the passenger seat.

She scares not just Dan but the rest of us too. He jerks his head up to face her.

"Where is your mind at? You barely got anything for the event which I should mention is being hosted by your father." She emphasises.

He just groans and goes back to staring out the window. Riya doesn't follow up. She can clearly sense that he is upset about it. She doesn't need to be told word by word to know that Daniel and his father don't get along well.

"When are you going to show us your dress?" George leans ahead between me and Riya. I am driving, so I can't punch him. *Shit.*

"It's a surprise." she squeaks. She didn't even show me what she bought. And I can't stop imagining how beautiful she would look in anything she wears. More so without the clothes, but that is a view I'd like to keep private only for myself.

"If you steal my idea of body painting a dress. I wouldn't mind it." Sid smacks George's head.

"Asshat." Sid mumbles.

"Thanks Siddharth." Riya rolls her eyes.

"How long is it going to take you, your highness?" George shouts from the living room of the suite.

All the boys are suited up and ready to head out. Except for my Raven. She made sure everyone else got ready and then went to get ready herself. She tied all our bows. It's been more than half an hour since then.

It didn't surprise me how nobody among us knew or didn't care about wearing bows. But when Riya snapped at us saying that if she's going, we better dress up because she didn't want to feel overdressed. Everybody shut up and stood still as she tied our bows.

A scream echoes from inside. "If you ask me that one more time George, I am going to stick my heel so far up your ass that even the ER team will have to cut it open to remove it." Damn. She's scary. Even George backs off. So she is SCARY. That's crazy hot! I giggle to myself like an idiot.

About twenty more minutes later she walks out of the bathroom in a navy blue sparkly dress which goes beyond her high heels. It has a slit high up her thigh which exposes her sexy leg and the dress dips in the front. Enough to see her perky tits sitting perfectly. Her hair black falling on her shoulder with perfect curls.

A small necklace with a single stone and beautiful dangling sparkly earrings. She spins around and I see the back of the dress and I immediately want to drag her into the bathroom and bend her over and fuck her brains out.

She twirls around to give us the entire show and I notice that the fabric is cut out enough to expose the dimples on her back and it hugs her in the perfect places, putting her ass on display for everyone!

"Wow!" Daniel says subconsciously and then looks at me when he realises what he said. I wouldn't blame him though. She looks spectacular.

"You guys look good too." Her eyes finally land on me and does she spot the drool on my mouth?

The boys are frozen. Standing and gawking at her. Like me.

She clears her throat. "Aren't we getting late now?"

I quickly turn around and adjust myself. Maybe I should have sized up two sizes in my pants. "Right. Dan...you're driving." I throw the keys at Dan. I can't drive because I'm painfully hard right now. These pants are barely holding me in. But my poor cock is fighting for its life right now.

We sit in the car and Riya sits besides me.

Fuck a life sentence. This is the worst type of punishment. I am literally fighting with Hades to keep my hands to myself and not claim her right now.

She smells good too. I want to make her come on my fingers.

She adjusts in her seat and her bare thigh rubs against mine. She folds her leg over to expose more of her leg. Fuck... She's going to kill me.

"You alright there James?" she whispers in my ear and I can feel her rusky breath on my ear and it makes my balls ache. I need to fuck her right now. I want to taste that delicious red lipstick of hers.

She's teasing me.

So I take off my jacket and fold my sleeves up to my forearms. I've heard it so many times that it turns on girls and the way she presses her thighs together tells me all I need to know.

I bring my mouth to her ear and whisper, "Two can play the game, *Raven*."

Chapter 11- Riya

My pussy aches for him. He's looking deliciously handsome tonight. I can't take my eyes off him and from what I can tell, many other girls can't either. So far, I have seen at least ten women *eyefuck* James.

We make our way through the crowd at the gala, Dan greets a couple of the guests he knows. But I feel a hand on my bare back ever since I walked in. James. If I'm not mistaken, he's basically eyefucking me ever since he saw me walk out the bathroom. Same goes for me.

His shirt is a perfect fit for him. Showing off his muscular body and the way the jacket hugs his shoulders makes me wonder how broad his shoulders are. I want to touch him. I want to do things to him.

I want to ride him.

What? No!

I swear to god, I can't think straight around this man.

"Would you like a drink?" James asks me. *One? Or ten?*

"Sure."

"I'll be right back." James leaves to get a drink and suddenly my back feels lonely. I look around, George and Siddharth are nowhere to be found and Daniel is still busy talking to someone.

"Drink?" a voice from behind asks me.

"That was fast, James." I turn around to find a handsome blonde towering over me. Fuck. He's gorgeous. Beautiful green meadow-y eyes. Chiselled jaw with a little stubble which definitely suits him. And a smell that drives me crazy. Yep. He's handsome as hell. The devil himself. I know I said that blonds are not my type, but fuck! This man is utter beauty!

"You know me?" He offers me a glass of champagne. I am sceptical enough to think that it might be drugged. "Relax. I just picked it up from the trays going around." He takes a sip from the glass and then offers it to me. "Here." I smile. "And she smiles!" he licks his lips and man does that make me wet. *I need to get laid!*

"So your name is James?" I accept the drink from him.

"Cole James Hariett." He offers his hand to shake and I shake his hand. But he doesn't let go. The pad of his thumb caresses the back of my hand and it sends shivers through my body. Yep. Definitely need to get laid as soon as possible.

"So, Cole..." I pull my hand out of his grip. "What do you do?" he leans towards me and whispers in my ear.

"I can do you." he leans back and winks at me. I find that equally gross and hot. If we weren't in public I would definitely throw him against the wall and kiss the hell out of him. What the hell is wrong with me? A stranger just whispered into your ear that he wants to fuck you and this is how you act? Great! Shame on you, Riya!

"That's one way of talking to a stranger for the first time, Cole." I turn around to look for James. Cole walks around in front of me.

"What's your name, Sweetheart?" Something in my stomach churns. It's not the butterflies of excitement anymore. When James called my sweetheart, it makes my heart flutter like a freaking butterfly. There is so much care when he calls me 'sweetheart' as opposed to now.

"Not your 'sweetheart'" I do the air quotes. I'm a little annoyed now.

This stranger Cole is very clingy. And it irks me a little. "Then what do you go by?" he flashes me a smirk which I'm sure would melt off women's panties. Not mine though. Mine are staying on. Because that is the only piece of underwear that I am wearing right now.

"I–"

"None of your business Harriett." James returns with two drinks in his hand. He hands me the whiskey and takes the champagne from my hand and puts it away.

Okay...

It is obvious they have beef among them. "You guys know each other?" If looks could kill, they'd both be dead by now. *Men.*

There's a little disappointment on Cole's face. And something else I can't quite put my finger on. His eyes stay focused on James. "Williams and I go back all the way to high school." he looks back at me. "Didn't know you were his date."his tone is suddenly rougher than a few seconds ago.

"I'm not his date." I say almost too quickly. I mean, James didn't specifically ask me to be his date. He said 'Do you want to tag along with us?' Okay. Maybe he didn't say 'with us'. But he also didn't specify that he wanted me to be his date.

Cole's expression turns mischievous. "I'll see you around, sweetheart." he runs his finger on my cheek before walking away. That guy is so Hot and Cold! I hate it! So indecisive.

"I'm not your–" and he's gone. "Asshat." James chuckles.

"Picked that one up from Sid?" I didn't even realise that. But I like 'Asshat'. Has a nice ring to it. I just shrug.

"He is an asshole though." James puts his hand on my back again and it feels like all is right in the world. Although, I sense a history here.

"Are you going to tell me a story about how you two fell for the same woman and she broke up two best friends?" James chuckles, but he's forcing it.

"Something like that." He doesn't elaborate and I don't push him either.

"His mother..." His nostrils flare. "Nevermind." he shakes his head. Okay, so it was a woman. Did James sleep with his mother? I don't think he is the type of man who would do that though. I know he is a fuckboy, but I'm sure that he wouldn't do that to his friends.

He takes a sip of his whiskey. He looks around and eyes widen.

"Excuse me. I'll be back in a minute." he takes two steps away before coming back and pulling me away with him.

"Where are we going?"

"Daniel." he chugs the rest of his drink and puts the glass on a random table. "And I can't leave you alone, can't afford another random asshole hitting on you!" *Jealousy?* Nah! No way. Why would he even be jealous?

He drags me through the crowd, my Jimmy Choo barely keeping up with me. We reach Daniel and he's talking to someone. "Sorry to cut in, Mr Martinez." James hugs the other man. I tidy my dress, so that I don't step on it.

Daniel is standing with an older man. Possibly in his 50s. If it weren't for the crows feet next to his eyes, I wouldn't have guessed his age. He looks...too fit! "Marcus! How have you been?" He slaps James's back.

"All good sir." James flashes him a fake smile which is very awkward and visibly fake. It's like he's not even trying.

I take a look at Daniel and he seems very uncomfortable.

"And who is this beautiful young woman?" This older man approaches me.

"Riya." I offer him my hand and he kisses the back of my hand. The way he holds my hand feels so off. And even the way he looks at me makes me uncomfortable. His grip lingers on my hand despite me trying to pull it away. Dan finally cuts him in and gently pushes him away from me.

"Dad." Dad? Shit! That makes sense. They have the same teal eyes. When I first saw Daniel, I thought he was wearing coloured lenses, but that is the colour of his natural eyes- teal! And his father has the same deep bluish-green coloured eyes.

Yet, his eyes seem so different from Dan's. Daniel's eyes are so kind and hurt all the time. Even in the car this afternoon, it seemed like he wasn't close with his father. I mean, his father does seem like an asshole. Who flirts with your son's friends?

"Riya. You must be hungry. Please." Dan leads me away from his father. James follows us.

"I'm so sorry about that." he whispers in my ear. He seems so embarrassed. One thing I have noticed about Daniel so far is that no matter how many women he has slept with, he is very respectful towards women. Complete opposite of his father.

"It's fine." I lie.

"No, it's not. This is the first time a girl ever accompanied me to an event like this and this is what he–" he exhales. I stop him and turn him around. I look around to make sure that everyone is out of earshot.

"It's not your fault, Daniel." I flash him a faint smile.

"I know but still–" I don't let him finish.

"Where is this delicious food that you were taking me to eat?" I change the topic.

Daniel chuckles. Running his hand through his hair. He looks a lot like his father, but besides that I see zero similarity. They're polar opposite.

"I know a better place, if you guys are up for it. But it's not fancy at all." He looks at me and then at James.

I shrug. I've had enough champagne anyway. "I'm down for the good place. Anyway, I'm bored of caviar and this fancy shit." I flick my hair like a spoiled brat but still a diva and both of them laugh.

James smiles eye to eye. An understanding smile. A smile thanking me. "You guys head out. I'll bring George and Sid." James turns around while Daniel leads me outside.

It's freezing outside, and I am standing without my jacket. Shivering. He offers me his jacket which I would reject under normal circumstances, but I'm freezing my ass off right now. I take his jacket and wrap it around me. Daniel is very quiet the entire time. I can tell that he still feels very embarrassed about what had just happened.

"So, I'm the first woman who accompanied you to an event like this?" I try to break the ice.

He just shrugs.

"Why? No girlfriends?"

"Girlfriends? FYI. I don't do dating and even if I did, I would date only one girl. I would want a monogamous relationship." He clarifies. *I don't do dating.* Of course, he doesn't! There's an awkward silence again.

"So, you have any siblings?" he chuckles now.

His teal eyes sparkle with joy. "I have a younger sister." His face lights up.

"Didn't see her in there with you..."

"She...um...she lives with my mother. In California." I want to ask more questions but I don't want to push him.

A few moments of awkward silence pass by so I smash the ice. "So, what's her name?"

"You talk a lot, don't you?" he snorts. I hear that a lot. "Her name is Vanessa. She's turning 16 in November. Thankfully her birthday is on Thanksgiving, so I might be able to fly down to her." he's smiling ear to ear now. He really loves his sister. That's so sweet. Me and my sister were just like this before.

Before God knows what happened. But I don't want to think about that. I let her know this morning that I am going out with friends and that I won't be able to go through today's plans. And have been dodging her calls ever since.

"So, what are you planning for her sweet 16? Isn't it a big thing here?" Dan nods.

He clicks his tongue. "It is. I'm still not sure what she wants. She's very picky. She plays Volleyball and one would think looking at her that she's a scary girl. But she's the girliest girl I know. She loves everything pink and purple and pastels. So I am planning something around that. But I haven't decided what to buy her yet."

"Need help with that?" I ask him.

"You don't strike me as the girly girl." he raises a brow.

"I like pink and purple and pastels. And I am totally a girly girl. And if you think otherwise I will beat your ass up." That gets me a big laugh out of Dan.

Footsteps approach us from behind. "I swear to god, I have never seen Daniel laugh like this before. Ever!" Siddharth comments as he walks with my coat in his hand. "What magic did you do, Riya?" he asked me.

"I told him I would beat him up and he thinks I am joking." All of them start laughing. *I am dead serious.* "Guys...I took taekwondo classes. Granted it was for two days, but I learned a lot!" I shrug.

"Sure, kiddo." Siddharth chuckles. I punch his arm and he groans, holding his arm in pain.

"Can't even handle a punch from a woman? Pussy!" George comments. Chauvinist!

"Chauvinist." Daniel mutters under his breath. And I snort a chuckle.

"She can throw a punch alright." Siddharth steps back.

"Come one, hit me, Queen." George takes a boxing stance.

"I'm not a jerk who goes around hitting people." I roll my eyes at him and a smug grin appears on his face.

"Why? Are you ready to admit that pussies are weak?" That gets him a punch from me. And I put all my strength in it. George groans silently, holding his arm. My dad taught me how to throw a punch and I grew up with cousins, so naturally, we fought a lot. I practised most of the WWE moves on them.

"Told ya." Siddharth squeaks still holding his arm.

"Remind me to never piss you off, your highness." I press my lips to not laugh. I take a look at James, who is silently observing everything. He licks his lips wet as he sees my eyes land on him. *Fuck me.*

Our car pulls up and we all get in when Dan drives us to the 'good but not so fancy' place. It's a taco place. And all eyes turn to us when we enter because obviously we all are overdressed. We take a seat at the booth. I scooch next to James. Dan, George and Siddharth are cramped up in front of us. We place our order for food, enough to feed a village. Because one thing I have learned from spending a day with them is that athletes eat a lot. Like a hell lot.

"Let's switch places." James whispers in my ear.

"Why?" I look around and see a group of middle aged men ogling me and my exposed legs. I don't fight with James and move inside the booth and James sits from outside.

It is so cold in the restaurant and the heater is barely working. James takes his jacket off and wraps it around my shoulders. I left my coat in the car thinking that it would ruin my outfit. Bad choice. It is still mid January!

"Thanks." His eyes lock with mine. There is a combination of lust and something I can't quite put my hand on. But safe to say, no one has ever looked at me like that. Like I'm the air they need to breathe to survive.

Someone clears their throat and breaks our deep eye contact.

"So, Riya..." Daniel asks me. "What's your story?"

"What do you mean?"

"I mean, where are you from? How did you meet dipshit over here? What's your favourite colour? I don't know...chick stuff." he shrugs.

"Cute." I try not to laugh at the chick stuff. "Really cute, Dan. Well, for starters...I am from India. Born and raised in Jersey until fourth grade and moved to India and back here for Uni. As for meeting dipshit, we—" I elbow him.

"Hey..." James gets offended and everyone laughs.

"I actually met him..." I can't tell him that they almost walked in on me when I was sneaking out of James' room after we did nothing but sleep because I was drunk. "I met him because of the interview thing. And my favourite colour...I don't have one. I can't pick just one." James smirks at me. Because he knows I lied about where I met him first. I intend to keep that between us.

"I thought that you were that crazy chick that tried to sneak out of M's bedroom that day. She was weird. Remember, cap? She didn't know what an honour it is to be noticed leaving our house in the morning." George chuckles. Honour? What honour? Ugh! I feel so embarrassed because that crazy weird chick is me.

James turns to look at me suppressing an obvious smile. "Yeah, she was really crazy." James teases me. So I kick him under the table and he groans.

The food comes and the boys inhale it. I ask them about where they're from and they each take turns telling me their hometown and *favourite colour*.

"But, I have to admit, in the three years that I have spent with Daniel, he has never spoken as much as he is today." George shoves his elbow in Dan's gut and he groans.

"That was a lot of talking? He barely said fifty words the whole day!" I love talking. Talking non-stop for at least five hours. On some weekends, me and my cousin sister back home, who is also my best friend, talk for hours on call without even realising. And before ending the call, we tell each other that 'I still had so much to tell you! I'll tell you next time.' Our record so far is about eight hours. *Meh*.

"Usually Dan's vocab consists of basically just *Hmm, fine, will do, Chauvinist, Fucker, fuck you* and *alright*." George elaborates.

"You take notes when I talk?" Dan genuinely asks George and I can't stop laughing my ass off here.

"Nah, it's your thing though. You talk less, no matter what. M talks less, but whatever he says makes sense and is always super serious and Sid here...he's the opposite of M, whatever he says never makes sense." I never thought that I would go to fucking gala and grab dinner with jocks. My impression about jocks was that they only love two things, their game and fucking women. I thought that that would be their entire personality, but maybe that's not the case. At least not with these boys.

I never had any athlete friends, so I never knew what it was like. I had friends, I still have friends, but all my friends are just intellectual nerds who don't have a single athletic trait. We rarely go to the gym, because our free time is killed by studying.

"What about you George?" I ask, shoving a taco in my mouth.

George flexes his bicep and that's when I notice how these guys have perfect athletic bodies. "I'm perfect. I say both, senseful and senseless things. I'm the whole package, baby." I can't stop laughing at how confident George is about himself. There's always one like that in every friend group.

I suddenly feel warmth and tingle on my thigh. It's James' hand. The pad of his thumb rubbing against my bare leg is sending shivers down to my core. I am not that horny a person, but this man makes me someone I'm not.

"What are you doing?" I whisper to him and he has a smirk on his face. He licks his bottom lip and that pulls a small gasp out of me. What is wrong with me?

"So, you let him call you baby and not me?" he leans down and whispers in my ear and I get a whiff of his woody scent. God he smells delicious. I know I should push his hand off my thigh and tell

George not to call me baby, but I want to tease James. I want to be naughty. So badly

"Georgie...sweetheart, could you pass me the water?" I lean my elbows on the table, pushing my breasts together. And that makes James' hand travel higher up my dress. His fingers are almost tracing the edge of my panties. And I am scared that his friends sitting in front of us might see that. I see George's face turn red in front of me. Dan chokes on his water and Sid is lost in his trail of thought but all I can think about is the hand looming on my thigh!

George passes me the water and buries his face in his food after taking one glance at James. I gasp as I feel him playing with the hem of my panties. My grip on the fork tightens and I butcher the chicken with my fork.

"Raven..." he chuckles and then stops doing what he was doing wanting me more. He was teasing me. Fucker.

I pull him closer to my mouth and whisper in his ear, "You wouldn't be able to make me come even if you wanted to, *James*..."

Chapter 12- Marcus

It's been a week since the gala. A whole week without meeting my Raven. She was busy with her work schedule and classes and study and didn't have time for tutoring or the interview stuff. And I have a slight feeling that she might be avoiding me. In the entire week, she has sent me three whole messages, which were-
Sorry I'm busy this week.
I can't do the tutoring.
Or the interview. See you next week.

That's all. Okay... So that's how it's going to be? Alright. Not that I'm holding my breath to see her again, or talk to her or even text her. It's fine. I'm fine. I'm more than fine. So fine that I am going to bang someone until I get Raven out of my mind.

"Let's hit a party. I heard the hockey boys are having one down the street. Wanna crash?" I enter the living room all ready for a party. Sid and George look at me as if I told them that I am actually a woman. Their jaws almost hit the ground. "What? It's fine if you guys don't want to come. I can go by myself." I walk across the living room and a huge muscular George pulls me next to him.

"Who are you and what did you do to my best friend? M? Where are you?" he starts shaking me. Sid starts mumbling which I think is either exorcism or black magic, both creep me out. And I'm saying that because one time when we got drunk, Sid sat me down and confessed to me that he can do black magic. From the way he was laughing after that I never dared to ask him if he was kidding!

I shake George off and adjust my leather jacket. "Are you coming or not, asshole? I don't have classes tomorrow, except for practice in the morning, my schedule's free." I get up and George is running up the stairs, skipping one at a time. Within two minutes, he's standing in front of me, with his party clothes on.

"Gotta look good for the ladies!" he shrugs as he pulls his matching leather jacket.

"You coming, Sid."

"Nah. I'm good! You guys have fun." He lazes around the couch watching Masterchef. Good for us. Masterchef inspires Sid to make really good food. If he wasn't a football player, he definitely could be a chef or even open his own restaurant.

We make it to the party and the hockey boys open us with wide arms. There are some beautiful women here as well. It hasn't even been a minute and George is already vanished in the hockey crowd.

"Has anyone told you how hot you are?" I feel a hand sliding over my shirt over my abs. Yes. It is exactly what I need.

I turn around to face her and she's a brunette. Big tits and a big ass. Grey eyes and did I mention that she is wearing nothing but a tiny skirt and a bralette. It's freezing outside! "Maybe you could remind me how much." Her hands immediately travel to my ass and I pull her closer to me.

This is exactly what I want. "How much have you had to drink, sweet– dear?" I don't know why I can't call her sweetheart. But I just can't.

"I just got here. Maybe you can get me a drink or two." she winks at me.

"Nope. Let's get out of here." I pull her closer to me and crash my lips on hers. She pushes into my erection which pulls a gasp out of her. "You like what you feel?" I ask her, smirking. I will admit, I love dirty talk. And I love it more when the girl reciprocates it too. But this one doesn't. She's just shy and looks away.

"You want me to fuck you, right?" I whisper in her ear and her eyes widen. She blushes, but doesn't say anything. Why do women think that men want to be in control all the time in the bedroom?

We like fucking a girl who like to be thrown around, but we love fucking a woman who likes to take charge and explore. At least I can say so for myself.

"Let's go." She holds my hands and waits for me. I lead her back to my place and I find Sid sitting right where I left him. He doesn't even bother saying anything. Just after we've reached the stair she starts running her hand up and down my arm.

I take her to my room and lock it from inside and corner her against the door. "You want me to fuck you right? You are going to have to tell me that, Dear. I won't touch you without your consent."

She bites her lip provocatively. "You have my consent." I smash my lips on hers and try to forget about how badly I wanted to taste my Raven's lipstick. When I go down on this woman, I want to forget how badly I wanted to make my Raven's legs shake just so that the sound of her anklets would echo in the room making music out of her orgasm. When I am inside this girl, I want to forget how badly I wanted my Raven to make her scream my name.

"I'm screwed." I say as I pull away from her. This entire time, I was imagining fucking my sweet Raven's brains out. "I can't do this." I tell her.

"What?" This girl in my bed shoots up from under the sheets.

I get up and find my pants and put them on. "I said I can't...."

"You can't be serious!" She thinks I am joking. But just thinking about how badly I want to fuck my Raven, makes me hard. I turn around to face her. "Holy shit. You are. I–"

"You can sleep here if you are tired." I throw over my shirt. I'll crash on the couch and pray that George decides to fuck on the floor instead.

"I can do oral stuff if you want."

"You want to blow me off?" I wonder how my Raven's tongue would feel around my cock. I remember how badly I wanted her lipstick around my cock. I am going to hell for thinking about this.

"Look under normal circumstances, I would take you up on that offer, but I'm not in the mood anymore–" *For you.*

"I can put on that red lipstick again if you want!" I may or may not have asked her to put on the red lipstick that Riya loved to wear. She quickly puts it on but for some reason, it's not doing it for me. It doesn't look the same. I admired my Raven's lips because she could spit fire through those, she challenged me, and it made her red lips even hotter. Or when she bit her bottom lip because she was thinking about something. Or when she rubbed her thighs together because I turned her on. God her thighs...*I'm screwed.*

I want to fuck Riya.

Chapter 13- Riya

I have never been so busy in my entire college life. This week was brutal. I was swarmed with schoolwork, ambassador duties, club stuff, and my job. On top of that Maura was trying to reach me to apologise and I have been avoiding her the entire time. I can't talk to her right now. I put my phone on Do not disturb. Literally the only time I used it was when I sent James those messages.

"I need a massage. Want to go to a spa?" Juju cracks her neck as she walks into the living room. She takes a look at the living corpse on the couch and gets scared. The living corpse is me. Yep, I look awful. Pulling all nighters for most nights, sleep deprived, caffeine deprived, zombie. "Screw that, YOU need a massage, babe." I just groan and nod my head.

"Want me to make your favourite popcorn and play that weird documentary about hoses?" I shoot and sit up.

"It's not a documentary about hoses, it's a documentary about firefighters. And I would love that. You're watching it with me, right?" I pull a pillow on my stomach and pull the blanket over my feet.

Within five minutes, Juju is sitting next to me with caramel popcorn and we're watching the Hose documentary. Firefighter Documentary. Slip of tongue.

"I still don't get why you have a thing for hoses." she stuffs her mouth with popcorn.

"Not hoses, nozzles. And I don't have a thing for either. Look at those muscular, sexy and sweaty firefighters. Are you telling me that you're not wondering about their package?" I chuckle.

"God, you're so gross. But I totally get that. The firefighter part, not the nozzle part."

"Again! I don't have a thing for nozzles." *I totally do.* I have a huge thing for nozzles. Especially garden hose nozzles. Back home, I was in charge of watering the plants and cleaning the outdoors, so I handled garden hoses and nozzles since I was a kid, and they grew on me. It's weird and I know it. And I'm not going to keep thinking about nozzles anymore.

"Ri…" Oopsies. She's going to ask me something I don't want to talk about. She even pauses the documentary. Definitely a discussion about a topic which I was avoiding. "About that trip to New York…"

I rub my fingers against my aching forehead. "I don't want to talk about it, please."

"Your sister had called me." she doesn't look at me.

I spring up my full attention. "When? And why are you telling me this just now?" I can't believe she kept that from me.

"She called me just before I came downstairs. And she was worried about you. And looking at you right now, I'm worried too. Are you okay?" Am I okay? Hell no! Would I rather pretend that whatever happened in New York between me and my sister never happened? Absolutely! Have I been trying to distract myself to not think about it by doing anything and everything? Yes! But I'm not going to tell that to anyone.

"I'm fine. And you should've told me that before, Juju. I can't believe that you did that." I am hurt.

"I was just about to tell you, but you looked like you were half dead, so I wanted to cheer you up before I told you. You have been down ever since you came back from New York and you wouldn't tell me why."

Why does everybody suffocate me? You can't hurt me and then ask me how I'm doing when I'm bleeding! Especially when you can see that I'm bleeding. Isn't the blood oozing out of my body enough of an indicator that I'm hurt? "Isn't it evident that I didn't want to talk about it then? I was going to tell you eventually. I wanted to process it myself, Juju. You know what? Forget it. I'm tired. I'm just going to go and sleep." I take my anger out on the wrong person.

"But–" I pick my bag and walk away. I don't have the energy to sit there and tell her how I was hurt. James and his friends distracted me well from all that. Maybe that's what I need. I need to hang out with them. I need distraction, at least until this wound clots!

I make my way to my room and throw my bag in a corner and text James.

You up?

He doesn't reply.

I was thinking, maybe since we don't have classes, we could work on the tutoring and interview that we missed this week?

It's been more than an hour and still no response. So I text Daniel instead.

Hey Dan, sorry to disturb you late at night, but could you let me know if you guys have anything planned for tomorrow?

He replies almost immediately.

No, we have practice early in the morning, but that's all. Why?

Alright, so you guys aren't going anywhere, right?

No, we're not. You stopping by?

Only if that's okay with you guys.

You don't need to be so formal with us, Riya. Of course we'd love to have you over. See you tomorrow then.

Yep, see you. And Dan...

??

Could you keep this between us?

Gotcha.

I want to surprise James. I can't stop thinking about him since the gala. His hand on my thigh felt so good. I pull out my trusty vibrator. Fuck, just thinking about his hand on me makes me wet.

I wonder how good it must feel to have him inside me. I flick the vibrator on and press it on my clit and James' lustful eyes appear before me.

At that moment, I knew he wanted me just as much as I wanted him. I remember when we walked out of the restaurant, it was pouring and we were all soaked before we made it to the car. James' white shirt was see-through and I could see his beautiful pecs. I could see the outline of his abs as the shirt clinged to his body.

Thankfully, I was soaked too, so I could also torture him just as much. His gaze travelled to the droplets of water that made their way from my lip to my cleavage. Fuck, I could imagine his tongue instead on those droplets. It barely takes me a few more seconds to orgasm. I see stars and everything goes white, before I am back on Earth. Panting. I really needed this. My body needed this release, because I notice how easy it is to drift off to sleep now.

An orgasm a day, will maybe keep your mental health at bay.

I get ready and head to James' place at around twelve, I'm sure they must be home by now. I ring the bell and a very wet Daniel opens the door. His hair is still wet, probably from the shower. He smiles looking at me. "You made it!"

I smile back, not trying to show that I was just checking him out. God, he looks hot! I just try not to gawk and smile at him.

"Come on in." He leads me inside to where George and Siddharth are sitting with some more muscular and hot men. Some with women on their laps.

"Riya, this is Mike, Josh, Jaren and Howard and that's Marina, Jaren's girlfriend and Evelynn, Howard's girlfriend." Dan introduces me to everyone. And let me emphasise how handsome everyone is! And their girlfriends...spectacular. Perfect hourglass body and well gelled nails, perfect flowy hair. They are the sheer definition of beauty! Marina is in a cheerleader costume.

Is it a criteria that everyone has to be devilishly handsome to be on Winston's football team?

I greet them. I am so awkward right now. If I knew they were going to have company, I wouldn't have come over. I have never felt so out of place before. What was I thinking? I mean look at me, and look at them! I am a freaking nobody compared to them.

"Oh my god, I love your anklets that make noise." Evelynn comments with a smile. I'm not sure if it is a Regina George smile or a genuine one.

"Thank you, they're my grandmother's." she passed on her jewellery to all of us cousins. I got her anklets.

"Antique!" Marina squeaks. Okay...I'm definitely not looking forward to that fun time anymore.

George and Siddharth give each other a *we're out of here* and go to the kitchen. It's weird how in sync those two are!

"Where's James?" I ask Dan.

"James? Who's James?" Marina shifts on Jaren's legs and plays with her blonde hair.

"Is there a James on the team, babe?" Evelynn asks Howard in her cute voice. Which I'm sure is not her real voice. It can't be! Unless she's a cartoon. But man these women are some characters!

"He's upstairs. I can call him, if you want." Dan comes to my side.

"No, it's fine. I'll go upstairs." I hear a few gasps, mostly from the girlfriends. "I have something to give him anyway."

During one of our interviews, James told me that his idol after his dad was Derek Vanderwals. And I'd heard from one of my classmates in the journalism class that Derek Vanderwals was going to come to Winston. He is a Winston alumni who is one of the best quarterbacks, NFL has seen. James' words, not mine.

He was interviewed by none other than one of my friends- Nina Gallenti. And I asked her for a favour to let me get Derek's signed jersey. So, right now, stuffed in my bag is Derek Vanderwals signed jersey. By the way, Derek Vanderwals- disgustingly handsome. Buffed body and that beard. Fuck, he was hot despite being fourty eight years old!

"Please...Please..." I hear a woman's moans from James' room. Is he watching porn? I wonder if he is jerking off, right now. God, why does that make me wet? Thinking about James stroking himself. I want to hear him when he's coming.

Something naughty in me pushes me to go and open his door. I want to see him jerk off. No, I want to be the one he jerks off to. God! He's driving me crazy.

Just as I open the door I hear, "Please...I want to come, Marcus." The door is half open and I see James on top of someone. Her arms are wrapped around his waist and he is shirtless. The woman under him is naked I realise. Who has amazing breasts by the way. I already took a step in and my stupid anklet made a noise.

I love the sound of my anklets, it relaxes me, that's why I wear them. But right now, I hate that I am being noticed because of them. It is like my personal notification for others.

"Shit, I'm sorry." I immediately bang the door closed. They noticed me! Why couldn't they lock the door?

I hear footsteps fast behind me, someone running up the stairs. "Don't go in th–" a panting Siddharth stops in front of me. I am too shocked right now to process anything.

"I–Um...I–" What do I say? He obviously knew what was happening up here and that's why he ran upstairs to stop me. I thought that I was feeling out of place a minute ago? Never in my life have I ever felt this embarrassed in my life. "I'm going to go downstairs."

I press my lips together and slowly walk downstairs, Siddharth behind me. I don't know why my heart feels heavy right now. I mean, I knew he was a fuckboy from the get go, but I feel disappointed.

Maybe I was a little charmed by his *Raven* and *Sweetheart* and *Baby*. Fuck! This is the number one reason why I don't do relationships. Although, I know this wasn't a relationship, but James used to make my heart flutter. I thought we had something. I guess that something is in someone right now!

I need to be alone with my emotions right now! There's too much that I need to process. "Sorry guys, I think I should head back. I just remembered that I have a bakery class." *Bakery class?* That's the best excuse I could come up with? Shame on me!

"What are you baking?" Mike asks me.

"Lies."

"What?" everyone says in unison.

"Pies. I mean pies. Apple pies. Pies." The embarrassment...it's too much! "I'm gonna go." I point to the door and start heading outside. I look at Siddharth's face and he knows exactly why I'm leaving. He probably saw the shock and disappointment on my face when I walked in on James making a woman scream his name.

"Did you give James what you brought?" Marina asks me in an accusatory tone. Does she think I was here to give him a blowjob? Because guess what Marina, he's probably getting one of those right now.

"No, I don't think he has time for it right now. He seemed very busy." And just as if it was timed, I hear running footsteps down the stairs. I don't want to talk to him right now. I don't want to listen to anything. I just want to go to my bakery class.

Girl, you don't actually have a bakery class! You can't bake to save your life!

"Bye guys." I'm literally speed-running-walking to the door and I am out in the blink of an eye.

"Riya...Riya...wait. Riya." I keep hearing, but my feet don't stop. I hear the front door close behind me. "Raven, please!" And I stop. Don't fall for his act. Don't fall for his act.

"Whatever you just saw right now..." Fuck! Why isn't he wearing a shirt? He's just wearing sweatpants and I can see that he's still hard. Did he not come in the brunette before? Why am I even thinking about it? Gross!

Perhaps it was all one-sided. All of it. "You don't have to explain anything to me, James. Since when do we owe explanations to each other? It's fine. I'm just late to my bakery class. I better get going." I reach my bag for the car keys and he spots the Derek Vanderwals jersey.

"Can we go inside and talk?" His voice mellows down.

It is my fault for not calling him, although I did text him. *Stupid Riya.* "I don't want to humiliate myself anymore, James. I'm sorry, I should've called before coming over. I just told Daniel since I– Nevermind. It's my fault. I'm sorry. Now, I better get going. The bakery class starts in fifteen minutes." Actually, no! It is not my fault. Just because I am busy and I don't reply to your texts continuously, he goes and fucks someone else? Was that all he wanted from me? To sleep with me? To fuck me?

He pulls out his phone and checks the time.

"So the bakery class starts at 12:38?"

"Yes. Now, if you'll excuse me."

"Five minutes. Just give me five minutes. We can talk in your car if you want."

God he's doing that thing with his eyes again. The cute puppy dog eyes. "Okay fine."

Fine, I'll admit it! I am a sucker for those deep ocean blue eyes of his. And if someone can make my heart melt with those puppy dog eyes, it's *James*.

Chapter 14- James

I fucked up. No pun intended. I had no idea that she was coming over. And I had no intention of bending the brunette over. But when I came from practice this morning, she was still in my bed. Naked. Playing with her tits. I am a man! Of course that's going to make me hard. But I told her to leave. I was trying to get her to put her clothes on, it's always the psychos that I manage to attract!

I heard the door open and the sound of those anklets, I froze there, on top of another girl whose name I don't know, but is moaning my name out loud for no reason. Probably for my teammates and their girlfriends downstairs to hear. I was really close to losing it, but I held it together. I pulled out of her grip and looked around for my shirt that I had taken off right after I entered my room before I saw her. I had told her to leave but clearly she was selectively deaf.

"Are you fucking serious?" she snaps at me. I know what I'm doing is cruel, but I can't let my Raven walk away from me like that. I saw the disappointment in her eyes when she saw us, even if our eyes met just for a split second.

I grab this woman in her undergarments by her hand and drag her down the stairs. My teammates clearly see us. I hear the front door shut. And I drag her towards the back door and leave her there. "Dress up and leave. I'm sorry for this." I apologise. I was the one who led her on!

I sound like a total dick right now, but I don't care, I just need to run after my Raven and make sure that this girl is gone when we come back.

Since when do we owe each other an explanation? I fucked up bad. I know what she must be thinking about me, but man, I don't like it when she walks away from me.

I spot a 49ers jersey when she is looking for her keys, but I don't say anything about it. I wonder if she got it for someone else?

Five minutes. That's all I get from her. We sit in her car and it smells like her, floral and leathery.

"Whatever you saw up there–"

"James. It's fine. I should've knocked. And I swear my eyes were closed. I didn't see anything." *Liar.*

"Alright. Fine. Okay. Cool. But what I'm saying is that–" She looks away. *How to act normal after being walked on while not having sex?* I doubt that she will believe me anyway. "So, why did you come by?" I know for a fact that we don't have any tutoring sessions or interview meeting lineup.

"Oh...right!" She reaches for her bag in the back and pulls out the 49ers jersey. "Here."

I take it from her hands and turn it around. It's a Derek Vanderwals jersey. And it's signed by him! Fuck! She got it for me? And I was being such an ass!

She doesn't even try to force a smile. Her disappointment makes me feel disappointed in myself. "I know you said that you admired him and he was stopping by at Winstons and one of my friends was going to interview him, so I asked in for a favour and here we are." She dares not to meet my eye.

"Can I kiss you?" Where did that come from? Her eyes widen and my heart races.

She scoffs. "You're seriously asking me that after you were buried inside someone else?" Damn, does that twist the knife further!

"I'm sorry you had to see that but I really wasn't...we weren't– it's not what you think it is!" I don't know why but it matters what she thinks of me. She matters more to me than I would like to admit.

"You don't have to be sorry, James. It's fine. I never expected to be your type anyway. I know I'm not as..." she blinks her eyes as if she's trying to hold her tears back. Fuck! How could I do this to her? "Seductive as her." She grips her dress that bunches up around her thigh and then her knit thigh high socks.

"Raven..." I hold her face with my hand and she lets me. "The only reason I was with that girl in the first place was because I can't stop thinking about you, regardless nothing happened. You were ignoring me last week. It was pathetic of me to do, I know and I am sorry but I swear nothing happened!" I explain everything like a high school teen.

She forces a laugh. "I wasn't ignoring you. I sent you messages."

"Three messages in total."

"I texted you last night as well, but clearly you were busy." Shit! I had left my phone in my room last night since she was sleeping there and I slept on the couch. And this morning I just left for practice without going into my room, waiting for her to leave. It is my stupid fault! "Anyway, your five minutes are up, I got that bakery class. So, I can't be late." she stares blankly at me.

I exhale loudly, irritated by my own behaviour. If only I had waited for her instead of assuming stupid things. I've never had this sort of connection with anyone before. Women usually want to sleep with me because they either want to be seen leaving the house in the morning or they want to weasel their way into me taking them to meet my father. Which is never happening.

Never!

But with Riya...I am not Marcus Williams, I'm James. Just James. And I love the person I am around her, so I'm not letting her go anywhere. "I'll go with you too. I really want to learn how to bake." I know for a fact that she does not have a bakery class.

She sighs, irritated. Good, I'm happy to know that at least my being affects her a little. I'll take whatever I can get. "I'm not taking you like this. You're only wearing your sweatpants." Her gaze falls to my groyne and she immediately looks everywhere but in my direction.

"Give me five minutes. I'll be right back." I open the door, but she turns on her car. Oh! I see how it's gonna be. I go upstairs to put more clothes on and she'll drive off. I get out of the car, keeping the door open so that she won't be able to drive off and walk over to her side and open her door.

"You're coming with me." I throw her over my shoulder. And her short dress rides up, exposing her blue lacy panties and her sexy ass.

"What are you doing? James! Put me down. Now! James!" She moves around. But that only exposes her ass more and more. Now I don't mind looking at her sexy behind for the rest of eternity, but I wouldn't want my teammates to even peek at her.

"Give me one second." I cover her butt with the Derek Vanderwals jersey and open the front door. Everyone in the room falls silent, including my Raven.

"Excuse me boys." I make my way through the living room and everyone's jaw is on the floor. When I reach my room, the brunette from before did not creep back in. Thank god!

"Five minutes." I put her down.

"You are an ass!" she grunts.

"And you have the most beautiful ass." I smack her behind and she moans. Fuck. Why did she moan? I was already aching to want to jerk off, but now my cock twitches in my pants and my balls ache.

Her gaze falls to my cock as it is literally standing upright in my sweatpants and it doesn't help that I am not wearing any boxers.

"James..." her voice mellows as she takes a step towards me. Her gaze locked on my erection. She's not even hiding it anymore.

"I'm going to need a minute to take care of that as well." I shrug.

She doesn't stop walking towards me until she is standing so close to me, a small movement and I could be inside her. Fuck. I would like that very much. But I am not going to push myself.

"You're really hard right now." Her gaze finally flicks up and she looks at me with her doe eyes, biting her lip. "Are you going to jerk off in the bathroom?" she licks her lips and fuck does that do things to me.

"That was the plan."

"Do it." She takes a step back and sits on the chair behind her. "Do it, in front of me." she pushes her thighs together and her knit cosy looking socks glide down a bit and I think about eating her out.

I walk towards her with a smirk. "You want to watch me jerk off, Raven?" She nods a no.

Her eyes darken. A darker shade of brown- a dangerous shade of brown. "I want you to jerk off to me. I want you to think only about me when you stroke yourself and when you finally come...I want nothing but my name on your lips." That catches me by surprise. This turns me on at a next level. For a moment I almost choke on my breath.

I lean down close to her mouth, inches apart. "Are you sure you can handle it, Sweetheart."

She presses her index finger on my lips and gently nudges me away. "Not. Your. Sweetheart."

I hold her hand and pull her up. As soon as her body presses against mine, she gasps. My erection pressed against her. She's playing with fire right now. A fire that will end up consuming the both of us into the deep taverns of hell.

"Are you wet for me right now?" she nods. Her gaze fixed on my lips. "Are you sure you want to watch me come?" I flash her my cocky smile.

"All talk and no show?" She teases me. God this woman drives me crazy. No woman. And I repeat no woman has ever made my balls ache so badly with just words.

I slide my thumb over her plump lips and do not miss the way her body hitches under my touch. "You have a filthy mouth, Raven." But I love that. She takes a few steps ahead and sits on the bed, legs crossed over.

I pull the chair in front of her and pull my pants off before sitting in the chair. Exposing myself completely.

I am so painfully hard that precum beads on the head as I give myself a gentle stroke. My eyes are on her and her eyes stay fixated on my hand and my hand grips my shaft a little tighter than before. I've never done this before. Jerked off in front of someone.

"Are you going to come for me?" she whispers in a rusky voice.

I keep stroking myself, up and down. Each stroke brings out a different expression out of her. First her eyes darken, second she bites her lips, third her thighs squeeze together, fourth her lips fall open, fifth her breathing fastens. I see it all and I love it all. "Fuck. I'm too close. And I can't stop thinking about your hands instead of mine." she raises a brow and I think I went too far? Until...

"Show me." she says and I am a goner. "Show me what my hands would do. Tell me what would make you come the hardest." My strokes start to speed up. Until I can't form sentences.

"You." That's all I can say. Before my balls clench and I am almost coming.

Her cheeks flush red, matching a similar shade of mine. "Say it." she demands. Bossy.

"My sweet little Raven..." I groan as fluid ejects around my stomach. Fuck, that was so hot. And we didn't even touch each other.

Hell, we haven't even kissed and yet she makes me see stars with just words. And her filthy mouth. Her fuckable filthy mouth!

"Not late for the bakery class, now? Are we?" I walk out of the bathroom into my room and find her snooping around. She was going through all the medals and awards I have in my room. I have always been good at sports and coding and have received several awards for it too.

"I rescheduled." By that she means she actually found a class.

"Alright. Let's go then. Where was it again?"

"Boston. I hope that's alright." It takes about forty five minutes to drive to Boston from here. Winstons is in Bradwick, MA. Meaning if you don't have a car around, you're probably screwed.

"Alright." I stand in front of the mirror and adjust my hair and I can feel her gaze on me. "If you want me, all you have to do is ask."

"I am not going to have sex with you, James"

"I wasn't referring to sex. I was talking about me."

She doesn't look away, her bold eyes stay on mine. "I don't understand." I walk towards her and she rubs her thighs again. Damnit!

I lean closer to her ear, teasing her. "With you, I'm sure there are other things we can explore, *Raven*."

Chapter 15- Riya

Was I hurt seeing him fuck someone else that he really wasn't fucking? Absolutely. Did I want to get revenge by making him strip in front of me and make him obey while I stayed fully clothed and not let him touch me? Yes. Did that torture me just as much? You bet it did!

I can't get the image of James groaning my name while coming. And I know for a fact that I am going to touch myself tonight, replaying it again and again, wishing it was him.

Have I done something remotely similar before? No! Did I ever have the confidence to talk dirty to someone before? No! Did I like talking dirty with James? Fuck, yes! I can only imagine what sex with him would feel like. His hand on my clit, his mouth on my breast. Sucking. As he made all the beautiful noises which are music to my ears as he tells me what all he wants to do to me. I loved it when he spanked me before. Maybe he could do it again? This time with less clothes on?

"Miss Riya? Miss Riya?" The instructor calls me. I look around and I see that everyone is near the oven with their batter. I looked up this class when James was in the bathroom, taking a shower and I was wishing that I was with him. No! Snap out of it!

"Yes. Coming." I quickly stride over there.

"You're drooling." James wipes the corner of my mouth with his thumb and it lingers around. I wish he'd slide it in my mouth to suck on it. What? No! Gross. I have to deboard this Marcus James Williams fantasy train, otherwise it's going to drive me crazy.

I push his hand off and he chuckles. A raspy deep chuckle. "You're drooling." Why is it so fucking adorable when men chuckle?

INTERTWINED

We sit in the car with two baked cakes and look at each other and burst out into laughter. We were the only two who walked out of the class with an edible cake. The rest of the old ladies' cakes were burnt, so they got mad and started a cake fight. Shoving the burnt cake down each other's throats. James and I grabbed our cake and walked out of there slowly.

We're gasping for our breath! "That was not what I expected from the old ladies. They were so sweet at first." Gertha was the first to start the fight. It was just between her and her friend- Molly and then she 'accidentally' threw the icing on annoying Janice, who thought it was Bert. And from there it escalated so fast that it turned into cake wars.

"Did you see when Janice threw the cake at Bert and it knocked him out? It was so funny." We are laughing our asses off. And I am not even faking my laugh! And he's not judging me for my laugh! Everyone and I repeat everyone, besides my family has made a snide comment about the way I laugh at some point. Even Juju. Although, it was funny before, but now it's just straight up mean sometimes.

"We're totally coming to this class again."

"Totally." We high five each other and seem genuinely happy in each other's company.

"Are you sure you're fine?" My cousin sister- Lara asks me. We're almost the same age. She's about six months older than me and never lets me forget that. But she's my best friend. Literally, my best friend. She knows about my first kiss, the boy I lost my virginity to, she helped me pick my vibrator, she knows about my weird obsession with nozzles and she is one of the reasons why I have that obsession in the first place.

She's that person who if I call and tell that I need her help to get rid of her body, she'll come over and help me first and then ask me what happened. Although, it's not like I have people locked up in the basement. Maybe I do. *Come on guys, I'm kidding. I don't even have a basement!*

"Yeah, I'm fine. I just want to punch the shit out of that fucking Keith. He's manipulating her and she doesn't see it." I groan.

She is working on her project while talking to me! She can multitask like hell! I will never understand how. "I doubt he could handle your punches. No one can. Trust me. I know! And why don't you talk to Maura about it? I feel like you two should talk it out."

I turn around in the chair. Sitting backwards letting my head fall down. "She's around him 24/7. Even when I call. God, why do they have to work together? I just hope that she doesn't give up her idea about her own fashion line." I groan.

"Do you want me to talk to her?" If anyone can talk some sense into Maura, it's Lara. No matter how supportive Lara is, she's brutally honest. *Brutally.*

"Let me talk to her first. Keep you as the last option. You know?"

"Just because I don't bitch and moan and beat around the bush, doesn't mean that I don't care about her feelings. I just say what needs to be said." She's not lying. If you ever want a reality check, Lara is your go to person. Everyone is super scared of her but at the same time we all know that she cares about us.

"Alright! You care. So, how's work going on? You still got the job?"

"Actually…" This is where her brutal honesty lands her in trouble. Lara is an architect and she is supposed to be understanding of her clients. But she can't stand incompetence and I totally feel that, it icks me too but she crushes her clients.

"Don't tell me…" there's a groan from her side.

"I swear it wasn't my fault." It was her fault. Her client wanted something brick and for the structure bricks wasn't good, it wouldn't bring out the beauty of the fountain? I think…I lost her after bricks. I don't know shit about architecture, but I do know she did lose her temper there. Calling the client a 'twat' wasn't the best decision.

For the next two hours I fill Lara in about everything going on in my life.

"So, you're telling me that you are friends with four super hot jocks and you haven't boned a single one?" Okay…I never said she had the most sophisticated wording either.

"No, I haven't *boned* anyone. Although…" I want to tell her about all the fantasies I have dreamt about James. But I know that I will never hear the end of it.

This girl has no filter. "You want to bone all of them? I mean I understand the appeal, but that'd be too much! Don't you think so?" she doesn't chuckle, so she does mean it. And I looked around just in case anybody heard her. *I am wearing earphones.*

"God! No! Lara. Geez. You and your mouth." She chuckles. "Nothing. I'm telling you nothing. You're going to sleep right now and keep your head out of the gutters."

"Oh my god!" She sounds as if she solved the most difficult puzzle. "You want to bone more than one of them?" That catches me by surprise. Did I ever fantasise about Daniel? I'd be lying if I said no. Did I ever fantasise a threesome with James and Dan? Yes. But in my defence I was only laying on top of Dan's naked body while James was…hitting it from the back. Maybe I should stop this fantasising stuff.

"I do not!" I say in the most obvious voice which not just her, but anyone can recognise is fake.

"Alright. Fine. I'll take your word for it. By the way, could you please lend me your JMs?"

"JMs?"

"Your blue Jimmy Choos..." she coos. I never let anyone touch my designer stuff. I repeat no one. Not my Chanel and Gucci Bags, not my Tom Ford and Armani perfumes and definitely not my Louis Vuitton and Jimmy Choos. I took a pair back home for the wedding and I have a lot more designer stuff back home, which no one is allowed to touch.

"Only if you parcel me your Bvlgari necklace." My uncle brought Lara a Bvlgari necklace on her 21st birthday. Okay, maybe all the women in our house are spoiled, especially me. I am a spoiled brat. Because for my 21st, I asked for a trip to Cabo and guess what, my dad sent over the money. So, in two months I'm supposed to be chilling on the beach sipping coconuts and margaritas and checking out hot men with Juju. And I can't wait for it! Thankfully the Spring break this year aligns with my Birthday- which is March 25.

My beloved father also sent me enough money to buy some designer goodies for me which I splurged on Prada and Dior and plan to spend the rest in Cabo. Like I said, I am a spoiled brat. Sue me. Doesn't mean that I am not down to Earth. I work part time in the library nearby for some extra cash. I like to live a bougie lifestyle, even though my unkempt nails and my messy hair would say otherwise. I like to save when possible and I do donate to charities anonymously. I am not that bad of a person, guys!

"Bitch." Lara groans over the phone and I am dragged back to reality.

"Tit for tat, sweetheart."

"I hate you."

"I love you too. Gotta go. But I'll talk to you soon. And stay away from my JMs." she hangs up without saying bye and it makes me chuckle. I get back to putting the books away in the library. One of the biggest pros about working in a library- there's peace in here.

And if someone is trying to disturb that peace, I can just kick them out.

Plus not to mention the free access to all the books I ever want. I put all these books back and ran towards my favourite section- Romance novels. I'm a delusional person who has fallen in love with almost all the male characters in the books I've read and they're the reason why my mind is so corrupt.

My phone buzzes in my back pocket. I pull it out to see a name which brings a smile on my face.

I opened the message from James.

Party at our house tonight. Wanna come? You can bring your friends too.

What time?

It starts whenever you come.

Cringe.

Around 10pm.

See you at 11 then.

I tuck the phone back and it buzzes again. I open to see another text from James.

It's a sexy themed party.

Wouldn't it be better if I didn't dress at all then?

The three dots appear and disappear and again appear and disappear. And again.

That party is reserved only in my room.

A few seconds later he sends another message- *And only for me.*

We have been texting and flirting like this the entire week. And everytime it only riles me up more and more. I open another chat and text Juju.

Party at the football guys' house at 10. You in?

She replies back in a few seconds with two thumbs up and three winky faces. I pick up dinner for Juju and I, on my way back. Spicy fried chicken is the only acceptable pregame food. Does it make you bloated the next day? Sure. But does it help you drink more? It sure as hell does! And I plan to let loose today. That call with Lara has put me in a fun mood.

I fish deep in my closet to find the sexiest of the sexy dress that I can find, just so that I can tease James. But there's one problem with that. Teasing him is starting to turn me on just as much. I look at myself in the mirror and I know that I look good. And trust me, I don't say that very often. This is the perfect outfit to tease him.

You better wear tight pants tonight, James.

Chapter 16- James

My eyes are super glued to the door. Every time it opens, a wave of excitement passes through me. I know for a fact that my naughty little Raven is going to wear something that is going to make me hard for the rest of the night. So, I already made adjustments for that. I am wearing my tightest jeans so that I'm not poking out of my pants. It's 11:15 and she's still not here. I'm starting to think that she's probably not coming. But then the door opens to prove me wrong.

She appears like a goddess and suddenly all eyes in the room jolt towards her. She flips her hair back with such confidence knowing that she is looking lip smackingly good.

Tasty.

Her black skirt covers enough to keep wanting more. Her silver heels string around and are tied around her calf. And her top. She's wearing a silver sparkly crop top, which dips low enough to know that one movement and she'll be out. She turns to greet George who is basically ogling her like every other guy in here. Damn. The back of her top is held by one frail silver string. One tiny tug and her tiny little top falls to the ground.

She looks around, probably and hopefully trying to find me. And when she does, she licks her signature red lips. And I am so glad that I chose to wear these jeans. She whispers something in the girl's ear who she walked in with. Which I am guessing is her roommate, Justine. She waltzes around the room until she is standing in front of me.

My voice is suddenly too high pitched for my liking. "You made it." That's the first thing I say to her? I swear to god, my body suddenly starts to disobey me infront of her.

She looks around the room, checking out other people's costumes. "Am I dressed appropriately for the theme?" She gives a quick spin, sticking her ass out in front of me on purpose and I have to clench my fists too hard to not smack her butt. I'm scared that by the end of the night I'll be bleeding.

"You look delicious."

She bites her lower lip and looks at me with those doe eyes. That fuckable expression. Umm..."Drink?" she asks me.

"Let me guide you to the good stock." I put my hand around her back and I'm one hundred percent sure that she just shivered under my touch. I wonder if I slip my hand into her panties, will she be wet?

Great, because now I'm even harder now. I guide her to the bar and open the locked cabinet. She bends to pull out a bottle of scotch and I can't help but take a look. I know it's not a very gentlemanly thing to do so I force myself to look up. I'm dancing with the devil here.

"This. Let's use this." She stands upright again, holding the whiskey bottle in her hand.

"You have a good eye." I take the bottle from her hands and her eyes travel up and down my body, checking me out.

"I sure do." She bites a smile and winks at me. What the actual fuck? If I hadn't clenched my ass right now, I swear I would be covered with precum right now. I want to fuck her right now.

"Glasses?"

"Huh?"

"Glasses. For the drinks." She presses her lips to not smile, but the corner of her lips rise anyway. She knows exactly what she's doing. I want to haul her over my shoulder and carry her upstairs and fuck her smug smile off.

I saunter over to the cabinet next to it and grab two glasses. She makes two drinks and guides me through the crowd to her friend. "James, that's Juju, my roommate and that's Jake, her boyfriend." She introduces me to them as if I didn't already know. I am not supposed to know.

"Hey man." Jake and I shake hands and give each other the *'your secret is safe with me'* look.

"So when do the playoffs start?" Jake asks me. "It was a good game this season though. Especially against UCLA. You guys crushed them." It was a tough game, but we had some good touchdowns from the get go and Dan handled the defence pretty strong as well.

"It was a team effort." Believe it or not, I hate football talk at parties. It's all I talk about during the day and even at night. But parties are the one place I like to leave it behind.

"But that touchdown that you made in the fourth quarter...Amazing!" Is it bad that I want to yawn? Not because I am cocky, but I am genuinely bored.

"Yeah. Thanks man. I appreciate it."

A cheerful hand slips on my shoulder and that beautiful sweet floral scent wraps around me. "Do you want to play beer pong and watch me beat your ass?" Of course. It's my Raven to my rescue.

"Sure."

"Me and Marcus vs you and Jake?" Juju wraps her arm around Riya. I'd rather team up with my Raven but before I could object, the game has already started.

I am an athletic person, I've always been. Football, golf, swimming, ice skating, shooting, I'm good at it all. Not to brag, but I am just as good at studying too. Looking for a genius? He's standing right here. But I don't like to show it off.

"Chug. Chug. Chug. Chug." Riya shouts from the other side. One thing I like to boast about myself is that I'm competitive. I remembered once I fell on my butt in middle school while ice skating and the hockey boys started making fun of me.

I skated till 2am until I was better at it than them. If I'd continued, who knows, I'd be in the hockey team instead of football! And I can clearly see that she's just as competitive. Jake and Juju, or as I like to call them the JJ couple, quit the game because me and my Raven were making it too competitive and it was no more fun. I have never had more fun.

"Drink up Mr Williams." she squeaks and turns around to the beats of music. I throw the ball and it misses and she wins.

Didn't I mention how competitive I am? Seeing her cheery dance makes me feel happy about losing for the first time.

She walks over and hauls me to the living room between the drunk dancing people. Did I mention how physically strong she is? Hell yeah! I really lose the person I am and become my true self when I'm with her! She...She never ceases to amaze me.

"Come on. Let's get dancing." She's waving her hair in the air to 'What makes you beautiful' by One Direction. I am not a dancer. The only move I know is a girl grinding on me. But her energy rubs off on me and I mimic her moves, her shoulders move and I move mine the same way and then she throws her hands in the air and jumps and before I know it, I'm dancing and shouting the lyrics with her. I throw my hands in the air and bop my head and I enjoy myself!

And it's like the odds are against me, the song changes to 'Under the influence' and her hips start swaying. But I'm not complaining, all I have to do is put my hand around her waist and pull her against me. She doesn't push me away. And I start to realise how bad of an idea it is to have her grind on me like that. It brings back memories from that party we met at.

All of a sudden she stops moving and turns around to whisper something in my ear. "I'll stop now. Wouldn't want you to pop out of your pants in the middle of the dance floor." She winks at me as she walks past, leaving me speechless and making me even harder. I am *literally* about to *pop off*!

We are all chilling on the couch, talking. Most of the people left at around 2am, and now it's just my roommates, the girls they're going to hook-up with, JJ couple and Riya. Riya sits in front of me, eyeing me as she sips her scotch.

The door slams open loudly and a girl in a skimpy dress walks in yelling 'where is that bitch.' I just pray to god that it's not for me. And thankfully it's not. She stomps over to Sid and the brunette he was about to hook up with immediately stands up. Raven and I are completely unaffected by this shenanigan and keep continuing eye-fucking each other. That is until her head turns to Sid who is standing in front of her with a hand on his cheek, because this crazy bitch who just walked in slapped him.

Riya gets up and stands between both of them. Her expression is darker than ever. God she looks hot when she's mad. And it turns me on even more.

"You stop right there." She tells the crazy girl who slapped Sid and the crazy bitch stops like hell froze over. Hell, anyone would. She's scary like that. Bossy too. Which I love.

She turns around to face Sid. "Do you deserve that slap? I just want to hear "Yes or No"." straight to the point.

Sid looks embarrassed. "No." He says.

I know for a fact that no matter how many women these boys and even I sleep with, we never give them any hope for a relationship and we sure as hell don't disrespect them. Sid has a little sister and he's always lecturing me about how to let women down respectfully because he wouldn't want someone to treat his little sister disrespected and karma and all. I did not need the lecture, but I know for a fact that he of all people did not deserve that slap. And that is his first slap!

As soon as Sid says no. My Raven pulls the hair of the crazy girl and drags her head to the open space in the living room and throws her head. Fuck! Note to self- never hurt Sid in front of her.

"You hit him, because you knew he wouldn't hit you back. Guess what bitch, he has an older sister who can. So, why don't you take on someone who can hit you back?" Older sister? When did that happen? Sid is just as shocked as me. Everyone is standing on their feet. Even George who finally looks up from his make out sesh. Which is rare, nope, it has never happened before. It is a celestial event.

"You fucking bitch." the crazy bitch screams and I'm not sure who needs help here. From the looks of it, it's definitely not my feisty and scary Raven.

Riya takes the same stance that she took that time she threw a punch at George. And George was complaining about his arm for almost 3 days. If she throws one at this girl, she'll be knocked out.

"What? Scared? Scared that I'll hit you back? This is not a cat-fight. I don't do those. You wanna throw your hands at people's faces? Guess what? I can do that too." Consider me a goner. I don't care about the people in the room and all the spectators. I just want to fuck her, right here, right now.

The girl on the ground is shivering and gets up. "You're crazy!" Says the crazy girl herself as she runs out of the house.

George gulps. "You're crazy." He looks like he saw a ghost. It's a look I have never seen on his face. And if George is calling Riya crazy, it means that she is CRAZY. But fuck does she make me go cray-cray with her craziness. Look at me, using words like cray-cray!

"Time for us to go." JJ couple gets up and Juju holds Riya's hands who shakes it off and walks towards Sid. She hits his chest, softly.

"Wait here." She walks to the kitchen and comes back with an ice pack. This is the second time she's icing a slapped face in this house. Almost makes me snort. Almost. I'm just happy it's not me this time.

Dan and his hook-up make way to his room right after George and his hook-up and JJ argue as Jake tries to pull Juju out of here.

Riya senses the uneasiness that Justine feels. "You guys head out. I'll head out after some time. I'll see you at home, Juju." she smiles and nods at Justine to let her know that she's fine.

Jake pulls Justine close to him. Away from Riya and I'm almost half tempted to knock him out. "Aren't you staying over at my place, babe?" He forces a smile.

"You should stay over, James will drop me off, babe." Riya hugs Justine. So she calls her best friend babe. Nope, not going to overthink it. Why does she have a problem when I call her that? I want to pout and whine like a baby.

"No, funny games. Make sure she gets home safe, Marcus." Justine glares at me.

"I will." I raise my hands to surrender.

Riya ices Sid's face for some time and tortures me by bending over and putting her ass on display for me.

"You okay there, cap?" Sid teases me. He knows exactly what's wrong with me right now.

Raven turns around to look at me and then looks at my eyes glued to her ass.

"If you want it, all you have to do is ask, Williams." She teases me and Sid acts like he's throwing up. I press my tongue against the hollow of my cheek. This girl knows exactly how to rile me on. "The ice pack, I mean." She wasn't referring to the ice pack, but I think I might need one for my balls. Poor guys are going to be blue until I jerk myself off tonight.

Sid presses his lips together and gets up and walks away, taking the ice pack out of her hands. "Thank you for that, Riya." He turns back and smiles at her. She nods her head and he is gone and we're let alone in the living room.

I saunter towards Raven, who flops down on the couch. Legs crossed. Thighs pressing. And that adorable fuckable expression on her face.

I lower myself onto her. Her sweet and floral scent overwhelms me and makes me want to bury my face in her neck. "You have been a bad, bad girl all night." I tilt her chin towards me and she bites her lip.

"Oh yeah? What are you gonna do about it?" she smirks. Fuck. I bend my neck backwards and try to find that one thread of control. But it snaps when she pulls me onto her and crashes her lips on mine. Sweet! She tastes so sweet...and a bit bitter- like the scotch. I want to smear that red lipstick off her face tonight. One way or the other.

Her lips are so hungry for me, matching my hunger. My tongue slides along her lips, seeking permission and her mouth opens up for me. I can never have enough of her. I am so engrossed in her that I forget to breathe. But then again, breathing is optional here.

I slide my hand around her waist and pick her up in one swift motion and she wraps her legs around my waist. Her tongue tells me just how much she wants me. Glad we're on the same page about that.

I carry her to the stairs and press her against the wall and she moans as my erection presses against her. I wouldn't be surprised if my balls turned blue from all the pain tonight.

She's panting and gasping for air, but at the same time wanting more of me as she pulls my neck towards her. "You room..." I trace my mouth from her mouth to between her neck and shoulder and it must be her sweet spot as I see her head fall back and she moans even louder. "Fuck...Williams...Do that again." I kiss her neck again and another moan escapes her mouth. I feel her legs around my waist loosen for a second.

"Are you wet for me, Raven?" I whisper in her ear as she shivers under my breath.

She unwraps her legs and stands and holds my hand and guides it under her skirt and up in her panties. Her eyes look directly into mine, no trace of shame anywhere. "See for yourself."

My fingers find the hem of her panties and slide inside. She's not just wet, she's soaked. I wouldn't be shocked if she leaked out on the couch. "I have been wet all night–" She presses her lips on mine and then comes closer to my ear and whispers. "–for you. I have been wet for you." And I lose whatever it was holding me back and pick her up in my arms and carry her to my room. I lock my room behind us and corner her against the door. Lips consuming each other. Fuck, I want to see her come.

"I want you to make me come." she commands but looks shy the next second. "On your tongue." Is it just me, or did her eyes become darker and hungrier? Hungry for me.

I get on my knees in front of this gorgeous woman who I have been fantasising about for weeks and pull down her skirt, which bunches down at her sexy high heels. She's wearing Black lace panties. I slowly slide them off to expose her, keeping her heels on.

"Your wish is my command, *Raven*."

Chapter 17- Riya

I just told a man to go down on me. Not just any man, I told one of the biggest fuckboys I know to make me come on his tongue. And he looks up at me, like he is genuinely thankful I asked him that. I love the sight of this. Those blue eyes looking at me hungrily, waiting to devour me.

His tongue starts grazing my inner thigh. Slow kisses tracing higher and higher until he's right where I want him to be.

"Fuck, you are so wet for me, Raven."

"I can't stand straight like this for long, Marcus." I'm wearing heels higher than the Burj Khalifa, or at least that's how it feels like. I tangle my hand through his hair. He chuckles when I tug on it. He grabs my right leg and puts it around his shoulder. Fuck, his shoulders are broad enough to hold me still. But I can tell that my heels are digging in his back. He doesn't complain though.

"Now, let me eat you out." He is skilled with his tongue. He first slowly plays with my folds, riling me on. Until he really gets into it. And when he slides his finger inside me, I did not expect it whatsoever. His hands are bigger than mine, so it is very different from how my fingers feel inside me.

"Fuck, you're slick." He slides another finger inside.

My head rolls back in unison to my eyes. "Oh fuck–Yes.". He curls his fingers inside me and his long fingers hit a spot inside me that I didn't even know existed. His tongue keeps playing with my clit. I push my hips ahead and shamelessly rub against his face until I feel a wave of liquid pool in my pussy.

I feel my orgasm building up as I keep rubbing against him. Craving him. I push his face against my pussy. He's mouth-fucking me, he's finger-fucking me and he's holding me in place so that I don't lose balance and fall.

He pushes his finger deeper and my back arches. "I'm going to come." I moan.

"Come for me. Scream my name as I eat you off." And that's exactly what I do. I scream his name as I shiver and ride his fingers. I feel the orgasm tear through me. My pussy clenches against his fingers and he groans and licks me clean. He brings his fingers to his mouth and licks them clean too. Why is that the sexiest thing ever?

"You taste so so good. One taste is not going to be enough, Raven." I am still panting. Recovering from my orgasm before he picks me up in a swift motion. I swear to god, this man lifts me up like I weigh nothing. He lays me on the bed on my back. "Clothes off!"

"So cocky..." I give him that same look that he calls 'the fuckable look'. I bite my lip to tease him and he is teased. He is more than teased. Because when I press my hand against the bulge in his pants, he groans with pleasure.

"Not so soon. First, I will take care of you." He pushes me back on the bed and takes off his shirt to reveal peaks and valleys between his pecs and abs. He's ripped. And by ripped I mean that he is rocking those eight pack abs. He has muscles even on the side of his ribs, how is that possible? I hold onto the belt hoops on his jeans and pull him close. I need to feel his ripped body with my own hands to know that it's real. I trace my hands up and down and he's smirking at me.

"It's real!" That gets me a laugh.

"You thought it was fake."

My hand travels lower and lower until I reach the button on his jeans and unzip them open. "So greedy!" he grins.

He kicks off his jeans and groans as if he can finally breathe now. I rub my hand against his erection in his boxers and no wonder he was in pain. He's huge, and must be cramped up in those jeans. His hand holds mine and pins me above my head. "First. I will take care of you."

"But–"

"Shhh..." Nobody in my life has ever shushed me. Nobody. "Let's get rid of this, shall we?" He holds the straps of my top. I stuck the top to my body with body tape, because I'm not wearing anything underneath. When I take my top off, Marcus stares at me as if he saw the eighth wonder of the world. "You are so beautiful, Riya! Every inch of you is art, a beautiful beautiful art." I blush at his words. I have been called beautiful before, but never when I was naked.

My breasts are fine. I always felt like they're a little small in comparison to my ass. But when Marcus takes one in his mouth. Fuck. It fits perfectly.

I moan and groan as he plays with my body. And when he goes down on me again, I am all but in pleasureland right now. His tongue teases me at my entrance. One hand playing with my clit.

And when he pinches my nipple, I am a goner. I hear a loud moan and I think it must be from either of the boy's rooms. But when the hand that was playing with my nipple just before came to my mouth, I realised it was me.

"I know I am skilled, but we don't need to tell my roommates how much, Raven."

"Then stop playing around with my nipple. I'm sensitive there." He's a brat because he brings his hand back to my breast and continues playing.

A raspy chuckle. "Maybe I don't mind telling them how good I am. Your moans and gasps get me off already." Man just thinking about how hard he is right now, gets half the job done. And the rest of the job is done by his talented tongue. After I settle down from my orgasm he crawls back up.

"You're a screamer." he chuckles as he flops down next to me.

"And your tongue deserves an award for giving the best orgasms." Another chuckle. He pulls me on top of him. And I bend down and push my lips on him as my pussy grinds on him. Fuck, he's really huge. I doubt if he'll fit inside me.

He pulls back from the kiss. "Keep grinding like that, I'm close." Oh no no! We can't let that happen. So I stop grinding and he's equally furious and laughing.

"Tease."

I smirk shyly. "No. I should return the favour, sweetheart." I start tracing sweet kisses down his torso. His stomach shivers when I reach his abs. God, he's built like a Greek god. No wonder so many women worship him as if he's a sex God. He is. When I pull his boxers down and free his erection, his eyes roll back. I wish I could take a picture right now, just so that I could touch myself later looking at it. Feeling proud that I made him feel like that.

"My turn." I wrap my hand around his cock. He fits perfectly in my hand. I start massaging him. Slow strokes at first as I see him bead with precum. I've been thinking about sucking him off, more so when he jerked off in front of me.

When I lick the tip with my tongue he groans my name.

Not Raven.

Riya.

Fuck.

That makes me squirm with pleasure between my legs. I finally take him in my mouth. Slow teasing strokes at first. That is until he wraps his hands around my hair and starts thrusting in my mouth. Gagging. I am gagging. Gasping for air, but who wants air? Because when he groans in pleasure and tells me how good my mouth feels, I want nothing more than for him to come in my mouth even if my eyes tear up.

"Fuck...I'm coming. Can I come in your mouth?" Is that even a question? I give a small nod so that I don't break his pretty dick. And he shoots in my mouth. I swallow his saltiness like a good girl.

I swipe my thumb across the corner of my lower lip and lick the drippings looking at him. "Fuck..." He pulls me closer to his chest and flips me over so that he is on top of me.

"Pleasure returned." he pants. And I can't help but chuckle. Is it too late for me to tell him that this was the first time I let someone come in my mouth? Nah! I'll just keep it to myself. "Ten minutes. Give me ten minutes and I'll be good to go again." His eyes turn naughty again. "Until then..." his hand travels to my clit and rubs small circles around it and my hips start moving to his rhythm.

"Are you good to go again?" he asks me. This man made me come two times in less than half an hour and wants me to orgasm again? And we haven't even fucked each other. Just oral stuff. Among the three one night stands that I've had, I never came once, never once saw a man so eager to make me come. Usually it was just making out, clothes on the ground, a little bit of touching each other until they were ready to go and that's it.

It was done after they were satisfied. They weren't half bothered if I had fun. That's one of the reasons why I stopped doing it. Because it is awkward telling a stranger you met a few hours ago, *Hey I didn't orgasm. It's great that you did. Could you go down on me?*

James's tongue nips my nipple and that pulls a moan out of me and brings me back. "Now that I have your attention again." He has that cocky grin on his face.

"Assshole." I hit his chest.

"Have you done that before?"

"What?" I act coy. No I haven't. I never even thought about it.

He flips me over as if I'm a pillow. I swear to god, the way this man throws me around turns me on even more. He's strong! Like really strong!

"Do you trust me?" I nod. "You are going to have to spell it out for me, Raven." he kisses my butt as I am on all fours. I should be embarrassed about my body like I always am, but for some reason, I am not! I feel shameless in front of him.

"I trust you." I spell it out for him.

He spanks me and I moan softly. "Good. Let me know if it's too much or if you want me to stop alright?"

"Yes." I can't see what he's doing, but I hear a pop sound. Did he suck on something? His finger. He wet his finger. I feel one wet finger on my asshole.

"You okay?" he asks me.

I clear my throat. "Yes."

"Good girl." He slides one finger inside and my back arches. Fuck, that feels good.

"Alright?"

"Don't stop." he moves his finger inside me. "That feels good."

"Yes?" he leans ahead and his teeth nick my ear, while his finger is still inside me. His other hand travels to my clit, soft circles around it. Mmmm....That feels good. He pushes two fingers inside my pussy. Fuck! That caught me by surprise and I jerked up.

"That good?" I can't contemplate anything anymore. All I feel is his voice in my ear, his breath on my neck, two fingers in my pussy and one in my behind. His fingers curl up inside my pussy and I cry out loud, words like, *Yes baby, just like that, fuck, that feels good, harder.*

"Come for me, Raven. Let me see you fall apart around my fingers? Come for me." He doesn't have to tell me twice, because I am already seeing stars. I clench around all his fingers as I feel my orgasm soar through me. This is what heaven must feel like, because Marcus James Williams is a sex god. Or finger god. Or tongue god. Because just as I am at my peak, he starts kissing my neck, under my ear, which makes it hundred times more intense. I don't think I have ever come so hard.

"Good girl." he kisses the back of my neck as I am shaking, soaring through my orgasm. After he pulls all his fingers out, I fall on the bed. Panting, exhausted, tired, drained of every ounce of energy.

"Come here." He pulls my shaking body closer to his body and holds me as he chuckles.

"I'm never using that word around you ever again." Asshole.

"What word?" he chuckles and his entire body shakes against mine. I hit him playfully. "Alright. Gotcha. Are you okay though?" This time concern in his tone.

"I've never felt this much pleasure. I'm more than okay." My eyes assure him and this time his lips find mine. My hands linger around his body. But before they reach his cock, he holds it back.

He brings my hand close to his face and kisses the back of it. "We don't have to. You look tired."

"Are you afraid because you said ten minutes and you're not good to go? I promise I won't judge." He's laughing now. But he doesn't say anything, instead he holds my hand and presses against his very erect and hard cock. He only needed ten minutes. Fuck, athletes have a next level stamina.

He pulls a blanket over our naked bodies. "But, let's not."

"But, I feel bad that I came multiple times and you only once." Am I tired? Yes. Do I have the energy to give him head? No. But do I feel guilty about it? Yes.

"It's not a competition, Raven. Nobody's keeping a count." He presses his lips on mine.

"But–"

"Shhh..." he does it again. And I want to snap at him for shushing me. But just as I am about to open my mouth to argue, he presses a kiss on my forehead.

Aww.

No! He shushed you!
But then he kissed your forehead!
Fuck!
Don't fall for Marcus James Williams!

Chapter 18- James

I broke my rule. Well, I half broke it. We didn't have sex, we did other stuff. But not sex. I just hope that when she wakes up, she doesn't regret what happened last night. What if she wakes up and thinks that I took advantage of her? I didn't, right? I mean we both were drinking all night. But we weren't drunk. I wasn't. And she didn't seem drunk either. But what if? I swear to God, I was too consumed by thoughts about making her come and the sounds that she made, made me lose my mind. So much so, that I was almost about to fuck her. But when she got tired, I realised what I had done. I didn't want to continue.

Next time, I'll make sure that we're both completely sober. I hope there is a next time, because I don't think one taste of her is going to be enough.

She shifts in my arms and her eyelids move. "Good morning, Raven." I pray that when she opens her eyes and sees me she does not say the words, 'I hate you'.

"Good morning." She cuddles up to my naked chest and my morning wood is erect. Fuck. Not now, Marcus Junior.

"Sleep well?" I ask her.

She nods. Her eyes are barely open, but she smiles when she sees me. "You?" she asks me.

"Better than ever." I really did. Until I woke up and the realisation of what I'd done, set in. I remember she said that she has only ever had drunk sex, although we didn't have sex, whatever we did was under the influence.

Damnit.

Does that make me just one of her other hookups? I hope not. Because last night was amazing. And that was the best blow job I've ever received. She said that my tongue should deserve an award, well her mouth deserves a Nobel fucking Prize then. My phone buzzes on the side table and I reach for it. It's a message from my coach. Finals are next week and it's a home game.

No pressure.

I opened his message to read just two words- *Bad news.*

I groan in the bed as I stretch my arms over my head. We had evening practice today, because both our coaches had some personal matters to tend to.

"What is it?" Riya wakes up and stretches her arms and legs too. "Ouch..Ouch..Ouch..Ouch!" she freezes her leg mid stretch.

"What happened?" I panic.

"Cramp in my calf." I know just how to treat it. A good massage and a hot bath and she should be all good.

"No, don't touch it. I can't breathe."

"Where is the cramp exactly?" She's starting to freak me out.

"If I breathe, I move, I can't move. Don't worry, it'll go away on its own." She starts taking slow deep breaths. And finally lowers her legs and exhales. "Better."

"A massage would've helped."

"If you'd touched my leg then, I would've chopped off your balls." And good morning to you too. I can't help but chuckle in this situation. Until I remember that I need to wake everyone up and drive our asses to practise.

Bad news meant, bad news for *us*. Coach knew that if we don't have morning practice on a weekend, the boys are going to be drunk. Which meant that he wanted us to go to practice. Ugh! I hate doing this.

"What happened?" Riya asks me as she sits up and covers herself with the duvet.

"Practice. I gotta wake the boys up."

"But it's only 6am. You barely slept."

"We're late. We were supposed to be there at 6!"

"Do you want me to go?" What? No! I want her to be here when I come back. So that I can finally fuck her this time.

She pulls the blanket up and sits upright. As if I don't remember what I saw last night? I could cast it out with clay. I know the exact measurements of her entire body. Her brows scrunch up.

"I'll be back before you know it. Why don't you get some more rest?" I don't have to say it twice, because she's already closed her eyes and pulled the blanket over her.

I pull my ass out of bed, naked.

"Nice butt." Riya says from bed in her sleepy voice. Fuck. I wish I could take her right now.

"I have a lot of other nice things sweetheart. I'll show you after I come back. Why don't you energise yourself with sleep until then?" She chuckles and closes her eyes again. I fish in my closet for boxers and put them on. Along with my sweatpants and a hoodie. I grab my winter jacket and just before I am about to step out of the door, I go back to bed and plant a kiss on her lips and head out.

You'd think that the boys would be fast asleep after some action late at night? Well, Dan and Sid are sleeping. But, when I am about to knock on George's door, I hear moaning sounds from his room. "Yeah, suck it like that, Vanessa." I hear him groan inside.

"What about me?" I hear another girl's voice from his room. He's having a threesome. When did the other girl come in? I'm sure he was with just one chick when I last saw him. But then again, it's George.

I bang on his door. "Go away, Sid. Not now. Unless you want to join. You don't mind, right girls?" I hear three girls' voices from inside. This fucker is having a fucking foursome. Then again, I wouldn't expect anything less from George.

"We got practice in 10. Zip it up and I'll see you outside in 5." I shout from outside because I have no interest in taking a look at the orgy that George is having right now.

"We better finish in 5 minutes, girls. Who's first?" I hear George from inside. I roll my eyes and walk away. I grab a coffee from the kitchen and Dan and Sid are right behind me with their mugs. They both just walked their 'dates' out and flopped on the table behind. I top them up with coffee.

The boys can barely keep their eyes open. We indeed had an eventful night yesterday. Sid's cheek is visibly swollen. Thankfully there's no bruising because of the icing. "Why is the coach busting our asses? He was going to buss them in the evening, right?" Sid is half asleep.

"God knows what crawled up Belkis' ass. I for once am not looking forward to this practice. He's busting our ass with the new defences." Dan holds his head in his hand, tugging on his hair.

I take a whiff of my coffee and let the aroma of it wake me up. I had to call up the rest of the team, just in case they didn't receive Coach's text. Half of the boys cursed me for ruining their morning and the other half cursed the coach and god. Well, I certainly wasn't at fault here. "It was my idea. Fritz has a good defence, so it's going to be already difficult for us. I really want us to win this one."

Dan groans. "Our only weakness right now is Nolan."

"Safety?" I raise my brow.

"How'd you say he is as a safety, Sid." Dan asks Siddharth, who is another safety.

"He is the weak link. I told the coach to try out Bundon instead, but he said it's too late now."

"Who? Issac Bundon? The sophomore?" I raise my brow. I don't like to dabble that much in our defence. I know Dan is the best at handling that, but as the captain, I can't help but make sure we don't fall short anywhere. Especially after having an awesome season and making it to the playoffs and now finals. It's all so close.

"Kid does have potential. Not gonna lie." Dan takes a sip of his coffee.

Just like his message said, practice was bad news. Especially for defence. Belkis is milking those guys. We are done with practice at around 12pm. It is snowing outside, but we are all covered in sweat. "I'll see you all in the evening." Belkis walks away and all the boys groan together.

George starts taking off his shoulder pads. "He needs to get laid. Maybe then he'll stop taking out his frustration on us."

"Facts bro." Kenny, our cornerback, joins the convo. We all hit the showers and it's just a bunch of guys who were hungover six hours ago and now are just sleep deprived. I know I promised Riya that I would show her a good time, but my ass hurts too badly to even walk properly. And just to add salt to my injury, George slaps my wet butt just as I step out of the shower. I'm one hundred percent sure that his hand is imprinted on my butt right now. He often forgets how he is the most buffed amongst us all!

George's personality is so sporty and hyper that he needs another sport to direct his energy towards. As if getting tackled in football isn't enough, he also trains for Brazilian Jiu Jitsu. I only ever went once with him…never again! He has way too much energy.

"Asshole." I mutter. And god does that bring back memories from last night. I was beaming with joy and pride and ego when she told me that she trusted me with her beautiful ass. And god, when she moaned my name as she came in my arms. Best feeling ever!

"Want to grab brunch before heading back?" Sid steps out of the shower with his wet hair.

"Nah. Riya's waiting for me at home." The boys look at each other. They escorted their dates from last night in front of me, which means Riya is alone at home. Waiting for me. I checked my phone before, there were no messages.

George places his hand on my shoulder. "You're just banging her, right?" No, I haven't banged her! At least not completely.

I'm not telling these asshats shit about her! "She's also tutoring me, fucker. Not to mention that interview and article thing." Dan raises his brow at me.

Dan packs his gear in his bag and applies oil to his hair. Fucker has the most lucious locks ever and never lets any of us touch his homemade oil. His mom makes it for him every semester. "Since when do you need tutoring? You're like the smartest amongst all jocks. Hell, if practice didn't take up all your time, you'd be a genius. Not that you aren't. Only one of us is managing to keep their GPA above 3.7 and it's none of us."

"3.75" I correct Dan.

He closes the lid and throws it back in the bag. "But, you clearly don't need tutoring. So what's that about?"

"I don't know. There's something about her." I can't quite put my finger on it. It's true that I do want to fuck her, but there's something more about her.

I witness something I have never seen before. George is afraid of a woman. "There's a lot about her. She scares me. And last night was just another demonstration of how scary she can be. If you like your balls to be attached to your body, don't piss off Riya." George shudders.

Sid backs him up. I can't believe that Riya scared George. Dude acts as if he's unshakable.

"Am I the only weird one who thinks that she's sexy when mad?" all eyes turn towards Dan. Including mine. Because no. He is not the only one.

"Don't tell me you want to bang her too. If so, maybe you two could ask her for a threesome. I doubt any girl would say no to that." My blood boils when George says that.

"I think the fuck not!" I rub my hair dry with the towel and toss it to the side.

"But do you really want to?" Sid asks Dan and I slow my pace, to listen to Dan's response.

There's a pause. "Who knows?" Fuck. I'm not even paying attention to where I'm walking and I trip on someone's gym bag. And I hear some soft chuckling from behind me. Either Dan is fucking with my head, or he is wanting to fuck the girl I like.

We make it home and I get a whiff of sweet and salty flavours. We walk into the living room and Riya is sleeping on the couch. My small blanket is around her waist, but one of her legs is folded out of the blanket. Fuck, she looks hot while sleeping like that.

George tiptoes to the kitchen, silently. Usually he is a loud mouth or blasts music after practice. Sid is silent too. Damn! They are really scared of my Raven. And that turns me on even more. I sit down next to her and pull her head in my lap and she wraps her arms around my waist. Her head lays on my cock and I'm hard. It's like this woman's existence itself makes me hard. It's unfair. I caress her hair and tuck them behind her ear.

God! She's so beautiful! She's my Aphrodite. And right now, she looks so much at peace. Her breathing is even and I feel her heartbeat and it churns something inside my stomach. I cannot take my eyes off her.

One thing I can never shake off from my mind though is when I saw her crying on the streets of New York. Her tears had soaked my shirt wet and the image will forever scar my heart. I cannot see tears in her eyes. Never! But weirdly enough, I want to always be the one who holds her when she wants to cry too.

"She made breakfast. Pancakes and bacon." George loud whispers from the kitchen. Dan sits close to Riya's feet and his gaze travels to her bare leg and her plump ass which is accentuated in this position. He was just fucking with me before, right? Man, I really hope so. Because the way he looks at her, makes my blood boil.

"She must be tired." I spread the blanket over her legs to cover them. Just then her head moves in my lap and her eyes open.

She smiles at me and blinks her eyes open. "You're back! I made breakfast." She sits up and that's when I see the oversized Ralph Lauren shirt she's wearing. It's mine.

It looks so good on her. My gaze falls to her legs, and she's not wearing any shorts. I wonder if she's even wearing her panties right now? She's clearly not wearing her bra, because I can see the outline of the nipples that I sucked on last night.

"It's really good." George exclaims with his mouth full of bacon. Riya chuckles and gets up from the couch and pushes the blanket away. My shirt just covers her ass, but I see enough to see her black panties, which I thank god that she's wearing because I would be pissed if Dan got a peek of it.

"I tried." She walks around and puts her hand on my shoulder and bends over the couch. George chokes on whatever food is in his mouth which tells me that he just saw Riya's lacy panties when she just bent.

"You coming?" She plants a peck on my cheek. And I almost came. Almost. I do some adjusting and make my way to the table. When she sits at the table, my shirt rides up, to expose her panties. Fuck, I can't eat like that and from this angle, I'm sure, Dan can see it too. When I look into his eyes, they're busy locating the food. Good. But for me, I'm busy focusing on my feast.

My Raven.

Chapter 19- Riya

Will you come to the game?
James sent me this message two days ago and I still haven't responded. I don't understand shit about American football. I've been avoiding him completely for the past two days. We sexted for three days after our hookup last weekend. But I've been avoiding him for the past two days.

Why? Because I can't get him out of my head. I can't stop thinking about his tongue on my clit and his finger inside me. I've become a sex maniac. Hell, I even bought a remote controlled vibrator, and orgasmed in public. Although it was in the closed and locked door of my study room in the library, I'll still count that as public. There were no windows or glass in the room, but what if someone knocked or heard it? Scandalous!

But the point is that all I've been doing these last five days is study, work and make myself come thinking it was Williams. And this has to stop. I can't stop imagining how good his dick will feel inside me. He is huge. I'm not even sure if he'll fit.

"So, what do you think?" A girl with glasses sitting across me asks me. I don't even remember when I got here, why I am here, much less what she was talking about or what she just asked me. I take a look around. I see two other boys and one other girl who just asked me something which I forgot, too. Because I can't stop thinking about James fucking me. This! This is why I need distance from him.

"Sorry, could you repeat that?" I adjust my glasses and take a look at the screen behind her. James also seldom wears glasses when studying and man does it make him look a hundred times hotter! It should be illegal to do the things I want to do to that man and the things I want him to do to me. I want him to keep the glasses on at least once when we fuck.

Back to reality! It's a presentation about the clinical data from the paper that we're presenting this midterm. I chose the paper, so they think that I know everything about it. I do, but still, they could use their brain, too, right?

I quickly glance through the slide and spot one thing lacking.

"In the entire paper there's only one thing which doesn't add up. And it was exactly about this figure."

"What is it?" Hailey, the girl with glasses asks me.

"The T-test results. They don't match with the figures. I ran them three times and they're wrong. The printed p-value is totally off." I take off my glasses.

"So, are we going to have to choose another paper then?" Borris, one of the guys asks me. Borris and Victor, both have been absolutely useless. Victor more than Borris. Dude literally does nothing and is just mooching the good grades off us.

"No, even if they calculated the wrong p-value, they don't use it anywhere further or in the results. So, it's better if we mention it once and move on from it." Hailey shakes her head and closes her laptop, concluding our meeting.

"Beers at Joanna's?" Victor asks Borris who nods and gives him a slap on the back. Joanna's is the only bar near our college. Okay, it's not the only bar, but it's the best bar, decent price drinks and good ambience. Only problem? Everyone at Winstons goes there on weekends. So, it's a pool of sweat and drinks on the ground. It's sticky and gross.

My phone buzzes and it's a message from Juju. I opened it.
Come home fast.

What happened?

Find out yourself *winky face*

I do not like where this is going. I'm sure that I ordered just one vibrator, which is...I check my tote bag and find the vibrator in there. What if she found Sebastian? My favourite vibrator!

I hope not. Yes I do name my vibrator. The bigger one is Sebastian, who's at home right now. And the one in my tote is Bradon. It's not weird guys. Girls name their dildos and vibrators just like men name their dicks. No biggie.

But James' was big. I mean his dick. Was huge. Snap out of it, Riya! Enough is enough. Don't make me slap you in public!

When I reach home, I find Juju and Jake sitting on the couch, cuddling like a cute couple. "What happened?" I looked around, but the house was not on fire.

"On the table." Juju doesn't even bother to turn around. There's a small package on the table. It's an envelope which was torn open, by Juju, of course. I peek inside what's in the envelope and it's three tickets to the game. The football finals. It's a home game. So, everyone I know is going to the game. Everyone! Literally even people who don't watch it are going. The game is tomorrow.

"You bought these?" I ask Juju, who finally turns around to look at me.

"No. Marcus sent them, with a note." I look around, but there's no note. "Here." Juju holds out the note. Of course she read it. "Sorry, I couldn't help myself. You know I'm nosy." Juju pouts. I snatch the note from her hand and open it.

I miss my face between your legs.

Never been more thankful that red is Winston's colour because it looks so good on you. But then again, which colour doesn't? Please come to the game? FYI- got tickets for JJ too.

I chuckle when I read the first and last part. JJ!

"Who's JJ?" Jake asks me.

"You showed it to him?" I blurt out. I hate this about Juju, she tells her boyfriend everything! Literally everything. I lost my v-card in Australia and Juju was one of the first ones to find out. But, what does she do? Tell her boyfriend. Every time I had drunk sex with someone, I told her and she told Jake. I found it uncomfortable, him knowing so many details about my sex life or my life in general.

    She throws a pillow at me. "You dirty dirty slut! You fucked Marcus Williams and didn't tell me." This! This is why I didn't tell her. Because she would tell this to her boyfriend.

    "Why'd you read the note, Juju?" It's not fair. I want to say. But she tells me everything about her life, yes her sex life too. Even though I am not interested in knowing all the tiny details, she doesn't leave out a single one.

    "Why didn't you tell me?"

    "Because, we didn't have sex!" I'm frustrated that I don't have any privacy here. I would've been fine if it was just Juju who read the note, but Jake? Why does he have to know? I don't like people knowing my personal life! I find it confining.

    "The note says otherwise." Jake shrugs from the couch.

    "I am not discussing my sex life with you, Jake." Then I turn to face Juju. "Not with you either! At least not right now." I grab the tickets and the note and head to my room. I pull out my phone and pull James' chat.

Asshat.

A couple minutes later, he messages back.

I thought you weren't going to use that word again.

    It was asshole! And no, I'm never going to use it again.

So, I'm assuming that you got the envelope?

I did.

So, I'll see you tomorrow, Raven.

Overconfident?

Nah, I'm just an optimist!

Good luck with the finals, James.

I tuck my phone under the blanket and change into my PJs. I grab my phone again to see a message from James.

If I look for you in the bleachers, will I find you?

I don't know why, but I am reminded of Taylor Swift's You Belong with me plays in my mind.

Maybe. I sent him. I wait for sometime, but he doesn't reply. Maybe he slept. So, I pull the blanket over my face and sleep.

"Juju, I'm not wearing that!" I run around the living room as Juju forces me to wear James' jersey that Jake bought. Slick bastard!

"It's either that or the Winston tattoos."

"None. I veto." I raise my hand.

"We veto." Jake chimes in and raises both their hands.

"You don't get a veto. And I'm either going to the game like this, or I'm not going at all."

"Jersey! There's nothing wrong with wearing their jersey! I'm wearing Siddharth's." she turns around to show me.

"Good for you. But I don't want him to get the wrong idea, Juju. So, no jersey." I mean we already did have almost sex, what else is there to misunderstand? I just don't want him to think that I'm some crazy woman who is obsessed with him. Because I am neither of those things.

"You won't be the only girl who he has fucked who will be wearing his jersey at the game. So stop being dramatic!" That reality check hurt like a bitch. She's right though. I am just any other girl who he has hooked up with. Who's to say that he didn't sleep with someone else after me? "I'm sorry. That was a little harsh." *You think?* Her tone mellows.

I shake off my head and the thought as well. "No, you're right. I am not the only one. I know that. And it's not like I am in love with him or anything. I just don't want to, alright? I'll do the Winstons tattoos on my–"

"On your face–"

"Arm. On my arm. That's all."

"On your face and wear Dan's cap and twin with me."

"On my arm, and no hat."

"Two tattoos on both your arms and the cap."

"Deal."

"Deal." It is always impossible to negotiate with this girl, but I am learning my way.

I put a Winston's tattoo on my arm and wear Dan's jersey number cap and of course, signature Winstons red shirt. James said that he wanted to see me in red…No! No! No! Maybe he has an infatuation or a weird fetish with seeing women in red colour. I'm not wearing red for him, I'm wearing red because I know I look good in it!

The game starts and it should come as no shocker but I don't understand shit about what's going on. I just tried to find number 18- that's James' jersey number. I know because he told me during the interview. I don't see him though.

"Why isn't Marcus playing?" I ask Jake, because clearly, among us three, he possesses the most knowledge about American football.

"That's because we're on defence right now. That's Daniel, our linebacker, our safeties, Siddharth and Nolan. Our cornerbacks, Joseph and Bianco. Our–"

"Alright. Gotcha." Jeez! How many people are there in a team? If there are this many people on a team, how are NFL players still this rich? Why do I care!

I see some players in red running across the field and everyone gets up and I shout and cheer because I thought that it was a goal or whatever it is. The amount of embarrassment I felt is unmeasurable. Because the next moment I am shown on the big screen. I want to throw the popcorn bucket over my head, but I just pretend as if I didn't see it. As the saying goes, the problem won't bother you if you act like it doesn't exist!.

"The other team scored a touchdown, Ri!" Jake loudly whispers in my ear.

"So they scored a goal?" Jake shakes his head in disappointment.

I just take a seat and watch the rest of the game in silence. Towards the end of the game, it is a close match with a competitive score. Until finally Jersey number 18 passes it to jersey number 56, which is George.

"Touchdown!" Jake stands up and throws his hands in the air.

"Did we make a goal?" I ask Juju.

"I think we did a touchdown. Kind of like a goal." She shrugs.

Jake slaps his forehead so hard that my head hurts! "Oh my God, babe. What am I going to do about you? After touchdown, we have an option if we want to opt in for a kick for an extra point. The kicker- in our team it happens to be Ace Grunt." I snort when I hear that name. Poor kid must be bullied so much in school. "He's one of the best kickers. He'll definitely make it to the NFL." Jake continues. My eyes are glued to the field.

Ace kicks the ball and it makes it through the two poles. And I know for sure that it is a goal. So I get up and shout and cheer like everyone. As soon as the match ends, all the players run on the field and lift each other and there's confetti blowing up everywhere. My eyes wander to find James in all this. I want to run and congratulate him. When I do finally spot him, he's being lifted by Dan on his shoulder. Dan puts him down and he finds me. Our eyes lock. I look behind twice to make sure that he is looking at me and not someone else.

What should I do? Thumbs up? Wink? Flying kiss? I do none. I just smile at him. I'm bursting out with happiness but I don't give a flying fuck about football. American football.

My happiness is short-lived as one of the beautiful cheerleaders wraps her arms around James and presses her mouth against him. I don't look back after that.

*She's cheer captain and I'm on the bleachers...*Stupid Taylor Swift. It was as if she saw my future. "Let's get out of here." I hold Juju's hand and pull her behind me. She was right, I wasn't the only girl who James had fucked (we didn't have sex) who would wear his jersey and cheer for him. Granted I am not cheering for him or wearing his jersey.

It takes ages for the crowd to clear up. And when we're finally just about to walk outside, Juju insists that she's hungry and wants to grab more food before going out. I remind her that we are going out to grab food. "My latin ass will digest it until then."

I want to correct her about so many things, but I don't bother. I just wait in a corner for Jake and Juju to grab food. There's a huge line. Like a really huge line. Ugh!

It's been almost half an hour of me standing in the corner, and these are the times when I hate being the third wheel.

"Hey..." I hear a familiar voice. I turn around to see Mr. Muscles standing behind me. Towering over me. Wet blonde hair and those green meadow-y eyes.

"Hey..." I totally forgot his name. I remember his middle name though, James...Ugh! Now I'm back to thinking about how that cheerleader was snogging his face.

He chuckles, looking down at me because he is that tall! "You forgot my name, didn't you?"

"And I know that you don't know mine." My eyes fall on his green Fritz jersey. It definitely brings out the pop of green in his eyes.

"I know it's not sweetheart." That makes me chuckle. "Cole," he says.

"Riya." I offer my hand to shake and he looks at it for a second longer which makes it awkward before he finally shakes my hand.

Last time I saw him, he was all dressed up in a suit and now–jeans and Fritz jersey. I'd say he's more of a jeans guy. It suits him better. And I don't miss the playfulness in his eyes when he looks at me. "So, does it hurt?" I ask him.

"When I fell from heaven?" He flashes me that stupid smug grin. *Cocky.*

"When you got your ass kicked by Winstons an hour ago." he chuckles and nods. I am a loyal Winston's student!

"It did hurt. I wouldn't mind you rubbing it to make it better." I don't know if I should be grossed out or turned on.

"You guys played well though. Couldn't help it that we were the best!" I shrug. Even though I don't know shit about the game, one of my friends told me that confidence is the key. You can bullshit your way through anything if you're confident enough.

"I didn't peg you for being a loner." My eyes widen and my jaw drops. I am not a loner!

Consider me offended! "Excuse me. I am with friends here. Well, friend and her boyfriend. But nonetheless, not alone!"

"Sweetheart, third wheeling is worse than being a loner." he chuckles. There's something about his raspy laugh which makes me smile. Ugh! I need to get my aura cleansed!

I roll my eyes at him and turn away, looking at the crowd. Where are the 'super urgent' phone calls when I need them? "Don't you have to be at a bar to sulk over your loss?" My phone is dead silent and I just want someone to save me.

"Or I could help you get out of third wheeling and make it a double date." My eyes jolt up in his direction. Subtle way of asking someone on a date, unless he's taking pity on me for third-wheeling.

"Are you asking me on a date Cole James Harriett?" I say playfully. His smirk tells me that he is definitely flirting with me. I should flirt back. I mean he's hot as hell. Granted I know nothing about the guy, but we are all strangers once. Some strangers just happen to be hotter than some others.

He leans his shoulder against the wall and tucks his hands in his pocket. He does have a charming smile. And he sure uses it often! "Why yes I am, Riya. Unless you don't want to be mistaken as conspiring with the enemy." He raises his brow. I love sarcasm.

"Don't worry about it. I don't care about football anyway. American football." I correct myself quickly.

"Harriett." A loud voice echoes from the back. Cole turns around to see a red James standing behind him. It must be from the game. But god he looks hot with all that wet hair and those gloomy deep ocean blue eyes. James strides towards us and all eyes turn towards him and whisper something inaudible.

"Williams." Cole turns hostile.

James strides towards us, his bag hanging on his left shoulder. "She's with me." James puts his hand around my shoulder and I hear a couple of gasps.

Oh hell no! I am not letting this happen. I am not going to be the captain's trophy! "Why don't we meet up some other time, Cole? I'll take you up on your date offer then." I slide off James's hand and reach in my pocket to pull my phone. "Why don't you give me your number? I'll call you." *Petty*. My behaviour is petty right now. Just because he kissed that cheerleader, I am agreeing to go on a date with a random stranger. Okay, a hot and sexy random stranger.

Cole puts his number in my phone and has that smug smile on his face. "See you sweetheart. You need anything, you call me." he winks at me.

James glares at Cole."She won't need to." I should stop this little game before it blows up in my face. I literally feel fumes coming off James. Or maybe it's his post game hotness? Who am I kidding, it's freezing!

"Wasn't talking to you, jackass." Cole strikes back.

"I will. See you Cole." I hate being around drama. This...I don't like.

James turns to look at me. "You let him call you sweetheart? And what's this about a date?" Is he jealous? Nah. He can't be.

"You don't have a right to tell me that, James–" Don't say it. Don't say it. "Especially when you had your tongue down someone else's throat." He stiffens and I immediately regret the words that come out of my mouth.

He backs away for a second before coming too close to me. I can smell the scent of his body wash and his cologne leather-y and fresh shampoo. Together, that's a deadly combination. "She came onto me! I swear to god! I didn't kiss her. She kissed me. And I pushed her off the second she came onto me." he sighs. "I did push her away and..." he looks around and there's people around us. Staring at him. And me. He pulls me further into a corner and whispers softly. "because she didn't do it for me." What?

"Do what? Fuck you right there and then?" That was harsh and I have no right to say that.

"She didn't make me hard, Riya." Oh! I look down at his jeans which cling onto his body like skin and that loose white tee and a Winstons jacket. God, he's looking smack-a-licious.

"Um...okay...I–" What do I even say here? I don't know what takes over me, we are still in public, given that we are standing under the stairs and people can barely see me over his huge back, but still-public. His eyes seem so innocent. So...

I run my hand down his arm and tug on his jeans buckle. "What about now?" he groans.

"Fuck, yes." Why does it make me horny, that I make him hard, by not even touching him, directly? "But. No." He flicks my hand off.

"Why?"

"I like you Raven. And not just for your body. I mean I do like you for your body, I can barely get it out of my mind, but I would also like to get to know you more." I almost laugh when he says that joke. But he doesn't laugh. Is he for real? Why would anyone want to get to know me?

"Why?" I ask and he chuckles.

He clears his throat and blinks his eyes faster. He is caught off guard just as much as me. "I didn't prepare for that. But all I know is that when you were ignoring me for two days, I wanted to do nothing more than just talk to you. That and think about ways to make you come. I think it might be my favourite thing to do." I look around to double check if anybody heard us. This man has no filter.

I am speechless.

"Why don't you go on one date with me? I promise to keep my hands to myself."

"Why?"

"You really like that word, huh?" he laughs in his deep voice.

"No, I mean...I'm just confused."

"Do you feel the same connection I do?"

"Yes." Without a beat.

"Then one date. Grace me with one date!" he does those puppy dog eyes again that I always fall for.

"Alright J*ames*."

Chapter 20- James

I am not going to screw this up. I saw her in the seat that I got the tickets for, and I knew in my heart that I had to win this. Especially when my Raven is here to cheer for us. But when stupid Zara kissed me, I saw the disappointment in her eyes and when I pushed her away, I realised that my body didn't react the way it would usually have to a girl, a hot girl kissing me.

"Shoot your shot, before you lose her." Dan suggested in the shower. After the coach gave the celebratory speech and all, I ran out of the shower. I was probably still dripping but I didn't care.

Alright James. She had no idea how happy those two words made me.

I'm going to put an effort into this date. Originally I'd picked a fancy restaurant to go to, but after George's comment about my boring date idea being the definition of 'how to lose a girl before you even get her' made me drop it.

Sid recommended going for something engaging. I googled 27 options for engaging dates. I don't know why half of them were for ages 60+ people. Shouldn't their definition of fun and engaging be a walk in the park? Or a stroll?

I asked Dan for backup and he told me that I know her better than these monkeys and told me for something adrenaline filled to which Sid replied pottery class. I wonder who hurt him?

I did write down George's idea of sex practice class which I first thought was just a joke. But when I looked it up, it existed. I don't even want to know why he knew about that class. But that class is for couples who are looking to reignite their passion which is definitely not an issue when it comes to us. The issue for us is how do we control it?

After all the debating, I settled on arcade. We'd have different options. And plus there is a bowling alley right next to it. And I happen to be good at bowling. Maybe I'll make a good impression.

She is kicking my ass at bowling. But one thing that I get a kick out of is when he bends down to pick the ball, her skinny jeans squeeze around her ass and it is the most beautiful picture.

She jumps around and screams and does her victory dance after she scores the fifth spare of the match. And I have to say that she is amazing. But I'm not far behind.

I pick up the ball and slide it along. Spare! She snorts and rolls her eyes. It's my fifth spare. But she is a couple points ahead of me. "Not so fast, baby."

"Oh! We'll see... This is not my best. I can do much better." She did not tell me not to call her baby. I can't believe that I am happy over the fact that someone is letting me call her baby.

"I'm going to kick your ass in air hockey."

She sticks out her tongue. "I'd like to see you try." She's competitive. I love that about her. She challenges me. And as a sportsman, I love it.

She is beating me at air hockey too. "There's something wrong with my disk." I picked it up to see. There is nothing wrong with my disk. It's the fact that I hate losing.

"You are such a sore loser." she chuckles. "I can't believe that you are an athlete." She's laughing out loud now.

"'I believe that losing is a choice and I don't like it. I love winning." I fly the plastic puck towards her and score.

"That does not count. You cheated!"

"All is fair is love and war."

"Oh! This is war..." It gets a little intense when playing air hockey and we even shoo away the four kids who wanted to play it. Well, I don't. Alright, I did too. I want to win. Like I said, I can't help that I am competitive. It's in my blood. It's in my sport.

"Haa! I won!" I throw the disc on the board and throw my hands up in the air. I shoot her airguns and she rolls her eyes. She is a sore loser, just like me. God, she looks cute when pissed. I know I said that I'd keep my hands to myself, but it's getting more and more difficult to do so. "I told you that I'd beat your ass." her eyes jolt up when I say that. She's trying so hard not to blush. God I love that dirty mind of hers. Maybe she liked being spanked? Making a mental note to try that next time.

"What are you thinking about?" I tease her.

"There are people around, or else, I'd show you." Where has she been all this time? I love her confidence. Fuck! That's what makes her even more sexy.

"I'll make sure to rent the entire place next time." I wink at her. "Are you hungry?" We've been playing for hours because we both didn't want to give up.

She pouts and nods her head.

"Let's get you fed." I wrap my arm around her and lead her through the arcade. It feels fun to be around her. She makes me happy. And hard.

We put on our winter coats and I drive us to a soccer bar. They have good food and I figured that she might be into the idea of watching soccer. Or as she calls it "The real football".

We sit by a booth which has a good view of the match. "Now these are my people. Who came here to watch real football!" I am too tempted to roll my eyes out of my eye socket.

"Want a drink?"

"I'm not 21."

"Oh!"

She takes off her coat to reveal her white top. "Yeah. But you can have one if you want. I'm not much of a drinker anyway." It is loose around her shoulders and puts her cleavage on display. I haven't been able to take my eyes off them since I first saw her. She looks around. "This is not what I expected from you though."

I panic. I made a backup reservation at the French place which is just a fifteen minute drive from here. "You don't like it?"

She chuckles looking at me in panic. "I love it. I mean, last time we went to this fancy place."

"That wasn't a date though." I corrected her. I was just trying to show off back then. But we ended up having a good conversation about everything.

"So, tell me about your family." I ask her as we scan through the menu.

She rests her elbow on the table and leans forward, readying herself. "After my dad didn't feel like coming back, because it felt like home, he decided to stay there. Sold the business he had here and started another one with his two brothers. I live with all my cousins and my uncles and aunts in this huge mansion and I am a huge family person."

"How many people live in the house then?"

Her eyes wander and she starts counting on her finger, my eyes widen after she counts seven but she keeps going. "Thirteen...wait. No. Now it's twelve. Including me and Maura. One of my cousins got married."

I cannot imagine how lonely it must be feeling living with just one roommate compared to how many people she grew up with! From the looks of it, her face lights up when she talks about her family. She must be missing them! "Damn! That's a lot of people."

"What about you?" she asks me cheerfully. I don't want to ruin the mood by getting into my family history. My family is not as cheerful as hers. At least not anymore.

"Are you guys ready to order?" The waitress comes to take our order. We order food and I am hoping that Riya has forgotten about her question.

"So... Are you going to tell me?"

I chug on the cold water. "I mean you can find my family on google."

She rolls her eyes and huffs sarcastically. "Of course, 'Mr. I'm famous'. But I'd rather know about it from you." She leans closer to the centre as if waiting for me to begin.

I clear my throat. I guess there is nobody who understands me more than her, so screw it! I'll just tell her. "I have a father who was a NFL star. That's all. We were a happy family. When my mother was alive."

She nods, carefully listening. And I can't help but feel warm at someone's genuine interest in me. In my story where my father is not the centre of attention. "What was she like?" She seems genuinely interested and her smile makes me want to talk more.

Every time I've mentioned my mother, I've only ever gotten pity from everyone. Even from my father. So, it made me not want to talk about it at all. No one wanted to talk to me about her, not even dad, because they thought that it'd hurt me more. In fact what hurt me more all these years is not being able to talk about her without getting pity from the other person.

So I tell her. I tell her all the memories that I can think of. All the memories I cherish! "She was a dedicated coder. Taught me so much about it. Coding takes me back to those days. When she would fight with my dad for my time and teach me how to code. They would play board games and whoever would win, would teach me their skill.

It was fun for me. It's not like they ever forced me to do it. I was genuinely interested in football and coding both."

She reaches for my hand and gives it a squeeze. "That sounds so sweet."

I continue reminiscing about the bittersweet memory. "My mom would make these tacos almost every Thursday. It was a tradition in our house. I guess it was because I loved tacos and if I ate a lot, I'd sleep right there and then. So they would feed me a lot of tacos and dad would carry me to bed and they would have their 'private time'" I do the air quotes and she chuckles, still holding onto my hand. "When I understood what they were doing, I felt yucked out and would still pretend that I was sleepy and go away." I laugh now. I hadn't thought about that memory for a long long time.

"How'd you know what they were doing?"

"I once ate less because I wasn't feeling that well and pretended to fall asleep. I came back down and they were half naked making out on the couch. I didn't make a sound and walked back upstairs and swore to never stay up late on Taco Thursdays." she taps on the table as she laughs out loud.

She smiles at me like she sees me. She sees the person I am. Not the son of a NFL celebrity and not the captain of the football team of Winston. She sees me as James. Her smile makes me smile. "Your parents sound like they were so in love!"

My smile fades immediately and I feel my heart race. "They were. Until..." I take a deep breath in.

"You can tell me some other time...there's no rush." She reads my mind. Nobody knows about what happened. Not the media. No one. "So, do you still have taco Thursdays with your dad?" There's a brief pause from my side. And it gets a little awkward. Because ever since that incident me and my father have drifted apart a little. Okay, we have drifted apart a lot.

"No. I don't" I say without any emotion whatsoever and Riya reaches for her glass.

"What's your favourite cuisine?" she folds her hands and raises her brow.

"Why? Will you cook it for me?" I tease her. I loved it when she cooked breakfast for us. I'm saying that because it was a nice break from the mediocre tasting protein pancakes that Sid shoves down our throat because he is a fucking health nut.

"Maybe."

"I love French cuisine." I tell her and she immediately hisses and shakes her head in disappointment.

I get that a lot. I cannot handle too much spice. *Only in food.*

My mother used to cook French food in our house every other day. It somehow became my favourite food. "So, you basically like bland food?" she snorts.

I correct her quickly. "It lets the main ingredient shine. And it's definitely healthier than Indian food!" That gets me an eye roll.

She retaliates back! "Sweetheart..." Holy fucking shit! The way it rolls off her tongue, makes me want to jump over and take her right here. "The Indian food you're referring to, doesn't even scrape the surface. It's not Indian food. I mean it is, but that's not all the Indian food there is in the world."

"That's all that Sid cooks. He likes to call it our 'cheat meals'" I use air quotes.

We bicker for sometime about Indian food and French food. And Raven promises to cook for me to prove me wrong. I am really looking forward to it.

I settle the bill which of course she fights me on. I tell her to get it next time and she laughs. It slightly bruised my ego but when I realised that she's just teasing me, I ran after her in the parking lot. She's swift like a deer but I finally catch her and tickle her into agreeing into going on another date with me.

Who knew dates could be so fun? Usually they would just be a lot of awkwardness, suit and tie and a fancy meal. But look at us! I'm in my jeans and a t-shirt and she's wearing jeans and a shirt. This is perfect! This is so comfortable! She is my comfort person.

I drive her back to her house and she picks the music on the way. It starts with MJ hits and then she does a 180 and plays Bollywood music, which I don't understand a word of, but the music...it's so peaceful! And sounds...rusty and old. But peaceful old. She vibes to the music and smiles and explains to me some of her favourite lines. I don't know why the road is so empty because we reach her house so fast. I drove below the speed limit all the way too! But because I am a gentleman I get out and open the door for her.

She steps out of the door and rubs her hand together because it's windy and freezing. She looks like she's wanting to say something but is hesitating. And I realise that I should end it with a kiss, right? I mean that's what I've seen in the movies!

She finally speaks after some glances. "I had fun tonight. Really. Beating your ass in bowling was the highlight of my month." My heart flutters. I have known her only for a month. Because for some stupid reason I was living under a rock!

"And beating your ass in air hockey was the highlight of mine." I stuff my hands in my pocket. It's freezing and I don't have my jacket on.

"I thought it was winning the game last week!"

I forgot for a second that we had won the game. I don't know why that win didn't matter as much. I mean of course it did matter for my career. It helped me draw the attention of some potential NFL teams, but personally it didn't change much for me. "It's right after the hockey thing. You are such a sore loser..." I snort remembering her face when she'd lost. Her cute and mad face suddenly mattered more to me than any trophy.

"Says you. You are an even bigger sore loser." she huffs and white air escapes her mouth. The mouth that I have been dying to kiss the entire night.

"Come here..." I pull her in my arms and she's acting cute and pissed.

"I thought you said you'd keep our hands to yourself."

"I never said anything about my mouth." A wicked grin appears on her face. Fuck, I am a goner.

"Good." she pulls my head down on to her mouth and her lips crash on mine.

It's so warm and sweet. Her touch, her scent, her taste. "Fuck. I want you so bad..." I say against her lips.

She pulls away. "Lock your car." And I do exactly that. She leads me to her apartment. Which is silent when she opens the door for me. "Juju is crashing at Jake's place tonight." She flicks the light on.

"Which bedroom is yours?" I ask her as we upstairs. She opens the door for me and I see stuffed animals. Half her bed is full of stuffed animals. "Cute." I take a look around. I see some designer stuff. Books. A lot of books. And her desk is cluttered with textbooks and makeup and jewellery.

"Sorry for the mess. I have an exam coming up and I was getting ready and all this." She picks up her purse from her bed and moves to keep it on the chair but it falls off the chair and empties its contents out. Something purple catches my eye and I bend down to pick it up immediately.

She races to pick it up first but I snatch it.

I'm glad I got it first. I hold the purple vibrator in my hands. She seems flustered when I trace my hands along the length of the silicone. "How often do you use it?" I'm dying to know if she's ever thought of me when using it and just that thought gets me hard.

She gets up and meets my eye and walks towards me. "Everytime I think of you." I squeeze my ass cheeks tight so that I don't nut in my pants. I'm that hard right now.

She walks close to me and closes any gap between us. Her breasts press against my chest and I feel her warm breath on my body. Too close. I am too close. She is too close. Her eyes do not stray away from mine. "Get on the bed." I command and she obeys and gets on the bed and starts stripping. I waste no time either.

I strip naked and push the soft toys off the bed and prop myself on top of her. "Let me know if it's too much, okay?" she nods her head. I crash my mouth on her. And it's like our tongues were destined to be together because they get along so well. One hand playing with her breast and another reaching down to her pussy.

I take her breast in my mouth and she moans my name.

"You look so beautiful, *Raven.*"

Chapter 21- Riya

"Don't stop!" I moan. Gripping the sheets with one hand and digging another one in his back. He strokes the vibrator around my clit and I feel a wave of pleasure building within. It is so different from when I use it by myself. Right now, I can feel his mouth on my breast and his other hand wandering on my body. His abs rubbing against my body. And it feels so good!

He brings his mouth close to mine and hovers it over. Building up the tension even more. "Come, for me, Raven. Come just for me."

He rubs the vibrator over and holds it still when he finds that one perfect spot. I feel a wave of pleasure soaring through me and I sink my teeth in the nook of his neck. I don't care if it hurts him right now. "I'm coming...fuck! That feels so good Marcus!"

After I finally crash from my high, he turns the vibrator off. I like how he learns about my body so fast. "Do you know how sexy you look when your eyes roll back when you come while shouting my name?" his darkened ocean blue eyes crinkle into a wicked smile.

I hit him on his chest as he falls next to me. "I do not shout!" He chuckles and falls next to me.

He pokes my nose. "You are a screamer. Especially when I do this..." He pinches my nipple softly and a some-what loud moan escapes my mouth.

"You think you're too silent when you groan my name as you nut?" that gets me a husky laugh. I never knew that I could be this comfortable naked. In my own body. Not like I can be naked in someone else's body. Unless I pull their organs out and use their skin as a catsuit. Which I don't even want to think about, because the thought itself makes me want to puke. But he has a way of making me feel comfortable around him. He doesn't judge my vulnerability and he tells me how beautiful I am!

His gaze fixates on me. "I'm not loud in bed." His eyes freeze on mine and a small smile spreads across his face.

"Let's see... shall we?" I pick the vibrator.

"It doesn't work the same on me..." He huffs and smiles. I climb on top of him and prop my knees on either side of the huge chunk of muscles.

I turn it on and press it against my breast which sends thunder down to my pussy. "Who said it's for you? You have me!" I press my lips against his and trace my lips down his torso. But he pulls my head up.

"Let me see you touch yourself when you suck me off." a wide grin spreads on my face. I fucking love it when this man tells me exactly what to do, just in bed. Just in bed.

"Yes captain."

"Fuck! Say that again!" Ooo...seems like I discovered something new here.

"Yes. *Captain*." I emphasise in a seductive tone.

"Holy shit." I lick the tip of his cock and his body shudders. I move the vibrator on my clit, in search of finding that sweet spot that Marcus had found before. I wish I could ask him for directions to that sweet spot.

"Do you like that?" I moan when he groans my name. I lower my mouth on his cock, my hands still trying to guide the vibrator to that sweet spot.

"You know I fucking love it." He thrusts in my mouth and the movement moves my hand and helps me find that sweet spot. I come up for air and my body shivers. I better mark it down. "Are you close?" he asks me.

"So close."

He grips his shaft in his hands and rubs it.

"No…" I remove his hand from his cock. I can't believe that I am feeling jealous of his hand because that is where my mouth is supposed to be right now.

"Greedy. You're so greedy for me. I love it!"

I chuckle and lower my mouth back on his cock. Slow strokes at first till I take him in and I'm gagging. "Fuck. I'm going to come so hard, Raven. Are you close?"

I just moan in response.

He grips the sheets as I see his abs clench and he comes all over my breasts and the pleasure sores through me at the same time.

We sprout dirty words at each other all night. Making each other come after taking a few breaks in between. But we don't have sex. Because whenever I tried to, he shot me down. It's not like he has a reason to shy away because of his size. Because trust me, he is the biggest I've seen.

Actually, no. I once dabbled in the wrong side of porn websites and reached the dark side. Though I'd closed the tab at lightning speed, I was scarred for life. It wasn't anything remotely bad as you guys think it is, but it was bad enough for me. That dude was just way too big, I don't know how the blonde still did him. But back to the point. James is the biggest I've had. Not yet. But you get the gist.

At one point, I'm scared if he thinks that I have a STD or something and I blurt out. "I'm clean. If that's what you're scared of. And it's not like we still won't use a condom."

"What?" his brow rises.

I don't know why but embarrassingly enough, I keep explaining! "I mean, I've never had unprotected sex with anyone. So, I don't have any STD's if that's what you're scared of. And even if I am clean, it wouldn't mean that we still wouldn't use a condom. Trust me. Unprotected sex is not on my bucket list either."

He chuckles and his eyes close and his cheeks squish. I should've taken a photo of him like that. From the chest and above. "It's not that. Do you remember the first time we met?" He tucks his arm under his head which flexes his bicep. Fuck, he looks hot!

"You know I don't. Did I tell you not to fuck me? Because if so, I was totally drunk then and I take my words back."

He laughs now. Again. Me. Naked. In bed. With a guy! Laughing? Mission Impossible. Yet here we are.

"I love how greedy you are for me."

"Not for you. For Lord Percieval." I stroke my hand over the length of his shaft.

"You named my dick? And Lord?"

"I mean...in my defence it is a majestic name and your *dick* doesn't deserve anything less."

"This is the biggest boost to my ego. It's through the roof right now." I can't help but laugh. And I notice the way he looks at me when I laugh. His eyes don't move off my face. Fuck! I might be falling for him. But I can't do that. I just can't. I don't want the heartbreak that follows. I am afraid of love because I am scared of heartbreak. Sue me! But I'm never doing relationships again. Ever!

"Hold your horses, sweetheart. Being this desperate doesn't suit your personality." I say and he laughs out loud.

"Come here." he pulls me closer to him.

"You want to cuddle?"

"Why not?"

Why? One thing I cannot tolerate is my personal space when sleeping. Even back home I'd make Lara, who I share my room with, sleep on the edge of the bed and I would sleep on the other edge. I don't cuddle. The only thing I cuddle when sleeping are my pillows and my soft toys.

"I'm all good. You can use one of my soft toys if you want to cuddle." I yawn. I feel the fatigue of our orgasm marathon set in.

"Like hell I am." he pulls me closer to his warm body and doesn't let me go despite my futile and fake efforts. God, he smells so good. He cuddles me close and we fall asleep like that.

Justine is the only woman on this entire planet who can dunk her tenders in her drink because 'they were too dry!'

I give her the most judgemental look ever. "That's just gross! I should totally reconsider our friendship!"

"Shh...you're distracting me! Did you see Will? He looks delicioso." She checks out the Aussie Indy race car driver. Juju is obsessed with cars. Like literally! I do watch F-1 with her and I am into F-1, but she is one of those crazy psycho obsessed car fans.

"You know that he's married and twenty years older than you, right?" I'm scared of what she might do if he's in a 50 metre radius of her. I'm scared for the poor guy.

She hits my leg and shushes me. "Age is just a number and marriage is just a contract." I roll my eyes at her.

"And jail is just a place." I laugh at my own joke.

"You know I'm not into younger guys! I would rather die than date someone younger than me..." Thankfully Jake is older than Justine. I swear to god, if a guy is even a day younger than her, she will refuse to date him.

"Yeah..yeah! I know! Immature men and all. But you know Sid–Siddharth, one of Marcus' friends. He's younger than us, but dude is more mature than half the boys on the team who are older than him. And he's totally your type too. If Jake wasn't in the picture, I'd totally ship you two!" I feel like Sid could be the calm to Juju's storm. You know, opposite attracts and shit.

She groans and dips the tenders back in the coke. "Thank god that Jake and I are together then! Because I would rather drink my own piss than date someone younger than me." *Never say never.*

I scrunch my nose, my lips fold in that weird way and I give Juju the most judgemental side-eye look. This girl has no filter. But I guess, she's like this just around me! "I'm going to hold you to that!"

Her eyes wander around looking for Will as she talks to me. "Honey, if I do marry, it'll be Jake. You know I have no space for any other man in my life!"

"As if he has space for any other woman in his life! You two are a match made in heaven!" *Literally. The JJ couple are inseparable.*

We watch the race, Will manages to win the race with a comfortable lead and Juju almost jumps out on the track when he lifts the trophy. Thankfully I am strong enough to hold her back and stop her from getting arrested or sued by Will.

We grab lunch together and chat about school and our upcoming trip to Cabo for my 21st. I was actually thinking of inviting James too. But I don't want to think about him today. It is our girls' day out! And we've barely had one. With assignments and midterms approaching, we're both swamped with work.

Justine comes from a lower-middle class family and she has had to take care of her expenses herself. Her family is so warm and welcoming. They all have the Latino charm. No, I'm not being racist. But I just think that her family are some of the sweetest people I've ever met. Whenever I've visited her family for any holiday, they've always treated me like their family. And after midterms and that Cabo trip, we were planning to go down and spend some time with her family for Easter.

"I looked up some great places for us to go around. A couple of museums, historic places, stripper clubs, cultural sites, awesome restaurants, etcetera" I choke on my pesto pasta.

"What? I'm never trusting you with the awesome restaurants part. Because the last time you took me to an awesome restaurant, there were three legs of a cockroach floating in my drink! But I am down for the strip club part." We both start laughing uncontrollably.

It is true, Juju is incapable of picking out good restaurants which serve edible food. The girl has the most unhealthy eating habits. As if I'm the one to judge! But she still has that perfect model-like sexy latina figure. With a plump ass and full breasts, luscious and juicy lips and those big doe eyes! She's the beauty queen. No, she's the goddess of beauty!

"By the way, when are you going to do the deed with Marcus? He doesn't seem like the guy who would wait that long to sleep with a girl." He would wait a lifetime for me to be comfortable enough to have sex with him. Those were his words. Not mine.

"I want to have sex with him, but he keeps saying no. I mean, it's not like we haven't done other stuff or seen each other naked, but he just...I don't know."

She chugs on her cocktail. "That's not like him at all. At least from what I've heard, he is a huge fuckboy and would fuck a girl, the first chance he'd get."

I try so hard not to roll my eyes. "That's George, not James. But I know. It is unlike him. And I am warning you! You better not tell Jake all this, or else I'm not telling you shit from now on!"

"But–"

I quickly add on. "No buts! Whatever we discuss about my personal life, stays between us! I feel uncomfortable knowing that he knows about my sex life." I show visible discomfort so that she hopefully understands.

"I won't. My lips are sealed." She zips her mouth and locks it.

"Pinky promise?"

"Pinky promise! Do you want to get the check? I want to go back and study."

"Sure. I'm tired too." It's starting to get dark already and I hate driving in the dark. I reach for my Chanel purse and pay the bill.

"I will never get over how rich your family is!"

"We're not that rich." We are.

"You have almost 50k worth of luxury stuff!"

"Excuse me! I have more than 100k worth luxury goodies, and that's just the stuff I have over here in Boston! I wish I could show you my mother and my aunt's collection back at home! They have the real shit! Especially my mom. She has the best fashion sense. Expensive, but good!"

Juju chuckles. She has a way of not making me feel guilty for having been born into a rich family. All the friends I've had before have found some way of making me feel uncomfortable for having the privilege. That I do not take for granted at all. "Her ring collections say it all… I think her one ring could probably pay for my entire tuition and her one necklace could cover my family's debt." Justine got a full scholarship for going to Winston and her living expenses are covered by her job. I pay more rent than her since I took the bigger bedroom. But I really admire and respect her financial independence. It's not easy doing that.

"Do you want me to steal it for you?" I ask her.

"And risk your mom's wrath? No thank you!" It's true. My mother has no chill! She is very very strict. Always has been. But my father, on the other hand, spoils me like anything and is the most chill dad ever.

I open my phone to check my messages. It has been going off like crazy since I walked in the class. I have 12+ unread text messages.

Of course it's James! Who else would text me like a creepy but cute obsessed person?

Aced that Biology test.
Thank you so much!
When do I get to return the favour?
I mean about the interview
Unless you have something else in mind...?
Like maybe...you could come over?
Or maybe I could?
Whatever works best for you.
Let me know the time.
I have practices from 4pm to 6pm, but I'm free after that.
Actually I have to hit the gym later at night! Shit! How about Friday night? I'm free then???
Okay I'm going to stop spamming you now.
Let me know what works best though

Okay! This guy is crazy! He couldn't formulate all this in just one text? And why am I blushing? Jeez! Someone might think that a dude just texted me to ask me to marry him!

Congratulations but I barely helped you study! You're already good at it anyway. And practices after the finals? Why? Also, Friday works for me. What did you have in mind? I could plan a date, if you want...Let me know.

He replies almost immediately–
Practices go on for a lifetime. They're never ending.
But I'd love to see what you'd plan for the date.
Do I need to wear a suit and tie?
If so, please let me know beforehand.

No suit and tie. I'm not in the mood for anything fancy. But dress to impress? Or don't wear anything at all...Yeah! Actually, no. I'd hate other women looking at what's mine...Just kidding. Wear something casual.

Noted.
Also, bring some tissues. We're going to need them, James.

Chapter 22- James

I am in a room full of old couples, who are either faking to be head over heels in love with each other, or maybe true love actually exists. It's a couples bonding exercise type of thing. It's a show, which is broadcasted on a small local channel. Guess what the name of the show is? Spit or swallow. And no...it is not the type of show that.

"Are you sure you want to do this, Raven?" I ask her one more time.

"I'm totally fine with it. But if you want to chicken out, I'd totally understand!" Bruising my ego? She knows how to hit the mark.

"I'm going to make you spit out everything and make you spill your secrets." That sounds gross. The theme of the show itself is gross though. Literally.

"Alright, couples, thank you for coming on Spit or Swallow, I am your host Jessi and I would like to welcome you all today. I will explain how the show works." The host takes over. "In front of each of you is a disgusting concoction of juice in a shot glass. You have to drink it and keep it in your mouth while the other person asks the question and if you are willing to answer the question, you get to spit it out, or else you have to swallow the vile drink. There's a twist this time..."

The oldies around us started to make some noise and hype him up. "We are passing out a refresher around each table. If you choose to spit out the drink, you can drink the refresher to cleanse your palate, if you choose not to answer the question and swallow the disgusting drink, you do not get to drink the refresher."

The middle aged couple behind us screamed. And I see the man brood over his wife.

"Ooo Yes!" Jessi laughs. "The questions are whatever you want them to be. You get to ask 25 questions each as there are 25 shots of disgusting drinks in front of you. Ranging from soy sauce to clove milkshake to anchovy smoothies. Yuck! I know, right? And you cannot cheat. You have to drink the entire contents and hold them in your mouth. No cheating allowed on my watch!" Just what I needed! The shot glasses in front of me has liquid ranging from pink to blue to poopy brown to black. The smell itself is enough for me to throw up. There's no way that I am swallowing any of this!

"This is fun, right?" Raven squeaks in front of me.

"I would have answered all your questions anyway. We didn't have to come here."

"There's no fun in that! I'd rather torture you into answering. Bring your A-game baby! It's war time!" She is so into this. I get my competitive spirit on too.

"Oh! Alright! It's game time, Raven. It's on!" I cracked my knuckles. I'm going to rain hellfire and win this game.

"Alright, ladies and gentlemen! Let's Spit or Swallow!" I will never get over the name of the game. They could do so much better.

"You go first. What do you want me to put in my mouth?" I ask her. She picks a red shot glass from in front of me. I take a whiff and it is so spicy, it makes my nose runny. Hot sauce! She's pulling out the big guns right from the beginning... Alright! I can totally work with that. I chug the hot sauce and keep it in my mouth. It is so spicy that it makes my eyes tear and sets my face on fire. My ears are heating up and I start sweating.

"Okay...Who is the one person you hate the most in your life?" The list is not too long...Cole and a woman whose name I don't know. I immediately spit in the bucket next to me and drank the cold refresher. It isn't of much help, but at least my ears have stopped burning.

"I don't know her name or what she looks like, but I hate her more than anything in this world. She broke my family..." I exhale. If she wants the truth, I am going to give it all to her. "My father once got drunk. Very drunk at one of his after-parties and this woman got all over him and he cheated on my mother with her. Someone took the photos and sent it to my mother who was distraught and..." I feel a lump in my throat and I feel a hand on mine.

It looks like she's feeling guilty for having asked that question, but I want her to know. My past, present, all of it. "It's alright. You don't have to tell me everything."

But I continue. "My mother and father got into a huge fight. Dad made sure that nothing was leaked to the press and he apologised to my mother too. He didn't mean to cheat on her. He was very drunk, but still...My mother and he fought. It was his last game before retirement. And my mother said that she won't go. I went with him instead of staying with my mother. She got into an accident on her way to the game and... So yes, I do blame that woman for everything and I hate her the most in this world." I had never told anyone this, but with Riya, I know I can trust her. It is just her! It is just us!

"Thank you for telling me. I know it wasn't easy. But I really appreciate it. My turn. What do you want to torture me with?" I shake away all those feelings. Somehow, it feels much lighter to share it with someone. "This one." I pick the glass with lemon juice. "You're a monster!" she complains.

I will agree, it was very evil of me to pick the lemon juice. And I cannot stop laughing. "You ready?"

"I hate you!" She picks up the glass and drinks it and keeps it in her mouth.

"Who was the boy who you dated before me, who broke your heart and what did he do?" I wasn't sure if she'd spit or swallow. Because she never told me anything about any previous relationship. But it was pretty evident that she had gotten her heart broken by some bastard who didn't deserve her and that's why 'she doesn't date!'

To my surprise, she spit her drink out in the bucket and chugged the refresher making a yucked out face. "I hate you so much for making me put that thing in my mouth!" She squeezes her eyes shut and the glitter on her eyes shines beautifully. She is looking spectacular by the way. Jeans and a translucent white shirt with a black bra inside, high pony and glittery eyes and my favourite- red lips.

"You have to answer now!" I laugh. "Who was he?"

"How'd you know there was someone? I don't remember telling you..."

"I took a wild guess. Come on, spill the beans, Raven."

"Alright." She adjusts herself in her seat. "He was my best friend. We dated in high school. He asked me to be his girlfriend after confessing that he'd liked me for two years. I said yes. A few months later, he broke up with me telling me that, 'he didn't see our future together.' He hurt me. I hurt him. End of story. I am over him though." Whoever that bastard was, was a fool. To let a beautiful girl like Riya walk away. I can understand why she tries to conceal private life and doesn't share much about her with me or anyone. I understand her trust issues now.

"That's why you should date men and not boys. He was a boy."

"And you are a man?"

"I am not a man. I am *the* man for you, Raven." I wink at her and she blushes. I am glad that whoever the scumbag she dated was out of the picture. His loss is my gain.

"My turn." She picks the glass with raw egg. That is so evil! She is a monster! She put the glass in front of me and smirks. "Drink up baby!" she suppresses a laugh.

I drink the egg and try my best not to throw up. That slimy texture doesn't help. I don't even hear her question before I spit the egg out. I chug the refresher and glare at her.

"So, what's your answer?" she asked me.

"You…"

"What?" She looks surprised.

"Can you repeat the question?"

"I asked, what is the one thing that you used to believe in or follow, but changed your mind about?"

"Oh! Yes. You." I clean the edges of my mouth with the napkin while her jaw drops.

"What do you mean?"

"Well, I used to believe that you were a sweet person, but you are so evil." I laugh sarcastically and she glares at me. Maybe it wasn't funny? I mean she is torturing me here. "Just kidding" I raise my hands to surrender. "I used to believe that I will never do relationships, but…You…made me change my mind." I am not a liar. And one thing I hate is leading women on. I never do that. I say whatever I feel. Especially in cases like these.

Her face turns blank and unreadable. "What do you mean?" It scares me for a while. Because what if she doesn't want a relationship or is not ready for one and I pushed her away?

So my stupid self clarifies it further. "I mean, I like you. And not just as a friend. And I would like to date you, if you'd want to date me…"

"James…I…You knew I don't do relationships. And I…"

"Hey…It's no pressure." I hold her hand. "You can take your time and think about it." The wait is going to kill me, but for her, I'd wait a lifetime.

"Alright."

We continue the game. She'd asked me if I had to save one out of Dan, Sid and George, who'd I save. I swallowed the soy sauce and it burned my throat. There was no way, I could pick between those fuckers. No matter how much we bickered, they are like my brothers. I can never pick between them. When I'd asked her about the person who'd hurt her the most, she refused to answer and gulped the sticky aloe vera juice. It was so slimy, it'd make me want to throw up. But I didn't want to push her for the answer. Also, it felt like I already knew the answer.

"Alright, couples...this brings us to the end of the game. Thank you so much for joining us and I hope you got some juicy answers out of your partners, or pumped some disgusting juices into them." Jessi really thought that it was funny. But that was the worst joke I'd ever heard.

We head out to my car and I open the door for Raven as she gets in. It is still freezing outside, so I turn on the heat and the seat warmer. "So, what's the plan for dinner?" I ask her.

"Oopsies...I thought that we would get full over here, so I didn't make any reservations for dinner." My eyes blink faster as I glare at her in disbelief.

"You thought that all those disgusting shots of hell were our dinner?" she shrugs casually, giving me the puppy dog eyes. "Buckle up, Sweetheart. We're getting actual food. The soy sauce in my stomach needs something else to complement it. I think I drank enough salt for the rest of the month." she laughs. I'm glad that she finds it funny. Because I am dead serious. I was surprised that none of the oldies there passed out or worse died of food poisoning given the disgusting food that was available there. Calling it 'food' is atrocious.

I take her to my favourite sushi place and when the server brings out our order of sashimi, she deliberately pours a ton of soy sauce in my dish. I cannot help but laugh out loud and that gets us creepy stares from other people in the restaurant. We dine and talk. Talking comes naturally when I'm with my Raven. I get the feeling that I want her to know every small detail of my life. I want her to know all of me. And I want to know everything about her too.

Her favourite colour- Yellow.

Her favourite place to go- The library.

Her dream- To help people with their mental health.

Her favourite person- Right now, it's her cousin Lara.

Her guilty pleasure- Me? No, I am just her pleasure. There's no guilt here. But her guilty pleasure is shopping for designer goodies.

When she talks I am unable to focus on anything else. When she's around me I don't care about anything else. She has the power to constrict the entire world into her, making it impossible for me to focus on anything else. And I think I am way past falling for her stage. After tonight, I should give myself a medal for not sprouting out the words-

I love you, Raven.

Chapter 23- Riya

Holi is also known as the festival of colors. It marks the triumph of good over evil and is a symbol of a new beginning. We burn logs of wood and with that log, we burn away all our worries. I have always celebrated Holi with my family. We would sit around the fire and eat and talk for hours. And the next day, with the ash, me and my cousins would play holi. Drenching each other in the ash. Supposedly, it is good for your skin and stuff.

But the real fun is always the next day. It's a festival called Rangapanchami. That is when we play with colours and torture each other. Back at home, we would target one person in the household and drench them with concentrated water colours, that colour stains you for days. And even to get it out 50%, you have to wash yourself for 3 hours.

It's all good fun though.

Thankfully, this year, there is a Holi celebration being organised by the Indian association. They are doing it the same way we used to do it back at home. Only difference, back at home, we would have a drink called thandai- it is similar in taste to lassi- the famous Indian yoghurt drink. But it is laced with weed. And everyone would have to drink a minimum of two glasses. It was compulsory in my house.

Before you judge, that is the only day in the entire day, when it is allowed to do that. Our God- Shiva, used to drink weed. But since it is a no-no in Boston, they are going to lace the drinks with alcohol. It won't be entirely the same, but I'll take it.

I had bought entry passes for me, Juju and Jake and had asked the boys if they wanted to accompany me. And the only reason they are coming is because there are water balloons filled with coloured water that you can throw at each other.

James however, is coming for me. It is said that the first person to apply colour on you should be your partner. And James doesn't know that. But I want to be the first one to apply colour on him.

I prepare myself and my skin and hair for the festival. The dress theme is to wear white clothes. It is impossible to get the colour out of the clothes, so I wear a simple white Indian kurta and white leggings. The event is outdoors and the weather has been in our favour. It is nice and warm and the sun is shining down brightly on us.

Perfect!

I oil my skin and my hair and tie my hair in a pony and ditch all my makeup. I opt for my worst sandals that I want to throw away and white tote bag and put my phone in a plastic cover. I'm holi-ready.

I walk outside of my room to find Jake and Juju standing outside in the living room in their all white clothes. Jake should not have opted for his white jeans!

The place is about half an hour drive from here. And since I want to get wasted, Juju said that she would be the sober police and drive us back. I really wanted to have fun with her!

When we reach the place, I scan our passes and find the boys and James standing in the centre, in all white and the only ones judging everyone else. There is Bollywood music being blasted in the garden. The lawn has been uprooted and the soil is dried and prepared for all the water it is going to be drenched in. I sneak behind James and pick up some red colour in my hand from one of the colour stands. I make sure that I tip-toe very quietly, since my anklets have dancing bells on them that make noise.

"Happy Holi!" I shout and smother the colour on his face. He is caught by surprise and turns around frantically. I'm not sure if he's red because of the colour or anger.

But I just can't stop smiling because I was the first one to apply color on him.

Maybe I shouldn't have done that. But that is what Holi is! I had even picked a target for today. George.

I don't know how to play white-holi. I can't tone myself down on festivals. But I guess I have to this year. My face falls and I don't even see the blue colour that is thrown on my face. James. "Let's get this party started!" George shouts. And Juju squeaks and Jake hoots.

The decoration done here is so similar to the one back in India. There are colour stands. And everyone over 21 gets a red band to get an alcoholic lassi. I am just a few weeks from turning 21 and all I had to do was flash my puppy eyes at the uncle and swear that I had a sober person who was above 21 to take care of me.

Indian uncles are the best when it comes to emotional manipulation. Indian aunties on the other hand...they're a rock that cannot be fazed by anything.

"Let's get something to drink first. Rule no. 1- We don't play Holi sober." I instruct everyone. "Let's get our shit on! And also have two sober people to drive us back." Dan sighs and that tells me that he is the sober police in their group.

We flash our bands at the counter and get our drinks. "Uncle, please make mine extra strong." I wink at him playfully and he chuckles and winks back.

I grab my drink and turn around dancing and swaying to the beats of a bollywood song. I see George's mouth wide open and he is staring at me. I raise my brows to make the creep stop staring at me. "Who are you and what did you do to my highness?" He asks and I can't stop laughing.

"I'm having fun! It's holi!" I shrug and chug my extra strong boozy lassi. Thankfully the sweetness of the lassi masks the alcohol, so other than the burning sensation, I don't feel anything.

"You're day-drinking at 11am on a Friday."

"Oh get off your high horse. As if you've never done it!" I take the yellow colour from the table next to me and throw it on George.

"Riya!" I hear in unison. I turn around to see that the yellow powder is splattered in everyone's drinks. I'm not going to apologise. The saying of this festival is 'Bura na mano Holi hai.' which translates to 'Please don't be mad or angry because it's Holi!'

I flash them an unapologetic smile and wave my shoulders to the beat of the song- Second hand Jawaani. And I feel all eyes on me. This won't work.

I turn around to the uncle and tell him to make extra strong drinks for everyone except for Dan and Juju.

"She's trying to get us fucked up." Sid says as he also joins me in my weird dance. That's what I need! The festive spirit.

The uncle making the drinks laughs and shakes his shoulders to match me and it seems like everyone is trying to get the gist of it now. The point of the celebration is to let loose and have fun! It's a Saturday tomorrow anyway, we can think about our actions then. But right now...we have fun!

The song changes to an even bigger banger- Let's Nacho. It means Let's Dance. I shout the lyrics of the song and throw my hands in the air and have fun. The uncle makes our drinks and tells me that he made mine special, with a playful wink. He tells me to have fun and the group disperses to the centre where everyone is dancing and throwing colors in the air.

We quickly chug our drinks and chime in.

I see James smile and dance and let loose next to me. I have never seen him dance this openly. I see him laugh and throw water balloons at the boys and me. Me and Juju are doing our own thing, dancing and throwing color in the air.

I pass the message around to everyone secretly that today's target is George. And the way everyone tortures George is brutal. But I do the worst possible thing to him. I sneak away and get the water colour powder enough to make 10 litres of water color, but I mix it in a small mug. It is so concentrated that it looks foul. And it is a dark pink colour.

George is white as fuck and he's blonde! His scalp is going to be stained for at least a week and his hair is going to be dyed pink. I signal the boys and everyone holds him down. George is the biggest amongst the guys, so James holds his hands back and Sid holds his shoulders and Dan just stands on the side, recording everything in my phone.

Mine is the only one in a plastic cover and the guys had their phones collected, because they didn't want it to get wet. I'm smart. But Juju and Jake hoot and shout as I pour the dark-colored water on his head. It drips and falls on James's hands and he immediately lets go of him.

Dan is on the floor laughing and George is hella pissed. Not angry-pissed, but friendly-pissed. "Oh! I'm going to get you for that!" He chases me and I run in the crowd. He chases me with a plate of purple colour.

He wraps his bicep around my neck and dumps the entire plate on my head and massages the powder in my head. Everyone else aims water balloons at me and I am drenched and the colour seeps into my head.

"Violet...you're turning Violet!" Juju laughs. *Hahaha.*

"I hope that was up to the level, your highness." He lets go of me and bows in front of me. Smug! But fun. So fun!

I am god knows how many drinks down. I lost count after 5 and I am a multicoloured person. My head is purple, my face is blue, my torso is every colour in the rainbow and thank god I had painted my nails black. We are exhausted and drunk at around 3pm. But I keep dancing. I mingle with every Indian group, even the aunties! Drunk me likes adventures! Or should I say horror?!

James picks me up like a baby, his arms are around my stomach and I keep waving my legs and arms at the aunty as he drags me to the exit. "Alright! I think we've had enough!" He says after I ask the aunty what University she got the certificate of being a bitch at. In my defence, she did tell me that I should lose some weight and not wear things that show cleavage two years ago! Oh! I didn't forget!

"But I...am having...so much fun!" I slur and smile. Those blue eyes...Oh how I could drown in them! I cannot stand straight, so I let myself fall into his arms. I know he will catch me. It feels nice to have someone who cares about you.

"Alrighty, Raven. Let's get you home."

I immediately let go of him and narrow my eyes at him. How dare he not take advantage of me being drunk? What am I even thinking?!

"Oh! No. No. No. No. We are not going home. We are GOING home!" I say smiling and nodding. George is just as fucked up as me and is being hailed on Dan's shoulder. Thankfully, Dan is the second most buffed guy amongst these men.

George shouts in agreement and suddenly I think that I said something very sensible and meaningful.

James scoops me up in his arms. "Alright. Let's GO home." I smile and nod at him.

I wrap my arms around him as I let my head fall back. I am so hungry and horny and drunk. I don't know what to focus on. So, I act on my instinct. "When we go back I'm going to fuck you so hard that you will forget your own name

James...Marcus...Williams...Marcus...James...Williams..." I say and keep smiling.

I wake up with a pounding headache on the bathroom floor of James' room. His arms are wrapped around my waist and I'm using his bicep as a pillow. He's buffed enough to do that. Muscular and squishy. I move closer to him. How did we end up here? We're both fully clothed and still covered in colour, but it's still dark, maybe it's still night.

So I snuggle close to James and wrap my arms around him and doze back. Only one scent envelops me. I have only one thought. One feeling. One name.

James.

Chapter 24- Riya

I wish I had balls, so I could kick myself in the balls to knock some sense into myself. How many times do I have to tell myself not to fall for him? I've recited the same line at least 150,000 times. So much so that I've annoyed Juju to not be in the same room as me.

I sit on the couch with Jake watching Ice hockey. I don't understand shit about the game. But I know that if I am left alone, I will text him for the twentieth time. We just finished the Midterms and my birthday is next week and so is the trip to Cabo. Juju is coming with me and I asked James last two days ago if he wanted to tag along and he still hasn't responded.

I can't help but think if I came off too clingy? I hope not. Or was I taking it too fast? Maybe I shouldn't have asked him. But if he doesn't want to come, he can just tell me that. I am a big girl, I can handle rejection. It's the silence that I hate.

"You're doing it again." Jake presses his hand on my thigh to stop me from shaking my leg again.

Justine walks into the room and sits next to him and he immediately takes his hand off my leg. "I have told her several times that if she doesn't want to think about it so much, just drive to his place and ask him yours–"

"Babe..." Jake cuts off Justine. "That's even worse. It's a rule that if a guy doesn't reply within the first two hours, he's probably banging someone else." James would never do that. Right? He felt the same spark? I mean, after that date at Spit or Swallow, which by the way is an awful name...I thought we connected. And at the Holi party, we had fun, right.

Granted I screamed infront of everyone how I was going to fuck him hard and didn't let go of him at all so he had to take me back to his place. And I passed out when we reached and he couldn't bathe me, so he got tired and since he wasn't exactly sober either, he took me to the bathroom and laid a bedsheet down and we slept there because I wanted the cold floor and wouldn't stay on the bed. His bed, which I had completely ruined the colour that I had on from the Holi party. But he stayed with me. He slept with me on the floor because I wouldn't let go of his hand.

I was...I am falling for him. Hell...I might even–

"Considering his history, it wouldn't be a surprise." Jake adds quickly.

"I think you should go and confront him. Face to face." Justine finally speaks in my favour.

"He's very busy on Thursdays. I know he is home on Friday nights. I'll drop in then." I get up and make my way to my room.

"You are making a mistake..." Jake shouts from the couch and I hear Justine mumble something to him.

"Wanna make a bet, Ri?" Jake asks me and I stop.

"What bet?" I am not a gambler, but I am just interested in knowing what he wanted to bet on.

Jake smirks at me. "Williams is banging someone else already." I try to force a smile too. It obviously looks very fake.

"Haha."

"I bet you two hundred bucks." I look back at him.

"Two hundred?"

"Yep."

"I'd love to win that money, but I lost my wallet the day before yesterday. I even had to block all my cards."

"Why? Because you know you will have to pay me?" Jake laughs.

"Nope, because I'd much rather keep that transaction in cash and I just happened to carry my card purse in my cash purse and I lost them both. And I loved my cash purse a lot, so you will have to wait till it arrives to pay me." I smile at him.

It was my favourite purse. It was a non-brand purse because it was custom made for me by a local designer in India. It was very beautiful and exactly what I wanted. But I don't think I made the point I should've.

I knock on James' door and a semi-naked Daniel opens the door for me. Wet out of the shower, towel around the waist, wet hair and droplets of water streaming down his perfect abs.

"Marcus is not here."

"Huh?" I force my eyes to face him! Come on, you cannot blame me for checking out a beautiful semi-naked man! "What? Yes. Wait– Why? Where is he?"

"He went back home a couple days ago and hasn't come back since."

"I texted him a bunch of ti–"

"Riya?" Someone called my name from behind. "What are you doing here?" I know I am here to get some answers from him, but how am I supposed to stay mad when his hair is all messed up and he's looking that cute? No! Don't be wavered by deep blue ocean eyes and those dark circles beneath his eyes. He looks tired. Not just physically, but he looked emotionally drained. The spark from his eyes before is gone somewhere.

"I–You–" Now is not the time to stammer Ri!

"Let's talk in my room." He walks past me and to his room. We make our way to his room and I sit on the bed. James takes off his shoes and flops down next to me with a huge sigh.

"I'm sorry, James...I shouldn't have shown up unannounced. I'll leave."

"No. Please. Stay. Riya, I..." he holds his head in his hands and I'd never seen him this distraught before. He said my name. Something's wrong. I feel a strange tug in my heart, it is as if someone fisted their hand in my chest and squeezed my heart from within.

"Is everything okay?" I put my hand on his shoulder and I swear to god I hear a soft gasp. Is he crying? Fuck! What should I do? I wish I could just google about what to do when people cry. I am not very good at consoling crying people. I hug him and pat his shoulder lightly and James cries. He isn't wailing, but those tiny sobs of his tear my heart to shreds.

I love him.

At this moment, I want nothing more than taking away all his pain. Murder whoever even brought a tear in his eyes.

James just keeps his head in his hands while I hug him and continue to softly pat his back. No words are exchanged, but none are needed for me to console him. He was there when I broke down and I have never been more glad that I showed up at someone's house unannounced.

"I want to sleep. Will you be here when I wake up?" he finally rubs his tears away and looks at me with such tired eyes that it shatters my heart further.

I kiss his forehead and lay next to him. "I'm not leaving you. I'm not going anywhere. You should get some sleep. Come here." I open my arms for him and he nestles his head on my chest, hugging my waist tightly. I don't even have to try to match his breathing because it is as if we are somehow in sync.

James after that nap is a different James. He doesn't talk about the reason for his pain. His sorrow. His tears

He's flirting with me as usual. I don't want to push him, because clearly he needs time to process it himself. But I hope and pray that he will at some point at least consider telling me.

"So, are we all set to go to Game Boys?" The sports bar- Game Boys, is a little far from Bradwick. It is one of the most famous sports bars which I absolutely hate. Because they mostly air american football which I don't understand whatsoever and the people there are sometimes...racist.

"Yep. Let's go." I step foot into the living room and find the boys ready as well. I didn't know that they were coming too. I thought that it was a date, or something like that. Not that I don't like hanging out with the boys. Trust me, they've grown on me more than I'd like. It's alright. I can work with that. But I thought that maybe, just maybe I could finally spit those words out to him tonight.

They were sitting there right at the tip of my tongue, and I couldn't wait to throw them around James. I can't believe that I will be the first to say those words. Not that there is any shame in saying what you feel, but I have always been careful with relationships.

Love can be your greatest strength and your biggest weakness. I'm just afraid of it being the latter.

It's all sunshine and rainbows when love is your strength, but the moment it becomes your biggest weakness...that's when shit goes down. But with James, I doubt that will ever be the case. He gets me in a way no one ever has.

I believe it was the time I'd stay over at James' place and we were both drowned in orgasm city. I'd cooked food for James and the boys and I'd needed some spices that I had at home. So I went home to grab them and Jake had made a comment about me eating too much and having a stomach that rolls when I sit down. I haven't always been confident in my body. I know I don't have a thigh gap and a slim waist, but I had an hourglass body that I embraced. I was starting to love my curves. I'd come back to James' place and make the food and serve it to everyone.

I barely ate two bites before I started playing with the food on my plate and made my way to his room. James followed me to his room with a plate of food in his hand and sat down on the bed next to me. "What happened? You barely ate. The last meal you ate was more than eight hours ago, Raven. You need to eat. And the food you made tastes so good. Seems like we should fire Sid and hire you as our own personal chef." He chuckled and pulled me on his lap. I didn't laugh and immediately got off his lap.

"Did I do something, Raven?"

"No, I didn't want to break your legs. Lol. I'm not as light as the girl who you are used to sitting in your lap." He pulled my hand and pulled me on his lap.

"Here." He put his hands on my waist and buried his face in the nook of my neck. "Insult me one more time saying that I can't handle you and you will have to bear the consequences, Raven." His deep glare burned a hole through my chest and his words pierced my soul. "And you are perfect. Trust me when I say that I have never met a woman like you. You have a body that I worship before violating it later. And don't let anyone tell you otherwise."

"But I have a stomach that rolls over when I sit. Do you still like me? I lifted my shirt enough to expose my FUPA. "This!" I held my lower belly in my hands. "I hate this."

"Come here." He walked me in front of the mirror. He put his hand on my lower hand and never in my life have I felt more embarrassed. "What is this?" he asked me in a dead serious note. I wish I could melt into water and vaporise. Or burn away like a vampire.

"My belly."

"And why do you have this?" Another tug to my heart. If I thought that Jake's words were harsh, James' straight up destroyed me and my self esteem.

"I-I-"

He looks at me in the mirror. "I'm sure you know biology already. But let me refresh it for you again. You are a woman and have a uterus. You have a body which is blessed with making the miracle of forming and nurturing a life within. So, naturally, it will need protection and that is provided by the fat layer on top of it. So don't ever apologise or let anyone judge you for being the beautiful woman that you are. And those stomach rolls...you have no fucking idea how much they turn me on. Maybe I haven't shown enough love." He put his other hand on my lower belly as well. Slowly tracing the hem of my panties and slipping his hand inside.

He did show me- multiple times.

That's the James I love. The one who makes me feel comfortable no matter what. Who accepts me as I am. Hell, who helps me love myself. And I fucking love James to pieces. I love every inch of his soul.

I love James.

Chapter 25- Riya

"It's fine, I got it baby." I planted a peck on James' lips and threw a punch at the man who just slapped me wide across my cheek. I heard ringing in my ears for a split second as his hand made contact with my cheek. It was so sudden and uncalculated that it caught me off guard and made me lose my balance on contact.

I hate violence, but that doesn't mean that I won't account for it when needed. And it was needed here. I needed to stand up for myself.

Let's rewind to half an hour ago. Me, the boys and James had gorged on 3 buckets of 'sultry wings'. It's their menu! I will never understand it and the reason for all the naming. Like, why do the mozzarella sticks have to be named 'spread your sticks' and the poutine fries called 'cum on my fries'. I mean, I agree it is smart. But it's just too dirty. I was on my second beer and the boys decided to participate in a game trivia that was going on in the bar. The crowd was a good mix of college students and middle aged men.

"Cricket!" I got up from my seat and shouted the answer and the entire bar stared at me. I heard a mix of sighs and groans from our table.

"The correct answer is baseball." someone else in the crowd shouted.

I get up from my chair and shout. "Bat and ball! You use it in cricket. Baseball is merely a third if not fourth copy of cricket. Forgive me for thinking that originality of the game mattered in the answer." My answer gained me a couple more gasps. There were a ton of Red Sox fans in there and I got myself some very nasty looks from them.

"Marcus. Zip her mouth shut. She won't only make us lose this game but get us permanently banned from this bar." George glared at me.

I went on. "Cricket is a hundred times better than Baseball. And nothing in this world can make me believe otherwise." Sid and Dan smacked their foreheads as I angered a couple more drunk gentlemen around us.

We absolutely did not win the trivia and the boys blamed me for their loss. "You guys are athletes, how should I know more about sports? It's your lack of knowledge that cost us the win today." I avoided any eye contact and chugged on an empty beer bottle. James laughed next to me. It was great seeing that smile back on his face. I didn't know what I'd do to see that smile again.

"I think it's time for us to call it a night." James didn't drink because he insisted on being the sober police and escorting us back home. The boys were wasted! Completely. "I'll go settle the tab." He went to pay the bill while I gathered my belongings and got out of my chair.

I saw a man in his early to mid thirties standing right behind me. I moved to excuse him, but he just stood there and glared at me before he uttered the words- "Go back to your country, you fucking cunt." Now I would lie if I haven't imagined going through such a scenario before. I've imagined being discriminated against because of my colour at least a thousand times. So you bet I had the perfect reply ready.

"Alright. But I fly first class only. Unless you are willing to pay for a chartered flight. First class should do it." I adjust my bag. And George, Dan and Sid are standing right in front of me, in a split second. Like a herd of lions protecting their ones.

"What?" The man asks as he tries to push the guys away, but they don't budge. I don't budge either. I keep on a brave face and pat their back to let them know that I got it.

"*You* want me to 'go back where I came from' right?" I use air quotes. I walk ahead until I stand right in front of him. "Then it's better that you pay for it as well. I'll have someone send over my required details for you to book the flight. Man, my parents will be surprised to see me. And don't forget, First class only. God knows that my back can't handle economy flights." Another step. "You see, I never even walked through those aisles before. But I just know that Economy is just not for me! Son of a bitch." I say with a smile. I meant every word of it, none of that was a lie. I've never flown Economy and I don't intend to either. Call me a spoiled brat, because I am! And I am a proud spoiled brat.

Because whenever I can, I do help out the people I can. Charities, donations, I've done it all, not just donating money, but also my time. I love volunteering at the local orphanage whenever I can.

James just reappears behind that man and before I can say or do anything, that man slaps me! "That should teach you some fucking manners!" I'd be lying if I say that it doesn't hurt. I can taste metal in my mouth. Which I'm guessing is my own blood. I swallow it and before I can think or do anything, my instinct is to stop James. He is an athlete wanting to go pro and can't afford to have any assault charges on his record. Me on the other hand. I don't take disrespect from anyone.

"James...Wait." I stop James, who has already swung his fist in the man's direction. But stops just before impact.

"It's fine, I got it baby." I plant a peck on his lips and form my right hand into a fist. Focusing all my energy into my arm, I swing my hand with all my weight at him and throw the mightiest punch ever. People who say that violence is disturbing are so fucking wrong. There is nothing more peaceful than violence.

"Man down!" George yells as the man I just punched falls to the ground. Not knocked out, but down with pain. The entire bar erupts with loud cheers and I cannot stop laughing. James, on the other hand, rushes next to me and holds my hand to examine. My knuckles are a little red and there are tiny spots of blood on them, but I feel exhilarated.

Siddharth keeps the man down on the floor as he tries to attack me again."You wouldn't dare." The owner rushes towards me and starts apologising.

I mean, I hit him too. So, I guess, it's alright. I won't press any charges. I take another look at the racist bastard before walking away with charisma away from the SCUM.

My bravado lasts merely three seconds after I get outside and I wince in pain, holding my knuckles.

"Wait here." James tucks the coat on me and tries to walk past me before I hold his hand to stop him.

"I need you. To be with me. Please James." I hug him from behind and he stops in his tracks. No matter how much I'd like to deny it, I am shaken to my core. And if it wasn't for James turning around to hold me in his arms right now, I'd crumble and fall to the ground, shattered in pieces. He just embraces me. His warmth engulfs my pain and insecurities.

I'd faced racial discrimination before. Mild. Yes. But this was very extreme. Just because I have more melanin and am at less a risk for skin cancer is no excuse to treat me any different.

James slowly pats my back and consoles me as I hear soft gasps. It is too late for me to control the tears that are streaming down my cheeks. "Shhh...You're alright. I got you. I got you." The only thing I hate the most in this world is crying in front of anyone. I'd rather cry alone until all the fluid and my blood runs dry than shed a single tear in front of anyone. But here I am again, crying in public in James's arms. "You are the bravest person I know, Riya. Don't let anyone tell you otherwise." He caresses my head and his words make me feel consolidated.

"Can you take me to your place? Please?" I manage to speak between my sobs.

The drive home is a quiet one indeed. The boys don't even make those loud annoying loud breathing noises that I hate.

"You have to teach me how to throw a punch, Riya." Dan tries to lighten the mood as we walk into their house.

"Sure. It'll be $300 per hour."

"Done."

"Okay..." I was joking. But he wasn't. "Next Saturday. I'll teach you."

"I'll see you then." They all disperse into their rooms, leaving me and James in solitude.

He doesn't say anything. In a span of less than five hours we'd both cried in front of each other and embraced each other. "James I..."

"Yeah. You should get some rest. You can head to my room. I'll bring some ice for your cheek." He walks towards the kitchen. I was going to say I love you. I don't know why, but I feel that I need to tell him now more than ever.

I head upstairs and sink in his bed. James returns within the next two minutes with an ice pack. He places it gently on my cheek. "Does it hurt too much?"

"Just a little." I lie. I am scared that I've broken my jaw. But the ice pack definitely helps. The swelling and pain has subsided considerably. "James...This morning...What'd happened?" I just cannot stop myself from knowing who caused him pain.

His gaze stays on my jaw, as he takes a deep breath, fighting his inner demons. It is as if he is contemplating his entire life choices. I stay quiet. It is too late to back out from what I'd asked him.

Another deep breath and he starts talking. "I had gone home. Got into an argument with my father. Well, not an argument. But he found out that I knew everything. He didn't know before that I knew everything- about his affair all those years ago. And everything went cascading down from then on. I got angry and I…I accidentally stepped on my phone and that's why I couldn't call you back or reply to your messages. I'm sorry." The look on his face is defeated and I hate it more than anything. I hold his face in my hands until his deep ocean blue eyes pierce mine.

I press my lips onto his. "You didn't do anything wrong. Do you hear me? You didn't do anything wrong, James." I press my lips onto his again. "I…" say it. Say it.

"I love you." I finally say it and his eyes deepen further. The air between us thickens. And he goes silent. "You don't have to say it back…I just thought that you should know. You are loved. By me. Immensely. You deserve all the love there is in the world, James. Mine is just like a small pebble in the ocean."

"Enough to send unstoppable ripples through my heart. Because I fucking love you too, Riya." I think now would be a good time to stop the time forever. I want to be in this moment forever.

Knowing that I am loved by someone who I love and respect is the best feeling ever. If I wanted to expose my bare self to anyone, it'd be James. If I wanted to give someone the power to hurt me the most, it'd be James. If I wanted to give someone the power to make me the happiest, it'd be James. I want him to be my everyday.

"Riya…" The way my name rolls off his tongue sends shivers down my spine. "I don't want to hold back tonight."

"I don't want you to." That's all it takes for the fire within to consume us until we are nothing but perished to ashes.

"I want to go all the way, Raven." his raspy breathing turns me on even more and I can feel his words pool in my panties.

I look into his eyes with a smile.

"*I trust you with my heart, body and soul, James.*"

Chapter 26- James

I love you- I thought of these words arranged in this order to be the most trivial thing. Yet here I am, utterly consumed by them, but more than the words, consumed by her. Her scent envelopes me and drives me crazy every time she is close by, making me want to devour her. Disrespect her body in the most respectful way. I want to do things to her I'd only thought of. But more than that, I want to do everything with her.

She is the bravest person I know. The strongest woman I know. I respect her just as much as I love her and I love her more than I love even football. The comparison may seem trivial but trust me when I say, after my mother passed away, nothing except football and Riya have ever made me truly happy. I know it is a crappy comparison, but football saved my life. It saved me from drowning.

"I trust you with my heart, body and soul, James." She says and the thread holding me together finally snaps and I want nothing more than to bury myself inside her deep.

I crash my lips onto her and hold her hands behind her back. Her tongue slides over my lip and my cock presses hard against my jeans. Her soft moans and pleadings make me even more hungry for her.

"Fuck, Raven..." I groan as our breathing gets heavier and sweat beads over our bodies. It is mildly warm in my room. My mind goes back to the night we first met, when she passed out on my bed. She was mumbling in her sleep that she has never slept with the same man twice, so I didn't have "sex" with her, no matter how badly I wanted to. Because deep within I knew that I didn't want to do it just once, not with her.

I could spend an eternity with her and yet that would still not be enough time.

Her hands glide under my shirt, tracing up and down my abs. I slowly pull her shirt over her head and undo her bra. Her perky breasts fall beautifully, nipples, hard as rock and her neck flushed. She is the epitome of beauty for me. Of course she has the body which I worship, but she has a heart, which understands mine in a way no one does and that's what makes our every touch and every kiss so much intense.

I'd fall for this woman in every universe in every body and form.

"I want you to make me come on your fingers." And of course her filthy mouth. I love all of her.

"Your wish is my command, Raven." I am so hard that if I don't force myself right now, I can come from her words. I slowly slide off her pants and discover she is soaked. For me. I have never felt more pride in my entire life. I slide one finger inside her and a soft moan escapes from her mouth. Her cunt is the sweetest thing I have tasted. Her back arches as I slide another finger inside her and she moans considerably loud. I love a woman who is expressive, especially in bed. And I love the sounds she makes for me.

"Harder. Faster.... I'm...so...god...so... close." I arch my fingers inside her and rub her from inside while my mouth takes in one of her breasts. I tug her nipple between my teeth, knowing full well that it is exactly what will tip her closer to her orgasm. She pulls on my hair in a way that it hurts so good, her nails scar my back (war scars) and she comes so loudly screaming my name that you could hear her scream in fucking Egypt.

"That's my girl!" I crash my mouth onto hers and finally pull the fingers out of her. I pull back to suck on my slick fingers which were buried inside her and damn she tastes so sweet.

"I want to taste it." her eyes look at me with such heat that I am surprised that I am not burnt crisp yet. I crash my mouth on hers, giving her a taste of what she wanted.

"What do you want next, Raven?"

"I want to see you come apart for me." Her shy smile and her confident eyes are such a deadly combination that I am a goner. I unbutton myself, slowly, deliberately. "You are such a tease." She pushes me back and climbs on top of me. I flip her over and hold her hands above her head. I know she loves being thrown around as much as she loves taking charge.

"Where do you want me to come?" She looks down, all shy and brings her eyes back up to hold my gaze.

"Inside me." she bites her lip and I can't hold myself anymore.

"Good girl." I pull a condom from the side drawer of my bed and quickly take my jeans and boxer briefs off. I am too hard to care about teasing her anymore. All I know is I need to feel her from inside, once and for all. I slide the condom on and lower myself on her. She spreads her legs for me, giving me enough room to be able to dig deep within her. "Let me know if it is too much for you or if you want me to stop."

"Yes."

I slowly slide myself inside her. We don't need any lube because my Raven is literally dripping her slick on the bed. She gasps and hugs me tightly. Digging her nails in my back.

"Fuck...you are so tight." She feels like what I imagine heaven to feel like.

"You are so big. I always knew you'd be too big for me." A raspy laugh leaves my throat.

"You are my biggest ego booster, Raven. Now take it all like the good girl you are and come for me screaming my name until I see your legs shake." Her eyes enlarge and her lips curve into a smile. One thrust and I am completely inside her. Her eyes roll back and another loud moan escapes her mouth. This is my favourite site. I want to capture this image in my head for the rest of my life. I want to bottle this feeling and keep it with me at all times.

"Oh my god, right there! Yes! Harder." I slowly increase my pace and she digs her nails in my back so hard that it's probably bleeding, but that just turns me on even more.

I push myself as deep as I can go and feel her clenching around me. It takes everything in me to keep going. "I love you, Raven." I say as I bury my face in her neck. Her scent...it's so overwhelming!

She pants and moans as I thrust in her every time. "I'm...I..." her breathing becomes faster, harder and her body shakes as an orgasm soars through her, robbing her of her ability to form her words except for her screaming my name. But I know exactly what she was going to say. 'I'm having the best sex of my life'. Too cocky?

I am unable to hold myself anymore as I let my release shudder too with groans and pants. We both catch our breath and I peel the condom off and dispose of it in the trash can. I slide into bed under the covers and she lays her head on my arm. "I was saying that, I fucking love you too, Marcus." God, does that bring a huge smile on my face!

After making my sweet Raven come for the fifth time, our bodies are covered in sweat and bodily juices. But I am ready for round two. Just as I slide another condom on, Raven flips me over and props herself onto me. Her knees on either side of me. Her clit rubs off on my cock and it rushes blood to my groyne. I hold her hips and slide her onto me.

She hisses as she slides down my entire length and I am back in heaven. Her walls stretch around me and squeeze me at the same time. My breath becomes heavy and my vision clouds as everything narrows down to her.

"You take me so well." I manage to say. Her raspy laugh and her nails digging in my chest, hungers me. I buck my hips as I thrust deeper into her and she shudders, trying to adjust to the last few inches.

"All of it. You will take in every last inch. You are mine. All mine." My grip on her hips tightens and she starts moving by herself. Such a good girl. Her head falls back and I miss my favourite view.

"Eyes on me, Raven." Her soft moans tell me that she is nearing her release. I hold her hips in place and start thrusting into her. Hard and fast.

Her eyes stay on mine as they start tearing up and her mouth tugs into a smile which tells me that it is a smile of pleasure. Tears of pleasure. I hold myself from coming so soon. She needs to come first.

I feel the sweat trickle down my stomach and my back and my legs. I see sweat trickling down her body. I follow every drop as it makes its way from between her beautiful breasts and to her navel and down her beautiful body.

"Come apart for me, Sweetheart. One more time." Her nails digs in my pecs. "Let go for me, Riya."

"You are going to be the death of me, Marcus." she says as her walls squeeze me, so tight, making it impossible to hold my release anymore. Her body shivers on me and she falls on my chest and I quickly wrap my arms around her. I find my release at the same time as hers and it feels like my hunger has finally been satiated.

"Good job." I whisper in her ear and feel her raspy laugh against my neck.

"I love you." I tell her one more time. I cannot believe that I get to have this amazing woman all to myself!

I am the happiest person on this planet as I make my way down the stairs to make breakfast for Raven. Our activities last night went on till dawn and just as promised, I did make her legs shake and she can barely walk now. I had to help her get to the bathroom to brush her teeth. And she was blaming me when she was the one who couldn't keep her hands off me. I know...everybody wants a piece of this! But sorry ladies, not anymore. I'm reserved for a special someone for the rest of my life. Although, I am very proud of myself.

My streak of happiness is interrupted by a couple of black eyes in the kitchen. "What happened to you guys?" The smile from my face has not diminished even a bit.

George groans."Your energy could be contagious." He fills his cup with coffee and walks away.

"I can almost imagine him doing ballet in tights. He looks disgustingly happy." Dan groans and walks away from me.

"Why do they got their panties in a twist?" I ask Sid as I pour a cup of coffee for myself.

"Bruh! Riya didn't let us sleep a wink! Next time you guys want to bone, book yourself a room or book one for us!" Sid frustratingly walks away and yet I can't help but feel proud and happy about last night. The grumpies would get over it.

"I'm making breakfast." That's all it takes for the jocks to get over it and crowd around the table.

"Is Riya making it?" Sid asks me with a cute smile.

"No. She's...she can't...I'm making it." Some nasty looks passed around followed by some hooting and cheering praise for me because it was very obvious what happened. Riya is clearly not the silent type in bed or outside bed to be honest. "Scrambled eggs and pancakes?" I ask the lot.

Sid walks around to stand next to me. "Are you sure you don't need my help?"

"I can crack the eggs for you." I offer my help. "And make the batter for the pancakes."

"Yeah! That'll be of huge help. It's best for the house if you stay away from fire." Sid squishes me over towards the fridge. I open it to find everything neatly arranged. There's proper order and everything is so clean! I grab a dozen of the eggs and get cracking. After taking out 15 egg shells out of the bowl and straining the egg mixture twice the eggs were shell-free.

"Also, do you guys want to go to the gym later?" I ask everyone.

"You're leaving her alone in the house?" Dan asks me.

"No I meant, you guys! Do you guys want to go to the gym later?" I am not at all embarrassed to shoo the boys out of the house so that I can enjoy some alone time with my woman. Without any ears around! Let her be as loud as she wants to be.

"I see what's happening here..." George suspects my intentions, which I swear are not innocent whatsoever.

"I'm booking a room for myself for the weekend. If you fuckers want to crash." Dan taps away on his screen.

I whisk the eggs in the bowl. "We're not behemoths. You don't have to sleep outside." I try to act coy.

"And listen to all of that again?" Sid shudders besides me, making me roll my eyes. "We're staying at that fancy 5 star hotel, right Dan?" George asks Dan.

"It's the inn close to our school." Dan hates spending his piece of shit father's money. And I understand why. He works at the public school as a part-time assistant football coach. He likes to keep his pride and self respect as a human by at least paying for his basic necessities out of his own pocket.

"They have a pool! Woohoo!" George throws his arms in the air.

"It's snowing next week." I mention.

"What's your point?" George asks me.

"Nevermind. Don't forget to bring a chisel and hammer when swimming through the ice." I pass the whisked eggs to Sid and start making pancake batter.

Breakfast is made and I quickly grab two plates and make my way to the room. I'm halfway up the stairs when I turn back to ask the boys- "So, you all will be gone when we come down, right?"

"I will kill you if you do it in the living room." George shouts from behind as I close the bedroom door behind me. There is a weird fantasy of George, it changes every year.

Freshman year it was having sex in the closet. The coat closet in the living room- with the door open.

Sophomore year it was having sex on the porch outside which is very clearly visible from the kitchen and the living room. Thankfully our porch is on the back of the house with trees covering it from all sides, but I still don't understand it.

Junior year he started doing it in the living room. I'm scared for next year. I just hope Senior year he chooses to just do it in his room!

When I open my room door I find Riya in bed, scrolling on her phone. Her face lights up as soon as she sees me and it fills my heart with immense warmth.

I make my way to the bed and put the tray down. "Hot tea for ma'am!" I give her the black tea she'd ask for.

"Thank you so much, captain." My head jerks up to see her bite her lip knowing full well what she is doing to me.

"You are being a very very naughty girl, first thing in the morning. That won't do. I guess I'll have to give you a glimpse of yesterday." She chuckles.

"I would like that very much..." she leans closer to me and whispers in my ear, "...captain." If it wasn't for the hot tea that she was holding I would bend her over and spank her ass until she begged me to fuck her.

I take a deep breath and grasp control of my feelings again. "You need to eat. For what I am going to do to you next, you will need a lot of energy."

"Ooo! That sounds...*exciting.*" She stresses on the last part.

"You have a very filthy mouth, Raven." She bites her lip and takes a sip of her tea. I lean closer to her and kiss her lips. "And an even filthier mind. And I fucking love you for that." She moans as I deepen the kiss. I pull away just as it was getting hot and she growls. That's for teasing me.

We have breakfast and watch a movie together downstairs. Play cards, fuck, order in lunch, eat, fuck, play another movie, ignore the movie and fuck again until we are drained of our energy and order dinner while playing the new season of Demon Slayer. I pause the anime to go grab dinner and come back with plates and cutlery.

"Did you see the meme I just sent you?" she asks me.

"I broke my phone. I forgot to order a new one. Do you want to go with me to get a new one?" I sit next to her and hand her the plate.

"Or..." she puts her phone away too. "Maybe, we can both be off our phones and just..." she kisses me. "Spend time with each other and then we can buy you a new phone. How does that sound?"

"Perfect." I smile so hard, it reaches my eyes. No phone would mean peace. Not having to worry and take responsibility for once.

She stands in the doorway of the bathroom. "You should go. I need to wash my hair anyway. You have tangled it way too much for one wash with conditioner. I am going to have to apply the conditioner at least three times. I'll be done by the time you come back from the gym." Raven convinces me to go to the gym. It's been two days since I didn't go and we just saw George's story on Instagram in the gym. It was a boomerang of him, shirtless and sweaty, shaking his head in disappointment with the text that read, "When you get kicked out of your own house."

I am going to kill him when I see him. But clearly, the boys are at the gym. "Are you sure?" I ask her one more time.

"Yes, now go. I need to wash my hair. I'll be here when you come back." She kisses my lips.

"I don't have my phone, so if you need anything, anything at all, call Dan, okay?" I kiss her lips and then her forehead.

"You're such a cheeseball." she chuckles.

"And you still love me." I smirk.

"And I still love you, James. Maybe that's why I love you." she shrugs.

"God, I love you so much, *Raven*."

Chapter 27- Riya

I have successfully managed to detangle my hair and condition them twice. That is when I hear the doorbell ring. I wonder why the boys would ring the bell? Also, it has barely been 45 minutes since James left. I guess he could not stay away from me. God Ri! Snap out of it and open the door.

I put on the bathrobe and make my way down to open the door. The doorbell rings again and again. "Yes...I'm coming." I shout and finally open the door. I see no one when I open the door. No sign of the boys. That is until someone walks into me. Someone tiny.

"Are you lost?" I ask the little boy. He reminds me of someone I know. "Where's your parents?"

He doesn't say anything, just walks into the house. Ohk... I can totally deal with a kid breaking into James' house. "Umm... excuse me kid. What's your name? Are you lost? Do you know where your mom is?" He stops in his footsteps and sits on the couch as if he owns the place. Still saying nothing.

He reaches for something in his pocket and for the first time I am afraid of a kid. Of course, he can't possibly pull out a gun from his tiny pocket. I close the door and make my way towards him. He pulls out his phone and opens the notes app and starts typing. 'I am here to meet my brother.'

"Your brother? George?" Dan has a sister and Sid has an older brother and a younger sister. Although, I am not sure if George ever mentioned his younger brother.

The kid nods and starts typing again. 'Marcus.' And my heart stops. Marcus has a younger brother? He never mentioned that to me. Even when I looked him up on google, I didn't see any mention of his mom ever being pregnant after him. But nonetheless, he never told me. I told him about everything. I presented my life to him as an open book to read and yet he...He lied to me.

"Marcus? Marcus James Williams is your brother?" I ask the kid and he nods. "What is your name?" I ask the kid.

He starts typing again. "Caleb."

"Hello Caleb." I try to smile. "Do you know sign language?" I learned sign language in my last semester in Australia. I used to volunteer at a children's shelter and there were some kids who were either deaf or dumb. I'd learned sign language to communicate with them and it just kind of stuck around. I learned Australian sign language along with American sign language. Because, isn't learning languages super fun? I like the advantage of being able to converse in a language that no one in the room can understand. It's being secretive openly.

Caleb signs 'Yes' to me.

I sign to him to tell him that James isn't home. He just shrugs and stays in place.

He keeps looking around and that's when his stomach growls. I chuckle softly and ask him if he's hungry. He just nods to me. "Give me two minutes and I'll be back." I rush upstairs to put on James' clothes and come back down to find Caleb listening to classical music. "Caleb..." I call out to him. "How old are you?" I sign to him.

"5." He signs to me. He has awfully mature taste in...everything for a five year old. His suit and pants stun me. But it's the classical music that knocks my socks off. Since when do five year olds listen to classical music? He's so much different than James.

"Do you want to eat chocolate crepes? I will add whipped cream to it as well." His face lights up and he cheerfully walks towards the kitchen. Maybe he is still a kid at heart, as he should be. For heaven's sake, he's just five. "Do you want to help me make the crepes, Caleb?" I ask him. His smile widens and runs towards me. "Do you like bacon with maple syrup? James...Marcus once told me that they were your mom's favourite." His smile drops immediately.

Shit! Maybe I shouldn't have mentioned his mother. Then it strikes me...Caleb is five years old, James' mother died five years ago. James resents his father for all the cheating, but what if it was not just that? Oh my God! It might be just me overthinking, but what if James's mom was pregnant when she got into the accident? And...

"Mommy liked it?" Caleb asks me. He doesn't sign. He asks me with his mouth. He can talk?

I try to hide my surprise. I don't want to scare away the kid. "Yeah. Your brother told me that once."

"Did you know mommy? Can you tell her something for me?" Caleb signals me to bend down with his tiny little hands. I squat down, so that I can see eye to eye with him.

"Sure." I try to smile at his odd request.

This time he speaks. His voice is so adorable, contradictory to his words. "I want her to come back. She left because of me and daddy and Marcus are sad that she is gone. So can you ask her to come back?" The little kid's eyes welled up.

"Oh sweetheart. Your mommy didn't leave because of you." I take his tiny hands into mine. "Your mommy loved you so much." And he starts crying after I say that. I feel a weird pain in my heart for the kid. Did James and his dad never tell him that? For fuck's sake! He's five years old. A five year old should not be saying or even be thinking something like that.

He clutches onto my hands and tries to hold back his tears. "Can you tell me more about mommy?" He calms down a little and asks me to lift him up. I put him on the table while I make the batter for the crepes. I try to gather everything James has told me about his mother. We spoke a little about her this morning and a little during breakfast. That's when he told me that she used to like bacon with maple.

I dip the tip of my finger in the batter and smear it a little on his nose and he starts chuckling out of control. "She also liked classical music. Just like you." It is the most adorable laugh I have ever heard.

"Really?" he asks me.

I smile and nod to him. James hates listening to classical music, because it reminds me of his mother. Caleb smiles to himself. "Do you want to help me crack open the eggs?" I ask him.

He throws his hands in the air and squeaks with joy. I roll back his sleeves and help him crack open the eggs. We crack the first egg and then Caleb cracks the second one on his own and I clap for him and he chuckles in an adorable kid-ish way.

The crepes are ready in no time with Caleb's help. He is a cleanliness freak and asked me to clean up after every time I poured the batter. He is very cute nonetheless.

We are laughing about how Caleb knows everyone's secrets in school because they don't care when talking around him, because well...he doesn't speak to anyone. Which I still find really sad.

"So now Holly and Becca are both crazy about John." he summarises.

My eyes widened in disbelief that I am this invested in kindergarten drama. But it's the way he tells stories. I can't help it! "But he likes Lilah!" I gasp.

"Yes he does."

"Damn!" I bite my tongue. "I mean, Oh my God!" I quickly corrected myself.

Caleb chuckles and bangs his hand on his leg. A trait he has in common to his brother. "It's fine. I know most cuss words. Marcus taught me some."

Did he? "Well, saying cuss words is bad. Don't listen to him and don't use cuss words. You are just a kid. Kids don't cuss." He nods like an obedient child. "Do you want more crepes?"

"Can you add melted chocolate and rainbow sprinkles along with whipped cream, please?" He makes the puppy eyes, again...similar to his brother. He has brown eyes, unlike James, who inherited his mother's blue eyes. Does his father have brown eyes? I never noticed.

"Sure I can, Caleb." I smile at him and his face explodes with joy and I get a happy dance out of him. A little booty shaking and wiggling. "Do you like chocolate chips with yours?"

"Yessss..." He shouts. Dan hides chocolate chips in room because Sid once gave them a choice to choose between chocolate and chocolate chips and well...George and James collectively chose chocolate. Dan was not happy about it so he started hiding chocolate chips in his room. How do I know? He told me to help myself with some once when we were having waffles.

I make a few more crepes and melt some chocolate for the crepes while Caleb tells me all about the drama in kindergarten. He is very smart for his age and can read people so well. I know I shouldn't feed off kindergarten drama, but I can't help myself. It is just so good!

"I'm all done. Let me get the chocolate chips for you." I fold the crepes in quarters, add whipped cream on top, add two strawberries on it which makes Caleb very very happy and drizzle the chocolate on it. It looks spectacular.

I make my way to Dan's room to grab the chocolate chips when I hear the front door open and close and some chaos that follows.

"Raven!!! Time for round t–" I hear *James*.

Chapter 28- James

There are some things that I am very very protective over- my brother, my Raven and my personal space. And it seems like all three are in jeopardy.

When mom got into that accident all those years ago, she was pregnant. Mom and dad had decided to keep it under the covers this time and they were going to announce it at his last game. He always used to say that my brother was going to be his retirement gift to him from mom. We were all genuinely excited for my brother to be born.

Frankly, if I ever wanted a sibling, before I had one, I'd always wanted a little brother. I could teach him football like dad taught me. We'd go golfing with dad and to Tech fest with mom. I'd bully him and bully anyone else who bullied him. When I dreamed of having a brother I'd dreamed of us all vacationing in Hawaii- mom's favourite vacation spot.

"We can only save either of them." The doctors had informed us. "The mother or the child. The mother chose to save her son, but she still wanted to make sure that you two were on the same page." Even on deathbed, my mother thought about the man who had cheated on her while she was pregnant with his child. I was on the verge of throwing up.

"I–I–I–can't. How can I choose? Your fucking job is to safely deliver my child while keeping my wife alive. I will not choose. You will save them both, or else I suggest that you find some good lawyers." Dad said in a very calm voice which was more threatening than if he'd yelled.

The doctor starts to sweat. "I assure you that we are doing the best we can. But when your wife arrived at our hospital, she was already on the brink of death. The baby's heart is still strong, the odds are in his favour. The decision is you and your wife's. And she has chosen to save the baby. Again, we are trying to save both of them but she has lost a lot of blood, if the baby stays inside, you might lose them both." I zoned out after that. Nothing made sense to me. I looked at my father's face and I was shocked.

Tears. I saw tears flowing down his cheeks. Just thirty minutes ago, this man was lifting the Vince Lombardi trophy and now he is having to choose between having to save his wife or his unborn child. I felt sorry for my father. He must be feeling so helpless right now. I wish...I wish I'd gone with mom. I wish it was me instead of her who was lying on that bed.

"Save the child." My father was inaudible. Defeated.

I jumped onto him thinking I must've heard something wrong. "What? Dad...how can you–"

"Save the child!" My father said sternly now.

"Dad!" I shouted as I saw the doctors and everyone walk inside. "You are a fucking monster. I am not letting my mother die." I tried to run past him and he held my hand and stopped me.

"If I chose her over the baby, she would never forgive me and she would never forgive herself."

"Well...now she won't even be there to forgive you or herself." I raised my voice at my father for the first time in my entire life. "You are a selfish person. You only care about yourself. And you are doing this just because you want to have a clear conscience for yourself." Poison. I was spitting poison. And it consumed my father, because I saw it on his face.

He'd won the last game of his life, but he'd lost at the game of life that day. "I will never forgive you. Ever." I walked away from him.

I was so consumed by anger, frustration and pain that I never got to say goodbye to my mother. I don't know if my father did though.

I'd never felt that helpless after that because I never gave one thing so much power to make me feel helpless, until I did. Until I fell harder than ever for her. Until I loved her. And I ruined it all.

I'd just walked inside the house and was very pumped up for round two this morning. "Raven!!! Time for round t–" I spotted my brother sitting at the table. "Caleb?!" Panic triggered in my brain, was my father here? Why was he here? I was not ready to talk to him. I didn't want to even see him for now. I needed space. I needed air. Suddenly breathing became difficult.

"James...you're here." Riya appeared from the stairs. "James...are you okay?" her brows furrowed as she ran towards me. I was clearly having a panic attack.

"Where is my father?" I managed to ask her.

She helps me sit on the sofa and gets me some water. I focus on her hand on my back and then on my breathing. It's fine. I can breathe. Only after I've calmed down does she tell me. "He's not here. Your brother came here by himself...I think...he took a cab by himself."

My panic turned into anger. How irresponsible could my father be? He let Caleb out of the house, let alone take the fucking cab to my place? Caleb doesn't talk. It's not like he cannot talk, but he hasn't ever since he was three. After he spoke a couple of sentences, he never spoke again. Not to our father and not to me.

I sometimes wonder, if things would be different had mother still been alive. Had that accident not happened. Had I gone with her and it was me who died instead of her. I could've driven her. If only I had not gone to the game with my father despite knowing about his indiscretions.

"Ri...Ri...choco chips." Caleb called out for Riya from the table.

"Yes, darling. Just a minute." Riya's face is unreadable. It is as if she is mad at me, yet she feels pity for me.

"Hello, Emem." Caleb signs to me and smiles.

I hold her hand. A little too tight perhaps. "He talks to you?"

"Ouch, Marcus! That hurts." she winces.

"Sorry." I immediately let go of her arm. I didn't mean to hurt her in any way. I just am baffled by the fact that Caleb talks to her.

"Hi Caleb. What are you doing here?" I ask him verbally this time, hoping and praying that he will talk to me as well. I walk towards the table and sit in front of him. Riya sits next to him and sprinkles chocolate chips on his crepes.

"Thank you, Ri." he smiles at her. Completely ignoring my question.

"You're welcome. Caleb." she smiles at him and pokes his nose. And he laughs. HE LAUGHS! The last time I saw him laugh, was before he learned how to speak. When he was a baby. And a small nose poke from Riya was all it took for him to laugh?

"When did you come here Caleb? How did you come here and why did you come here?" I ask. My voice is tougher than before. His smile immediately fades away and he stares down at his plate of food.

Riya clears his throat and my gaze shifts to her. "He came twenty minutes ago. I called Dan a bunch of times too, but his call was going straight to voicemail. And he came here to meet you, Marcus. If you could be a little nice about it. He is *your brother* after all." Riya's eyes darken even more. It is clearly visible that she is mad at me.

"Riya, you don't know, but Caleb doesn't–"

"Caleb." she shifts her gaze back to him and smiles. He looks the same as he does back at home when me and dad argue. "Do you want to take your plate to Marcus' room and watch your cartoon while eating?" she asks him.

"He's not going anywhere but home this instance." I stand up from my chair. I love Riya and I know she is trying to help, but I will not tolerate anything when it comes to my brother. I will protect him with everything I have.

Caleb gets out of his chair and hugs Riya. Is my brother scared of me? No that can't be, right? I've done everything I can to protect him, to make him happy and yet he has never once smiled at me like the way he smiles at Riya. "Ri, I don't want to go home." she smiles back at him. It is so weird how she can smile at him yet glare at me at the same time.

"Don't worry. You can stay here for as long as you like." She caresses his head. "Why don't you go to Marcus' room and eat the crepes there?"

Caleb picked up his plate and started walking towards the stairs. Riya stays silent until she hears the door of my room close and then she gets up abruptly out of her chair.

"What is wrong with you?" She yells at me.

"What is wrong with me? What is wrong with you?" I shout back at her. "That is my brother, Riya! I will not–"

"Exactly James! That is your brother! A brother you never told me that you had!" She sits back down in her chair. Looking defeated. And then it strikes me. The only people who know about Caleb are my father and Daniel. I never got the courage to tell anyone else. I mean, how could I? I am ashamed of myself that I could not be the brother that he deserves.

"Riya...I...I was going to tell you but–"

She didn't even look me in the eye. "But you didn't. I trusted you with every little secret. And I am not saying that you didn't tell me anything at all, but when were you going to tell me that when your mother–" she takes a look at the stairs and lowers her voice. "That when your mother got into that accident all those years ago, she was pregnant with Caleb? I told you everything about my sister and you know how much family means to me yet you lied to me."

"I couldn't tell you because I am not a good brother." I shout. "I am not a good brother, Riya." I mellow my tone this time. "I could never tell him anything about our mother. I would yell in front of him. I would fight with my father in front of him. And I let him believe that he is alone. I..." my throat constricts. I have always thought these thoughts but I could never say them out loud. Not even to myself. Because if I did, I wouldn't be able to look myself in the eye.

Riya rushes to me and holds my face in her hands. "James...Your brother...you know him better than anyone. All he needs to hear or in fact all he has ever wanted to hear was that he is not alone. That his big brother will always be there for him." her hand caresses my face.

I blink off my tears. "I wasn't there when he needed me, Riya. I wasn't...I didn't tell him anything about her. I couldn't. I couldn't bring myself to talk about mom without breaking down before."

"James I know—"

"And when I saw him speak to you, laugh with you. I...I felt jealous. Envious. Rage. I need space. So back off!" Words spit out like hot fire from my mouth. She suddenly takes two steps back from me. I wish I could take them back. But it is too late. Am I jealous? Yes. Am I envious? Yes. Do I feel a little bit of anger? Yes. My brother said her name before mine. He refused to share his laughter with me. And he was laughing and talking to someone who he'd met not even an hour before. Water pools my eyes and I fall on my knees. "I'm sorry. I didn't mean it."

She keeps backing away from me. "No James...I got it. I heard you loud and clear." I could hear the lump in her throat reflect the pain in her words. She was holding back her tears.

"I feel pathetic." My words are barely audible. Even to me.

"It is not my fault that you chose to hide a huge part of your life from me and him and didn't fucking talk to him. I didn't do any magic on him or force him to talk to me. He just felt safe with me. It's sad that he felt safe with me within an hour, yet you couldn't do it in five years, just because you didn't have the balls to feel your pain and process it. Just because you were a coward your brother can't speak to anyone!" Her words stung like a bee stung an allergic person. I had gone into an anaphylactic shock. I couldn't believe what she was saying. I know I hurt her with my words, but if my words were a small cut, hers were bullet holes.

The next words that came out of my mouth were purely out of spite. I never meant them. And I never would either. Yet, I said them. "You have so much to say about me and my brother, huh? You are so brave when it comes to your sister then! You couldn't even tell her the fucking truth to her face! Well, if you had used your own fucking advice, maybe your sister wouldn't be such a bitch to you."

Her face is red, with anger, with pain, with embarrassment. Tears roll down her cheeks. And I did that to her.

You hurt me, I hurt you...

The reality of what I did to her hits me. No...What have I done? I screwed up big time!

"How... dare you...bring my sister...into this!" her voice breaks. "You fucking lied to me! You didn't even tell me that you had a brother to begin with! And yet you have the audacity to yell at me and make accusations? You know what? We're done. I'm done with you! I knew from the beginning that everything was a facade. The show you put on! It is my fault I fell for it. But don't worry, your every single word made it very clear to me where 'WE' stand!" She grabs her phone and walks towards the door.

I trust you with my heart, body and soul, James.

Her words keep echoing in my mind.

Stop her.

Don't let her go.

I freeze.

"I'm sorry..." I mumble, standing still. She doesn't even wait to hear those words.

I open the main door and run behind her.

"Ri...Ri..." Caleb comes running down.

I hear a tumbling noise and I run back to the stairs. "Caleb!" I shout. Fear set inside me at the sight of blood. Flashbacks of mother being wheeled into the ICU. *'We can only save one...'* I hated the sight of other people's blood after that. My hands start shivering. I grab the table cloth lying nearby and press it on his head. He is bleeding profusely.

I keep yelling out for Riya. And I hear the engine of her car start and she leaves. She drives away. I was going to ask her for help. I didn't have my phone on me either. I didn't get to buy a new phone.

"Where's your phone, Caleb?" I ask him. He points upstairs towards my room. Fuck! I need to apply pressure to his wound! Only if Riya could've fucking stopped for two seconds to listened to me. But no! She had to let her ego take over. Not that she was the only one in the wrong. I wasn't entirely honest with her. But if she had waited even ten seconds more to listen to me, she could've helped me with Caleb. If not the second chance, at least help me with Caleb.

I hear another car pull into the driveway immediately. Is she back? Thank God!

"Riya!!!" I shout, not moving an inch and keeping a constant pressure on Caleb's forehead. "Riya! I need your help. Run in here! Fast!" I shout again.

I hear heavy footsteps bang into the house. "M..." I hear Daniel's voice. George and Sid are right behind him.

"What happened?" Dan asks me as he helps me pick Caleb up and carry him towards the car.

"I just need to get Caleb to the hospital, right now."

George doesn't mutter a word. He gets in the car and drives us to the hospital.

INTERTWINED

We come back home after I drop Caleb back at home. He needed two stitches on his forehead and sprained his wrist falling down. Thankfully there was no internal bleeding and he should be fine within the next three weeks.

"Where was Riya?" Dan finally asks me. I don't want to think about it right now. This always happens to me. Just when my life is at my peak, I am forcefully knocked down. The game of life always has a point over me. Never letting me win!

"And why is she calling me?" Sid asks me. His screen displays Riya's name and her photo from Dan's father's ball. She is smiling in that picture. We had fun at that ball to be honest. Even if I don't want to admit it, I fell for that woman when I first laid my eyes on her at that party, I fell deeper for her at the ball and I have been a goner for her ever since. Only for us to end up like this.

I couldn't tell her about Caleb. And I admit that it was my lack of trust in her that I couldn't bring myself to tell her about Caleb. No, it wasn't my lack of trust in her, but maybe it was my lack of trust in myself. I was too ashamed of myself. She wasn't wrong when she said that I was a coward.

"M...she's wanting to talk to you..." Sid pulls me out of my thoughts.

"I can't talk to her...not like this! Not over a call. I need to see her in person and sort it all out."

"M...!" Sid shouts at me. "She cut the call before you could finish yo—" I realised that the call was on speakerphone.

I am up and out of the house with the keys in my hand before Sid can even finish the sentence. I don't know how much she heard, but I need to tell her. I need to tell her what I was going to say before, but couldn't.

I keep chanting the entire drive–

"I'm coming to you baby! Please hold on to us. There still exists a WE. And above all, I'm sorry, *my Raven.*"

Chapter 29- Riya

Life never throws just one punch. There's always the first one that you never see coming. And then there's the one you can feel is coming, and you even see it coming, but too late. And it's often that second punch that knocks you out. But if you are like me and you endure the second punch too, life will throw a rocking hard third punch which is a skull breaking punch. There is no escape from it. The first two punches might give you false hope that you might be able to handle the third one too. But nope. The third one knocked me out cold.

I come home shaking and crying while driving all the way. *He hurt me, I hurt him...*

Juju runs towards me when I enter the house. She probably heard my not so subtle sobs. "Ri... What happened? Why are you crying?" She wraps her arms around me.

"It's over..." I sob in her arms. "We...we're over. Just like that. I...I..." She hugs me tighter. "I had really fallen in love with him and he...he lied to me."

"What? Do you want me to break his bones?" I visibly see her nostrils flare.

I don't care about his bones, he broke my heart! This is exactly why I didn't ever want to fall in love. I feared the heartbreak that came along...But...I...I thought that we were different. I thought we were game!

I just keep sobbing, gasping for breath. "I know babe...I know..." she pats my head and rubs my back. "I know...Love conquers our deepest fears, but your deepest fear was love. I know!"

"I really loved him, Justine." I fall to the ground. Broken and frail.

The last time I'd dated a boy in freshman year of high school. We'd broken up because apparently I wasn't enough for him. Or maybe I was too much. It wasn't like I was head over heels in love with him. But I did love him. We were best friends for two years. He'd just transferred to our school. I was his first friend and he became my best friend.

'I really love you. Would you like to be more than friends?' he'd asked me. I had always loved Karthik as a friend. Correction-best friend. And when he confessed his feelings to me, it felt like I owed him the relationship. I did love him. I wasn't in love with him. But I loved him. And when he told me that 'He didn't want to continue this relationship with me because we would never work out in the future', I didn't just lose a partner, but I lost my best friend too.

'I never loved you anyway.' I'd told him. I was angry at him and I was hurt. I always say things I don't mean when I'm heartbroken. The truth is I did love him. Not deeply. But I liked spending time with him and holding his hand and hear him talk about his life. I loved that even after getting into a relationship, we still remained best friends. But when he told me that he never considered me his best friend, I was shattered. I regretted every word.

I started to feel guilty for hurting him so bad that I ignored the pain I'd felt. But he moved on. When I was stuck there for two years. I feared love after that. I feared that if someone I barely loved could break my heart so badly, what would happen if I found love that consumed me and that love broke my heart?

Well, I did find out.

It hurts like a bitch.

"I just want this pain to go away, Juju...I..." I gasp for air. "I can't bear the pain anymore!" I keep crying.

The only one who can soothe this pain is the cause of the pain itself.

When he'd called my name, I wanted to stop. I did stop for a split second, my legs had become so heavy as if I was pulling an entire car with my legs.

My heart wanted to stay and listen to him.

But my brain told me to have some self respect and leave. If only...If only I had listened to my heart. I don't know why but I feel regret. I feel guilt for some reason. I know that I said things I didn't mean, but he hurt me. He broke me in the worst way possible.

I trusted him. I hadn't trusted anyone in a long long time and yet, he gave me a reason to restore my fear of love again.

"Do you want some soup?" Justine asks me.

I pick myself up. "No, I'm sweating like a pig for some reason."

"Riya...I know you loved him and I don't know entirely what happened, but are you sure you don't want to give this another shot? Just know that I am here for you, no matter what, babe." She hugs me tighter. And I feel myself break more so.

My chest physically hurts from all the pain. My eyes feel dry. My nose is runny. And my emotions are all over the place.

"Thanks, Juju. I know that I can always count on you." I wipe my snot on her shirt.

She steps back and chuckles. "You need to shower."

"I already did." I tell her.

"With girly products. You need a bubble bath and champagne...or whiskey" she adds quickly. "Whatever you want." She rubs my shoulder and I am glad that I at least have her by my side. I don't know what I'd do without her.

I will dehydrate myself if I get in a tub. "I don't want a bubble bath, but the whiskey does sound good right now." I don't want to think about anything and I definitely don't want to feel anything but numb right now.

I walked towards our alcohol cabinet and grabbed the cheap whiskey. I want my head to hurt tomorrow. I want the worst hangover possible, then, I won't be able to think about anything else. Maybe then I will wake up tomorrow and think for a minute that this was all a bad dream. Maybe then I will forget that all this happened, even if it is for a minute.

"I'm gonna head to my room. I just need some time to myself and...maybe a cold shower."

"Wait!" Juju shouts from the back. I wipe my tears and look at her with confusion.

She runs towards me, it's just a few steps but she's already out of breath. She really needs to work out. "Jake is in your bathroom. I'd completely forgotten. For some reason, there's no hot water in my bathroom, so he's using your bathroom to clean up." I sigh. "Do you want some soup?" She asks me sheepishly.

"It's fine. I want to take a cold shower anyway. I'll use your bathroom and can you call the management and let them know?"

"Already did. They said they will send someone by four pm."

I take a big swig of whiskey and head to Juju's room. I strip in the bathroom and break down again. I take another big swig of the whiskey and pick myself up off the floor. I splash some water on my face to wake myself up from this dream. It has to be a dream. There's no world where James and I would hurt each other like that.

But we did.

An hour. That's all it took for him to throw me away. To throw *us* away.

I step into the shower and let the cold water wash over me. We were so happy not even two hours ago. I was consumed by my orgasm with his arms wrapped around me in his bed. Just when we had finally confessed our feelings...It feels like our story is over before it even began.

But I don't want it to be over.

I was happy. With him.

I am happy with him

Until you weren't...my inner voice whispers.

But fights happen with every couple.

But your's happened before you two could even call yourself a couple, she whispers back.

'Shut up!' I shout. I pick up the bottle of whiskey and take another swig.

I let the cold water wash away my thoughts, my memories that my inner voice was starting to taint. I washed off the taint. And when my teeth start to clatter, I step out of the shower.

I wrap a towel around my chest and walk out of the shower. I'm sure Juju has one of her robes lying around in her bedroom. I walk outside in her bedroom and I feel chills all over my body.

It must be from the cold shower, but Juju's room is hotter than the fucking Sahara desert. I feel another chill as I take another step.

I wipe my tears and drop my towel on the ground when I find her bathrobe. I quickly put it on and tie it around the waist. Jake was using my shower, so I cannot go in my room. I look around for my phone and it is inside the bathroom, on the floor, next to the pile of my clothes. James' clothes. I go inside the bathroom to pick up my phone to see if there was any message or anything, from James and—

Women have better sixth sense than men. It is not scientifically proven. Nonetheless, it is a fact.

We carry pepper spray when travelling anywhere, and hold onto keys or anything sharp when walking home at night. Hoping that we never have to use it. We try to prepare ourselves for going to a war when going out at night.

Make sure you never leave your drink unsupervised, don't take drinks from other people, and *never* drink to the point of passing out when out. Make sure your phone never dies, especially when you are alone. Keep a shortcut for dialling the emergency number. The list goes on and on for the things that girls and women do when they leave their house.

But nobody told me that all that preparation was necessary even when you are in your own sanctuary. Your own house.

I pick up my phone from the bathroom floor and I unlock it to see if I had any messages. That's when I get that ominous feeling again. I walk out of the bathroom into Juju's room and I hear it lock. My heart sinks. I have a murmuring feeling in my stomach and the urge to throw up.

"So...Justine told me that you finally let Williams fuck you." Jake stands in front of me in nothing but a towel wrapped around his waist. I can see the outline of his erect cock pushing against his towel. And his eyes are dark. Cold. The hair on the back of my neck twinges and I feel colder than before.

"What the fuck, Jake? You cannot talk to me like that and I most certainly don't have to tell you shit. I'm out of here." I walk towards the door but he holds my arms and pushes me back.

I hear loud music from outside. Break up songs, played at full volume on TV speakers. "Where do you think you are going?" He grins in an evil way. It is so loud that it makes it impossible to hear anything else in not just the living room, but the kitchen too. It is one of the reasons I bought that expensive speaker. Because whenever Jake stayed over, they would make enough noise to traumatise me for a lifetime. I got that speaker to drown them out.

I see the way his eyes scan me up and down. I've never felt so violated in my life. I feel dirty given the fact that I've just showered twice in the past hour. "Don't you fucking touch me, you piece of shit!" I walk past him and grab the handle of the door to unlock it. He wraps his arms around my waist and jerks me against his body.

"Let me go!" I try to wriggle out of his grip but to no avail. I gather all my strength and turn around and punch his face. He falls on the ground and I run towards the door.

He grabs my foot and pulls me back. My anklet digs into my ankle and it breaks off as he pulls me, causing me immense pain. It makes me lose my balance and fall on the ground.

"Juju!!!!" I shout at the top of my voice. "Justine!!!" I yell again. "Justine!!! Hel–" Jake pulls me by my feet and picks up the towel I'd used before and pressed it against my mouth. Tears flood my ears as I try to escape his grip. His knees hold my hands underneath him, immobilising me completely.

His nostrils flare in anger and his chest heaves with impatience. "I have held myself back way too long! I wanted to be the first one to fuck you, but you just had to be a whore. And then fucking Williams!" He clicks his tongue and shakes his head side to side slowly. In a villainous way. "Bad move, Riya." he lowers himself on me and drags his tongue across my neck and I have never felt more repulsed in my life. It feels like someone is hammering nails in my body wherever his tongue touches.

"Let me go!" My screams are muffled by the towel. He grabs my hands from under his knees and holds them above my head and locks my feet underneath his. "Please!" I beg Jake this time.

He chuckles hoarsely. His eyes narrow on my body as they scan me. "Well..if you are begging...I shall give you what you want, darling." His smile is ugly and vile. I freeze when he loosens his towel and I feel his cock against me. I wriggle. I wriggle hard, but his grip is too strong and he has completely immobilised me. I try my best to free myself from his clutch.

Screaming, shouting. Yelling. "Shhh...You are just making this more fun for me, darling." I am wearing nothing underneath the bathrobe. One tug and the bathrobe slides off my body along with my shame. I lie there naked, defeated, lost. Jake's eyes light up with lust at the sight of my body. I try to turn around to cover myself up. I try to hold the bathrobe between my legs, but he pulls it off as well.

His gaze travels up and down my body like I'm his prey and he's waiting to hunt me. "Let me clean Williams off of you." he forces and glides his tongue over my body. I have never found human touch so repulsive in my life. I keep screaming and yelling and wriggling and kicking, but nothing is working in my favour. I cannot just stay there and let him rape me.

Then it strikes me– Jake is raping me! My brain goes into panic mode. I start to move faster and with more force as I feel his hand reach between my legs.

I'd be wet if it was James who was touching me, because I know for a fact that James would never ever force himself, not just on me, but on anyone. But it is Jake's hands on my body, and his fingers inside me. I feel bile in my throat and pain between my legs. It is more painful than the first time I had sex, as he moves his fingers violently.

"Oh! You are so fucking tight!" Jake groans in my ear and sweat beads my forehead and tears burn my eyes, fear coats my heart and shame consumes my brain.

I cry this time and force my eyes shut. Maybe I won't feel this. Maybe this is just a nightmare. Maybe if I close my eyes tightly and think of something else, it will get rid of this vile feeling. But his hands on my stomach still linger there. I still feel them. This is not a nightmare. This is happening. "Now I know why Williams wanted to fuck you so many times…Oh! How my cock would love your pretty little cunt! It's so much better than Justine's." His words feel foul and repugnant.

I keep pleading him to let me go. I keep crying, but he doesn't budge. Seeing me fall apart only feeds his animalistic behaviour.

He holds himself at my entrance and just as he is about to insert himself inside me, we hear a knock on the door. I open my eyes and wriggle faster and harder and scream louder. "Juju!!!" The towel still muffles most of my screams. He presses the towel harder against my mouth. "Juju, help!" I keep screaming.

I hear the door unlock, Juju must've used the key to unlock the door. She is very claustrophobic and has a phobia of being accidentally locked inside her room so she hides her bedroom door key outside the door in the pot next to it. How very creative! I was reminded about the key everyday for a year, but never had to use it once. Crazy how she had to be the one to use it.

Everything after that happens in a matter of two seconds, just as Juju opens the door Jake flips me over. He does it so fast that I lose balance and my hands land on his chest as Justine walks in. The towel from my mouth falls on his mouth. I look up and Juju looks at us with shock. Tears stream down my cheeks and I get up and run towards her. I quickly tie my robe and hug her.

"Juju!!!" I sob.

Jake gets up and quickly wraps his towel around him. "Justine..."

"What the fuck was going on over here..." Justine whispers loudly. Switching her gaze between me and Jake. Then our attires. Jake's expression changes so fast that I am scared. Not even a minute ago he was grinning evilly and now his expression matches mine.

"Juju...he...he..." I cannot bring myself to comprehend what had just happened, let alone form sentences. "He...Tried to..." I sob again. I cannot form sentences. I cannot believe what was happening to me.

"Will someone fucking tell me what the fuck was going on here?" Justine screams and I flinch. I had already gone into panic mode.

I started replaying everything that had just happened and I get stuck on one part over and over again.

I face Justine. "You told him?" I ask Juju. My voice is barely audible, but she hears it.

I see her nostrils flare. "You don't get to ask questions here. You tell me Ri. What were you doing sitting on top of Jake, naked!" Her tone is harsh and accusatory.

She broke her promise again. She'd promised me that she wouldn't tell Jake anything about me and James again. "Did you tell him about me and *James*?"

Chapter 30- Riya

"You dare ask me that when I just found you fucking my boyfriend!" Juju snaps at me. She starts shaking and shivering. Jake rushes and wraps his arms around her. How dare he act innocent? How dare he touch another woman after what he tried to do to me? After what he *did* to me.

I finally snap and push him away from her. "You want the truth? Here's the truth, Justine! Your boyfriend tried to–"

"She forced herself on me." Jake stuns me again. "You saw it too, right babe? She was sitting on top of me and she had muffled my mouth with the towel and she–" he looks away, acting as if he is in pain. He wipes his non-existent tears.

I feel my breathing constrict and get shallow with every passing second. Until I realise that I am not breathing at all. "He's lying, Juju." I say softly that nobody hears it. Then I scream. "He is the one who tried to rape me." I wrap my hands around myself and let the tears stream free.

"Riya!" Justine shouts and takes two steps away from me. "Jake would never do something like that. And rape? Don't you dare use such words for him. He could never!" She defends him and my last thread snaps. Now I will set everything ablaze.

"So you will believe that I forced myself on him? Me? He is fucking stronger than me. For fucks sake! Get your head together and think! How could I overpower him, get him hard and fuck him at the same time? I was in the fucking shower and I–"

"She was drinking." Jake leaves to go to the bathroom and returns with the whiskey bottle. "She was drunk. I didn't know that she was taking a shower in here and when I came in here she told me that she needed me to keep her company and she started to undo her robe and…and…" he acts traumatised. It makes my blood boil even more. He is not the victim here. He is the perpetrator!

"She started stradling my thigh and when I tried to escape and…" He looks away blinking his eyes and I cannot believe the show he is putting on right now! "She fucking punched me." he tilts his head to show her his cheek that I had punched. Perhaps not strong enough. "You yourself have seen how strong her punches are!"

This piece of shit!!! He should be writing a fucking book or a should audition for a TV show. "I couldn't hit her back. You know I don't hit women, right?" Justine walks towards Jake and hugs him and caresses his now swollen cheek. I am crushed in the worst way possible today. "When I fell to the ground, she climbed on top of me, locked my arms and legs under her knees and stuffed the towel in my face and tried to…but thank god baby! Thank god that you barged in at the right time! You saved me." Jake flashes me an evil smile as Justine hugs him tighter. Why can't she see the devil behind that face? That smile said everything. It told me that I lost.

But I am not giving up. Not so soon. "Are you done with your crap story? Because I am going to call the cops on you and report you. I am not letting a rapist walk free." I don't have the energy to explain anything to Justine. I shouldn't have to explain anything to her. She is supposed to support me.

"Juju…" I walk towards her and try to shake her out of her trance of love. He has trapped her. I can't let her date a rapist. I just can't. "Juju…he's lying to you babe. Look at me." I force her face towards me. "He came inside the room and locked it and when I tried to leave he said stuff about James and I lost it. Yet, out of respect for you, I just tried to leave. But then he grabbed me from behind and that's when I punched him. He pulled me and tried to…" I couldn't tell her what exactly happened. "Please Juju, you have to trust me. You–"

"Leave." She says quietly enough for me to hear it. But I thought I must've misheard.

I keep on telling her what had happened, "When you twisted the key to open the door that's when he–"

"Leave!" She shouts this time.

"Juju..."

"It's Justine for you." She cannot even look me in the eye anymore.

"So you want to choose a fucking rapist over your best friend then?" I raise my voice at her for the first time.

"Please..." She exhales painfully. She turns her face to look back at him and he quickly changes his expression from the smug grin to being sad and hurt.

"You don't even have the balls to say what he is? A rapist! Well, since you have made it pretty clear where we stand. Then I will see you in court." I say out of venge. But I meant every word of it. By hook or by crook, I will have Jake punished.

"The court?" Jake asks as his eyes widen and the fear is evident on his face.

I take a step towards him, wiping the tears off my face. And I see him flinch slightly. "You chose the wrong bitch to take advantage of, fucker. I will make sure that your ass rots in jail for the rest of your pathetic life. And trust me when I say that I will make it my life's mission to make sure that it happens. And not even your little bitch can save you from that." I grab my phone and waltz out of the room.

I walk in my room and lock the door behind me. I lock all the windows and close all the blinds too and I run into the bathroom and empty my stomach. After I've emptied the breakfast, the vile feeling doesn't creep out of me. Instead it seeps deep into my bones until I am repulsed by my own reflection. I dry heave in the toilet bowl as the nauseating feeling doesn't fade.

I don't know what to do. Even Justine turned against me. I...The one person who I told me that she was going to be there for me no matter what. I jump into the shower and grab the loofah and start to rub it over my body. I soon realise that Jake had used my bathroom, what if he used the loofah too? I immediately throw it away and scratch my body where I'd used the loofah. I cannot let even a single cell of that man remain on me.

I scratch and scratch my body to the point where I can see small red dots appearing on my skin. I am bleeding everywhere he has touched me. The sensation of his fingers inside me repulsed me. And I run to the toilet and throw up again.

I cannot breathe, I take shallow and fast breaths but it feels like the air is not flowing into my lungs. My head feels dizzy. I try to take deep breaths but I feel my body shaking and shivering. I pull my knees closer to my chest and try to concentrate on my heartbeat. This is probably one of the worst panic attacks I've had. I sleep on the bathroom floor unable to breathe, shaking, broken, used, tainted.

Dark thoughts keep creeping in my mind. Pain. I need physical pain to distract me from the emotional pain I am feeling. I need to escape the whirlwind of emotions I am caught in. Even if that escape is for a split second. I need to escape. I desperately need an escape. I am feeling everything yet I am numb. I need to feel something else. I take the stone exfoliator and I bash it on my left hand. Pain. I finally feel it. A distraction.

Excruciating pain. I think I might've broken my bone. But at least it distracted me. Mission accomplished?

I step out of the bathroom and dry myself and put on fresh clothes. Full clothes that cover my entire body. My loose turtleneck hoodie and loose flared jeans. I start packing my suitcase. I cannot stay here anymore. I will lose myself if I do.

I pack all my essentials. And I will hire someone to move the rest of my stuff. But I am never stepping foot in this apartment again. I text the landlord as well and let him know that I am moving out by next week and that I don't know what Justine was going to do.

I take two deep breaths and then one more. "You can do this." I clutch onto my Louis Vuitton bag and close the door behind me. I make sure to lock it and take the keys to my door with me.

I drag my suitcase down the stairs and walk by the kitchen towards the main door. "You're seriously leaving?" Justine gives me a nasty look. I don't take off my sunglasses at all because I don't want her to see that I was crying. She and I were through the minute she chose her rapist boyfriend over me.

"Yeah Justine. I'm like seriously leaving." I say in a taunting tone. "Because I like...seriously got raped by your boyfriend." I continued with the tone. I still can't believe that all of that just happened to me.

She puts down her mug of what must be coffee with cream and sugar. She has one every morning, then one in the afternoon and one in the evening. Her brows furrow in worry and there is sympathy on her face so contradictory to her words and her behaviour. "Riya, I've always seen how you act around Jake. I've had my doubts about your intentions towards him for a long time now." Just when I think that I am at my lowest, God proves me wrong yet again. I feel her hand shake on my shoulder and maybe it is in my imagination, but I feel her pat my shoulder slightly as I feel her hand linger a second too long.

My tears make everything hazy. Tears of anger and betrayal. "Then all I can say is that you are fucking blind and the worst friend ever! You two deserve each other. Oh and also, I am moving out by next week."

"You can't just get up and leave!" Justine yells again. Her expression changes so fast that I am surprised.

"Watch me." I smile through my tears that I hide behind my sunglasses as I walk away. It is starting to get dark outside as the Spring sun is setting and it is cold.

I pack my suitcase in my car and just sit in the car. I have no energy or will left to go to the police station and file the complaint about everything that has happened. I will have to live through it all again and I cannot do it. Not right now. I look up hotels nearby that I can crash at and then it hits me. I had lost my wallet. Shit! I had cancelled all my cards and haven't received any cards. I am also a stupid person who doesn't keep any cash saved for emergencies. Shit! I check my backup purse to see if I have any cash whatsoever left in my purse.

Twenty-one dollars. That's all I have. Tears stream down my cheeks. Way to kick a person when she's down! If I had to choose one day which has been the worst day of my life, it has to be today. I rest my head on the steering wheel and cry. I cry my heart out. I cry through the sunset and I cry through the moonrise. I cry to the point of dehydration and I have no more tears left. But the pain doesn't subside. I cannot stay here like this for the entire night. I need to leave, what if Jake comes down here?

I dial the first person I can trust who would be able to help me.

"Siddharth?" I sniffle.

"Hey, is everything okay?" He asks me.

"Is...Ja– Marcus there?"

"He is here..." he must've moved closer to the boys because their voices are more audible now.

"M...she's wanting to talk to you..." Siddharth must've told him before he picked up my call because he didn't mention my name to him.

"I can't talk to her right now, not li–" I immediately cut the call. I don't want to listen any further. I cannot listen to any of it. Not anymore. I cannot hurt myself listening to whatever Marcus was going to say after that.

This time I laugh. Uncontrollably. Like a lunatic. Like I've finally lost it and gone crazy and perhaps I have...who knows? Life is laughing in my face right now, so I am going to laugh back in life's face. I lost. I lost everything today. I might've even lost a part of myself.

No! I will never lose myself. I am the only person I can trust! I tell myself out loud, once and for all. I just need to find a place to park my car where I won't be kicked out.

I dial another number that I never thought that I would call.

"Hello?" he picks up on the first ring.

"Cole?"

His voice is very loud at first. He probably must have company. "Riya! This is very unexpected. What's up?"

"I know it might sound very weird but is it okay if I just park my car in your parking area for tonight?"

"Is everything okay?" He asks me softly this time.

My voice breaks and I don't lie to him. There is no point in lying anymore. "No. Nothing is okay. But I just...Nevermind it was stupid of me to call you like that. Goodnight Cole."

"Riya! Wait. Wait. Wait. Don't hang up" he rushes. "I am sending you the location of my house. You can park your car here." my phone pings immediately after with a message from Cole. It is the location of his house. Not too far. It is a twenty minute drive from my place. I gather myself and start my car.

I am about to press on the accelerator when I see a black jeep pull up in the parking lot. I don't need to wait for the person to get out of the car to know who it is. The little chipped paint just above the headlight, was from when I was trying to park his car. I'd offered to pay for it immediately, but he said no.

He doesn't even bother turning off his car before he jumps out and runs towards mine. I feel myself wanting to run into his arms and cry. Maybe he is here to tell me that this entire day didn't happen.

I can't talk to her right now. That's what he'd said. Before even listening to what I had to say. He...He broke me.

He knocks on my window and I don't look at him. "Open the door, Raven. I want to talk to you. I need to talk to you." he begs. But I can neither drive off nor unlock the door and throw myself in his arms. I refuse to even look in his direction. "Please Raven." His voice is still soft. "Riya." he says and it twists the knife in my heart.

I roll down the window. Still refusing to meet his eyes. Because I know the second I look in his eyes, I will break down again. And I am too broken to be broken more. I feel ashamed and used and more than that, I feel defiled. Defiled by Jake's hands and his...

"I'm sorry." His voice is sincere. "I'm sorry Raven. Please. At least look at me. Please...Riya. Just one time." I can hear his soft gasps. He is crying.

"Jam–Marcus...Please. I...Please don't do this. Not today. I feel disgusted today. Please just let me be. Just for today. Please." I try my best to hold back my tears, keeping my eyes straight ahead.

"I made you...I..." he mumbles something under his breath. He wipes his tears. "The bags! Are you going somewhere?" He asks me.

"It doesn't concern you anymore. Goodbye James." I say as I finally drive off. One last look. I get one last look of him in my side mirror. He falls to his knees, holding his head in his hands. Crying. And all I keep saying is, "Hold onto us. You are my biggest weakness, yet you are my biggest strength, *James.*"

Chapter 31- James

I made her feel disgusted. I broke her...I broke us...It's all my fault. I feel the cold breeze swift by, setting my face ablaze. The tears on my cheeks freeze. And I am alone. Once again.

I see her car disappear on the road. My feet stay still. Holding onto the hope that maybe she will come back. Give me one more chance. Give us one more chance.

As a quarterback, I have never used the concept of holding onto hope. In the game, you write your own destiny. The game moves according to the strategy you have. One wrong move and everything goes down the drain. Even then, I have never even thought of anything like 'hope'. Because there is no point in holding onto hope if someone or me doesn't go ahead and snatch that ball.

Control. That is what I have had in games. Sometimes you choose to give it up. Strategy. But here, there is nothing I can do. Nothing. She couldn't even look me in the eye anymore. That said more than enough for our relationship. I walk towards my car and get in. Just before I was about to pull out of her parking lot, I see the lights of her apartment flicker.

Why did she have a suitcase with her? And she looked like she'd cried right until I showed up. Her eyes were swollen red. Was she crying because of me?

Something wasn't adding up. Even if she was crying because of me, why was she going out with her suitcase? She has an exam tomorrow, so clearly she's not going on a last minute vacation. And even if she is, she would go with Justine. Every cell in my body is telling me to go upstairs and talk to Justine. But I am scared that she might throw boiling water at me for breaking her best friend's heart.

I can text her. Ugh! I need to buy a fucking phone. I refuse to act on my instinct since that didn't get me anywhere last time and drive to the closest Apple store.

I drive back home and put my sim card inside the new phone and start it. Thankfully my paranoia had me back up all my contacts on my account. So as soon as I log in, I go to Justine's contact and send her a message.

Hi.

At least the message is sent. So, she hasn't blocked me yet!

Five minutes later- Nothing. No response from her. I go to my call logs and see missed calls from the most unexpected person. *Harriet.* I would rather die than call him back. But something was not adding up here. He'd called me right after I'd left to see Riya and then again before I'd reached her place. He was the last person on this planet who I'd call, let alone text. But I do anyway.

He picks up after the second ring, "Marcus..." his voice is more jolly than ever.

"This better be important Harriet. I'm not in the fucking mood right now." I really am not. He clears his throat. Dragging the silence. Building my anticipation. "Now would be a better time to speak, Harriet. Or else I'm—"

"Riya is here."

"What the fuck are you saying?" My blood boils. "If this is another one of your games, Harriet. I swear to god I will put you six feet under the ground myself." I am too emotionally disturbed by everything right now. And him saying even her name, is making me vengeful. He needs to keep her out of our shit.

"This is not a game, Williams. She'd called me to ask if she could park her car in my parking lot. That's all. And she…" he takes a long breath.

"Spit it."

"She was crying when she called me. Look, I don't know what happened between you two, but I thought that I should let you know that I told her to come to my place." I realised that I was probably not at my lowest before. Because this right here, twists the knife further, cutting off my air supply.

"She'd lost her wallet…" It clicks. She had told me and I'd joked that finally she would let me pay for dinner now. She was looking for a place to crash. That's why she had called Sid. That explains the suitcase. But the question remains. Why?

"What?...She's pulling up in my driveway. Look man, no rivalry here. She's your girl…or was. Whatever the thing, I thought that I should let you know. And my job ends here as your friend. Now I am going to tend to her as her friend." and with that the fucker hangs up on me.

What the hell was going on? What has happened between the time that Riya left from my place until the last I saw her? Because something has happened for sure. And I need to know.

I call Riya and as I expected she doesn't pick up my call. She said that she'd felt disgusted. Was it really me who made her feel disgusted? Ugh! My brain is chewing me up. All these thoughts. They are drawing the worst conclusions possible. Thoughts I fear. What if something bad happened to her after she left my house?

What if she had gotten into an accident? But her car looked fine. What if she was mugged? But she had already lost her wallet. Maybe she got into a fight with Justine? But what happened that made her leave her house? What if she was…?

No! No. I don't even want to think about it. No. I'm sure that she'd gotten into a fight with Justine. That's all. Yes. That's all.

If she doesn't want to pick up my call, I will go and ask her in person. I just need to make sure that she's okay. I grab my keys and am about to jump in my jeep before her words echoed in my mind.

Please just let me be. Just for today. Please.

I have never felt so conflicted in my life before. I am torn between wanting to respect her wishes and needing to make sure that she is okay. Her wants are more important than my needs. For me at least. So I lock my jeep and go back inside in agony.

Right now I wouldn't mind selling my soul to the devil if that means that I get to know that she is safe. *My Raven.*

Chapter 32- Riya

Cole didn't ask me any questions. He didn't force me to go and stay inside his house. I quivered in the night, not from the cold but from the nightmares. I wake up at dawn from another nightmare and drive to college at 7 in the morning. I don't even bother telling Cole that I am leaving, because when I wake up, his car is gone. Early morning gym, I guess. I am grateful that he let me stay here.

I have an exam for which I haven't studied at all. I write enough to pass the exam and I leave. While exiting the class, I bump into someone accidentally. Okay fine, I didn't bump into her accidentally. I walked all the way to the other side of the campus to find her. I wanted to talk to her. One last time. When she wasn't around that piece of shit.

"Justine...We need to talk." I approach her with good intent. She couldn't have forgotten years of friendship in one night. Could she?

She crosses her arms and looks in the distance. "If you are here to apologise about last night, I am all ears." Her expressions don't match her words. It almost feels like she cannot look me in the eye. As if she's...but her words are the venom that sucks the life out of me.

"Excuse me?" Apologising? For what? My blood is boiling. I was here to reconcile our friendship, and she dares to ask me to apologise?

So I change my mind. "I am here to tell you that I am going to file that complaint against your rapist boyfriend." That is not at all why I came here to talk to her. I wanted her to be by my side. I need my best friend.

"Don't you–" she looks around to see if people heard us. "If you do that, I will have to tell the cops that you are making this all up and that Jake was with me when all that happened." her words do not falter. Unlike my entire life. Which is breaking apart. Piece by piece. I am in utter disbelief and hurt beyond I can imagine. "Alright. Thank you for being the best friend I needed." I say sarcastically. "I was also here to tell you that I cancelled that trip to Cabo." It was my 21st birthday this weekend and my dad had bought both of us a trip to Cabo to have fun. I had been looking forward to that trip so eagerly, but I cancelled it last night.

It was the first thing I did. Thankfully dad had selected the refundable option, so I was refunded the entire amount for the trip. How could I go and have fun when all of this had happened? How could I pretend that I was happy when I wasn't? I didn't want to pretend. I couldn't anymore.

"Alright then." She has tears in her eyes. She looks at my bandaged hand from yesterday that I had injured myself as she walks away. Just like that. I stand still. Watching life pass by.

"Riya?" I feel a hand on my shoulder and I flinch. Scared. "Are you alright?" those ocean blue eyes stare into my soul. "Raven, if there is anything–" I don't hear anything past Raven before I run in his arms and hide myself from the world. I don't say anything. And he doesn't either. He just holds me there tightly. Tears stream down my cheeks and my sobs get louder. Pulling more and more attention.

"Raven..." his voice stings in my heart like poison. Numbing my heart even more. Yet, making me feel. Feel something. Anything. Proving that I am still alive and all of that happened.

"I...I can't hold it in anymore. Please...Help me." *Help me.* Those are probably the bravest words I have ever said in my entire life.

When I take two steps back and assess his face, I notice that we have similar dark circles under our eyes. "What happened, Riya?" I wipe my tears and try to be strong. I need support. I can't do this alone. If I am going to go through with this. I need a lot of support.

"Will you help me?"

His eyes mellow and concern is all over his face. Yes. I am asking my ex to help me to put the man who sexually assaulted me behind the bars. "With my life," he replies. We clearly still loved each other, but if he is going to help me we need to keep those feelings aside and work together.

"Thank you. I will text you— wait you don't have..."

"I do." he waves his phone. "I bought it last night."

"Alright. I will text you the place and time to meet. I have some important stuff to deal with right now. And then I will–"

"Whenever you want. I will be there. You could call me to the deepest pits of hell to help you and I would still come." My heart softens a bit. But I cannot let it waver just like that. It was broken once and I cannot give him the power to break it again.

"Well, right now it feels like I am stuck in a place worse than that. But thank you." I force a smile.

"Why do you need so much money?" my sister shouts again.

"I told you I wanted to buy a new Chanel bag." I lie to her. I have found a new place to move into. It is a spacious one bedroom kitchen apartment. Not too far from school. Better area, better security. The only problem was they wanted my bank statement to show that I have more than enough money to move in immediately. I have enough to pay the security deposit and rent. And after getting the security deposit for my previous apartment, I will have more than enough. I even got my refund back for the trip, so all I need is a couple more grand in my bank and that will seal the lease.

"Ri..." she takes a long long pause. "Alright. I am sending you the money."

"I will send it back to you as soon as I get my new cards." If I had my card, I could easily transfer money from one bank to another.

My bank account has been locked since the transaction frauds. And I had to call the bank to let them know that this transaction was going to be made by me. Losing my wallet cost me a lot.

"I also have something to tell you." she shies off.

"What is it?" I ask her.

"I am sorry. For that day. I know I shouldn't have—"

"It's alright." We never apologised to each other. And I know that she was acting out of character because of the issues between her and Keith. She probably took out her frustration on me. I know my sister. I know how much she loves me.

"That's not all..." another long pause which makes me feel nauseous. If Keith had something to her, I would smack him straight across his face this time. "He proposed to me...and I said yes!" She squeals as she tells me the last part.

"What? When did this happen?" I felt bad for being left out of her life.

"Last week. He even asked me if he could help me in any way with setting up the company. And he has been acting so differently. It's like he finally understands and respects my dream. And I can't tell you how happy I have been these days. Oh Riya! If only you could see my face right now. It's hurting from me smiling too much." she sniffles.

"I'm very happy for you." I really am. All I ever wanted for her is her true happiness. And if Keith has somehow gotten his brains polished enough to see the potential my sister and her clothing line has, then that's all I want. "Congratulations!"

"You should come here. We will go out and celebrate! You, me and Keith. I promise you, this time will be different." she promises. I'm sure it will be.

"I can't. I'm going to Cabo this weekend. Remember?" I lie. I cannot bring myself to tell her about everything that is going on in my life. Especially not right now when she is so happy in her life.

"Oh right! Have fun with Justine!" She cheers for me. And I try to sound just as cheerful and hide my sobs.

"I will. And how's the company doing? I saw some designs on Instagram and I loved them!" She finally worked and released some of her designs and people were going crazy over some of them. I knew that she could do it.

"Oh my God! We already have so many people reaching out to see more of our designs. I have some models lined up as well. And can you believe that they approached me? I am flabbergasted. It feels too good to be true." Under normal circumstances II would immediately reciprocate the same energy! But I'm just too exhausted to do it.

We talk for some more time and finally end the call on a good note. I feel like the worst sister not being able to tell her what was going on in my life. I just don't want to rob her of her happiness. And along with that, I myself don't know what I am going to do with this matter. I was going to talk to Jam- Marcus about it and ask his advice. Well, I wasn't going to tell him the entire thing, just enough to know what happened. Because I don't want James to end up in jail for murder.

I sign the lease and can move in the next day, so I have to find another parking spot to crash for one more day. But I will deal with that later. I want to meet Marcus before sunset and sort everything later. I text him the time and place and he responds almost immediately with a 'Yes'.

We meet at the least popular cafe in the area because that ensures that there is no one around. Although the coffee there is the worst, that is Marcus' problem because I am not much of a coffee drinker anyway.

"Hey...I could've picked a better coffee spot. But I'm not complaining." He says too fast. I had picked the booth farthest from the counter so that no one would be able to hear us.

I flash him a forced smile and he does the same. He takes a seat in front of me, takes off his jacket and adjusts his legs and my gaze travels to the part where his T-shirt is too tight on him. His pecs and arms are screaming and threatening to tear out of his shirt, but now is not the time to focus on that.

He orders an iced coffee in the chilling weather and we both wait in silence for it to arrive before I start.

"So...What did you need my help with?" he asks me, getting straight to the point.

"Yesterday..."

"Riya...About that, I am very sor–"

"I am not here to talk about us." I am rude. I know I am. Because I can see the hurt in his eyes but he quickly sweeps it away.

"Alright..."

"Yesterday when I left home. Something happened." His face stays blank. As if he knew that something had happened.

"What happened?"

"Before you came and before I had called Siddharth, something had happened." I clench my bandaged fist as I force myself to recall the horror. He rests his hand on mine, to console me. And I feel a lump in my throat. I see his eye fixated on my bandaged hand.

"What happened, Riya?" He is serious too now, yet I can see concern in his eyes. And something else as well. Fear? Perhaps.

"I had gone home and I had to use Justine's shower and I was sad and drinking and when I came out, I felt weird. And..."

"And?" his voice was almost a whisper of fear.

"Jake..." I see him clench his fist as soon as I say his name. "Jake came into the room and he tried to..." my voice is barely audible, but he still heard me. He could hear my soul crying, yearning for consolation.

"Tried to or..." he immediately put two and two together. I had never doubted his ability to read my mind. Not never. Because he couldn't read my mind yesterday.

A soft sob escapes my throat as I stare at my feet. Praying that my tears don't fail me by falling down. "He did...But he..."

He rushes over to my side and wraps his arms around me. It is as if I can feel the world melt around us into nothing until it was just us. Safe. I finally feel safe.

"Raven..." This time there was anger in his voice. Vengeance. "I want you to tell me in detail what happened. Don't skip out on anything."

"Marcus I can't relive it. Please don't ask me to do that." I would rather pour melting lava down my throat than relive even a second of that incident.

"I need to know how much of a painful death that fucker deserves." I hold onto his arm, my hand barely being able to grasp onto his entire bicep.

"Please James...You won't do anything stupid. That is not why I asked for your help."

"I can't help you if I don't know what happened entirely. Please Raven. Tell me."

A gasp does escape my throat this time along with some tears. A gasp of his name. "James..."

Chapter 33- James

This is my hell. As soon as his name leaves her lips, I know that my worst fears came true. I can feel anger I've never felt before. I have never had the urge to kill someone so badly before. But I don't want to just kill him. I want him to suffer. I want to break every single bone in his body. I want him to beg me for the mercy of death.

I knew what I was asking her to do when I asked her to tell me every single detail. But I needed to know. I needed to decide how to make him suffer. She tells me every tiny detail. Every word that had left his mouth. And after she finishes telling me everything, I immediately wrap my arms around her.

I myself am in tears. He did that to her because of me. All of this happened because of me. If only I had told everything about Caleb, maybe we wouldn't have fought and she wouldn't have left. Maybe if I had apologised a little early and stopped her. I let her walk away from me. If only...if only...if only... It is all my fault.

"I'm sorry Riya! I am so so sorry babe. I..." loud sobs escaped my throat. Guilt consumes my soul.

"James..." she wriggles out of my embrace and holds my face in her hands. "If it is anyone's fault it is his. He is the only one who should have to apologise. Not you. Not anyone else. Only him. And I will never ever forgive him or Justine for this. I thought that at least she would understand"

"Did you ask her to–"

"She told me that she would testify against me." She looks down at her hands in disappointment. With that, my heart withers away. She went through all of that in less than a span of 12 hours and yet she is still standing tall. I feel ashamed of myself as I feel my legs quiver. I can't even fathom the fact that what is making my entire body tremble with fear just by listening to it, she had to live it.

"I'm sorry, Riya. I..." I start crying as I feel the dam of my tears overflow. "I am so sorry that you had to go through that and I am sorry for the role I played in it." Guilt. Shame. Regret. I am feeling the worst of the worst things. But I know that she must be feeling even more grim. I don't want to burden her with my emotions as well. I would rather help carry some of her baggage right now.

"I am not saying that what you did or said is justified. But I wasn't entirely right or kind either. And I just don't want to think about any of that. Ever. I just..." she sighs. Ever? Were we done forever? No! She asked for your help, James! Focus on that right now. Please don't be selfish here.

"What do you need help with? I wouldn't mind going to jail for murder." I am not joking. What would be a joke would be me just sitting idly and doing nothing to Jake. Not breaking a single bone in his body.

"Marcus...I need your help with finding a good private detective." My brain starts to churn up some ideas as to where she was going with this. And every single one screamed trouble. Trouble for her.

"I will not let you put yourself in harm's way. Let me handle this." She stands up immediately and in anger.

"I didn't ask you to take over or make decisions for me. I asked for your support. That's all I meant by wanting your help." I have been hearing words for the past half hour but I have barely registered anything.

She walks past me and towards the front door. I can't let her walk away this time. I grab my jacket and run behind her and hold onto her hand. "Please, give me some time to register it."

She looks at me with two sparkly tears. Her nose flushed red as she quickly swiped her hand across her face to wipe her tears. "I was the one who went through it. You think I had the time to 'register it'?" She walks out of the door again. As I stand there I watch her take every step away from me.

She asked for my help and all I could think was how I didn't have enough time to process information. I was selfish again. I underestimated her again.

"I'm sorry." I stand in front of her, gasping for breath. The cold evening air fills up my lungs. She looks at me with her big and beautiful brown eyes which I get sucked into like a quicksand. Her gaze melts my heart. "I'll find a good detective for you. But Rav– Riya let me help you. No, let me be there with you. Let me be something you can lean on. That's all I want to do. I know you are capable of doing anything you put your mind to. I am not doubting your ability here. I am just asking you to let me be there with you if not for you."

She sucks in a sharp breath. "Why do you think I meant by 'Please help me?'" a faint smile appeared on her lips. It is the faintest smile, but I'd take it. I will take everything over her tears.

I walk through my front door and immediately get a whiff of chilli. So much so that I start coughing. "Turn on the exhaust!" I cough towards the kitchen. I see George with a mask on, goggles, spatula and his camera. He has been very much into being a social media influencer since last week. He'd gained ten thousand followers in the past month itself. And I wouldn't be surprised if he knew all those ten thousand people.

The smoke fills up the entire house and soon enough the fire alarm goes off.

"Shit." George quickly puts away his phone.

I hear loud thuds through the smoke and soon enough more white smog is sprayed onto my face. The sprinklers go off and there is nothing but pure chaos around me and inside me. Sid comes to the rescue with a fire extinguisher. "I am never leaving you fuckers all free in the house ever again. I'm gonna start chaining you to your beds."

George is quick to follow up on my insult. "Kinky. But sorry M, I'm not into you."

Asshole.

"I'm going upstairs. You guys better clean this up before I come down." I shoot one cold glare at George. "And I am not kidding this time." He opens his mouth to say something but I shut him up. "Keep it to yourself. Not today, George." I walk up the stairs. I can hear the fire extinguisher go up in the air, meaning Sid was probably concerned and knows that something serious has happened. And boy is he right!

I flop on my bed and just then, my phone rings. "I don't really like hearing your voice so much."

"The feeling is mutual, Williams. Unfortunately, I don't want you to think that I am hitting on your girl or something. She asked me that herself." He is obviously trying to play games here. A game I hate the most.

"Spit it out now, Hariett." My blood boils.

"She asked me to meet her and had a huge favour to ask. I am standing outside the restaurant that she asked me to meet. I did ask her if you know that she's contacting me, but she told me not to tell you anything."

"Text me the address."

"Okay. Bye." And he cut the call. I almost have the urge to throw away my phone. But no! Last time my phone wasn't working a lot of shit happened. I thought I was the only one who she trusted and asked for help. And out of all the people that she asked help for, why did it have to be Hariett? Why? I know that I did say a lot of things that I didn't mean, which nonetheless hurt her. But it wasn't just me who said hurtful stuff. Ugh!

Frustration. The inability of having zero control over anything frustrated me. I have often felt this way when playing. I remember when back in high school, we were playing against Teresa High School and their defence was so good that we were unable to do anything. Their middle linebacker- Torris Becker was scouted by the Blackhawks immediately after he graduated High School. I feel like I am back in that game. The game is Riya who I desperately want to win over and Hariett is Torris Becker.

The only problem here is that we lost that game. And I don't want to lose my Raven. Under any circumstances. I am willing to do whatever it takes.

A few phone calls and I had already arranged a private meeting for her with the private investigator. He is one of the best. And trust me when I say that I had to crush and throw away my ego entirely to make this arrangement.

I dial another number and wait for the person to pick up the call.

"Riya..."

Chapter 34- Riya

I knew that hiring a private investigator wouldn't be enough. I need some security. At least for my peace of mind. I called Daniel to ask his father a favour but he redirected me in a very interesting direction.

"Cole. Thanks for coming here." I invited him to the Italian place near his place.

He is dressed casually. Denim jacket and jeans with a white tee. Classic. "No problem."

He takes a seat in front of me. I am more nervous than ever. I don't feel even 1% of this nervousness with James. Marcus. Because obviously, I trust him and more than that, I knew that we still– No. Don't go there.

"So..." Cole takes a sip of his water. "What was the favour?" He flashes me an uncomfortable smile. Telling me that he isn't feeling any different.

"Let's order food first."

Twenty minutes later–

I have exhausted every topic from my small talk jar. Cole is the worst at small talk. That I'm sure of now.

He gets straight to the point and I am wondering why I keep straying off the topic. Maybe because he will ask me 'Why?'. And I'm not sure if I will want to answer. "I've eaten well. Now will you tell me what favor do you need? Is it really that bad? Do you need to take care of a body?" I see his big gulp travel through his throat as his adam's apple bobbed.

"Well..." Just ask him already! It's not like I am not going to pay! I am just asking for a simple service request... "You got one part of it down."

"What?!" Cole sprouts out of his seat. Scared.

I recalculate my words and what he had said before and quickly realise my mistake. "No. No. No. No. Not like that. Please sit down." I look around and there are a lot of eyes on us now. Stupid Cole. I'm sure Marcus would never react like this.

What?! How did he come into all of this? Clear your head Riya!

Cole calms down and sits down. His entire attention is on me.

Now is the time to spit it out, but I don't know why I'm hesitating so much. I didn't feel any of this when asking for help from Marcus. Maybe because I didn't feel like I was burdening him or as if I didn't have a right to ask him. But with Cole...

"I need security. Could you ask your brother?" I blurt it out.

"What?" Did I say it too fast?

"I said that I need to hire a bodyguard and I heard that your brother, well your step brother works in a security firm and he could help me." I explain properly.

I am unable to read his face. I am not sure if he is angry or disappointed or both. "I heard you clearly I meant to ask how did you know all of this? And why do you need a bodyguard? Is everything okay Riya?"

I don't bring Dan into the conversation, given how he and Marcus are best friends and Marcus and Cole have a history. That's a pond I'm never going to dip my toe in. And I already have enough on my plate. "I just want to know if you will be able to help me or not. I just need a bodyguard for a few months. Just let me know if it is possible for you to do it or not Cole." I don't want to beat around the bush anymore. Now that the cat is out of the hat, it is time to be straightforward.

He hesitates a bit. "I know you don't get along with your brother that–"

"Half brother." he corrects quickly.

Maybe this was a bad idea. "Half brother...that well. I'm sorry. I shouldn't have bothered you with any of this. I will find someone else. Sorry for wasting your time." I get up to leave. There is no point in pushing him. I don't want Cole to do something that makes him uncomfortable.

"I'll do it." Cole takes his jacket and puts it around me. "I'll talk to my brother."

"Thank you so much. It means a lot to–"

"Only if you tell me what is going on." He completes. There is no way in hell that I am telling Cole what has happened. At least not until I process it myself.

I take off his jacket and give it back to him. "I guess that means that I will have to find someone else to do the job then. Thank you for your time, Cole." I walk out of the restaurant without any regrets or having nothing to look back to.

"Riya...Wait..." Cole calls my name as he is out of breath. "I'll do it. I'll talk to Quaso. I'll see what I can do. You don't need to tell me anything." He wraps a cashmere scarf around my neck. I'd completely forgotten to grab that on my way out.

"Thank you Cole."

A wide smile stretches across his face. "At least let me drive you home then."

"It's fine I drove here anyway." *And I don't have a home anymore.* I almost tell him. But there is no need for him to know those details.

If you keep the heater of the car turned on the entire night, the car runs out of battery. I learned that the hard way. Halfway through the night, the battery died and I slept through the cold in the parking lot of my new apartment. Thankfully there were almost no passersby and the parking spot for 402 is in the corner, secluded from others. Sorry 402 for taking your parking spot and thank you for not having a car or being out of town.

The move into my apartment was a smooth one. But more than half of my stuff was still at my old place. I'd already called Sid and Daniel to help me get it and they are on their way to my apartment right now. I get my battery recharged and drive back to that nightmare of a house. I pull up near the entrance with my empty car to load up my stuff and I see a black Jeep parked right ahead of me. No one inside.

My blood pressure shoots up and panic sets in. I run up the stairs without caring to close my car door or waiting for the elevator.

I was right. Blood. There is blood on the couch, the kitchen top, James's knuckles and Jake's face. I run towards them and pull James away from Jake. Broken nose and probably a broken jaw and definitely a broken arm and those fingers...his right hand is completely shattered. "No. James! Let him go! James. Baby, look at me." His eyes are not the usual mellow and calm. They scare me to my core. It's like a storm in the ocean. Dangerous. As if it could swallow everything within.

James gets away from him and hugs me. I can feel his heartbeat. Mine still beats faster than his. I take one more look at his face and his eyes melt. If I were wearing my Taylor Swift glasses I'd be able to see the hearts in his eyes. "Please don't hurt yourself anymore...Please." My voice breaks. And now when I look at him, there are tears in my eyes which I'm not scared of letting go. As long as he holds me, I'll be fine.

"Didn't think that you would weasel your way back into this house like a slut." Jake huffs. And I immediately tighten my arms around James. Because if I don't hold him back, he will kill Jake. And

I am not exaggerating whatsoever. "A snake can shed its skin, but it's still a snake." Jake's evil laugh prickles my ears.

"That's what you got wrong Jake." I wipe my tears and face my worst fear. Jake. Eye to eye. "I'm a porcupine. You picked me up thinking that I was cute, now you will see how I will dunk my quills into you. Now I will show you what real torture is." Jake looks battered up. His face is swollen and purple already and his nose looks disfigured.

Jake takes two steps closer to me and before I can even blink, James is standing in front of me. "I guess that wasn't enough of a lesson for you, huh bastard? If you even dare to breathe the same air as her, I will fucking kill you. And I'm sure that by now you know how capable I am of doing that." James holds my hand and leads me out of the house. I don't say anything. I simply follow his lead.

He walks me to my car and finally stops. "You stay here, we'll go get the stuff. Sid and Daniel are on their way here anyway." I can't help but caress his cheek.

There's a small cut on his lip. I bet that stings. A small bruise on his cheek, which is darker than the colour of his eyes. My eyes fill up again. "Don't cry for me Riya. I don't even deserve your tears." He pushes my hands off his face and walks away. Leaving me confused again. Did I do something wrong? Did I say something wrong again? I thought we were past this. I thought that we could again...

Sid and Daniel are here in the next two minutes. They don't ask me a lot of questions either, except for what furniture they need to pick up. I give them a list and within 2 hours, I have all of my stuff packed in three cars. I go to take one last look but I stop outside the main door. I can't go in there. And I cannot believe that I am leaving Justine with a rapist. Don't worry Justine, I will unmask him in front of you.

When I come downstairs, the black jeep is gone. I walk towards my car and find a note with a number and a name. It's James' handwriting. Must be the P.I. I told him to look into it. But he could've given this information to me himself. "Are you ready to roll?" Daniel loads up the last of my designer bags and closes my car door.

"Yeah." I shove the note into my bag and get in my car.

The boys unload all of my stuff into the new apartment. And I see Daniel checking out all the rooms and windows. "Okay...creepy Daniel! What are you looking for?"

He opens and closes the window several times. "There are no locks on the windows. And your door has only one lock. There is also no proper lock on the bathroom and the lock on your bedroom is pretty loose too." I did not notice that all, because I was sold on the security in the building. Facial recognition cameras, no one allowed inside without my permission and residence privacy.

"Okay Mr Bodyguard." I taunt him. Since when does he care about all that?

"I'll be right back." Daniel rushes out without hearing another word and I hear Sid crash on the couch. I almost thought that he broke it. "It's not broken." he shouts from the living room as if he read my mind. I lock the door as Daniel leaves and head to the living room.

I nudge Sid, poking him, urging him to get up. He lets out an annoyed sigh and stands up. I walk towards the kitchen ahead of him. "You're helping me arrange the plates." I start unboxing everything. He saunters into the kitchen groaning again.

"You have two plates." he picks up the plates. "And they are paper plates." he tosses them towards me. An annoying frown appears on my face.

My patience snaps when he picks up the paper plates and throws them in the trash can. "Why would you do that?" I shout at him. He is taken aback by my sudden change in behaviour. I shock myself too. I rarely snap like this. He quickly takes out the plates out of the trashcan and places them in front of me. Both of them had small holes in the middle that I hadn't noticed. "I'm sorry. I didn't mean to shout at you like that." I mellow my tone.

His hand finds my shoulder and gently taps it as if to console me. Console me of the pain he doesn't even know about. "Is everything alright, Riya?" He asks me after a minute or two of silence.

I ponder over who to tell and how much to tell. Of course Sid is someone I trust, he is like a brother to me. "No." I managed to say.

"You can tell me whenever you think you're ready." There's a faint smile on his face and I am glad that he chose to give me space. We unpack the rest of the stuff in silence and about twenty minutes later, the bell rings. Chills run through my body as I am back in Justine's room. Jake on top of me and Justine knocking on the door. If she had knocked even a second late, I know Jake would have forced himself inside me. One second. I was saved by that one second.

"I'll get that." Sid scooches past me and opens the door for Daniel. There is a huge plastic bag in his hand. He empties it on the kitchen island. There are locks and screws and screwdrivers. So many of them.

"What is all that?" I ask him.

He looks at me with a guilty face. I know that expression very well. It is the same expression James used to have when he did something that he didn't want to do but was forced to do. "Did he put you up for this?" I ask Dan.

"What?" Dan screeches in a high pitched voice which was high enough to compete with Ariana Grande.

"Where is he?" Dan's eyes wander around as fast as a bullet train. "Is he downstairs?" I walk towards the window and peep outside to see if I can spot his car. He is standing outside his car in the cold. There was a sudden temperature drop yesterday night! And he's without a jacket.

I rush outside the door and down the stairs not giving a damn about the elevator or stopping to listen to what Daniel had to say. He's staring at his shoes and then back up at my window.

"Marcus!" I shout from a distance. His head immediately jerks up. And I see a slight smile on his face. Or maybe I just imagined that.

I rush downstairs and run towards him and we meet halfway through. "What are you doing here?" I ask him. Stupid question. I realise.

"Daniel said he needed help." Lies. I can tell that he's clearly lying because he pouts his mouth and does not look me in the eye.

I take a deep breath, contemplating whether I should say the next words or not. But I say them anyway. "I want us to be on one team, Marcus. I don't want there to be this much awkwardness between us if you are going to help me. And..." I am tired of repeating the same thing again and again. "I want you to tell me. If something I do or say bothers you, I want you to tell me right there."

His eyes meet mine and there is an innocence in them. "Why did you meet Cole yesterday?" That was not what I was expecting at all.

"How'd you know?" he does not answer and goes back to staring at his feet that he kicks slightly in the ground. "I was looking to hire security." His brows furrow and he finally looks at me and there is concern on his face. "It was for my peace of mind. So, I reached out to Daniel and he told me that Cole's brother–half-brother works in that field and could help me out." A deep sense of relief washes over his face.

"You could've–"

"I know. But you have already helped me a lot. In ways you don't know. Even with the PI. I didn't want to be a burden on you. Now that I don't have any right on you. Now that there is no...us." I dared not to look in his eyes after saying that, but I feel the chills of disappointment coming from him. It isn't the sudden spring cold, it is a wave of sheer disappointment.

He holds my hands in his and I still cannot look into his eyes. His hands warm mine and his gentleness warms my heart. "Even if there is no us, you have every right on me. Because...even if you..." I feel the lump in his throat.

He grabs my hands and gives them a soft gentle squeeze. It feels so good. So warm. "Even if you ever fall out of love with me, you are it for me, Riya. I love you. I always have and always will. And I ask you only one thing in return, not your love, but your hardships. You keep all of your happiness and let me help you carry the hardships." It was that easy to break me now-a-days. Because as soon as his warm words reach my brain and are configured by my heart, I am already crying.

And among those sobs, I kept saying three words, "Thank you...Thank you James." Not Marcus. *James*...

Chapter 35- Riya

It has been three weeks since my last meeting with the PI and he asked me to give him a month before he gave me some concrete information. He'd only ever contacted me once before and asked me to hire security. For reasons that he would explain altogether. Luckily, Cole's half brother hooked me up with a great security company. My bodyguard- Ian, was so discreet that sometimes even I wondered if he was there or not.

I had zero plans for my birthday. None. Whatsoever. That was until Dan, Sid and George crashed at my place with beer and whiskey. When I told them that I had no intention of partying, they told me that all we were going to do was drink in silence and get hammered. And we did. Get hammered. So hammered that I called James 57 times and yelled at him for not coming to meet me or giving me any gift of any sort. I did regret all of it the next day, but a guilt ridden Dan got up from the carpet of my living room and gave me the box of jewellery that James had bought for me.

I was dissociated after that week and isolated myself so much that even when my parents had called me and had asked me about my strange behaviour tons of times but I couldn't muster up the courage to tell them what had happened to me. I felt...ashamed. Knowing well that it was I who was wronged. Still, ashamed.

I'd just lied to them that the stress of the senior year was getting to me and that I wanted to be left alone. And it had hurt me just as deeply as it'd hurt them that I shunned them out. They'd even asked Maura to check up on me. She was on her way to come and meet me in person and it took an hour of convincing to get her to turn her car around and go back. She was finally happy with Keith and things were starting to look good for her. If she came here, it would just pull her down.

I would have to tell everyone eventually. But not now. Not until I obtain substantial proof.

I did file a police complaint against Jake for sexual assault. I'd opened myself. I'd become vulnerable. But the complaint was resolved mysteriously and the police officer in charge had quit his job and moved to some unknown place with his entire family.

The reality itself was so disturbing that I knew that there is something about Jake that I should be scared of. There is something that I need to uncover. Something that might require balls to face.

"I didn't know that you could master that drawing. It took you...an entire 43 seconds to draw it this time." The girl sitting next to me peeps into my tablet. I had drawn four mountains, the sun between the valley in the middle and a river flowing through the middle. A house next to the river and four trees next to the house. Three birds in the sky and two clouds. That was probably the 80th time I was drawing that same thing. It somehow soothed me.

"Hey...I'm not judging." She quickly backed her statement after my silence. "The drawings are pretty and this journalism class is hella boring. So, I get it." She smiles wide at me.

I just look at her confusingly. This girl–woman is probably the most beautiful woman I have seen. Slender yet slightly curvy figure and a face carved to shy Aphrodite. High cheekbones and sharp jawline. Very full lips, cat eyes and the longest natural lashes I'd ever seen on a woman. "Sorry, I didn't tell you my name. I'm Jamilah." she offers up her hand. And her warm chestnut complexion highlighted her features even more.

I give her a faint smile and shake her hand. "Riya." I say.

"Sorry Riya, I'm very chatty. I usually just talk to myself on the camera. And when I try to have a conversation with a real human, I just start babbling." she goes on and I cannot help but smile. I was like that before I went too silent. She smiles back at me and then it clicks me

"Are you jams_skincare?" I remember George was once raving about a skin care routine and bought almost all of the skin care products after watching her video.

She flashes me her teeth, telling me that maybe getting recognized is not something she is comfortable with. "Yeah...that's me!"

"No wonder you have such amazing skin!" We both break out into a big laugh and get attention and a 'throat clearing' from our Professor.

"Silence. Ladies." We both looked at each other and suppressed a smile. Thankfully, class is over in the next fifteen minutes after the Professor had to run out for a cheese emergency!

"I hope her diarrhea never ends!" I shrug and Jamilah breaks out into a huge laugh. I cannot help but stare at her as she laughs in a way that I have seen models do.

"Sorry, but have I been living under a rock? Because why haven't we met before?" she taps my shoulder. Did I mention that she is very friendly and easy to talk to as well?

My stomach gurgles as soon as we make it out of the hall. And Jamilah turned to look at me, giving me an innocent and lonely look. "You want to grab lunch together?" I ask her. And she does those small jumps in excitement which somehow make me happy from within. It makes me feel that I am not alone. That I have a friend. I didn't realise until now how much I was yearning for a friend. A female friend.

"I'd love to!" Her face lights up with genuine happiness.

We walk to a nearby Thai restaurant and order food for ourselves. "So, what are you studying?" I ask her first.

"I'm majoring in Poli Sci since I want to go to Law School after this. But people don't really assume that I'd want to be a lawyer or that I have the potential. Everyone around me just presumes that I will always be an influencer." There is a moment of silence as she swirls around her glass of water. I cannot stop myself from admiring her long, slender fingers. Gold rings in her ring and index fingers.

She finally looks at me, after the silence prolonged and gives me a smile that reaches her eyes, but is clearly fake. I wonder how many times she had to do that. Smile when all she wanted to do was cry. "Don't get me wrong...I love being an influencer. It pays my rent and my tuition and for all the stuff I have. But..." A gulp.

"Is it easy to smile like that?" I voice my thoughts. Her eyes immediately caught mine and the smile from her face waned. As if I'd caught her lie.

"I'll admit it. You are the first one to be able to catch my lie." She ponders over what to say. So unlike her usual self that I'd met half an hour ago.

I understood how uncomfortable I must have made her. Maybe now she doesn't want to be friends with me. "I'm sorry. I shouldn't have..."

"It takes one to know one." She looks at me with a smile again. A real smile. A painful smile. "I suppose..." she took another sip of her water. My eyes water up and I felt a strange pang in my chest.

As if I am ousted.

As if my facade is finally recognized.

I thought I had been very good at hiding it. I thought I was able to bury my emotions. That no one but my pillow and my blanket knew the horrors that I relived every night when I'd wake up covered in sweat and tears, panting, gasping for breath. As I'd imagined Jake crawling on top of me...trying to...I felt dirty and rubbed my body excessively with a loofah. That was my every night routine, unless I was drunk and passed out. I have scabs all over my body from trying to get rid of that feeling of being touched in a way that repulsed me.

"I'm sorry." she says as she just watches me stare down at my feet. Sweat clings to my back as I feel it trickle down. Goosebumps on my entire body and all the color from my face fades.

I never thought I would be able to talk about it, but somehow I feel ready now. Ready to tell someone. Anyone. "I was almost raped. Three weeks ago. By my best friend's boyfriend." I have zero thoughts in my mind but my mouth isn't able to stop from spilling my darkest secrets. "I was saved because of her, not by her. And after all that, her boyfriend claimed that it was me who forced myself on him and she believed it." I finally stop and I don't dare to look up and see her reaction. Pity. I know it is going to be a pitiful look. It has to be.

A hand caresses my sweat drenched cold palms. I flick my tear filled eyes up to her and another smile. She is smiling! But it isn't a happy smile. It is...She is angry. She doesn't pity me. She looks vengeful. "Thank you for sharing it with me." She gets out of her seat and doesn't let go of my hand.

"Where are you going? The food isn't even here...Unless..." She doesn't want to be friends with someone like me. "It's alright." I smile at her. "I can understand."

She growls silently. "I wish I could slap some sense into you right now." she finally drops her inviting smile. "You don't understand anything. Just because she was your 'best friend'" she does the air quotes. "Does not mean that you can let her trample all over you." she tightens her grip on my clammy hand. "And we are going to chop that man's no....he's not even a human. We are going to chop that reptile's dick off." She says sternly.

"I think calling him a reptile is an insult to reptiles." I finally get to hear her genuine laugh. She sits back down and keeps her attention on me. Her laugh fades and she keeps her gaze on me. Waiting.

I am not sure how much I'm supposed to tell a stranger who I'd just met 30 minutes ago, but her eyes twinkle as she holds my hands in her. "If you ever need anything. Anything at all, I want you to call me." She pulls out her phone and gives it to me. I type in my number and save the contact with my name.

She gives me a missed call and I quickly save her number as well. "And if you ever need my professional help..." she smiles at me. "I have a 100% discount code especially for friends." I smile wider.

I doubt I would ever need a lawyer or even publishing regarding this case, the last thing I want is for everyone to know what happened. But I really appreciate her thought and offer.

We discussed how our Journalism Professor should have been used in war as a weapon, because she would put everyone to sleep and compared her to Jigglypuff from Pokémon over lunch. And when I bid her goodbye, I felt like I finally now have a friend. Someone who will have my back, no matter what. We made plans to meet over the weekend for a coffee date and Jamilah suggested that we go to a pottery class after that.

I get home and change into my PJs and my phone beeps.

A message from *James*.

Chapter 36- James

Have you ever jumped into a pond thinking that it must not be that deep, but when you dunk your head inside to see how deep it goes, you cannot even see where the light disappears?

Fear settled in my nerves when I'd received the report from the Private Investigator. Who said that he was dropping off the report with me because the information it contained would put the reader in danger. I'd urged him not to give the report to Riya. I read his report along with his note that he was going into hiding for a few months.

I could feel the bile rise in my stomach as I read his report and by the time I'd finished it, I had emptied my lunch in the toilet bowl. The first thing I did was text Riya.

You need to come to my place ASAP.

I immediately call Justine. Her call goes straight to voicemail. I try again, it rings this time, but she doesn't pick up. I try one more time and she answers. "What do you want, Marcus?" She sounds annoyed. But I don't give two fucks about that right now. I have to make sure that she is safe.

"Where are you right now?" I ask her. My concern for her is genuine. Despite what she had done to Riya. I would never let a woman suffer like that. It would be inhumane to not check up on her.

"I'm meeting up with Jake for coffee. Why?"

Terror sets in my gut when I hear his name. That man is more dangerous than we anticipated him to be. "Don't meet him for coffee. Go home and lock your door tightly from within. Don't open it for anyone. Especially not Jake. And don't go to tonight's party with him. No matter what. Please Justine. I'm saying this for your own safe–"

She retaliates, despite my genuine concern for her. "If this is another one of your games Marcus. Save it! I will not stand by and just watch you and Riya frame Jake to be someone he is not! You're making him sound like he's some serial killer. And it was your whore of a girlfriend who–"

"One more word against her Justine and I will rethink my entire decision of wanting to save your pathetic life." I cut the call. I cannot explain this to her on call. But I tried to warn her. I tried my best to warn her about her drug-dealer rapist boyfriend. I have to go to that party tonight. But before that I have to make sure that Riya knows how deep of shit we are in.

Who this is all tied to. My hands still tremble as I hold that report in my hands.

Fifteen minutes later, Riya is inside my house. In her pink pajama set. Hair tied up in a bun and pink sandals. Looking beautiful as ever. But worry on her face.

Fear.

Before I can say anything she rushes upstairs and into my room. Thankfully no one is home today. George and Sid were hitting the gym and Dan...I am not sure what his plan is. But he isn't home. Which I am thankful for.

I follow Riya to my room. Her footsteps steadfast and her breath unusual. She flops on the bed with her head in her hands and I close my door behind me. Perhaps, walls have ears too.

"Hello to you too." I try to make small talk before I drop *THE BOMB*.

"I got a message from the PI that–" her eyes drift to the papers on the bed. "What are these?" I quickly saunter over and pick those papers out of her hands.

"Who is this?" she stares at the image of a man from the report. "Is this..." her confused face tells me the disappointment she feels in me.

"Yes. This is the report from the PI and that is why I called you here." She shifts to face me. Something is bothering her. But I don't know what.

I sit beside her. Arranging the papers back in the order I had received them in. She watches me closely. Silence fills the room as she waits for me to tell her why I'd sent that message.

"Jake is a drug dealer." I tell her and she cannot stop staring at me. And that stare isn't because of my handsome face. I know a worried stare when I see one.

"What do you mean?" The horror on her face is clear. Her face goes pale. I know that Jake used to live with her. She is probably running through all the memories where she could find any connection to this. To accept this as a fact.

I give her the paper that shows his bank account and his "client list". But that wasn't what had sent chills down my spine. It was who he'd gotten the drugs from. How he'd gotten them and what the cost was. After I explained everything to her. She shot up to her feet and was at the door.

She turned to find her sandals that she'd thrown off when I'd told her that Jake had bought $50,000 worth of drugs.

"We have to go to her right now. James...take me to Justine. I need to make sure that she's okay." Riya is clearly panicking. I try to get a hold of her, but I scare her even more. So, I take two steps back, ensuring that the pain isn't reflected on my face.

I tell her to take a few deep breaths when I see her hyperventilating. I approach her slowly with caution, announcing my every step. She takes deep breaths and keeps looking into my eyes.

"I–I need to check on her…I–" she keeps taking deep breaths along with me. I will never forgive Jake for what he did to Riya.

"Riya I did call her to tell her but she–"

She snaps at me, going back into panic mode. "I don't fucking care what she thinks of me or whatever she has done to me. All I know right now is that as a woman…fuck that. As a human! I need to make sure that the bastard is locked up and away from her." She is angry. Very. Yet there are tears in her eyes.

I am going to kill Jake. Or at the very least I am going to be the cause of his death.

I know what she meant though. As soon as I'd read it and finished throwing up, I'd first texted Riya and called Justine to ensure the same.

"Riya…"

Her expression looks defeated. "She is…was my best friend once, James. I can't just let her…I need to make sure she's okay. Can you please take me to her?" Her tears stream down her cheeks. She was right now in a fight or flight mode.

The adrenaline rush.

I want to hold her in my arms and tell her that I am going to make sure that nothing happens to anyone. I just want to hold her in my arms and take all her pain and suffering away. Perhaps, I just want to hold her.

Perhaps I am a mad man, who just wants to always be by her side.

The Investigator's note keeps flashing in my mind. If he had to go in hiding just because of the fear of being entangled in all of this. We are already a part of this. And we need to take care of it. With a calm mind.

I hold Riya's shoulders and shake her hard. "Raven." I jolt her back to reality and out of that panic. "Look in my eyes." She does. And two fat tears fall on my forearms. They weigh awfully much for the size of mere two tears. "Take deep breaths. In." she takes a deep breath in. "And now out." and after a few breaths she is calmed down.

"We need to call the cops on Jake." she says. I had thought about that possibility as well. But knowing who this is all tied to. There is a good chance that we would be silenced one way or other before the case is even registered.

"You need to listen to me very carefully. I have a plan." During the fifteen minutes it took Raven to get to my house, I'd sorted through every option that we had. But, if we want to escape this unscathed, we need contacts. Contacts of people we should fear and run the opposite way.

I explain to her my entire plan. She listens carefully. Nodding when she agrees with me. At the end she pulls out her phone and taps a few times and shows me the message she had received.

"That's why you were freaking out when you came over?" I ask her. She simply nods. This is perfect. This was exactly what we'd needed for our plan to be a success.

"He sent it to me a couple minutes before I got your message and the timing seemed so off. But one thing I am not sure of is who does this number belong to?" I scan my eyes over the message one more time.

The message from P.I. read-
(953)467-5678- Q
Use it as your last resort.

I scan through the report and only one name reminds me of Q. It seemed like Riya figured it out too. "Querida!" We say together.

This is a tight rope that we are walking, and I don't want to put her in danger. But thankfully she has arranged the necessary security measurements. Yet, I find it very unsettling because I know it is not enough. I am just glad that she moved out of that house.

I need to go to that party tonight. No matter what. The date for the handover is tomorrow. What if Justine refuses to listen to me and goes to the party anyway? The handover is tomorrow!

I get up and start changing my clothes. The party is at Beck's. The place will be jam packed because Winston's hockey team has won three times in a row. And it being a superstition at Winstons that any team that wins three matches in a row has always made it to frozen four. Everyone is going to be hella hammered tonight, which would give Jake the perfect opportunity to execute his plan.

I reach for a white t-shirt and my baggy jeans. I spray on some cologne and I observe Riya observing me. She doesn't say anything. She just looks at my every movement.

"You are coming with me to my place so that I can get ready for the party too!"

"No way!" I bite back. "You are not going anywhere near that man, now that we know how dangerous he can be. No way in hell, Riya!" I am not risking anything. Especially not her.

"What if Justine is there? She will only listen to me. I have to go! You can deal with Jake however you want, but not Justine. I will not let anyone malign her name because of the man–the piece of shit she's dating!" She retaliates. It is true. The only person who might be able to handle Justine, is Riya. I don't think she will listen to anyone else. But Jake is a dangerous man! What if...No! I will keep her in front of my eyes all the time.

I will not let go of her. Not this time. "Alright." I give in.

We get ready and head over to her house. It seems cozier than her place before. More sunlight and more cuteness. She walks into the closet that I only get a peek of and it is a walk in closet. There is some unarranged furniture inside and everywhere in the house.

I know she will never ask for help even if she needs it. I walk over to the couch where an unmade TV stand rests. The TV is still in the box. The instruction pamphlet is right next to it. I take a look at it and get to work. All that is left is to fit the glass which is very heavy and requires two people. One who can balance it and the other one to screw it in place.

"I'm ready." She steps out of the closet and sees me trying to balance the glass in one hand while trying to screw it with my other hand. She rushes to my help and holds the glass from the other side. "That is very expensive!" she squeaks.

She holds the glass from one side while I tighten the screws. She flashes me a bleak smile and I offer to help her with the other incomplete furniture projects. "Oh! Thank you, but I can–"

"I know you can. But I would love to be Bob the builder for one day. I have too much free time anyway." I scoff.

"Thank you."

We walk towards her car and she asks me to drive. I see her hold her hands together. Is she nervous? Stupid question! I want to hold her hands and tell her that this is going to be over once and for all. But I wonder if I have the right to say that anymore.

"So, how's the interview assignment going?" I ask her.

"Oh right! I'd completely forgotten about that. It's going…well. I am just making stuff up at this point." Should I be worried? "Not that you should be worried about it. It won't be published anyway. Don't worry, I'm just writing well enough to pass." she forces herself to laugh.

"I see."

"How's your Biology class going?" she asks me. I take a quick peek at her.

"Oh you know how smart I am!" I boast. And she laughs. This time she laughs for real!

Score!

"That you are." she chuckles. "Umm..." She hesitates a bit. "How is your brother?" she asks me. I had asked everyone not to tell her about Caleb's accident the day she'd left. She already has too much to deal with and this would just add more to her worry. Plus, I am making progress with both him and my father. Believe it or not the person who gave me the PI details was my father. And we are trying to bridge the gap between us.

At least for Caleb's sake. We are even going for dinner next weekend. Caleb doesn't like the cold and thankfully the weather is supposed to be warm next week. Perfect for a day out. I have even planned a surprise picnic for us. I wonder if Riya would like to go. Maybe I will ask her if everything goes well tonight.

But Caleb and I are getting there. He's not talking with me so far, but he's laughing with me. We mostly talk about mom. I never knew how much that kid was starving to be noticed. How much he craved to know more about mom. It was my fault. I wasn't a good big brother.

But I want to change that. I don't want to continue being the bad big brother. Me and dad reminisce about the old days in front of Caleb and tell him how much mom loved him. How much she cared about him. I even dared to share the taco Thursday truth with my father and he burst out in a laughter.

I hadn't seen him laugh in five years. For the first time in five years, I saw life in his dead eyes. For the first time, I didn't regret going back home. For the first time in five years, it was difficult for me to actually leave home.

Riya clears her throat and I realise that I hadn't answered her.

"We're..." I wonder how to complete that sentence. "A family again." That feels right.

"I'm glad! Caleb is very sweet." She smiles at the road. He hasn't shut up about Riya since we got him home. And because of him father has been keen on meeting Riya. In a good way of course. But I screwed up.

"He misses you." I tell her. She turns to look at me and smiles.

"I miss him too."

"And..." I take in a deep breath as I pull up at Beck's house. I put the car in park.

"And?"

"And I miss you too, Raven."

Chapter 37- Riya

There are very few things that I remember from the past few weeks. But as I sit in the courtroom and hear the judge give Jake 45 years in jail, I feel exhilarated. I feel free. Mama squeezes my hand tightly and gives me a faint smile.

I feel like I can finally breathe. It wouldn't have been possible without the support of my family. Jake is dragged away and he gives me the stink eye as he is dragged away.

I feel like I can finally breathe.

I turn around to see Justine sitting on the last bench. She is the first to leave. And James is sitting right behind me, he smiles at me and nods. Bian, and Jamilah and the boys are next to them. I run towards Bian and hug her tightly.

Among all the women in here, I spot one in a black pencil skirt and a white shirt and black blazer. Wearing sunglasses and a dark nude lipstick. She picks up her diamond studded white alligator birkin and makes her way out. I excuse myself from everyone and run to chase her. She's also wearing white Louboutins, matching the black ones that I'm wearing.

"Wait." I holler.

She stops and pushes her sunglasses down and looks at me.

"You are a mighty soul." she says as I approach her. I smile at her and she smiles back. "How'd you know that it was me?" she asks me.

I shrug, stating the obvious truth. "You are the only one who is dressed up like the badass mafia bitch!" She scoffs and laughs. So elegant and tall. She's so beautiful! She brushes her shiny red hair back.

She raises her brows, as if challenging me. "In normal circumstances, people would run away from me. I also spot a badass bitch." she pushes her sunglass back up and offers me her hand. "Querida." she says. "Pleasure to meet you, Riya."

I shake her hand firmly. "Thank you for your help." I tell her.

"Rest assured. Giovanni is dead. So, you all should be fine. His..." she pauses. Rethinking "...organisation is also taken down." It sends chills down my spine. Her aura is so cold yet so powerful. Yet some sense of relief washes over me. Some relief to my unconscious that there won't be a constant fear looming over my head. But what if Jake gets out? What if he does something from inside?

I have watched enough shows and movies to know that criminals can have their contacts outside hurt people. People who cross them. I am one of the reasons why Jake is going to jail. What if he asks someone to kill me? Or worse yet...finish what he started with me? Do I stay locked inside my house fearing that one day I might be violated again?

I know I shouldn't butt in because that is a dangerous world to be associated with, but I ask her anyway. "Did you...Are you the one?"

"No." she says sternly. "But don't worry...I will find him. And when I do, I am going to send him to the deepest pits of hell." her jaw tightens and I think just for a second. Wasn't Giovanni the bad guy? So, wouldn't anyone who killed him and destroyed his operation be a nice person? Perhaps that is not my story to tell.

"Thank you for your help." I tell her.

"Thank you for believing in me." she tells me with a smile. It's weird how she's so hot and cold. But all this wouldn't be possible without her help.

"I hope to meet you again someday, Querida." I actually like her. Perhaps, it's the way she carries herself. But it's just so...respectable. She seems like the woman who you would see on TedTalk and be inspired by.

She laughs. Not giggle or the feminine laugh. She laughs and even though it's very loud, it's still so graceful. I could never! "Nobody has ever said that to me before. I like you. Thank you for your time, Riya."

"Hey...if you ever need my help..." I wink at her.

She smiles sheepishly. "I'll keep that in mind. But I think you already did help me. In more ways than you can imagine." she shakes my hand with both her hands and smiles. "Thank you." And she disappears into thin air. Just kidding, I see her walk out the front door. Mom, dad, Maura and Keith are waiting for me when I turn around. I rush towards them and we do a group hug.

"You were so strong." Dad tells me and I almost feel myself tear up.

"You really are strong, Riya." Maura chimes in. "I'm sorry you had to go through it alone." she sobs.

"You were there when I needed you the most." I assure her.

"I'm sorry too." Keith says softly and I smile through my tears.

When we'd reached that party, James and I had rushed inside to find Jake and Justine. He didn't let go of my hand, not for a second.

I'd called Justine multiple times before that, but her phone was switched off and it scared me even more. I just prayed that I wouldn't find her here. But I still kept looking.

"Riya?" I turn around to find Dan standing behind me. Are Sid and George here too?

"What are you doing here?" James and I ask him together.

"I...I...I'm here...with..." he stutters. "With a...friend." his eyes keep wandering as if he's too distracted. He's here to bang someone. Noted. "What are you doing here?" he asks us. Right. James pulls me towards the kitchen and rushes towards the stairs leading upstairs. Did he spot Jake? Why is the layout of this house so weird?

James pulls me closer to him and whispers in my ear. "He's with some girl. Black hair. That's all I saw." He quickly informs me. That could be Justine. I take in a deep breath as we stand outside the door and James knocks. No answer. I knock louder and impatiently this time.

"This room is occupied. Fuck off." Jake screams from inside. I try to take in deep breaths as I feel my hands and feet sweat profusely.

"Step back" James lets go of my hand and prepares himself. He's going to kick the door down. He kicks the door down in one kick! Just how strong is this man? Now is not the time!

We rush inside and find Jake kissing a half naked girl. Her clothes are gone and she is just in her bra and panties. And from the looks of it, she is neither Justine nor conscious. Sick bastard. James pulls him off the girl and I quickly rush to check her. She's either passed out or drugged.

"You sick piece of shit." James punches him hard and Jake falls to the ground.

"You bitch! You ruin everything, don't you?" he says, looking at me. James picks him up by his collar and spits foul words at him. "First Justine and now this. You will pay for it!" he swears.

I carefully put the girl's clothes back on and try to wake her up, but she doesn't respond at all.

"What is going on here?" Dan walks in. He takes one look at the girl I'm dressing and Jake and James and fuels up. "Piece of shit!" he strikes Jake and he falls to the ground with a thud. I'm guessing Dan probably knows this girl?

Now is not the time for those questions. I run to the bathroom and return with a glass of water and spray some water on her.

"Is Bian okay?" Dan asks me. Her name is Bian.

"She's unconscious." Dan grunts. I have never seen Dan this angry. It is so unlike him. By the time he reaches to throw another punch at Jake, he is knocked out cold by James. There is blood on the floor, coming from Jake's nose which looks disturbingly broken. But he deserves it.

The girl in my arms...Bian flickers her eyes open and mumbles something.

"Are you okay? Do you know where you are?" I ask her. She is forcing herself to keep her eyes open. This fucker drugged her! The party has barely started and unless she poured an entire bottle of whiskey down her throat at 3pm, she shouldn't be this drowsy.

God knows how many women he has done this to!

All the commotion draws more attention and more people walk in the bedroom. Until finally Beck makes his way through and flops on his bed, holding his head in his hands.

This could be Justine! I shiver. Nonetheless, this is still a woman! I'm glad that James broke down the door at the right time. God knows what would've happened and this woman wouldn't even know what happened to her.

Jake was all over the news and social media in the next two days. Bian had filed a police report against him. And after her 7 other girls filed rape charges against him.

I wanted to check up on Justine after everything that happened. She remained unreachable.

But if she still couldn't see the true face of Jake, then she was blind and a disgrace to being a woman if she sided with him again.

"I can't tell you how thankful I am!" Bian holds my hands. "If it weren't for you and Marcus...I don't know what would've happened."

I smile at her and pull her in for a hug. Bian is so sweet that anyone who troubles her is a criminal. She is so calm and so nurturing.

"If only we'd gotten there before...we could've avoided it altogether." She puts her hand on my shoulder and smiles.

"You did avoid the worst! And for that I will always be thankful!" She is too sweet! And her voice is so calming that it sounds like a melody.

My eyes tear up and I pull her in for a hug. "I'm just glad that you are fine!" she squeezes me tighter. And we go our separate ways for our classes.

Jake had raped 8 women. 9 including me. I should come forward too, right? I shouldn't be ashamed. He is the one who should suffer. But I'm scared of how my family will react. I want them to hear it from me first. I have to woman up and tell them. I can't hide it from them for the rest of my life, especially if I want to be one of the reasons that Jake goes to jail.

I attend my classes and make my way to my car and find Justine standing by my car. In a hoodie and sweatpants. She looks like she has been through hell. A few women make nasty eyes at her and pass some snarky diss comments. But she doesn't say anything. Which is so unlike her. Justine never takes shit from anyone.

"Hey..." I drag along and she spots me.

"Hi." she says quietly and quickly lowers her gaze.

"How are you?" I ask her. Stupid question, I realise.

She scoffs. I have never seen Justine like this before.

"I came here to apologise to you." That was the last thing I was expecting from her. "I'm sorry Riya." She looks up and meets my eyes.

"I see..." I don't know what to say. I can't just forgive her that easily. She did leave me when I needed her and on top of that she made things worse for me. She dug this hole for herself, now she has to marinate in her own choices.

I walk towards the door and she holds my hand. A little too tightly. A soft gasp escapes her throat and she lowers her head even more. "I really really am sorry, Riya. I...I..."

I pull my arm out of her grip and get in the car. "I don't want to hear it. But thank you for the apology Justine." She keeps staring at the ground. I will not forgive her until she looks me in the eye and apologises.

I get in the car drive off and see Justine standing there. Crying. It hurts me to do this, but she hurt me more. I roll down my window and let the air blow away my hair. April has started nice and warm. It feels good to feel the warm breeze and to breathe freely. I just want to close my eyes and soak this moment in, but I also don't want to die.

My phone pings with a notification and it pops up on my console.

It's *James*.

Chapter 38- Riya

James had again asked me to join him and his family on the surprise picnic that he had planned for them. He assured me that he asked me only because of Caleb and it would really make him happy. And I agreed to go on this trip only to see Caleb.

Okay fine! Now that the hard part is over, almost. I thought that maybe James and I could sort some things between us. He said he missed me and I didn't say it back and I want to, but I am too proud to say it.

I put on denim overalls and a white shirt and tie my hair in a ponytail. Isn't this the classic picnic dress? James is supposed to pick me up from my house and then we are going to head to his house and then to wherever he planned the picnic. Mom and dad were staying with me and Maura and Keith had left for New York again.

"What do you even see in that guy?" Dad asks me. He has been at it for days. He thinks that James could have manned up and stepped up.

I roll my eyes at him and mom tells me to ignore him. "Dad...I stopped him. He was about to kill Jake. If I hadn't intervened, he would've killed Jake."

Dad sips his whiskey and rolls his eyes at me. I see that I probably learned how to roll my eyes from him.

I tie my shoelaces and put my jacket on the shoe stand. "I'm just saying." Dad shrugs. "He could've done something to show us that he will take care of you after we are gone. If he wants to take you out on a date and date you, that's the least he could do after everything that you've–" dad goes silent and I freeze in place. I blink away my tears. Dad has always been overprotective over me.

INTERTWINED

Like I said- I am a spoiled brat. My dad has never denied me anything, fulfilled my every wish. When I'd asked him and mama to come to meet me, he'd dropped everything and gotten on the first flight to Boston. No questions asked.

He held out a box of Belgian pralines and a box of Swarovski in his hand as he greeted me.

I had hugged him so tight that it scared him. I'd broken down in his arms. I had cried to my heart's content. "I am going to kill that motherfucker." My dad had said with tears in his eyes.

That was the first time I had heard my dad use an English cuss word and see him cry. I'd asked dad to swear on my life that he wouldn't do anything reckless that would take him away from me. Only then did I go to bed. Even then I was scared that he would do something.

Mama had fallen to the ground. They held me in their arms for 5 hours. I timed it. That night, I had put my head in mama's lap and she had stroked my hair until I fell asleep.

I had woken up that same way. Dad had slept on the couch and that was the first night in weeks that I didn't have any nightmares. I'd informed them about my entire plan so far and they'd told me that they were proud of me for being so strong. It was probably the first time I'd heard it since the incident.

I tighten my shoelace angrily. James has done a lot for me and it hurts me how my dad makes such comments on him. "Well, if you have so much to say about him, maybe you should just ask him then, dad!" I grab my jacket and bang the door close behind me. I take a deep breath, but it's just...ugh! I go back inside with my shoes on and say sorry to my dad and come back out.

James texts me just on time that he is here.

I rush downstairs and find him waiting outside his car in baggy jeans and olive green shirt and a Chiefs cap. It is not cold outside, in fact it's very warm, but I still get chills on my body. He looks too good. And his stubble definitely suits him. It draws more attention to his sharp jawline and it's not too shabby.

"You look beautiful." he says as he opens the door for me. I just smile at him awkwardly, knowing that I should've said it back. But he's just looking too beautiful right now.

"Music?" he asks me as he drives us both to their house. I won't lie that I am not nervous. I am sweating in all the places possible. I know that his father was some big football player, but I don't see him as a fan. I am meeting him as James' friend. Or what if he introduces me as his girlfriend? What do I say then? I am not his girlfriend. Yet.

"Sure." Maybe the music can help me relax a bit. And what does James do? He puts on hip-hop and the speaker was so high that I'm sure I just had a mini-heart-attack.

I wish I loved football. I really wish I did because I have run out of all topics to make conversations with Mr Williams. And although he told me to call him by his name, the Indian in me just can't!

"So did you also have a phase where you got those gold braces, Mr Williams?" He laughs in the same way that James does. And I have to admit that for someone his age, he looks too fit and too handsome. I wonder if James will also look the same way when he's that old.

A gush of warm wind washes over us and sends ripples through the pond. I can tell that James is really putting in effort in everything. He is busy skipping stones with Caleb while Mr Williams and I have been making small talk for the past 30 minutes while sipping champagne. I either need Caleb here or I need to be drunk. I just can't make small talk anymore.

"You mean the grills?" he chuckles.

I nod at him as I empty my glass for the 4th time and he fills it up again. "Yes. I did for a very short time. And my wife told me to lose either one of them, so the grills had to go." He talks about his wife with a smile. And his crows feet crinkle as he smiles. His eyes shine too.

"Riya..." Caleb comes running towards me and I quickly put my glass down and catch him as he jumps into my arms. I feel Mr Williams stiffen next to me. Caleb still only talks to me but he giggles with both James and Mr Williams. Mr Williams pulls Caleb in his arms and starts to tickle him. Both of them break out into laughter and James comes and sits next to me.

Thankfully Mr Williams hasn't asked me anything about my relationship with James, because I really don't have an answer right now.

"Ri...ri..." Caleb chuckles "Help me." He is laughing so much that his eyes tear up.

"Here comes another tickle monster." James joins in and tickles Caleb even more.

"James...No...Please...stop. James." Caleb chuckles loud. And James freezes in place. Caleb talked to him! He picks up Caleb in his hands and stands up and spins him in his arms.

"James. Stop. James..." Caleb chuckles. Caleb also calls him *James...*

Chapter 39- James

My father hasn't shut up about Riya. Does she know how to do black magic? How does she charm the Williams men so easily? All in all, I have been advised to stop being a dick and "go get my girl." There were definitely sparks flying all over the place between Riya and I but instead of talking about our relationship, I coward out.

I even managed to get the stink eye from her father who was waiting for her downstairs as I dropped her off. I don't know what I can say to get his approval. I know for a fact that he hates me. Hate is probably a light word. But perhaps I understand his hate. Everything happened to Riya because of me. Because I fought with her. It was my fault up to some extent. But I was going to make up for it.

On our drive back from the picnic, I dropped off dad and Caleb home and drove her home. She was quieter than usual. Until she finally asked me, "What happened to Caleb?" I never told her what happened that day. She already had too much on her plate and I didn't want her to think it was her fault.

"He fell down the stairs." I tell her and pray that she leaves it at that. But knowing Riya, she probably won't.

She stayed quiet and didn't ask anything after that. No follow-up questions.

Just before I turn around the block of her house she tells me. "You know I still am scared sometimes…That he might come for me one day. That he might send someone out for me one day." She sent away the security after everything was settled, but I can understand why she feels uneasy.

The man who Jake was involved with wasn't just any other drug dealer. He was a very dangerous man. I can only imagine the connections he might have if he has been in that world for some time now.

I cannot stand the sight of Riya shivering in fear, especially fearing the man who assaulted her.

And I am going to do something about it.

I had received a message from Riya's father to meet him for dinner. Apparently he had some concerns regarding my intentions with his daughter that he wanted to address. I won't lie, but her father is very intimidating. He made a reservation for us at the fanciest place in Massachusetts and trust me it is next to impossible to make a reservation here even a month before.

"Sir." I shake his hand and take a seat in front of him. Riya told me that her parents were leaving for India at the end of this week.

He signals me to take a seat and the waitress brings us water and the menus. "Riya told me that you play American football? How is that working out for you?" The way he says *American football* reminds me of Riya. I assume that Riya inherited her hate for American football from her father.

"Yes Sir I do. I am the quarterback for Winston." I panic and forget to tell him that I am also the captain, but I doubt that it matters to him anyway.

"And what are your future plans?" He asks me as he orders a whiskey on the rocks for himself and I just stick to water. I'm already nervous as it is. Riya is the spitting image of her father. Same nose and same eyes, only her forehead doesn't crinkle so much.

"I intend to graduate with my Computer Science degree and go pro in football. Sir." I stress on the degree and Computer Science aspect more, hoping that maybe it will make a good impression on him because football is not going to work in my favor.

"I see." He clears his throats and looks me dead in the eye. I will admit that in my life only coach Belkis has managed to scare me to death with his gaze, but Riya's father scares the living shit out of me. "So, my daughter is not in your future plans?" Fuck!

I did not expect that turn in the conversation. I gulp hard, thinking what I should respond, but words fail me. As if to save my ass the waitress arrives with the whiskey. Blue Label 21 years old, neat. I myself prefer 21 years over 25 years Blue Label. But that is not what I should be thinking about right now.

"That will be your daughter's choice. If she shall have me as her partner, it will make me the happiest man alive, but if she doesn't, I will respect her choice. Sir." I want to pat myself on the back for coming up with that response.

I see a faint smile on that man. Faint. But I will take it. "So how is your father doing? The last time I met him, he was an aspiring football player." Riya's father had met my father in the past?

"I went to the same University as him." Mr Nayan adds. I had zero idea. "I'm surprised Riya did not mention that to you. Of course I only met him a couple of times at parties, but I remember his spirit and love for football." He chuckles softly. Or maybe I just imagined it. I wonder if my father remembers Mr Nayan. It'll be great if I can hear some stories that will humanize him for me.

"You seem to share the same passion for football I see."

"Yes sir." I answer.

"You can call me Chandran." He tells me and I know that this is a trick question because Indians don't call the elderly by their name. I learned that from Riya. She wouldn't call my father by his name whatsoever. It is a form of respect for them.

"Thank you Sir, but is it okay if I call you Uncle?" Well played Marcus!

"Of course Marcus." he nods in approval.

By the time the main course arrives, the mood has lightened significantly. That is until he drops the bomb on me. His eyes go two shades darker and his jaw tightens. "As you might have seen, I have raised my daughter with a lot of love and care. And..." There it goes. "I don't understand that if you two were in a relationship, wasn't it your responsibility to take any action against everything that happened to her? Why did she have to go through it alone? Where were you, Marcus?" He hates me.

I can't tell him how much I beat himself for that eerie single day. I have no excuses. I just lower my gaze and leave my fork in the plate.

He exhales sharply. "I will never be able to look at myself in the mirror the same way again. I failed to protect my daughter. I know that she might seem strong and she is, but there is a lot that she doesn't tell anyone. She is a lot like her mother that way." I doubt that.

"I'm sorry, Sir." I say it like I mean it.

"I have seen how scared she is to step out of her house alone, fearing that..." he stops and takes a deep breath. "How can I trust that after I leave, nothing of this sort will happen to her again? I know it is not one person's responsibility to look after her. But how can I sleep peacefully knowing that she doesn't have anyone to rely on, Marcus? Can I rely on you for that?" He asks me directly. I have always seen my father's friends be very protective over their daughters. I would often just laugh at it, not understanding why. But I think I know now.

"I–"

"I know what you did."

I am confused as to what part he is talking about? Does he know that Riya and I had fought and she had left angrily and that was why...

"Will you be able to live with that decision?" He asks me, the intimidating expression now replaced with that of concern.

I am very confused. "I spoke with Carlos as well." he says and my shoulders stiffen. And suddenly I am very attentive.

The PI I had hired had sent me a number that I could use only in life and death situation. The sentence that Jake got was not fair. It wasn't fair to Riya. It was not fair to all the women that he'd raped. It wasn't fair to all the women he'd harassed. All of them were living in fear that one day he'd get out and do something.

"I see." I fold my hands on the table.

"You know that you ordered this kill. And regardless of who kills him, his blood will be on your hands. Will you be able to live with that?"

"Yes." I say without missing a beat. I know for a fact that if Justine hadn't knocked on that door, Jake wouldn't have stopped. Jake is a vile man, who rapes and assaults women and even...God I cannot even say it in my head, let alone say it out loud. Something that nobody knows. Something that couldn't be disclosed. Something that only Riya and I know. Something that we let Jake get away with.

I know that it makes her feel guilty. I know how badly she wanted to disclose it, but she didn't. A decision that weighs heavily on her heart. A decision that keeps me up at night. Jake doesn't deserve to live like this. People like him never change. Second chances are not meant for people like him. And I won't regret having his death on my conscience. I won't regret it one bit.

I huff and smile at him. Mr Nayan thinks that I am a bit odd. I can tell it by his expression. "I won't be able to look myself in the eye if I don't do this. I cannot just let her sit in the fear that one day that bastard will get out or do something to her. Sir."

He stares at me, as if trying to understand me. He nods at me and smiles.

I had to sign up for an advertisement to collect the money to order the kill on Jake. Turns out Carlos Ignacio Ortiz does much more than Hardware programming and making ammunition.. He is one hell of a scary man. But now that I have dipped my toe in that world, I might as well make use of it. After making the deal with him, he told me that it would take at least three weeks to get it done.

Finals are in three weeks and practice has been tougher. And with all the offers I was warding off this year, I decided to sign up with a sports agency. Too much has happened in this semester, and I swear to god that I cannot wait for it to end.

I finish my class schedule for the day and head to practice when my phone pings. It's Riya. She wants to meet me.

Is this a dream? Is this the light that people talk about that shines brightly at the end of the tunnel? I reply immediately and we set a place and time to meet.

I head to meet the coach and ask him if I can head out early and to my surprise he says yes. Never in the time I have known this man has he allowed any of the boys to flunk any part of the practice. He coaches us as if we're preparing for war. "It's nice to see you smile again, Williams." Belkis says as I walk out of his office. I pinch myself just to make sure that this is not a dream.

I shower quickly and borrow some perfume from Sid. I didn't pack mine and I don't want to smell like myself when meeting my Raven.

I rush to the library fifteen minutes late and find her sitting by the window table. Waiting. For me.

She looks so beautiful! My Raven

Chapter 40- James

I can tell that something is off. She has barely said anything in the hour that we've been here. Is there something on her mind? Her silence now scares me. Her father's words echo in my mind- Riya doesn't share her deepest emotions. She keeps to herself even if it eats her from inside.

But after everything that we've been through, I hope she trusts me again.

I trust you with my heart, body and soul.

She'd told me this once upon a time. I don't want to be the same person who she said that to, but I want to be someone better. Someone who trusts her just as much. Someone who knows how much she can handle by herself, and someone who will always be there if she needs me. Because I need her.

"You can just say whatever is on your mind." I break the ice. The silence was just too deafening. "I swear that it's fine if you don't miss me back." I want to smack my head so bad right now for saying that. "And we can work on..." I take a deep breath. I have to continue with this now that I have started it. "...Us if that's what you want." I quickly add.

She forces a smile. "Why didn't you tell me about Caleb?"

"Riya...I...that was stupid of me and I never thought that you and I...that...us...we...that you would ever want to be with me let alone love me and I was afraid that you would judge me and my family and leave me. I know that was stupid of me to think, but I have never told anyone about Caleb. I was always scared for him. That people would drag him through hell...the media...press...people...I'm sorry." I exhale as I finish sharing my side of the story.

"I am not talking about that. I am referring to the day I...we fought and I left. Caleb fell down the stairs that day, didn't he? When you were shouting out for me..." she pauses. I see the visible gulp that she swallows. "Was it because you needed help with Caleb? You didn't even have your phone that day." she sniffles and presses her hands together on the table.

I put my hand on hers and she sniffles. "Baby...it's all over. There's no point crying over spilled milk."

"I should've stopped." she says, not daring to look me in the eye. I don't know who told her, but whoever did is going to get it from me. "I'm sorry James." she sniffles and gathers her bag and gets up to leave.

"Wait...what? Hey don't go." I try to get a hold of her but she's gone. I chase after her and stop her. She can't just leave a middle conversation.

"You're mad at me for not telling you? You were the one who left, Riya." I say softly. The last time I raised my voice at her, it all went to hell. "And I am not blaming you for anything. I was going to tell you eventually, but you had a lot on your plate to deal with. I didn't want to add more. And it wasn't your fault. You didn't push Caleb off the stairs. And he's fine now, so it's all good. Okay? You don't have to burden yourself with it. He is doing just fine."

She sniffles and still doesn't meet my eyes, but she nods. "Who told you?" I ask her.

The only ones who knew were the boys and my father.

"Who?" I ask her again. Calmly.

"George." she says. I inhale a sharp breath. I am going to kill George. He had no right to tell her. She holds the sleeve of my jacket and looks at me with teary eyes that punch me in the gut. "I forced him to tell me. Well, I blackmailed him. Nonetheless, he did not disclose any of it voluntarily."

I know that George is scared of Riya, but is he actually scared of her? And what did she blackmail him with? None of that matters right now. What matters is that I don't want Riya to blame herself even for a second.

I grab her hand in mine and reach for the other hand. I tilt her chin up, until she is looking at me. "Can we press reset and start our relationship anew? I love you Raven. I really do. And I know that we both made mistakes in the past, me more than you. But can we please forgive each other and move on? Will you ever be able to forgive me, Raven?" She breaks down into sobs. I pull her close to my chest and pat her back slowly.

We both are broken people who have been broken to mold each other.

She pulls the collar of my shirt down and presses her lips on mine. I inhale her floral scent sharply and tangle my hand in her hair and pull her closer to myself. Does this mean yes? Does this mean that she still loves me? Does this mean that there is still a *WE*?

"I need you, James." she pants between our kisses. Her place is closer than mine. She grabs my hand in her tiny hand and leads me to her car. "Do you need me?" she asks me before turning on the ignition of her car.

I caress her face with my hand and tell her. "Let me show you how much."

We make our way to her house, keeping a safe distance between us. A distance too long for my taste. A carefully calculated distance that still kept me in the range of her scent. She closes the door behind her and looks up at me with those beautiful brown eyes that I yearned for!

I close the distance in one step and rest my arms on her shoulders, cornering her against the door. "Riya…" I exhale, wanting to crash my lips on her and devour her right this second, but I also know that we have a lot to talk about before. And I don't want to force her into anything.

Her breath hitches visibly and she breathes faster, I quickly take a step back and grant her space. "Are you okay? I'm sorry…"

She keeps shaking her head. "I'm fine." she keeps saying. I hold back my tears and bear the stabbing pain in my heart when I realise that she is not saying it to me. I don't want to spook her by going too close. I'm afraid that I might scare her. I don't want Riya to be scared of me. I can't bear the thought!

"Riya…Raven…It's just us." I say from a distance. "We don't have to." I smile at her and she looks back at me with tears in her eyes.

She falls to the ground, holding her face in her hands, sobbing and crying. I bite my tongue so hard that it bleeds. I can taste it. My blood. But even that hurts less than watching the woman I love break down. I move closer to her, announcing my eyes step, until I softly wrap my arms around her. I feel her gasps and tiny chokes against my chest. I tell her to let it all out.

"Every time I close my eyes, it's like I'm back in that room. Jake is crawling on top of me and I am fighting him off. Bleak. I really try to forget it all, James. I just…I'm scared." I slowly pat her head and her back, trying to console her in the best way possible.

"You're not only out of that room, but you're out of that house now. Anyone who tries to harm you will have to go through me. And I know how to tackle people in a way that will break their bones. You're safe now, Riya." I tilt her chin to face me. "I know it is going to take time and I know that things will never be the same. But you have to wake up now babe. The sun has risen and the night is over." I force a faint and weak smile at her.

The nightmare is now over Raven.

Chapter 41 - Riya

The nightmare is now over. I tell myself every waking day. James has been a huge help the last few days since my breakdown. He held me, or at least the pieces of me. I tried putting the pieces back to how they were before, but they don't fit that way anymore. It is difficult trying to find your own self, trying to build your own self. I have been going to support groups and even had my first therapy session. I have been somewhat scared to be in close proximity with a man.

I know that not all men are the same, but the one who broke me was a man. No, he was not a man. He was a predator. He is a predator. But I have to move on with my life, because if I don't I know that life will leave me behind. And I don't want to be stranded alone. It sucks!

So I shake all these thoughts away and get out of bed and brush my teeth. I shower and get ready and head to class. With finals looming over my head, I need to catch up on the things I couldn't focus on. I have the interview assignment for my Journalism class submission due this week and I haven't even started writing the final article.

Hell, I don't even know what I'm going to write about Marcus James Williams. Maybe I can write about how he is a gentle and caring man, or how he loves to watch anime. Perhaps I should focus on his game that I know nothing about or how his passion for coding that nobody seems to appreciate. I carefully jot down all the points in my notebook, ensuring to exclude any personal details about his family.

Jamilah takes a seat next to me. Today is the last day of classes before finals week officially begins. "My interviewee was so particular about everything! I should've just asked her to write the article herself. She's a Communications major and represented Winston Uni in the UN debate team. Like, I get it Jessica! You want to highlight how each of your arguments was neatly designed to have the perfect balance of productive and filler words, but I do not need the statistics of every sentence you speak! How's your stupid article coming along?" She groans. I chuckle softly. Jamilah and I have become pretty close friends, from meeting just in class, we have taken our friendship to random weekend plans.

"Good morning to you too." I say.

She chuckles. "Sorry. It's just Jessica pisses me off in a way nobody does! And trust me I deal with cyber bullies ALL THE FUCKING TIME!" she stresses.

"Yeah, that really sucks. I'm surprised you haven't told her to fuck off soon enough." Jamilah is a very sweet girl. When you first meet her. As she gets comfortable with you, her real self starts to show. She is a typical lawyer. And the girl can bitch! She showed me some of the "conversations" with her cyber bullies and trolls and if someone sent me messages like those, I'd cry. She hits the nail where it hurts. And the thing is that she knows where it hurts!

"I know right!? Unfortunately, at the end of the class, the interviewee also gets a form where they rate us and that is going to decide our grade. I need straight A's to get a scholarship for law school. So, everything lies in the wicked witch of the west's hands. I hope she drowns in her own tub!" I stifle a chuckle.

"Drown?"

"I don't mean 'drown and die'! I just hope that she at least chokes on some of her statistics and I hope that my face flashes in front of her eyes as she gasps for air!" The expression on her face scares me a little. But I like her! She was there for me through the entire Jake situation. She really helped me spread the true colour of Jake using her online superpowers. She is the reason how all those girls that Jake had assaulted before know that he is being ousted!

"Wouldn't wanna be Jessica! But thankfully my interviewee is a nice guy." James is a nice guy.

"Lucky bitch! You don't have to rub it in my face!" We both break out into a laugh just before Cruella aka our Professor steps in the class in her Dalmatian coat.

Literally! She's wearing a dalmatian coat! It is a knockoff, I can tell easily, but it suits her personality.

One rejoices life and mourns death.

One rejoices life and mourns death.

One rejoices life and mourns death.

I am rejoicing in his death. I do not mourn it.

I really tried to.

All I could think about was what he did to me and wanted to do...

I am rejoicing in his death. I do not mourn it. Not one bit!

Jake is dead.

He was beaten to death by his new cellmate. His new cellmate was in for murder. Muder of rapists. Apparently his wife was once raped in front of his eye by some criminal gang leader and since then, he swore to find and kill every rapist.

God bless his soul—He, who killed Jake.

I am rejoicing in his death. I do not mourn it.

I am free.

Free.

Free of the fear.

Free of the torment.

Free of my nightmares.
Free at last.
Free.

Have you heard the phrases, 'Love sustains you', 'Love nourishes you'? Love and love and love...

I know that I am capable of sustaining myself, of nourishing myself, of caring about myself, of loving myself. I know that I don't need anyone to tell me what I can and cannot do. I don't need anyone's opinion about me for me to get to know myself better.

I don't *need* anyone's help. I *want* it.

I've realised the biggest difference between need and want- the availability of *choice*.

I want love in my life. I want someone to sustain me. I want someone to nourish me. I want someone to care about me. I want someone to love me. I want someone I need. I want someone who needs me. And thankfully only one person makes the list.

It's time to suit up and go get my man!

It was no shocker to me when my article wasn't selected to be published. And it screwed up my entire plan of grand gesture. But thankfully, I have one thing- money. I bought a small column in the same paper for that week's paper. And by buying the column, I mean that I buttered up one of my colleagues who was in charge of the column, I promised to buy her dinner.

One thing college students will do anything for is good food! Although I'd heard that Winstons has better food when compared to other Universities, I refused to believe that dry chicken and unseasoned food should be allowed to count as good food.

The space was obviously shorter than before. I know I couldn't pour my entire heart into it, but I wanted to pour just enough.

It has been two days since my article was published in the paper. Everyone in the University knows that I am madly in love with Marcus. I did not write anything of the sort, but I wouldn't say that it's entirely wrong either. There has been no word from James. No text. No call. No meeting. Nothing.

I know he held onto me when I'd given up, he held onto the hope of us when I never thought there could be an us anymore.

It's my turn to keep faith now. In us.

I check my phone for the hundredth time. No texts. No calls. I bang my phone on the desk and go back to studying.

My stomach growls in retaliation. I've been studying for 7 hours without a break. I place a quick order on doordash and go back to studying. The Biology finals are going to be the death of me!

The bell rings just on time as I close my laptop and flop on the bed. I open the door totally expecting the food delivery person. I don't even bother tidying my hair or blot my oily face. A very handsome football player stands outside my door, holding my food order.

"Please don't tell me that your grand gesture was to sign up for doordash delivery, just so you could wait for me to place the order and deliver it to my house and that is why it took you two days to respond because I hadn't placed any order on doordash?!" I take a breather and he keeps smiling at me.

"If there was a competition of grand gestures, I'd win!" I say too quickly in my defence. James breaks out in a huge laughter.

"You win." He drops the food to the ground and closes the distances between us in one stride and swoops me in one arm and crashes his mouth on me. I don't think one second before I tangle my hand in his hair and we are heavy breaths and tongue and two bodies starving for each other. He pushes me against the wall and presses his body onto me. Grinding against me, while his mouth proclaims me in the purest and most innate way possible. Our bodies mesh together in need of the other.

I bring my other hand to his neck and his hands wander on my body, settling on my waist and the crook of my neck. His lips trace hungry kisses from my mouth to my neck and a loud moan escapes my throat. We realise that the door is wide open and the neighbours are hearing everything.

But I don't give a damn right now. I need him. I need James. He grabs the food in his left hand and pushes me inside the house, while not breaking the kiss. And when he finally pulls back he smiles at me. He traces his thumb across my lip with hunger in his beautiful blue eyes. With love in his heart. And me in his arms.

"I love you Raven, with my heart, body and soul." he smiles and his ocean blue eyes sparkle like the rising sun lights up the ocean.

"I love you James, with my heart, body and soul." I think we can make it this time. James and I. Us. I love him.

I love James.

Epilogue-

Summer break has been the honeymoon phase of our relationship. And George and Dan have had a lot of complaints. Noise complaints to be specific. We'd mostly stay over at my place, but on the rare occasion that I stayed over at James' and had sex, I was guaranteed angry looks from George and Daniel for either ruining their sleep or their orgy or whatever it is that George does.

But in the time that James stays over at my place, I teach him cooking. He's a quick learner. He even planned a dinner date for us because he'd just mastered the recipe of homemade pasta and I have to admit that it was so good! And I actually got a medal made just for him for not burning the house down.

And for that, he thanked me all night. As I lay on my stomach, the loose sheets cover my back and my ass as my hands lay under the pillow and I admire the eight packs that walk out of the shower with wet hair and just a towel around the waist. I feel the sweet ache grow between my legs.

I groan into the pillow in frustration and he jerks his head towards me. The wet hair splatters on his forehead. "What happened?" concern clear in his voice.

"You're going to get your ass whooped." I flash my sleazy smile and he matches mine.

"I wouldn't mind that." he takes slow strides towards me.

"Oh no!" I shake my head. "I didn't mean by me. I meant Belkis is gonna whoop your ass."

He looks at me as if I just told him that I am a man with a dick. He makes a grossed out face and gets up, I quickly grab his hand and toss the blanket aside as I sit upright. "I am not letting Belkis anywhere near my ass– or you," he says in an angry tone. "Why do you want the oldie in our bed anyway? Please don't tell me that you want to bring anyone else in our bed, Raven." he says in anger and I let him vent out, holding in my laughter. He grabs my neck and pulls me closer to him and my nipples press against his bare chest. "I do not share what's mine." his eyes darken.

I stifle a laugh and look at him. "You gonna let me talk?" Maybe I am rubbing off on him in more ways than possible. He has started to blabber around when he's nervous. I trace my hand down his rock hard abs and look up at him and bite my lip, knowing well enough what it does to him.

He grabs my hands and holds them back and leans on top of me. "Talk about another man when you're naked and next time I will punish you, Raven." A wicked smile curves my lips. A devious one. I know that I am still sore from last night, but I wouldn't mind knowing how much I can push him.

I whisper softly in his ear, "Maybe then I should be the one getting whooped by Belkis. Would you like the sight of that?" I bite down his ear softly and his gaze jerks towards me and he pins me down.

He exhales loudly on top of me. "You are a bad bad girl. And bad girls get punished." He glares at me and flips me on my stomach in one swift motion. "Now let me show how much I hate other men's names on your lips without your clothes on."

He lifts me by my waist and props me on my knees, holding my hands behind my back and pushing my face into the pillow. Just as I think that he is going to fuck me from the back, I feel a palm hit me on my ass. A loud moan escapes my throat. A moan of his name.

"Good girl. My name is the only one that should echo in this room, Raven." he says as he spanks me again. And again. And again. Hitting me in a way that pleasures me. It doesn't hurt me. I don't know how he's doing that. "Now take all of me and let me hear who all you want to be fucked by."

I hear the sound of the towel drop to the ground and turn around to see him stand butt naked, all hard for me. "All talk and no show?" I tease him more. Maybe I love being punished?

His low growl makes my body shiver as he stuffs himself inside me in one swift motion. A fill so perfect as if I was molded just for him. Every inch of my soul is filled with him. Every inch of me is filled with him. "Let me put on the show, Raven." he groans in my ear as he pulls out and thrusts in harder, making my eyes roll at the sweet ache.

"Tell me Raven, say the name." He pulls out with a force and thrusts back in as I feel him deeper than before. My back arches in agreement to angle myself so that he hits that one spot.

Heavy breaths and heavy thrusts. He is not gentle whatsoever. And I love it. The thrusts speed up as I feel him deeper. "Fuck...Harder. Deeper. More." I manage to say words that I hope make sense to him. I grab his hand and put it around my neck and he pushes me down.

Thrust. "Say." *Thrust. Thrust. Thrust.* Faster. Harder. Deeper. More. Just what I want. "The." His groans grow louder, as I feel him pulsing inside me, I can feel that he is so close. "Name." He groans in my ear.

Speech. I need to say something. He wants me to say something. He is asking me something. Perhaps telling me something? No, he is ordering me something. And I will obey. Just this once.

"James..." I moan as the tension builds between my legs. His thrusts become more uncontrolled. More feral. He's close. Just like me. I can feel it. His hand reaches between my legs and his thumb strokes my clit. My body jerks and a series of moans escape me. I try to hold back the tension, but it's too much. Too much.

"Let go." he says in my ear. "Let go for me." he says again.

"Fuck. Marcus." I pant as I feel my release shudder through me. Engulf my very existence and take me on a tour of the universe. The stars, planets, the fucking ducks, I see them all. He pulls out of me and I jerks off the liquid on my back. The sticky, hot liquid that I would rather take in my mouth. He has been eating pineapple for me lately. Every day.

He pulls me up by my throat and licks my ear. "What were you saying again?", his eyes are still feral.

A peaceful smile tugs my lips. A satisfied smile. A loving smile.

"I love you."

His eyes immediately soften and his grips around my loosens as he plants his lips on mine, claiming me. All I was saying before that coach Belkis was going to whoop his ass because I was going to fuck him hard and he was going to end up being late for practice. Guess, I got what I wanted anyway.

I pull away from him and gawk at him. He looks so beautiful, and I wrap my arms around his neck, but my pussy aches in rebellion. *I've had enough!* I can hear her scream. I am still throbbing between my legs.

"I have a surprise for you tonight." he kisses my forehead and gets back up and puts on his clothes.

I grab the pillow and throw it at him and narrow my eyes at him. He laughs in a playful and naughty way. "I love you too." he says and my heart relaxes.

James left me nothing but a note saying that he wants me to wear something Indian. That is so vague.

I put on my loose cream kurta and matching dhoti pants as I wait for him. When the door opens, it knocks my boots right off. James in a loose black kurta and cream dhoti pants makes my jaw drop to the ground. "Are you trying to kill me?" I say as I step towards him slowly. He chuckles in a way that makes my heart flutter. The air from my lungs has been stolen from me. He literally looks breathtaking!

James reaches in his pockets and pulls something out. I don't even have to know what it is before he is holding them in front of him. The sound of the dancing bells tells me exactly what it is. I run towards him and jump him as I inspect the anklets carefully.

The design–it's so beautiful. Even more so than the previous ones. The way I'd lost the last ones made me not want to wear them again. The sound of the dancing bells only brought the worst memories back. Of Jake on top of me. Me trying to fight him off.

I try to force a smile despite the gut wrenching memory. He drops his hand to my face and tilts my head up to face him. "You don't like them?" His face drops.

I shake my head and take the anklets from him. They're beautiful. There are more dancing bells on this one. I look up at him and guide him to the couch. I raise my foot on the couch and hand him the anklet and pull the dhoti pants to reveal my bare ankle. I signal him to put it on.

He takes the silver anklets from my hand and slowly hooks it on my ankle. His hand softly grazes my skin and sends shivers down my spine. The anklets are so beautiful that it makes my heart ache. The design is similar to the previous ones. Just has more intricate detailing and more dancing bells. Creating a deeper sound that soothes me. He thought about me. Like he always does…

It makes my heart melt.

I pull up another foot and he hooks on the other anklet and tinkles the dancing bell on it. "I missed these." he looks at me and smiles. He leans his head, bringing it closer to my feet and gently plants soft kisses on my feet, making my entire body shiver with happiness and lust and love, narrowing everything to the touch of his lips on my skin. I pull my feet away but he holds them back. I immediately hiss as he keeps holding on to my feet. In our culture we only let people younger than us touch our feet, or someone inferior to us. And he is in no way inferior to me.

We might not stand shoulder to shoulder, physically, because he is way taller than me. But James has always looked at me as his equal. Never once letting me doubt myself that I am less than him in any form. I am his just as much as he is mine.

"There's one more thing." he scrunches his brows. I keep my hand hooked on to his hands as he reaches for his pocket again and pulls something.

A wide smile spreads across my lips. "I heard that it wards away the negative energy." He holds out a black thread in front of me. I rest my chin on my knee as I observe him tie the black thread around my left ankle. I wonder where he found out about that. The black thread is supposed to act as an evil eye.

My heart mellows this time. I love this man. I am in love with every inch of Marcus James Williams.

He smiles softly. "I love you too, Raven."

About the Author

Rika is the pen name of the author and she prefers to keep her identity hidden. She wants her name to be known by her work. Rika is a female author and along with writing novels, she enjoys writing poems and quotes. As much as she loves writing, she loves reading even more. And when she's not writing or reading, she is cooking something in her kitchen or baking cookies for her friends.